THE FAL

Gordon Kent is the pseudonym ... both of whom have extensive personal experience in the US navy. Both are former intelligence officers and both served as aircrew. The son earned his Observer wings in S-3 Vikings during the Gulf conflict. After service in the Mediterranean, Persian Gulf, Pacific and Africa, he left active duty in 1999. They live in the United States and Canada.

Visit www.AuthorTracker.co.uk for exclusive updates on Gordon Kent.

Praise for Gordon Kent

'A lot of thrillers these days, you come away feeling like you've been in a simulator. Gordon Kent straps you into the real thing. Enjoy the ride!'

Ian Rankin

'"*Night Trap*" is the real straight Navy stuff. Better strap yourself to the chair. I loved it.'

Stephen Coonts

Told with all the authority of inside knowledge . . . an absorbing tale of international skulduggery.'

Irish News

'Consistently excellent . . . loaded with gunfights, snappy dialogue and the aerial hijinks of supersonic jet fighters. The high testosterone doses satisfy, but best is the complex and clever web of motive Kent weaves for the mole.'

Publishers Weekly

By Gordon Kent

Night Trap
Peacemaker
Top Hook
Hostile Contact
Force Protection
Damage Control
The Spoils of War
The Falconer's Tale

Gordon Kent

THE FALCONER'S TALE

HARPER

Harper
an imprint of HarperCollins*Publishers*
77–85 Fulham Palace Road,
Hammersmith, London W6 8JB

www.harpercollins.co.uk

Published by HarperCollins*Publishers* 2008

1

A catalogue record for this book
is available from the British Library

ISBN 978 0 00 717875 9

Set in Meridien by Palimpsest Book Production Ltd,
Grangemouth, Stirlingshire

Printed and bound in Great Britain by
Clays Limited, St Ives plc

To those who didn't cross the line

1

A steady, cold rain fell from low clouds on the naked rock of the hillsides and became white waterfalls plummeting to the coarse grass below, soaking the thin soil and filling the streams and rivers.

Piat had walked up the valley from the road at Horgsa without wetting his feet, but the stream between his legs now roared. Where he stood to cast on a tongue of gravel, the water rose around his ankles and then his shins, pushing heavily against him. The river came down the mountain behind his left shoulder and curved in front of him before running into a long, slow, deep pool forty meters long, and from there falling away into a canyon.

His hands were slick and nearly numb on the cork grip of his rod, and when he raised his arm to flick another cast over the river, more water ran down from his wrist to his armpit, soaking his old wool sweater.

After a long, slow retrieve, he cast again, then pulled the line with his rod just as the fly struck the water so that it moved an inch on the surface before sinking. A sea trout struck just after Piat thought he had missed again, the pull before the first leap sending a shock down the rod to Piat's wet hands. Then the fish jumped again, three quick jumps, pulling line off the reel after each one, and then ran away upriver.

Piat, burning with adrenaline, steadied himself by replanting his feet. One of his wellies filled with water. The big trout took almost a hundred feet of line in a continuous stream from Piat's reel, and then the weight on the line changed. Piat's first thought was that the fish was gone—a fraction of a second's pressure on the rod, and then he could tell that the fish had changed direction, running in at him and his submerged gravel beach. Piat began to reel up as quickly as he could. His reel was too small, too light for this kind of action, but he knew what he was doing, and he pulled line and reeled up and raised his rod as high as he could, risking his footing in the rising stream and filling his other boot with a considered advance into the deepening water.

The fish leaped again and then again, the leaps shorter, farther apart, and Piat caught up with the line on the reel and started to use the rod to work the fish. It felt his first real effort at control and reacted like an unbroken horse, fighting the rod with a new series of short jumps and fast pulls that served only to tire it faster. Piat had time now, and he ratcheted up the drag on his reel to make the fish's task of taking line off all the more difficult. He took his first careful shuffles toward the safety of the bank. He was in too deep, and when his heel caught on a rock in the gravel, he almost went down—he turned his head, caught his balance, and the fish was moving again, this time toward two straggling weed beds to his right. He tried to turn it, using the strength of the rod and the line against the fish, but even now the fish was too strong.

Piat took a long, gliding step up the bank, his filled boots clumsy. With his feet planted, he risked a strong pull and turned the fish. The sea trout leaped once more, its silver length flashing across the low gray clouds.

He didn't have a net, and it took him more time to get the fish up on the gravel above the water line. The trout was a little smaller than he had thought; the poetic clarity of its last leap had suggested a much larger fish, but he wrestled it under his arm and hit its head with his knife handle. It thrashed, and he hit it again until it was dead.

Only after he had its guts out and his hands and knife clean did he take off his socks and wring them out. He had nothing to dry the insides of his boots, so he dumped out the water and the gravel, used the socks to towel his feet and the insides of the wellies, and wrung them out again before pulling a dry pair from his pack. The change was immediate—even rammed back into wet rubber boots, his feet were warm.

The rain slowed. He poured himself a celebratory cup of coffee from the thermos in his pack and admired the fish, now lying on a patch of grass.

While he sipped his coffee, the rain stopped altogether and the low cloud blew off down the river valley toward the sea. In a minute, the vanishing curtain of rain and cloud revealed the vast landscape of the valley and the rise of mountains beyond. Before his coffee was gone, he could see for miles across the river, the mountains high and snow-capped to his left and the river valley descending in deep-cut canyons to his right until it vanished a mile away where it crossed the road to town. He was content. A rare feeling for him.

He poured a second cup of coffee and watched a distant falcon soaring above the river. A flicker of color on the most distant hillside caught his eye and he glanced up to see one of Iceland's many buses stopped on the high road above him, hardly more than a white dot amidst a tumble of rock. It was well over a mile away. A ray of cold yellow sun flashed off the windscreen; it must have been that that had diverted him from the falcon. Even without binoculars, he could see a passenger get off, and paranoia made him suspicious—there was nothing to get off the bus for out here except fishing. Perhaps serious rock climbing.

He went back to his study of the falcon, finished his coffee and changed his fly. His hands were warmer and more nimble after holding the coffee. He smiled when he saw the fish on the grass, considered bagging the rest of his fishing and going back down the valley to his room, but he had paid the last of his diminishing supply of cash for three days' fishing on this river and he didn't want to waste it, although this first fish satisfied his need. He had caught a *good* fish.

He wished he had waders. He looked at the river, now moving with considerable speed, still beautifully clear despite the press of water.

I need waders, he thought. But he didn't have money for waders. And they couldn't be bought anywhere short of Reykjavik.

He made several lackluster casts. The wind had changed and developed flaws; the combination made casting tricky. He moved to his left along the rocky shore and cast again. As his eye followed the fall of the fly, another dot of color caught his attention. The bus passenger had donned a yellow slicker and was coming down the hillside. Piat had climbed that hillside himself, and he wished the late-season hiker luck in negotiating the steep, sodden marsh that passed for a trail, with grass tussocks surrounded by ankle-twisting holes you could go into to the knee. He noted that the hiker did not have a rod.

Piat fished automatically until he focused again to discover that he had moved to a place with no weed and no wind—and no fish. The casting was easy, but to little purpose, and he reeled up and started back to the beach. The pale sun became stronger at his back. Out in the river, a fish rose noisily. Piat looked up to see the size of the ring, checked on the hiker's progress with the same glance, and was startled by how fast the hiker was moving. He was almost down to the base of the hill, walking purposefully.

Piat went to his pack and took out binoculars. He took a

careful look. Then he carefully dried the lenses with a cloth, replaced the binoculars in their case, and put them in his pack with his thermos and the fish wrapped in a plastic sack. He broke down his rod, stowed it, pocketed his reel, and started back down the valley. No one watching him would have thought him hurried or panicked.

The streams really were full, and Piat remembered having crossed four on his way up from Horgsa. He crossed the second one that he came to with trepidation; the third was running so heavily that he turned and followed it rather than crossing. He knew that the stream should bring him down the glen to Horgsa. A narrow track ran along the side, cut so deep into the turf by rivulets of water that he had to catch himself constantly to keep from falling. Patches of gravel were like rest stops. Even a few steps on solid ground felt like a holiday.

Piat pushed on, crossing a boulder field and passing over the last crest before all the land fell away to the sea three miles distant.

He did not look back.

The stream he had followed roared along to his right, sometimes close beside him and sometimes more distant as he followed the gentlest contours. He had a sense that he was too far to the east and might have a long walk on the road once he reached it, but he relished the thought of a walk on the shoulder of a paved road, no matter how narrow, and his unease was growing.

The hillside suddenly became steeper and the stream fell into falls, straight to the plain more than a hundred feet below. Piat stood at the top for several minutes, watching the falls and trying to gauge his chances of either crossing the stream above the fall or making his way down the cliff. He didn't like either, but neither did he relish the notion of backtracking up the long hillside behind him. He felt that he was being watched.

He started down the cliff, following another deep-cut track. Luck revealed an old road that seemed to spring from nowhere and ran along a hedge of boulders for a hundred meters. Piat couldn't imagine what conveyance could have climbed a road so steep, or how much effort it must have taken to hew the road. Just as suddenly, the road vanished into steep rock fall, but he was around the very worst of the cliff and he began to move cautiously straight down, grasping handfuls of grass at every step.

The last of the climb down took twenty minutes. When he at last reached the base of the cliff, he jumped across a feeder of the waterfall stream into the backyard of a local farmer. He crossed the yard into a farm road and walked down the hill past an old byre full of Icelandic sheep. In half a mile he was on the main road, and in fifteen minutes he was waiting at the bus stop.

Only then did he look down his back trail. Even with binoculars he couldn't find the yellow slicker, or the man who had been wearing it—a man he had seen several times through various lenses, and never met. Nor did he wish to. He cursed the loss of his fishing.

The bus arrived on time. Piat climbed wearily aboard, paid his fare, and settled into one of the high-backed seats after placing his backpack in the rack.

He was just opening his book when a voice said, "Hello, Jerry." It was a voice he knew, and it belonged to a man he didn't want to see just then. Mike Dukas.

"Hello, Mike," he said.

"Good to see you, Jerry."

It was a day to see people he didn't want to see. Piat had been walked, gently but firmly, from the bus to a private car, and from the car to the lobby of the Kirkjubaejarklaustur Hotel, and from thence to the bar. In the bar, a bright, modern, Nordic bar with good Norwegian wood counters and clean glasses hung from wooden racks, sat Clyde Partlow. Piat knew a great deal about Partlow, and he didn't like him much.

"I wish I could say the same, Clyde." Piat shook hands, not *quite* ready to cross the social line and refuse.

"Sun is over the yardarm, Jerry. Want a drink?" Partlow indicated the bar and the bottles with a proprietary hand that indicated that Piat could help himself—and that Partlow had complete control of the hotel.

Piat walked over to the bar, feeling his wet socks inside his wellies and the weight of the fish in the bag on his shoulder. He'd cleaned it—it'd keep for a few hours. Odd thing to worry about. He knew he was rattled—rattled by the men who had picked him up, rattled by Partlow, who looked prosperous and well groomed, rattled that they had taken him so easily. It was unlikely he was even going to eat the fish. He poured himself a stiff shot—more like two shots—of twenty-five-year-old Laphroaig. It looked to be the most expensive scotch on the bar.

Partlow raised his glass. "Old friends," he said.

"They're all dead," said Piat. He drank anyway, a little more than he had intended. "Okay, cut the soft crap, Clyde. What do you want?"

"As you will, Jerry." Partlow reached into an expensive leather bag and retrieved a file. "A project has resurfaced one of your old agents, Jerry. We'd like you to bring him in."

Piat struggled with the scotch and the adrenaline to hide his relief. It could still be a trap—they could still arrest him or turn him over to Icelandic immigration or any number of other things. But the file looked real, and it all seemed a little elaborate for an arrest. In fact, now that his hour-long panic was beginning to subside, it had *all* been too elaborate for an arrest. He hit his panic with a little more scotch.

He circled to the chair that had been placed opposite

Partlow, slipped his fishing bag over his shoulder to land on the floor, removed his rain jacket, and sat. "Who?"

"Not so fast, Jerry. You are aware, I think, of your status with us—nil. In fact, you are a wanted man, aren't you? So try to keep your usual greed in check, Jerry. First, I want your agreement that you'll go and fetch this fellow for us. Then there will be some documents to sign. Then we'll talk about who it is."

Piat looked at Partlow for a few seconds, and his hand holding his scotch began to shake. Piat took the plunge anyway. "If I'm a wanted man, Clyde, then you'd better arrest me, hadn't you? Because otherwise you'll be in defiance of an executive order about dealing with known felons, won't you, Clyde?"

The two men glared at each other for seconds. Partlow shook his head. "Really, Jerry, you are wasting my time."

"I'm not the one who just got kidnapped, *old boy.* So thanks for the scotch. I'll be going now. I paid a mint for the fishing that Mike Dukas interrupted." Piat rose to his feet and started to don his jacket, thinking—*now we'll see what cards he really has. Fuck, my hands are shaking.*

Partlow took a deep breath, sucked in his cheeks, and blew it out in a little explosion of petulance. Rain came against the big plate glass windows in rhythmic surges. "You know, Jerry, whole years pass when I don't see you and I almost forget how much we dislike each other."

Piat zipped up his coat. Partlow looked sleek and well dressed, and Piat felt every pull in his sweater and every tear in his rain jacket. "I never forget, Clyde."

Partlow shook his head. "Fine, Jerry. Fine. Point to you—I overplayed my hand. I'll pay you handsomely to bring in this agent, and I'll drop the line about 'wanted felon.' Now be a good fellow for once and sit down."

Having scored his victory, Piat had a hard time believing it was true. The shaking in his hands didn't improve. Much the opposite. He had to struggle to get his jacket back off—a pitiful performance that made him feel even less secure in the face of Partlow's careful grooming and assurance.

"How much?" Piat said, reverting to his time-honored role as greedy man of action.

"Five thousand dollars. In and out. You can be done in two days."

"Ten thousand," Piat demanded.

Partlow shrugged as if the subject pained him. "If you must."

"Okay. Who is it?"

Partlow took out a sheet of paper. "I think you are familiar with the terms."

Piat read it—a standard agency document for the recruitment of agents. Piat had always been on the other side of the document before—the case officer making the recruitment. Case officers were carefully trained professional spies. Agents were their amateur helpers. Mostly riffraff and rejects. *That's me these days,* Piat thought to himself.

Partlow slid over an envelope. "I was sure you'd insist on getting money in advance."

Piat cursed under his breath, but he took the envelope and scrawled his name on the agreement.

"Excellent. Welcome back, Jerry, if only as a lowly agent. You understand confidentiality, etcetera?"

"You'll be running me yourself, Clyde?" Piat already disliked being an agent.

"Of course not, Jerry. I run a department. A case officer will come to deal with you and your needs. He's waiting outside until you and I are finished."

"I smell a rat already, Clyde."

"As you will, Jerry. Your man—Hackbutt." Clyde made a show of checking Piat's signature before he handed over the dossier.

"The nerd? Christ, Clyde, what do you want him for?"

"Nerd?"

"Nerd. A hopelessly antisocial geek, Clyde. Who specializes to the point of obsession."

"I don't think you ever used that phrase in a contact report, Jerry."

"No, I don't think the agency pays its officers to write reports explaining what a bunch of fucking basket cases their agents are, Clyde. Nonetheless, he's a handling nightmare and a freak. I take it there is sudden movement in Malaysian oil futures?" Hackbutt had been a small-time informer in Malaysia. Good enough at what he did—report on the oil industry—but useless otherwise.

Partlow looked at him from under his heavy gray brows. He steepled his fingers in front of him. He was clearly trying to decide what to tell Piat. "He's now into falconry—the birds, you know." Partlow started in a patronizing tone. "Falconry is the use of birds for hunting—"

"Thanks, Clyde, I know what falconry is. Eddie was always into birds—I smuggled him a couple as part payment for one of his best reports. But no *way* am I getting from here to Jakarta and back in two days."

"Mull." Partlow said the word as if delivering a sentence of doom.

"Mull? Where's Mull?" Jerry thought the name could even be local. When Icelandic names weren't an endless chain of harsh consonants, they were often quite simple.

"Scotland, Jerry. The Isle of Mull is off the west coast of Scotland."

"Scotland? That's as cold as this place. He used to be cold all the time in Jakarta." Jerry finished his scotch, rose and poured himself another. Ten thousand dollars and relief from arrest—he had a lot to celebrate. "Whatever—I'll need a passport."

"Absolutely not. Your case officer will walk you through immigration."

"Christ—really? You can do that? The world has changed."

"The gloves are off, Jerry. People in Washington have realized that we are the most powerful country in the world."

Piat shook his head. "Most people in Washington couldn't find their asses with both hands, Clyde. Okay. I go, I meet this guy, I set him up with—who? Same guy who's running me? That right?"

"Yes."

"Fine. And no doubt wait around to make sure they get cozy?"

"Absolutely not, Jerry. You set him up and go home."

"That's all?"

"That's all." Partlow had returned to sounding smug. Piat didn't like it, or him, but the money was good.

"So no chance for a little salmon fishing here before I go?"

"Jerry, sometimes I think you are not quite sane."

"The feeling's mutual, Clyde. Okay, I guess that's a no. When do you want this done?"

"There's a military plane leaving from Keflavik in three hours. I want you on it."

"What about my fishing equipment? My luggage?"

"I'll see to it that it's returned to you when your assignment is complete."

"Be careful of my rods." Piat looked out the window at the vividly green grass. The hotel had the largest lawn he had seen outside of Reykjavik, as if a lawn was itself something to watch on one's holiday. He felt the weight of the fish in his bag again.

He said, "Dukas? He staying here?"

Partlow thought a long time before saying, "Yes."

"And you're sending me to Scotland with this case officer, right?"

Again, Partlow took his time answering. "Yes, Jerry," he said with mock patience.

"Okay." Piat got to his feet. "I'd like to fetch some clothes."

"No. You can buy them en route."

"Not outa my cash, you won't."

"Fine, Jerry. As you will. I'll have your case officer take you shopping. Otherwise, we're done?"

"Yeah."

Partlow got to his feet, looked Piat over carefully, and then walked to the bar's main door to the lobby. Piat followed him to the concierge desk.

"I'd like to leave something for one of the guests," he said. He ignored the heavyset man who appeared by his elbow and crowded his personal space.

The concierge nodded. "A package, sir?"

Piat thumped his bag down on the counter. "Dukas—Mike Dukas. Not a package. A fish. See to it he gets it for dinner."

Regrettably, the concierge said, Mister Dukas had already checked out.

Mike Dukas was sitting at a table in an airport bar that was so atmospheric it felt like a film set for the kind of movie he wouldn't go to see. Still, he knew that the rest of the world might find it warm and comforting and sweet, or at least a relief from Scandinavian modern. The motif was Olde Englande and the beer cost six-fifty a bottle. Dukas, begrudging the money but thirsty, figured the high price was really the admission charge to the Charles Dickens Theme Park, Iceland.

Dukas had kept his khaki raincoat on but placed his waterproof hat on the table. A small puddle had formed around it. Now, he sat with his right elbow next to the hat and his lower lip pushed against the knuckles of his right hand, watching Alan Craik saunter toward him. Craik was smiling. He looked relaxed and pleased, and also, Dukas conceded, handsome in a sort of rugged, fortyish, Hollywood way. What the hell, who cared about looks, anyway? (The ravishing blonde two tables away, that's who.)

"I think we did that pretty well," Craik said as he slipped into a chair. He was wearing some sort of weathered corduroy sport jacket and a nubbly shirt, and he had tossed a waxed cotton coat (veddy, veddy English) over the back of his chair.

"Piat didn't think so."

"Not pleased to be jerked away from fishing?"

"It costs five hundred bucks a day to fish here, he told me. For salmon, anyway."

"If you all got to the point of talking about fishing, I'd say he wasn't too upset."

Dukas shrugged. Craik ordered a beer. He said, "Partlow telling him what this is about, you suppose?"

"One assumes. Now if they'd just tell me what it's about. How about you tell me what it's about, Al?"

"I told you over the phone—if I knew, I'd tell you. All I know is Partlow was looking for Jerry Piat for an operation, and you keep up with Jerry Piat. Our part was to bring him in, period."

"You're trusting Clyde Partlow?"

"Not with anything important like my wallet, but yeah, as little as you and I are involved, yeah."

Dukas drank the last of his beer and stared gloomily at the bottle. "I don't get you helping a shit like Partlow."

"It's called 'I'll scratch your back now and you'll owe me one.'"

"I wouldn't *want* Clyde Partlow to owe me one." Craik shrugged. Dukas gave up trying to save money and ordered another beer and then said, "This is a fine mess you've got us into, Stanley." He waited for a response, got none. "Well?"

Grinning, Craik said, "You know what a working group is?"

"Mrs Luce, I *am* a Catholic."

"Okay, I was at a meeting of a working group—sixty people in a big room sharing secrets. Or *not* sharing secrets, as the case may be. Although, with all the bullshit that's been said since Nine-Eleven about agencies not sharing intelligence, in fact the amount of sharing that actually goes on is astonishing. Anyway, Partlow is a long-time regular at this particular working group; I'm a regular now because of my new job. When we took a break, Partlow made a beeline for me and asked me if you weren't a friend of mine."

"'Oh-ho,' you said to yourself, 'this is suspicious.'"

"No, I said to myself, 'Clyde Partlow is a good guy to do a favor for.'" Craik was silent for several seconds. "Now Partlow owes me one. And he owes you one—what's wrong with that?"

"I was building up debts from assholes like Partlow when you were in Pampers." Dukas waited while a fresh bottle of beer was put in front of him. "You've changed."

"Older and wiser."

"Where's the Al Craik who used to say, 'Damn the torpedoes, we're going in without a country clearance'?"

"You know what the shelf life of a collections officer is? Short. I figure doing a favor for somebody like Partlow might give my sell-by date a little leeway."

"I feel like I don't know you so good anymore."

"Yeah, you do. Same old lovable Craik, only I've wised up about Washington politics. Anyway, Partlow came over to me and asked about you, and I said why and so on, and he finally dropped Piat's name like he was passing me the secret combination to Bush's wall safe." He slipped into a Partlow imitation, cheeks puffed, head back. "'Might your friend Dukas know how Piat could be reached?' So I said I'd check. And I did. And here we are."

"Why?"

"Ah, da big question! I love da big questions! I dunno, Mike—Partlow has an operation that he wants Piat for, that's all I could get. It's on the up-and-up—it's got a task number; and it's passed the working group. It's kosher." He lowered his head, smiled. "But why would he want an untouchable like Piat?"

"You mean it smells."

"N-o-o-o—"

"If it's passed the working group, you heard it discussed."

"Unh-unh. Discussion is general—tasks and goals. Peons like me not to know."

"That's sure what I call sharing information." Dukas wiped a hand over his face. "Man, I'm tired. You at least got a night's sleep. You know what you have to do to fly to Reykjavik from fucking Naples? Now I gotta do it in reverse. You of course feel great and look great, you bastard."

"A healthy mind in a healthy body."

Dukas sat looking at him, lips pushed out, eyebrows drawn together "You're the guy who used to lecture me about honor, duty. Idealism. Now you're running errands for one of the most political shits in the business." He shook his head and held Craik's eyes. "What happened to that fine rage you used to work up when other people did things for slimy reasons?"

Craik's smile was tentative, apologetic. "My last fine rage got me a call from my detailer saying that if I didn't can it, I wasn't going to make captain."

"And now you're a captain."

Craik nodded. The same small smile was still on his face "'Honor, duty, idealism.' Right." He looked up. "But I believe you gotta pick your battles and your battlefield. And lost causes get you nowhere. Isn't it okay to scratch the itch of my curiosity about Partlow's wanting Piat, and maybe have Partlow owe me a favor at the same time?"

Dukas stared at his friend, then finished his second beer. Setting the bottle down carefully on its own old ring, he said, "It sure is comforting to know you're still an idealist."

2

Piat had never had a case officer before. Case officers are the men and women who recruit agents and then handle them—long hours of manipulation, a shoulder on which to cry, a voice when it is dark. Piat was used to being the shoulder and the voice.

"Dave's" was not the shoulder or the voice that Piat would have chosen. Dave was clearly the man's cover name—he didn't always respond when the name was called. His voice was rough, assertive, yet with a surprising repertoire of high-pitched giggles and nervous laughter. He had had trouble parking his rental car. He had shown considerable resentment while walking Piat through some shopping in Oban. Piat had been tempted to start coaching him then and there.

Two hours later, Piat sat next to the man on the cafeteria deck of MV *Isle of Mull* and tried not to gnaw on the sore ends of how little he wanted to do this. He'd taken the money, and there wasn't much he could do about any of it, but it smelled.

Partlow should have run him himself. They loathed each other, but Partlow was a competent case officer and would have made sure that things got done on time and under budget. Dave was so clearly a second stringer that Piat wanted to ask him what other agents he'd run—if any. It was as if, having recruited Piat, Partlow was now distancing himself from the operation. That wasn't like Clyde. He didn't usually let go of anything once he had it in his well-manicured hands.

Piat was sure that if he wanted to, he could ditch Dave at Craignure, the ferry terminal he'd already noted on the map of Mull. And then he'd walk. It was a tempting thought. Dave struck Piat as the type who'd order a lot of searches done by other people and spend a lot of time in cars. Piat thought it might be fun to walk away. In Piat's experience, the way to lose Americans was to walk. It worked on Russians and Chinese, too.

He'd been paid half the money and he'd discovered that the Agency really didn't have much on him—or had buried the evidence to protect themselves. He could probably manage a day's fishing before he flew—

Pure fantasy. He had one passport—his own—and they'd come looking for him. Mull was an island cul-de-sac with only a couple of exits.

Ten thousand dollars for two days' work, no matter how dirty, would get him back to Greece. If he was careful, the money would see him through the winter. By then it was possible that he would find something in the antiquities market to sell.

Because Dave had taken the window seat, Piat got up and pulled a sweater out of his bag. It was a very nice sweater—Burberry, more than a hundred pounds in Oban on the High Street. Piat had never been able to resist spending other people's money. He had purchased a wardrobe that would last him five years—good stuff, if you liked English clothes. Piat liked anything that lasted. He pulled the sweater over his head and added the clothes to his list of positives. He could leave Partlow holding his baggage now—there was nothing in it worth as much as the clothes he had just encouraged Dave to buy for him. Scratch that thought—Piat wanted the rods back. He sat and admired his wool trousers and smiled again.

Dave didn't even look up. He was reading *The Economist* with an air of self-importance that Piat longed to puncture. He shrugged internally. Why bother? Piat took out a guide to the early European Bronze Age and browsed it, trying to separate the useful facts from the clutter of drivel about prehistoric alphabets and runic stones. The early European Bronze Age was the hottest market in antiquities. Piat tried for fifteen minutes, but the book didn't hold his attention.

Why does Partlow need me? Piat chewed the question. Hackbutt was a handling nightmare—did Partlow know that?

He looked at the cover of his book and wondered if any of the Roman authorities had commented on the world before Greece. All too damned speculative. He allowed his eyes to skim past the usual photos; a bronze breastplate, a helmet, a spectacular sword with an early flanged hilt, some badly decorated pottery. He knew all the objects. They decorated major museums. It needed a remarkable coincidence of durability, placement and luck for anything that old—the second millennium BC—to be found in northern Europe. Even to survive.

Partlow is doing something around the rules—above, below, whatever. He had to be. He'd involved Dukas—Piat went back with Dukas, not exactly as pals but with some respect. He'd involved Alan Craik. Piat didn't love Craik but he had seen him in action. Dukas and Craik were buddies. Dukas and Partlow were not buddies at all.

And Hackbutt was into falconry—and Partlow had said right out that's why they wanted him. Most of the Arab bigwigs were into falconry, too. No big leap of logic there.

Like speculating on what classical authority might have a bearing on the Bronze Age, speculating on Clyde Partlow's motives from the deck of the ferry wasn't getting Piat anywhere.

I can find a partner and a dig when I get back to Lesvos. Worst case, I'm a few thousand richer, and I have some new clothes.

Piat shrugged, this time physically. It made Dave glance

up at him from his magazine. For a moment their eyes met. Piat smiled.

"I'm trying to read," said Dave.

Piat nodded, still smiling. He started to prepare himself to meet Edgar Hackbutt, bird fancier, social outcast, and ex-agent.

Piat swung the rented Renault down into Tobermory's main street, reminding himself to get over to the left, toward the water. The morning was brilliant, with thin, pale-blue mare's tails high up against a darker blue sky. The tide was in, and big boats rode alongside the pier; as always when he saw them, he thought, *I could live on one of those*, but in fact he never would. Too much a creature of the land, or perhaps too suspicious of the predictability of a boat, too easy to find. On land, you could always get out and walk.

He drove along the waterfront, brightly painted buildings on his right, memorizing them—hardware store, chandler's shop, bank, grocery—and then pulled up the long hill out of town and around a roundabout to the right, heading not down the island's length but across its northern part. A sign said "Dervaig"; he followed it, passed a chain of small lakes (*Mishnish Lochs, fishing, small trout*—he'd pretty much memorized a tourist brochure) and, with a kind of fierce joy, drove the one-lane road that twisted and switchbacked up and down hills. He played the game of chicken that was the island's way of dealing with two cars driving straight at each other: one would have to yield and pull into a supposedly available lay-by. Locals drove like maniacs and waved happily as they roared past; tourists either went into the lay-bys like frightened rabbits or clutched the wheel and hoped that what was happening to them was an illusion. Piat, flicking in and out of lay-bys, waving when he won, giving a thumbs-up when he didn't, had the time of his life.

He climbed past a cemetery above Dervaig and, following a map in his head, turned left and south. Halfway down the wide glen would be a road on the right; from it, a track went still farther up and then briefly down. At its end, Dave had assured him, Hackbutt's farm waited. Piat drove slower, head ducked so he could look out the windscreen. He'd have said that landscape didn't interest him, but in fact, it fascinated him, only without the sentimentality that led other people to take photos and paint watercolors. He always saw possibilities—for escape, for hides, for pursuit. Here, the sheer scale of the place surprised him: this was an island, and Tobermory was almost a toy town, but out here was a breadth of horizon that reminded him of Africa. Even with the mountains. The glen was miles wide, he thought, the mountains starting as rolling slopes that careened abruptly upward and became almost vertical climbs to their summits. *Strong climber could shake anybody up there.* The landscape was brown and green and gray; grass, not heather; bare rock and bracken. *You could walk and walk. Or run and run. If the footing is okay.*

He found the road to the right and drove it more slowly; it was ancient tarmac, crumbling along the edges, potholed, hardly wider than the car. He came over a rise and almost ran into a goofy-looking runner, some old guy wearing what looked like a giant's T-shirt that flapped around him in the crisp wind. Hardly noticing him, the runner plodded on. Piat thought, *I could give you half a mile and still get there first.* After another mile, the road forked and he went right. *Almost there.* When he had gone half a mile farther, he pulled up just short of a crest and got the car into a lay-by and stopped. "Please do not park in the lay-bys," the tourist brochure had said. *You bet.*

Piat got out and spread an Ordnance Survey map on the hood, traced his route from Tobermory, found the fork, followed with his finger, and judged from the contour lines that if he walked over the crest, he'd be looking down on

Hackbutt's house. Or farm, or whatever the hell it was. His aviary, how would that be?

He had borrowed a pair of binoculars from good old Dave—Swarovskis, 10x50, nice if you didn't have to carry them very far—and walked the hundred feet to the top of the hill. He made his way into the bracken and moved toward a rock outcrop, keeping himself out of sight of the house he'd glimpsed below, until he reached the outcrop and put his back against it and turned the binoculars on the house.

It could have been any house on the island—central doorway, two windows on each side, a chimney at one end, second storey with two dormers. The color of rich cream but probably stone under a coat of paint, possibly an old croft fixed up but more likely built in the last hundred years. At the far side of the house, clothes blew in the wind on a circular contraption with a central metal pole. Behind it, as if to tell him it was the right house, were pens and little shacks like doghouses that he took to be sheds for the birds; beside a half-collapsed metal gate, a dejected-looking black and white dog lay with its head on outstretched paws, beside it what was apparently supposed to be a doghouse made out of boxes and a tarp. The bird pens seemed to have been set out at random, the hutches put together by somebody who didn't know which end of a hammer to hit his thumb with. *That'd be Hackbutt, for sure.*

Piat studied the place. He hoped to actually see Hackbutt so he'd go in with that advantage. They hadn't seen each other in fifteen years; let the other guy feel the shock of change. Hackbutt would have an idea he was coming but wouldn't know when: Piat had sent him a postcard with a picture of a bear on the front, a nonsense message on the back signed "Freddy." From "ready for Freddy." It meant "get ready;" the bear was the identifier, an old code between them. Would Hackbutt remember? Of course he would. In fact, Piat thought, he'd piss his pants.

After fifteen minutes, nobody had appeared near the house. Piat eased himself around the outcrop and walked back through the bracken to the car. He leaned on the roof and trained the binoculars around him, idling, not wanting to go down to the house yet. *Apprehensive? Cold feet?* He looked down the road. The goofy runner was coming back. He was making heavy going of it now, his feet coming down as if he were wearing boots, his hands too high on his chest. The too-big T-shirt blew around him. He had a beard and long, gray hair, also blowing, the effect that of some small-time wizard in a ragged white robe. Smiling, Piat put the binoculars to his eyes to enjoy this sorry sight, and when the focus snapped in, he realized with a shock that the runner was Hackbutt.

The last time he had seen Hackbutt, he'd weighed about two-thirty and had had a sidewall haircut, smooth cheeks, and eyes like two raisins in a slice of very white bread. Now, there was the beard and the long hair, and the face had been carved down to planes that made his eyes look huge; his skin was almost brown, and he had lost a lot of weight—so much that his legs looked fragile. The T-shirt, Piat realized, must be one of his own from the old days.

He still can't run for shit, at least.

Hackbutt toiled up toward him. Piat moved around to the rear of the car and leaned back against the trunk. The runner came on, his breathing hoarse and hard, his eyes on the crest. He was going to pass Piat without looking at him, Piat knew—eye contact had always been hard for the man, confronting new people a torment. Now, as he came almost even, Piat said, "Hey, Digger."

Hackbutt was the kind of nerd who actually did double takes. He might look like a wizard now, but inside was the same insecure fumbler. Still running, he looked aside toward Piat, looked away, then *really* looked back and, finally believing the evidence of his eyes, came to a stop with his mouth open and his T-shirt flapping. "Jack?" he said, breathing hard. He'd always known Piat as Jack Michaels.

"Hey, man, you look good. Putting in the miles, that's great." Piat was still leaning on the car. He held out his hand. "Sight for sore eyes, Digger."

"Jeez, Jack, this is—" Hackbutt took a death grip on Piat's hand. The guy was really strong. "I got your card, but I didn't know when you were coming!" He grinned. "Wow, this is unbelievable!" Then they both said it was great, and unbelievable, and a long time.

"You look good, Dig. Lost some weight, haven't you?"

"Some weight! Sixty pounds, Jack." His breathing was getting better and he was able to stick his chest out. "Surprised?"

"Amazing."

"Jeez, Jack, you haven't changed. You look just the same. You look *great*."

"Little older, little grayer." He grinned at Hackbutt. Piat was surprised to find he *was* pleased to see him. Good old, easy old Eddie Hackbutt. "Let me run you down to the house." That was a slip; he shouldn't have admitted he'd already seen the house. Hackbutt, however, didn't notice; he was too busy shaking his head and frowning.

"No, no, Irene wouldn't like it. I can't give in like that. Anyway, I'm just coming up on the big finish—over the hill and then I sprint to the front door."

Piat thought that would be worth seeing. Most of his concentration, however, was on Hackbutt's "Irene." Partlow's file had said nothing about a wife, had mentioned only a "companion," name unspecified. "Keeps your nose to the grindstone, does she?"

Hackbutt's face darkened. "No, it isn't like that!" This was new—he'd grown a spine in fifteen years. "You'll have to meet her." And Hackbutt turned about and started his painful plod up the last hundred feet of the hill before his final sprint.

Piat sat behind the wheel without starting the car; he wanted to let Hackbutt get home and tell "Irene" about meeting good old Jack. The house was no more than a third of a mile away—give the man four minutes. Five, so he could get out of that T-shirt. And Piat wanted to think: he'd made a mistake. He'd thought he'd told himself that Hackbutt would be changed, but he'd thought only that he'd be more like Hackbutt—fatter, nerdier—and not that he'd have reinvented himself as a skinny, bearded exercise freak. Or been reinvented by a woman named Irene, who now took on an importance that Piat hadn't even guessed at.

Losing my touch. Or getting rusty.

He started the engine.

Irene Girouard wore a long dress, as if she had something to hide, but otherwise she was very much in evidence. Piat thought that her first initial, I, probably summed her up, so he didn't need the confirmation of the wallful of photographs that greeted him as soon as he was taken into the house.

"Irene's a photographer," Hackbutt said. His tone said, *I'm crazy about Irene.*

The photographs were all of Irene, taken by Irene. Irene's left eye, Irene's chin, Irene's right knee, Irene's vagina (oh, yes), Irene's left breast in profile, full front, and close-up, emphasis on big nipple. Piat decided that the long dress wasn't meant to hide her but to refer curiosity to the photos.

"I'm doing an installation in Paris any time now." Her voice had a hint of something foreign. "I just need to get my shit together and then it's go any time I say so. Hackbutt's gathering found objects for me."

Hackbutt smiled. "Irene's going to be a household name."

"These are all, mm, you?" Piat said.

"I don't fuck around with false modesty. Yes, that's my cunt, if that's what you want to ask. The photos'll be assembled on stuff we've found, mostly animal bones, to make a humanoid construction. I'm fastening the photos to the bones with barbed wire from an old fence he found."

"It's called *I Sing the Body Electric,*" Hackbutt said.

"Whitman," she said.

Piat thought of saying *Whitman Who?* but didn't, aware that he didn't like the woman at all, that she was going to be a problem, and at the same time finding a woman who took pictures of her own vagina perversely interesting. She also had a big, hearty, apparently healthy laugh, as if despite all the photos she was as sane as a stone and he ought to get to know her. For the sake of saying something, for the sake of having to put up with her, he said, "Are you going to cut the parts out of the photos when you, mm, barbed wire them to the stuff?"

"God, no, that would be so *calculated*!"

That was just the central hall of the house, as far as they'd got at that point. There had been introductions, a pro forma question about something to drink—they didn't drink tea or coffee, but they had water "from the hill" and juice, source not given—and then the photos, Hackbutt saying, as if they were the reason for the visit, "*These* are Irene's photographs."

There was more of Irene throughout the house, Piat learned. Nobody picked up after him/herself, apparently, so parts of both of them were left where they fell: the living room, just to the left after you came in the front door, was thick with art magazines, falconry paraphernalia (Piat had bought a book in Glasgow, so he recognized the jesses, at least); batteries, probably used; a battery charger, plugged in but empty; a sizable number of animal bones; a plate that had held something oily. Four spindly plants in the windows, yearning for a sunnier climate. The kitchen, next behind the living room, was furnished mostly in dirty dishes, a camera, burned-down candles. Piat, himself scrupulously neat, wondered if he'd dare to eat anything that came out of it. On the right of the central hall were, first, a small bedroom

("You're going to stay, aren't you, Jack?"), then a closed door that led, he supposed, to their own bedroom, which he hoped they wouldn't show him. He imagined dirty laundry in shoulder-high heaps. At the end of a corridor, another closed door hid what Hackbutt called "Irene's studio."

Then it was out to see the birds, which were to Hackbutt as the photos were to Irene. They were hawks and falcons, different types that Piat couldn't distinguish; hooded, silent, they sat on perches and occasionally turned their heads. Hackbutt insisted on feeding two of them for him to watch, and he demonstrated their training with one of them and an old sock that was supposed to represent a rabbit. Hackbutt almost had a glow around his head; his eyes were those of a fanatic. Partlow, he thought, had chosen well—if Hackbutt could be recruited.

"I *wish* I'd known you were coming," Irene said when she'd decided they had spent enough time on the birds. "We could have had lunch."

"I thought I might take you to lunch."

She laughed that big, healthy laugh. "Oh, Christ, you can't *do* that in this godforsaken place! We don't eat human food. We're fucking vegans, nutcases. I go in a restaurant here and the smell makes me barf before I sit down!"

"Maybe," Hackbutt said, "maybe, honey, we could have a salad or something."

"I don't think Jack is a salad type." She looked Piat up and down. "He looks like a carnivore to me."

"Raw buffalo, mostly," Piat said. He added no, no, he wouldn't stay; no, thanks; no; but he had some things for them in the car he'd meant to bring in. Just sort of getting-reacquainted stuff.

He hadn't known why, but he'd thought Hackbutt would be poor. On a city street, Hackbutt could have passed for one of the homeless, but in his own context, he looked *right,* neither poor nor rich, certainly not needy. And Irene, no matter what she was now, had known money, he thought. The accent, a casual remark about "when I was at McGill," a long-cultivated air of rebelliousness without penalty—no starving in garrets, please—told him she was doing a trapeze act over a very safe safety net. And the net, it turned out, was named Mother. "Oh, Mother sent that in her last Care package," she said of a CD player. Said it with contempt, but then socked a CD into it and said she hoped he liked bluegrass. He didn't, in fact, but knew it would do no good to say so.

He brought in the plastic shopping bag he'd filled in a supermarket in Oban, feeling not like Santa Claus but like the guest who's brought the wrong kind of wine. He'd been wrong about Hackbutt; he'd underestimated him. Now he'd pay with the embarrassment of the wrong gifts.

"Oh, friend, this is *so* wrong for us," Irene said as she took out a tin of pâté. And the crackers. "God, they've got *animal fat* in them!" And the Johnnie Walker black, which had always been his gift to Hackbutt in the old days. "Oh, Eddie doesn't drink anymore, do you, sweetie? Ohmmmm—" Big wet kiss. Ditto the Polish ham, the smoked salmon, and the petits fours (white sugar *and* animal fat).

"You think I'm a nut, I know you do," she said. She ran her fingers through her long, untidy hair. "You're right. I am. I'm a crank. I've turned Eddie into a crank. *But we're fucking healthy!*" She grinned. "And I do mean *fucking* healthy." Hackbutt looked shy.

Piat decided things were awful and it wouldn't work. Dumb Dave wouldn't be able to run Hackbutt with Irene around; Irene would be running Dave in about twelve hours. But if it didn't work, at least not to the point where Piat got Dave and Hackbutt together, he was going to lose half his ten thousand bucks.

"Actually," Piat said when Hackbutt went off to the john, "actually, Irene, you've thrown me a curve."

She smiled. Whoopee.

"What I mean is, I have a sort of, um, business to talk to Hackbutt about."

"Oh, Jeez, I never would have guessed." She gave that big laugh. "Sweetie, of *course* you've got business to talk to Eddie about! The first thing he said when he got your card was, 'He'll want something.'" She tipped her head, smiled with her eyes a little scrunched up as if he was giving off too much light, and played with her hair. "What kind of thing do you want?"

"You his agent?"

"I'm his damp crotch, and don't you forget it. Look, Jack, Eddie's a wonderful man, but he needs somebody to take care of him. Don't come here thinking you can push him around. Okay?"

"I never pushed him around in my life."

"Somebody did."

Piat opened his mouth to say something that would have been ugly, then thought better of it and leaned back—they were in the small living room, he on the sofa in a bare spot in a pile of mess—and said, "What did he tell you about me?"

"He said you were a great guy."

"That sounds right."

"But he won't tell me how he knew you, so that part doesn't sound so great, does it?"

"We used to bum around together in Southeast."

"Southeast?

"Asia."

"Yeah, he said he knew you from Macao. So, what *did* you two do together?"

"This and that. Some deals."

"You were in oil, too?"

"I was in a lot of things. We just bummed around together, had some laughs, some drinks." He thought he'd launch a trial balloon. "Some girls."

She didn't like the balloon. "Eddie didn't know his cock from a condom till he met me." She gave all the signs of talking a better sexual game than she actually played, he thought. But you never could tell.

Piat shrugged. "We were guys together, how's that? Pals."

She looked at him. She put her chin up, ran her fingers through her hair. She said, "You look to me like bad news." She laughed. "I like that in a man."

By then, Piat was hungry and annoyed, and when Hackbutt came out of the bathroom, he said he had to go. Both of them protested, but he could see that she wasn't going to let him talk to Hackbutt alone, and there was no way he was going to go into his recruiting pitch with her there. He could see Partlow's five thousand growing wings. He was damned if he'd let it fly away. "I'd like to come back," he said.

Oh, great, yes, great idea, sure!

He gathered the handles of the shopping bag in his fingers—they absolutely didn't want the stuff—and said, "I'll come back tomorrow; how's that?"

Oh, sure, wonderful idea, yes, they'd even have lunch.

"But I want to talk to Digger alone."

That was not so well received. Hackbutt looked pained; she looked insulted.

"I need one hour with Hackbutt. Then he can talk to you, Irene, and then the three of us can talk, but first it's just him and me, and the girls have to stay at the other end of the dance floor. Nothing personal."

Hackbutt said, "Honey—" and looked at her. His face was flushed, as if he liked being fought over.

She said, "Just gonna be guys together?"

"Something like that."

"Unless you can offer him eternal youth and a lot of really cute chicks, I can make him a better offer than anything you can say. Can't I, sweetie?"

"It isn't a competition."

She looked at him and then at Hackbutt and then at Piat again, and she fluffed her hair and said, "I need a bath, anyway. An hour'll be about right."

They all smiled and touched each other and said tomorrow, then, right, yeah, tomorrow. And Piat went out to his rented car, but to temper the humiliation of seeming to have been chased away, he detoured by the dog.

It was still lying with its head on its paws. It watched him come, then cringed when he put out his hand. Piat squatted and extended the hand, but the dog pulled back, then got up and went into its hovel, dragging a length of chain behind it.

Frowning, Piat made his way to the car, still feeling like an asshole because he was carrying back all the gifts that Hackbutt was supposed to be pathetically grateful for. And because Irene had made it very clear just who was Hackbutt's *real* case officer.

When Piat wheeled the rented Renault into the grass in front of Hackbutt's house next day, he was better prepared. During an evening much clarified by the Johnnie Walker he'd bought for Hackbutt, he'd scolded himself for poor preparation and overall laziness; then, the personnel work done, he had decided what he must do. It all came down to two things: learn to like Irene Girouard, because she ran Edgar Hackbutt; and accept the new Hackbutt, consigning the old one to history.

Now, as he got out of the car, he grinned as Irene appeared in the doorway. She was in another long dress, blue denim, fairly waistless. Piat was wearing a black polo shirt and a sweater and a pair of khakis. He waved. She waved. He took a plastic sack from the car and loped up to the door. "I'm going to try this again," he said, holding out the bag.

"For little ol' me?"

"For both of little ol' you." She hesitated, holding the storm door open for him. He had to go past her, face to face. Going by, he bent his head and kissed her, quickly, lightly. "Good to see you again."

"Edgar's with his birds."

"Good chance for me to talk to him?" *Make it a question,* he told himself; *get on her good side.* When she didn't answer, he said, "What's your dog's name?" *People like you ought to like their dogs, right?*

"No idea," she said. "He kept hanging around when we moved in." She was taking things out of the sack. "Greek honey—well!" He'd found the gourmet shelves at the Island Bakery in Tobermory. "Oh—!" She had something clutched between her breasts. "Porcini cream!"

"Organic."

She gave him an odd smile. "You're a quick learner." She pulled out other things—balsamic vinegar, olive oil crushed with blood oranges, a set of hemp place mats. She was pleased, maybe only with the effort and not the things themselves, but she was pleased. "Sure, why don't you go talk to Edgar. I'll get naked."

And if that wasn't a peace offering, what is? She made sex so overt, however, he was suspicious. He thought that maybe she was performing her sexuality, not being it. Maybe for her it was like a language she'd learned on paper but couldn't get fluent in. If so, if they actually got to it, there would be a lot of drama—costumes like crotchless panties, oils and perfumes, sound effects like yum-yums to go with the obligatory blow job and glad cries for orgasm, real or simulated probably the latter. And afterward, the reviews: You were so good. Was it good for you? Was I good? But maybe it wouldn't be like that at all. But either way, he already wanted to know.

He was only going to be with them for a few days, and then he'd be on his way, so it wouldn't be endangering his own operation if he took what she seemed to be offering.

He went out the rear door and stumbled because of the unexpected step down. Nobody cut the lawn at Hackbutt's, but a path was worn between coarse grass and a bed of nettles, which Piat knew from Greece and managed to avoid. He tried to remember how to get to the bird pens; giving up, he shouted, "Digger! Digger!"

Hackbutt appeared, much closer than expected. "Jack! You did come back!" His hands were covered with red goo. "How nice. I won't shake hands." Part of the nettle bed was between them. "I'm cutting up some pigeons."

Piat steered around the nettles and joined Hackbutt in the remains of an outbuilding. There was bad smell and a lot of feathers. "Where do you get the pigeons?"

"A kid shoots them for me with an air gun."

"That doesn't sound so vegan."

Hackbutt shrugged. "Raptors aren't vegans." He had a bucket on the ground half full of pieces of pigeon, partly plucked, bloody. On a rough table that had started life as something else, he was chopping a dead bird with a cleaver.

"Can't they do that for themselves?"

"Sure. They love to do it themselves. But you got to train them *not* to do it, so they'll bring you game birds if you fly them at them." He whacked off a wing. "Falconry's a sport. Like shooting. There's a quarry—in the old days, the object was to bring in game to eat. See, it's hard to get a carnivore to bring meat to you instead of eating it itself. Like using a tiger for a retriever." He whacked off the other wing. "You see Irene?"

"She was off to take her bath. I brought you some sort of veggie stuff. She seemed pleased."

"Oh, that's good." He swept the edge of the cleaver across the blood on the table, then held the bucket under the edge so he could push the blood into it. "Irene's a wonderful gal, Jack. I want you two to like each other." He wiped his hands on a rag. "She changed my life. They talk about people reinventing themselves—she reinvented me. Really. I'm still not much, I know that, but I'm a hell of a lot more than I was."

"You were always a good guy. And a good agent."

Hackbutt looked pleased and said, "Well—" but didn't really rise to it. In the old days, he would have been like a cat, doing everything but arching his back. He picked up the bucket and pushed past Piat. "The birds are a full-time job. It's fun, and I love my birds, but, Jeez, man, it's your life!"

He went along the pens, talking to birds he told Piat were immature, making noises to them, tossing pieces of pigeon to them. He strapped a guard over his left arm and enticed a young falcon to perch on it by holding up a pigeon neck with the head still attached, and then he gave it to the bird.

One of the cages was twice the size of the others. So was the occupant. Alone of the birds, the giant received a whole pigeon. Piat watched as the big bird held the head down with both feet and tore out pieces of meat from the neck, plucking as it went, feathers drifting down and now and then getting stuck to its beak.

"I thought you had to teach them not to rip the prey to shreds?" Piat asked.

"She's different. Jeez, Jack, can't you see how big she is? Bella's a sea eagle, Jack. I'm in a program for them. We get the chicks—long story there—and raise 'em by hand, then release 'em in the wild. Helps rebuild the population. They're nearly extinct. Isn't Bella great?" Hackbutt smiled like a parent with a bright toddler. "I love my birds!"

"You told Irene I'd want something," Piat said.

Hackbutt was picking up another piece of meat with a gloved hand. "Well—yeah, I apologize, Jack. I just meant—"

"You were being honest. And you were right. I want something."

Hackbutt looked at him and then turned so that Piat could see the bird better. He should have said something like *What?*, and in the old days he would have, but now he kept his mouth shut.

"How much did you tell Irene about what you used to do?"

"Nothing! Honest to God, Jack, nothing. I signed that paper, didn't I? I swore I'd never say anything and I didn't."

"What did you tell her I do?" He put it in the present tense because he wasn't going to tell Hackbutt that he was long out of the CIA and in fact a kind of renegade.

"Nothing."

"She must have asked."

"Oh, she said something like, 'Does he work for the government?'"

Irene was a lot smarter than that, Piat thought, although maybe she was one of those people who paid no attention to the worlds of war and politics and tricky shit. Still, she'd have heard of the CIA. "What did you say?"

"Oh, I just said, 'Sort of.'" The sea eagle had finished the pigeon and now snatched the next one from the glove and put it under one foot, then tried to disentangle the other foot from the remains of the head. It looked like a swimmer trying to shake water out of its ear. The mangled head fell to the ground and the bird started on the new prey.

"Tell you what, Digger." Digger had been an early code name, from the Digger O'Dell of an old comedy program; it had become a nickname when Hackbutt had become more than an incidental source. "I know that anything I ask you to undertake, Irene's got to know about—right? I see that. I acknowledge that's the nature of your relationship. It isn't usual, but we go back and—you two are bonded, right?" He was talking bullshit, but this was his spiel.

"Bonds of steel," Hackbutt said. "I heard that someplace. It says it all. It's love. It amazes me, but she loves me. *Me*. Thanks for understanding, Jack."

"I do understand, Digger, and I respect it, and I respect

you as a man. That's why I'll shut up right now if you want me to. I *do* want something; I want to offer you something, but I'll keep it to myself and we'll have a visit and we'll part friends and that'll be that, if you want." It was like ice-skating where you know that the farther you go, the thinner the ice gets: had he now gone too far?

Hackbutt, finishing with the bird, was offering it its regular perch; it seemed to want to stay on his arm, but he urged it, moving his arm, nudging the perch, and the bird moved over. Hackbutt picked up the bucket. Down the ragged line of pens, Piat could hear birds stirring as they smelled the blood. Hackbutt said, "I told myself I wouldn't do any more of that stuff. Not that I'm ashamed of it! But—" He came out of the pen and latched the makeshift gate. "I'm a coward, Jack. It scares me, what could have happened some of those times."

Piat had watched him handle the sea eagle, the bird's vicious beak four inches from his eyes. *You used to be a coward,* Piat thought.

"This wouldn't be like that." Piat shook his head. The old Hackbutt had merely provided information. He had been that kind of agent—records of meetings, oil contracts, stuff he heard at the bar from other geologists in Macao and Taipei actually not running much risk but always sweaty about it. "This wouldn't be dangerous. But I don't want to push it on you, Digger." They walked along the pens. Hackbutt stopped at the next gate. "It's just that you're the only man who could do it. Correction: the *best* man to do it."

"I don't want to go back to Southeast, Jack."

"This wouldn't be in Southeast," Piat lied watching him feed another bird. The older ones, Hackbutt had said, would be flown before they were fed; Piat could see him having to spend all day trying to get Hackbutt to say yes. Still, he made himself go slow. When Hackbutt had focused on the bird for ten minutes and nothing more had been said, Piat murmured, as if it had just come to him, "Doing a big art installation must be expensive."

"You better believe it. But worth it." This bird was restless and maybe dangerous; it flapped its wings while on his arm, and its beak flashed too close to Hackbutt's face, Piat thought. "Irene's going to be a household name. She has her own website. But that costs money, yes it does. Just moving an installation around from gallery to gallery costs a lot. Just the insurance! Plus we've got ideas for a coffee-table book of Irene's art, and she's into video now, maybe a DVD of the making of *The Body Electric.* She shot a lot of video of me boiling up a dead sheep I found. There're these great shots of the bones sort of emerging out of the flesh—sort of stop-action."

"The galleries pay for that?"

"You kidding?" Hackbutt laughed. He was wrestling the bird back to its perch. "Don't make me laugh."

"So where's the money come from? Irene's mother?"

"That's a sore subject." Hackbutt trudged along with his pail. "Between you and me, they had a big fight. Her mother doesn't understand about Irene's art. She hates feminists. We have to do everything ourselves. Irene's a free spirit."

"The project I have in mind might be able to help with that." Piat caught Hackbutt's head move out of the corner of his eye, and he said quickly, "Maybe you could support Irene's art and she wouldn't have to go crawling to her mother."

Hackbutt put the bucket down and folded his arms over his skinny chest. "You better tell me about that."

"I don't want to tempt you to do something you don't want to do, Digger."

"It's legit?"

"Oh, shit yes, well, if that's what's bothering you— Yeah, this is top-drawer, Dig. Have I ever bullshitted you? You know I was into some shitty stuff in Southeast; so were you, smuggling those parrots—"

"Irene doesn't know about that!"

"I'm just saying, this isn't anything like that. This is US policy. The most important kind." He lowered his voice as if he were going to pronounce the secret name of Yahweh. "*Anti-terrorism.*"

"I told you, I haven't got the guts for that stuff."

"Not that kind of 'anti-terrorism'. This is sort of social. It's a matter of contact. And maybe recruitment. You remember how that goes. Shmoozing. If anything starts to go down, the whole thing'll be moved to other people."

"I'm not very social, Jack."

Piat knew that, and he was looking at Hackbutt's wild hair and his scraggy beard and his bloodstained clothes and thinking that anything social was going to take a total makeover. But that wasn't his problem "You'd be fine."

"Why me?"

It was the moment he had been aiming toward. It was either going to make everything else a piece of cake, or it was going to end it with the finality of the cleaver. He leaned closer and almost whispered, "The birds."

Hackbutt didn't get it. He looked as if he didn't get it and he said so. Piat, his own arms folded now because he was cold, the early sun behind clouds that were piling over the whole sky, said, "You're an authority on falconry. No, you are, Dig, don't deny it. But you also love the birds. That love comes through in everything—when you handle them, when you talk about them. It's great—it's nice, it's a good quality. It's what makes you right for this project and it's what would make the project easy for you. See—" He looked up where the sun should have been and saw only a bright smudge behind deepening gray. "The means to make contact with a certain guy is through falconry. He's like you—he lives for the birds". Piat hoped it was true. He could push invention only so far.

"He flies them."

"Exactly."

"Is he an Arab?"

That caught Piat off guard. It was an obvious leap—It was the guess on which he was building the tale—but not one he'd expected Hackbutt to make. "You're getting ahead of me, man. What's the rule—we find out when we need to know?"

"Sorry."

"No, no—" He put his hand on Hackbutt's arm and then let go. "It would be meeting this individual and talking birds with him, letting him get to know you a little. Then, if that goes well, then the powers that be maybe would make a bird available to you to give him or something. Then—"

"What kind of bird?"

"Well, I don't know birds, Dig—"

"Do I get to pick the bird? There are some *fantastic* birds out there, Jack, I'd give my left nut just to handle one of them! Is that the way it would work?"

"That's the way it *could* work, I guess. You're the expert here, after all. Sure, I'd think you could maybe write your own ticket about that." Would Partlow buy it? Did it matter?

Hackbutt was hot-eyed. "There are some *incredible* birds out there! But Jeez, man, they cost thousands—I mean, big five figures!"

Piat knew he was overstepping his bounds. Still, what the hell. "The US is the richest country in the world, Dig."

Hackbutt looked away, his mouth working. Was he calculating figures? Almost without voice, he muttered, "Wow," and picked up the bucket. He unlatched a gate and then turned back. "I don't want to seem mercenary, Jack, but—Irene's installation, and everything—what kind of money are we talking? For me?"

On firmer ground, Piat said, "Fifty thou?"

Hackbutt's lips moved: *fifty*.

"If you score."

"God, I'd love to do that for Renie. God, that'd be great."

They went down the pens, feeding and handling birds, Piat lying back, letting Hackbutt think it over. They were heading for the farther pens where the older, trained birds were, and Hackbutt said as if out of nowhere, "Let's trot it past Irene. I think it's a fantastic opportunity. Incredible." He beamed at Piat.

A woman after her bath was always attractive to Piat. There was something about the skin, which seemed whiter, cooler, enormously tactile. If you added to this the baking of fresh bread, the appeal was overwhelming. He wanted to put her on the rug and go to it. Unfortunately, her husband was standing next to him.

Irene smiled at him as if they had a secret. "Almost done," she said. She was back in the day's long-skirted dress, without jewelry, little makeup that he could see on her broad face. She was a fairly tall woman, not Rubenesque or heavy but strong. Vegetarianism hadn't made her thin the way it had Hackbutt. "Surprised?' she said.

"The bread? I guess I am. I didn't figure you to cook." Piat *was* surprised.

"I'm a damned good cook. I do great country ham and shit like that, or I used to."

"Bread smells fantastic." He was laying it on too thick, but the smell of the bread—he pushed his mind back into the role of case officer.

"Baking bread is an art." She opened the oven, looked in, poked something. "Did you boys talk?"

"We did. Now you two need to talk." That seemed to please her.

Hackbutt went into the small living room, leaving the two of them in the kitchen.

She took the bread out and put it on the already littered table. One loaf was a low-mounded oval with coarse salt and something else on the top; the other was more ordinary, but both were beautifully browned and high. "No tasting," she said. "It has to cool." She came past him, stopped where he was in the doorway. She kissed him lightly on the lips. "So do I." She smiled. "All things in good time." She went out.

When he left, Piat paused at the dog again. This time, it sniffed his extended hand, then looked at him. He tried to pet it, but it withdrew its head; something like a warning, no more than the sound of the most distant thunder, came from its throat.

"You're a tough sell, doggie. Thank God you're not the falconer."

Explaining Irene and her importance (tactically, not sexually) didn't go down so well with Dave.

"It was great until she got involved," Piat said as if he hadn't planned it that way. "Then I had hell's own time with it."

"What the fuck did you even let her near it for?" Before Piat could answer, Dave shouted, "It's not the way you do it! You don't recruit the fucking girlfriend!" His broad face was red. Dave had been to the Ranch and had taken the courses, and so he knew at least in theory how things were done. Piat again had the feeling that he hadn't put the theory into practice much.

"This 'girlfriend' is different."

"You deal with the guy alone and keep her out of it. That's how it's done!"

"There'd be no deal if I had."

Dave made a contemptuous sound. Piat said, in a voice that meant *See how hard I'm working to keep from calling you a stupid asshole,* "Dave, you don't know this guy or this woman. They don't do things without each other."

"You've blown security and you've saddled me with a big fucking problem. I've got to run this guy!"

"Yeah, now thanks to me, you do."

"Christ, if I'd known you were going to tell the girlfriend, I'd have aborted you right the hell out. Jesus, what a bush-league thing to do. You know what Partlow would do to you if he knew?"

"Yeah, Dave, I know what Partlow would do. He'd say, 'Well, if that was your judgment call, okay.'"

"He wouldn't! He'd tell you you blew it and to get lost. Now *I'm* stuck with it." Dave was standing by the window of his room in the Western Isles Hotel, his fists clenched, his face blotched with rage. He was scared, Piat realized. Scared because he was going to have to do something that wasn't in the book. Dave said, "You're a fucking loser."

Piat didn't miss a beat: he didn't raise his voice or get red or insist on the challenge of eye contact. He said, as if he were lecturing a beginning class, "You get to him through her, at least at the start. Hackbutt will take a lot of stroking. Pass some of it through her. It'll please both of them and—"

"Don't tell me how to do my fucking job!"

Piat waited for him to stop and then went right on. "Hackbutt'll need a makeover. Clothes. A decent haircut. You're going to have to teach him how to—"

Dave lumbered toward him. "Get the fuck out of here! Stop talking to me! Get lost!"

Piat waited for him to come close. He thought it would be nifty to put Dave on his back. Maybe Dave saw that that was a possibility, too, because he pulled up before he was quite close enough. He shouted "Get lost!" again. Piat looked him in the eye and, in the same tone of somebody doing a routine, file-it-and-forget-briefing, said, "You're meeting Hackbutt at lunch tomorrow. I've made a reservation at a restaurant called the Mediterranea in Salen, partway down the island. Noon." He waited for Dave to take it in. "The hardest part of all was getting Hackbutt to agree to anybody but me as his CO. It took me an hour.

You're going to have to turn on all the charm when you meet him, Dave."

"I know how to do my job."

"Hackbutt's prepared to dislike you, because you aren't me. Hackbutt thought it was going to be me. He's a one-man man."

"That's fucking laughable—that we'd trust a job like this to you." Dave jabbed with his finger, but not very far, because there was always the possibility that Piat was fast enough to catch a flying finger and break it. "You're an agent! You're nothing but a goddam pissant agent! And don't you forget it!"

Piat put his hands up a little above his waist, palms out. Dave's hands jerked as if he expected a blow. Piat said, "There's an old Patsy Cline song—'Why Can't He Be You?' You might want to give it a listen to understand Hackbutt's position. Or you can just go on being an asshole and lose him and then you can tell Partlow why your agent won't work with you. I won't be around to blame, unfortunately for you. Lucky me. See you at noon tomorrow, *Dave.*"

Piat went out and closed the door very softly.

It rained most of the night and was still raining when they started for the meeting with Hackbutt, a depressing dribble from the low overcast, as if the universe above was saturated and had to let the water leak out somewhere. Dave was driving. Piat, in the left-hand seat, wasn't sure how he was supposed to get back to Tobermory after lunch if Dave took off with Hackbutt, but there was a bus, at least; asking Dave what he had in mind would prove too explosive, he thought, and anyway he didn't want Dave to get the idea that he could plan Piat's day.

Dave was still angry; maybe he'd been chewing on the scene in his room all night. He had bitched about the island roads all the way down, and he had come close to hitting another car more or less head on because he hadn't gone into the lay-by that opened next to them, and instead he had thought the oncoming car would be terrorized into getting out of his way. It hadn't been.

"Nice move," Piat couldn't resist saying when they were as far off the road as a stone wall would let them. The other car was vanishing behind them. The passenger-side fender was crumpled against the wall, and Piat couldn't have opened his door more than inch even if he'd wanted to.

It hadn't helped that another car had passed and the driver had laughed.

When they got out in the drizzle at Salen, Dave was in the silent phase of anger. He didn't bother with his raincoat but hunched his shoulders and walked toward the restaurant—if you can't punish somebody else for being stupid, punish yourself. Piat regretted having said what he'd said, because he knew he had made things worse, and it would all rub off on the meeting with Hackbutt. He didn't know why he cared that the meeting go well, but he did. Maybe for Hackbutt's sake. Maybe some vestigial pride of craft.

"Reservation," Dave growled to the smiling man behind the combination bar and reservation desk.

"Name?"

Dave ground his teeth. He didn't know Piat's cover name.

"Michaels," Piat said. "Jack Michaels."

"Oh, yes, right—we chatted on the phone about running." They had, in fact; now they chatted a bit more while Dave secreted bile. Piat had run a route the day before that this young man had suggested. "Fantastic," Piat said now. "Great scenery. Great run." The young man talked about hamstrings.

Hackbutt wasn't there yet. They sat at a table for four, from which the young man whisked a table setting. Dave folded his arms and looked around as if he expected somebody to call him a bad name. Piat ordered a glass of Brunello and bruschetta, which wasn't on the menu but didn't raise any eyebrows. He tried to mollify Dave by offering him some of the toasted bread when it came, but Dave simply looked at it. He wasn't going to allow himself to enjoy anything.

Hard on poor old Hackbutt.

"We could order," Piat said when Hackbutt was twenty minutes late.

"We'll wait."

Piat shrugged and asked the young man if by any chance they had some roasted pepper in olive oil. He was enjoying that when at last Hackbutt stumbled in, looking as if he'd just come from Lear's blasted heath—hair soaked and tangled, beard dripping, ancient drover's coat glued to his legs by the wet.

"I walked."

All three of them were standing by then. Hackbutt looked only at Piat. Piat saw Dave stick out his hand, and he said quickly, "This is the guy I've told you so much about, Digger. You two will really get along." He ducked out of the way of Dave's paw and went behind Hackbutt to help him off with the enormous and very wet coat. Hackbutt tried to turn to keep eye contact as if it were his only contact with reality. Piat gently turned him back and eased the coat off his shoulders, preventing Hackbutt from putting out his own hand. By the time he was able to do so, Dave had withdrawn the offer and was pulling back his chair.

"Siddown," Dave said.

Hackbutt looked at Piat for permission. Piat nodded. Hackbutt sat.

So did Piat. He picked up his fork and stabbed it into a piece of glossy roasted pepper and prepared to say something light and conversational about the weather, and Dave said to him, "You're done here. Bug out."

Piat looked at him. Dave, he thought, was incredible. He put the pepper in his mouth and picked up his last piece of bruschetta and mopped up some of the olive oil. When he looked at his old friend, Hackbutt's face showed frozen panic.

"You hear me?" Dave said.

"I did."

"You're done. Head out." He jerked one thumb toward the door. "Look for a Land Rover."

Hackbutt at last managed to open his mouth and wheeze, "Yeah, but—Jack, Jeez—"

Piat was on his feet. He patted Hackbutt's shoulder. "Everything'll be fine. It'll be great." He glanced at Dave and saw an expression of malice and triumph. Dave, he knew, was right—the case officer's the boss—but my god! he was a shit. Piat walked the few steps to the entryway, picked his raincoat off a hook, and opened the door. It was raining harder. He didn't look back because he didn't want to see Hackbutt's face.

He went out to the road and started looking for a Land Rover, found one around the corner of the restaurant. Partlow was just visible through the rain at the wheel. Piat climbed in the passenger door.

"There we are, Jerry," said Partlow. "Probably the easiest ten thousand dollars you ever earned." He put the car in gear and started out of town. The big chassis barely fit the single-lane road past the old inn that dominated the north end of Salen.

"That's it?" asked Piat. "And you're sure *Dave* can handle this from here?"

Partlow changed gears. "I'm sure Dave can handle him as well as anyone, Jerry." There were headlights visible on the long hill down from Aros Mains, and Partlow pulled into a lay-by to let the other car pass.

Piat considered a number of bitter replies and realized that, whatever mistakes Dave made, he himself was out of it. For two days, he had returned to the world of being a case officer. He had allowed Hackbutt's needs to become the horizon and limit of his world, just as he always had. The shoulder to cry on. The voice in the dark.

All done. Never again, and all that. He took a deep breath and let it out.

"So, now what?" Piat asked. He was gripping the hand-hold over the passenger window a little too hard. Partlow was driving fast in the rain, taking curves too aggressively, and with what Piat saw as a reckless disregard for the possibility of further oncoming vehicles on a single-lane road.

"I take you back to the hotel. You check out and take the ferry back to the mainland. And goodbye."

Piat trod hard on his anger. Partlow's dismissal was a little too much like Dave's. *Stick to what matters.* "When do I get my money? And my rods?"

"Why, immediately, if you like. Really, Jerry, your constant paranoia depresses me. You are done. You were hired to perform a service and you did a fine job. No hard feelings, I hope?"

Piat eyed an upcoming double hairpin turn with some misgivings, but he said, "No, Clyde. For once, I have no hard feelings." He shrugged, mostly at himself. But Partlow was clearly pleased with the progress of the operation, and he probably had money just lying around—"Although I did lose a thousand dollars' worth of fishing in Iceland, a trip I had planned and anticipated for some time."

"Jerry, just come out with it. I take it we're leading up to a demand for more cash?" Partlow sounded like a loving but aggrieved parent.

"Well." Piat's grasp on the handle loosened as Partlow reached the two-lane road that led into Tobermory. "Well, to be frank, Clyde, I'd think you could get me an airplane ticket and refund me the value of my trip to Iceland."

Partlow sighed. "I had intended to add fifteen hundred dollars as a success bonus, Jerry. Is that sufficient? You can purchase your own ticket."

Piat watched the town of Tobermory spreading out below them as they drove around the traffic circle. "Throw in the car for the rest of the day," he said. "Let me have the car. I'll go fishing."

Partlow sighed again. "Jerry, sometimes I think you aren't quite sane. It's raining. It's cold."

"So you won't leave the hotel. It's a spate, Clyde. Give me the money and my rods and I'll get an afternoon's fishing here. And no hard feelings." Curious how easily manipulated Partlow was on this. It had never occurred to Piat before that Partlow wanted his approval. But he did. *Interesting.*

Partlow turned and looked at him, as if assessing him. Almost certainly *was* assessing him. Then he smiled. "What the hell. Just don't run off with the car, Jerry, okay? It's a rental, and I signed for it."

Piat smiled. "Clyde, why would I run off with the car?"

Piat spent thirty minutes with Partlow signing forms. It amused him that Clyde was so punctilious on his forms—another sign that the man hadn't spent enough time running real agents. Perhaps that was the root of his insecurity. Piat complied cheerfully, however, especially when he discovered that he could sign all the forms in a cover name. He acquired sixty-five hundred dollars in large bills and retrieved his fishing gear and his battered backpack.

In his own room at the Mishnish he called Irene. Hackbutt would still be at the restaurant; Piat's responsibility to the operation was over; what better time to get her to join him? Except that nobody answered at the farm. He called airlines at Glasgow and discovered that, as he had suspected, he couldn't get back to Greece for twenty-four hours. Irene was vanishing over his horizon—Hackbutt would get back to the farm soon; complications would set in. He shrugged. In an hour, he was in the car, which he loathed as too big and too flashy—and too damned short to carry his rod already set up.

He had ideas about where to go to fish—he'd virtually memorized the green tourist brochure in his room. He sat in the car, watching the rain over the sea, and tried to remember how fishing worked in Scotland. You had to buy tickets—there was virtually no public fishing. At least, that's what he'd read in the brochure. A glance at his watch told him that it was two p.m. He shut off the car and went back into the hotel.

The windows of the bookstore were full of children's books and travel guides to catch the tourist's eyes, but as soon as he was through the door and out of the rain he saw the case of flies and the corner dedicated to fishing. The floor was old wood, the ceiling low—it was an eighteenth-century shop front, or perhaps two joined together.

A pretty young woman stood behind the counter, perhaps sixteen years old—a little young for Piat, but a pleasure to see. "I wonder if you could tell me about the fishing," Piat asked. "I have the afternoon."

"Would you be wanting the trout, then?" she asked.

"Salmon?" Piat asked, a little wistfully. "Or is there sea trout fishing here?"

"Some, aye. My da would know better." She spoke quite seriously—fishing was a serious subject here. "He's in the back. Shall I get him, then?"

She made Piat feel quite old. "Yes, please," he said, like a boy on his best behavior.

She vanished into an office in the back. Piat began to browse. The front of the store was full of books for tourists, with maps and walking guides and a whole series of books on the genealogy and history of the island. All locally printed. He flipped through one, a walking guide with historical notes. The antiquarian in him automatically counted the hill forts, the duns, the standing stones—the island boasted a strong archaeological record.

"Are you looking for sea trout?"

Piat turned from the book rack and saw a tall man, gaunt, with a huge smile and a shock of black hair. He did not have the expected accent.

"Yes. Sea trout," said Piat.

"Not what they used to be, I'm afraid. Had some Americans catching them in the Aros last year—they come every year. Aros estuary. I can give you that for this evening, but there's no point in going there now. The tide's down."

Piat nodded. "How much?"

"Five pounds for the estuary. It's best fished two hours either side of high tide. I wouldn't even start on it until six. I'm Donald, by the way."

"Jack," said Piat, shaking hands. He'd been Jack for two days. The lie came automatically, and Piat thought *Why'd I do that?* "I'd like to fish this afternoon, too."

"You have a car?" Donald asked. Donald spoke the way Clyde Partlow wanted to speak, with no trace of an island accent—like someone who had gone to all the best schools. Eton. Oxford. Maybe Cambridge. "I don't guarantee you'll get any fish, but Loch Làidir is available." He seemed wistful. "It's quite a climb from the road."

The man was already filling out a bright orange card. "Leave this on the dashboard of your car."

Piat watched him for a few seconds. "Where am I going?" he asked.

"Oh, yes. Right." Donald flashed his gigantic smile again. "Do you know the island at all?"

"I can get from here to Salen," Piat replied with a shrug. "I've driven over near Dervaig."

"Right. You'll want a map." He pointed to the rack of Ordnance Surveys. He rattled off driving directions. "It should take you less than half an hour to get there. Then the climb—you see this stream?—strenuous but worth it." His forefinger covered the mark on the map. "Just follow it up to the loch.

Nothing in it but wee trout. The sea trout come up the other side, from the sea, of course. Once you reach the loch, it's still difficult going—rock all the way round. But there's a gravel beach on this shore. I'd fish there, by the crannog."

Piat saw a tiny island on the Ordnance map, with the word "crannog" in minute italics. "What's a crannog?" he asked.

Donald laughed. "A local oddity. An artificial island. Built long ago. You have waders?"

Piat shook his head.

Donald considered him. Piat knew that Donald had just written him off as a novice.

"I forgot them," he muttered.

"You really will need them." Then, cheerfully, "I suppose that you could just skip about on the shore. The loch is very deep in places."

With a sigh for the money, Piat chose a pair of heavy rubber thigh waders from the fishing equipment. He wondered if the bulky things would go in his pack. He noted that the shop had light waders—very pricey. But they'd fit in his pack, and in effect, Partlow was paying. *What the hell.*

Piat paid.

The climb to the loch *was* spectacular. The terrain was very like Iceland, with shocks of coarse grass over gravel and volcanic rock. There was a path at first, but it soon divided into hundreds of sheep tracks, all going in the same general direction up the stream. It took him almost an hour to climb over the last crest and look down into what had to be the caldera of an extinct volcano. The shingle of gravel was clearly visible across the loch, and so was the crannog, seen at this distance as a humped island with a single tree growing from it, the tree visible for a mile in any direction because it was the only one. Again, Piat was reminded of the immense vistas of Africa.

Beyond the far lip of the caldera was only sky. High above,

an eagle circled. Piat drank a cup of tea from his thermos and started down. The sense of openness—freedom, even—Piat couldn't think of the origin of the tag, but the words *above him, only sky* ran around and around his head. The Bible? The Beatles?

It was three-thirty before he arrived on the gravel and set up his rod. He fished the shallow water between the gravel and the crannog for fifteen minutes, hooking and releasing a half-dozen minute brown trout. Then he put on the light, stocking-foot waders, a wet task in the rain, and pulled his boots on over them. No choice there. His boots were in for a pounding.

He worked the seaward end of the gravel, moving slowly into the deeper water. The loch itself was quite deep and very clear, so that when the watery sun made momentary appearances, he could see the complex rock formations in the depths. Right at his feet was a hollow cone of rock thirty feet across and so deep in the middle that light couldn't penetrate it, some sort of ancient volcanic vent. He cast to the edge of the vent and immediately caught a strong brown trout, perhaps a pound, which he watched rise from the depths to seize the sea-trout fly. As far as he could see, the loch was short on food for fish and long on fish, but watching the predatory glide of the brown to his fly was pure joy.

A younger and braver fisherman could walk out along the vent's top ridge to fish the deeper water. Piat actually considered it for a moment while he landed the brown trout before deciding that the creeping cowardice of age was going to win this one. He released the brown. He'd eat in a restaurant for his last meal on the island, and they wouldn't want to cook his fish.

The crannog rose like a temptation, only fifteen or twenty meters off shore, the perfect platform from which to fish the vent, and whatever further wonders might lurk in the loch beyond. Piat climbed out of the water on the shingle and eyed the crannog. The water was too deep to walk out directly—he'd be over the top of his belt at the midpoint, soaked to the skin and cold. But there were stones under the surface of the water, two sets of stepping stones. The stones themselves were well down, but he *thought* he could move from one stone to the next without going over his waders.

Piat knew he was going to attempt it. He laughed at himself while he drank some tea, because his failure to accept the lure of the vent ridge meant that he was going to try and prove himself on something just as ridiculous. Partlow had thought he was crazy for fishing in the rain. Piat raised his cup of tea to Partlow. Then he stowed it, put his pack under a particularly large clump of grass as the best shelter from the rain available, and studied the stones one more time.

The left-hand stones looked more accessible. They started in deeper water but stuck up higher and seemed to have larger and flatter tops. Piat waded out to the first stone and stepped up. The surface of the stone was covered in a dark olive slime and his hiking boots slipped badly. He moved cautiously to the next stone. The water came to the middle of his knee. He used his rod as a staff, heedless of the wetting of his reel, and took a long gliding step to the third stone. It was less slippery, and he paused to rest, sweat already pouring down his chest under his sweater.

The fourth stone was clearly visible now, a darker and larger stone that marked the halfway point. Piat knew the moment his boot touched the surface under water that this stone was slippery, and then he was in the water, his waders full and then his mouth. The water was cold—so cold that it hit him like an electric shock—and the bottom was ooze, not rock, so that his feet were sinking and he had no purchase.

Piat had long experience of his own panic reflex and he beat it down, kept hold of his rod and kept the other hand in contact with the stepping stone until he had control of his brain, and then he used the strength of his arms to pull himself up on the rock, heedless of the temperature of the water. The wind on his head was like a new shock of ice. He'd lost his hat, which was scudding across the loch on the surface of the water. Mud and ooze billowed around his thrashing feet. He pulled himself up by the strength of his arms, heaving the weight of his full waders to the rock.

He fell again, just one stone out from the shore, but he was prepared this time, and his fall merely caused him to sit down hard on the stone and take a new batch of cold water over his waders.

Close up, the crannog was composed of small, round rocks the size of his fist, raised in a low mound. Underneath the water, the mound of rubble continued, although he could clearly see a beam or heavy rafter of wood deep in the clear water of the leeward side.

He stripped. He wrung out each sodden garment and put the wool socks and the jeans and sweater back on under the now empty waders, made a bundle of the rest of the clothes and tied it around his waist. He was warmer already—his jacket and the waders were windproof, and the wool was warm even when wet. Just to make a point to himself, he made some desultory casts into the deep water beyond the crannog. Something made a sizeable silver flash on his fourth cast—

Gone. A sea trout, without question. A good fish. He cast again, and again, trying to relive the moment of the earlier cast and remember just what he had done, eventually wondering if he had imagined the whole thing. His head was cold, and that wasn't good.

Time to go.

The crannog interested him, even while he stood shivering on it. Between casts and retrieves, he tried to imagine how it had come here, how much effort it would have taken people (how many people—a family? Two families?) to build—and why. For the fishing? And when?

He left his boots off for the return trip. With his socks worn *over* the waders, he had reasonably sure footing and made his way without incident. He was losing too much heat from his head. He drank the rest of his thermos of tea and ate a sandwich made of the leftovers from his attempt to find presents for Hackbutt and pulled the plastic bags over his head, and then his cotton shirt, now wrung out, and then another bag. Better than nothing.

The walk back out was easier than he had expected. Perhaps because it was downhill, or the psychological effect of having his car in sight from the moment he climbed out of the caldera, but the climb down served only to keep the worst of the chill away. The Land Rover's heater was a magnificent, efficient machine and he was warm before he negotiated the mountain pass on the road back to Salen. The heater almost made up for the width of the monster, but as he negotiated lay-bys and oncoming headlights, he cursed the car again. Darkness was falling. He drove carefully, passed the Aros estuary with regret, and went straight to the hotel.

In the morning, he stopped at the bookstore on his way to his car. Donald was already at work and greeted him enthusiastically. "Did you get anything?" he called, as soon as Piat was through the door.

Piat recounted his adventures. He had recorded his catch on the tickets and produced them.

Donald laughed. "You climbed on the crannog, then?"

"Who built it?" asked Piat.

Donald shrugged. "We have some books—people always want to know. There are four of them on the island, more on the mainland of course." He pulled out a battered Ordnance Survey map and flipped it fully open. "One here, on the Glen Lochs—that's quite a walk. Some fishing if you like wee browns. One here, on Loch Frisa. The one you climbed, of course, down south. And one just above the town, here. Quite a story to go with the local one."

Piat had watched Donald's thick fingers moving over the map, thinking automatically *no cover, no cover, visible from the road.* "Hmmm?" he said. "A story?" Piat was a good listener.

"A local man, a farmer, had the notion that he could build a dam on the loch above the town and regulate the flow of water—perhaps he intended to build a mill. What he did in fact was to drain the loch. The crannog was revealed as the water ran out—and they found a boat, completely intact, all sorts of other objects."

Piat made interested noises throughout. "Where are they?"

"Oh, as for that, you'd have to ask Jean or my daughter. Perhaps in the museum?"

Piat left with two books on crannogs, one an archaeological report from a dig on the mainland and one more general. He stopped at the museum, but it was closed.

He made the ferry line with seconds to spare, checked in at Lufthansa two hours early in Glasgow, and landed in Athens via London and Munich in time to eat a late dinner on the Plaka and fall into a hotel bed. He had nine thousand, four hundred and twelve dollars and some change, a new wardrobe, a new historical interest, and a return ticket to Glasgow. It'd been cheaper that way. *What the hell,* he thought as he lay in bed. *Maybe someday I'll go back.*

The next day, he splurged and caught the high-speed ferry to Lesvos, saving twelve hours. He called Mrs Kinnessos from Piraeus and told her that yes, he would be taking the house for another six months, even at the summer price, and he was absurdly pleased when she offered him a discount for his constancy. By the time the ferry reached Mytilene, he had made himself the middleman on a deal for some

Roman statuary from the Ukraine headed to the United States. His cut would be seven hundred euros.

Molyvos seemed ridiculously crowded after Mull. He sat in the chocolate shop half way up the town with his laptop open, drinking Helenika and thinking about sea trout and crannogs.

3

A week later, Clyde Partlow was sitting at a computer in an office that was, by CIA standards, big. Not as big as the director's, but big. No private dining room, but a private john. Partlow was a somebody, so all the more reason that he read reports direct from the computer screen. Partlow sneered at the old fogeys who still insisted on hard copies and who had to telephone for help if their screen coughed up an error message. After his fashion, Partlow was with it.

His right hand was on a mouse so that he could scroll down easily. On the screen was something that called itself a "draft contact report," typed into a template so that the form number was at the top and the headings were boxed. The ones that interested Partlow were the operation number and the "task number served." Together, they interested him deeply.

He began to read. Almost at once, the slight frown of concentration that had puckered his smooth, sleek face deepened to a scowl of concern. Another paragraph, and the scowl began to take in anger, then anxiety, then despair. He scrolled down faster, clearly glossing text, whipping to the next page and then right to the end. He read the final paragraph and then sat back and pressed his forehead. He breathed deeply and rubbed his fingers and thumb back and forth across his forehead as if smoothing the wrinkles that the reading had created. He breathed out, the air expelled in little puffs, lips pushing out and in. He shook his head.

Partlow hadn't got where he was by wasting energy on his feelings. He'd never been known to blow up at anybody and he'd never been known to weep with gratitude or joy or even grief. He gave congratulations well and he censured well, right up to and including firing people. They always left thinking that there was nothing personal about good old Clyde. So now, instead of doing what his adrenal gland and the atavistic, caveman part of his brain wanted to do, he sat back and read the entire four-page document with care.

When he was done, he called up his address book, picked a name, tapped it into his telephone and waited. When a voice at the other end said, "Defense Intelligence Agency, Petty Officer Clem speaking this-is-not-a-secure-line, sir, to whom may I direct your call, *sir*!"

"Captain Alan Craik, please."

Mike Dukas was sitting late in his office because he was the Special Agent in Charge, Naval Criminal Investigative Service, Naples, and he and about half of his responsibilities were behind schedule. Down the hall, his assistant, Dick Triffler, was spending valuable time filling out paperwork for a three-year antiterrorism self-study that nobody would ever read; beyond him, two special agents were together in an office, trying to hammer out the charges against a sailor who had got drunk and beaten up a Turkish police cadet.

Dukas heard the ping of his secure telephone; he hit the button without taking his eyes off what he was reading. He was always reading now—reading or writing or going to meetings; the good days of getting out into the field were over. He sighed, looked up at the screen of the secure telephone, and read, "From: Defense Intelligence Agency, Captain Craik."

He hit the talk button and said, "Al, that you?"

The answer came like static from deep space, Craik's voice laid over it like an alien signal. "Mike?"

"Yeah. Al?"

"Hey, Mike."

"Would you like to move to a conversation, or you want to stay with IDing each other?" He heard Craik laugh, and then they spent thirty seconds on how-are-you-how-are-the-kids-how's-your-wife. Their spat—if that was what it had been—in Reykjavik was forgotten. Then Craik said, "I just got off the phone with Clyde Partlow."

"Better than getting on the phone with Clyde Partlow. Now what?"

A barely perceptible pause, but enough to sound a warning. "He wants Piat back."

"Oh, shit. What the hell for?"

"Wouldn't I like to know! Of course he didn't say. He just asked if I knew where I could get hold of Piat again."

"And you said, 'Oh, sure, my pal Dukas carries him around in his back pocket.' Right?"

"I said I'd see."

"Al—" Dukas had been trying to read a report while they talked; now, he tossed the stapled papers halfway across his desk. "I'm not Piat's personal manager."

"Chill out, okay?"

"Once, as a favor, I found him for you. Twice is too much like a job."

"I think he wants him again because something's wrong."

"Contact didn't work."

"Or it worked for a while and then it went bad. It's been more than a week, after all."

"Piat could be anywhere."

"Yeah, but I'll bet you know how to reach him."

Dukas saw his number two, Dick Triffler, appear in his doorway, and he waved him in and pointed at a chair. "So maybe I know an address in cyberspace where sometimes he takes messages. So?" He mouthed "Al Craik" at Triffler, who raised his eyebrows.

Craik's artificially tinny voice said, "Get a message to him."

"What—'Go see Clyde Partlow'? That wouldn't even get him off a bar stool."

"Persuade him."

"Al, I know where you're coming from, but why should I persuade Jerry Piat to do anything? The man's a loner, a renegade, a goddam outsider! He doesn't want to go see anybody! Piat's opted out and he knows the price and he's willing to pay it."

"Will you try?"

"Al, I got an NCIS office to run!" He winked at Triffler. "Sitting right here is Dick Triffler, who would take my place if I took the time to persuade Jerry Piat. Do you want the US Navy to have to depend on Dick Triffler?"

"Say hello for me."

"Al says hello."

Triffler smiled. "Tell him I said hello."

"Triffler says hello. We all cozy now? Okay. Listen, I'll do this much: I'll send Piat a message. If he's willing to listen, I'll try to talk to him. By phone. But I can't devote my life to this, Al. Neither can you, for that matter. It isn't as important as running the Naples office of NCIS. It isn't as important as being the collections officer for DIA."

"It's important enough for Partlow to have messaged the head of NCIS to ask for special cooperation, attention Michael Dukas, NCIS Naples."

Dukas flashed Triffler a look of disgust. "This was your idea?"

"This was Partlow's idea. He asked me to call you before the message got to you so you wouldn't take it the wrong way. Mike, I know it's an imposition; I know you're working your ass off; but so am I. I'm just the messenger here. Don't take it out on me."

Dukas sighed. "So Partlow wants me to bring Piat in. Even if I have to take time away from my job. And NCIS has already said that's what I should do. Are you in it with me?"

"Not this time. I got no authorization, no orders."

"You know, I thought I might actually take Saturday off this week and take my wife to Capri, which I've been promising to do for two years?"

Craik made sympathetic noises, and they tossed stories about overwork back and forth, and they parted friends. Dukas, when he had hung up, looked at Triffler with an expression of disgust. "I've been drafted," he said. His hand was still on the secure telephone.

Triffler, an elegant African American who played Felix to Dukas's Oscar, merely smiled. "Al got another wild hare running?"

Dukas grunted and held up a finger, as if to say *Wait until I check something*. He picked up the phone, and, shaking his head at Triffler's pantomimed offer to leave, called his boss in Washington. After a few pleasantries, Dukas said, "I hear I'm being ordered to run an errand for the CIA."

A brief silence, then his boss's voice: "Not my doing."

"Higher up the line? The DIA?"

After another hesitation, "Higher than that."

When Dukas had put the phone down in its cradle, he turned to Triffler. "What's the Pentagon's interest in sending me to do the CIA's work?" He cocked a cynical eye at Triffler. "You remember Clyde Partlow?" Dukas told him about the Iceland trip and the new request to find Piat. "Piat isn't exactly my asshole buddy."

"So you send him an email, and if he doesn't answer, you're off the hook."

"Well—" Dukas hitched himself around toward his pile of paper. "Apparently I'm getting orders to bring Piat in. I may have to leave the office."

"And put me in charge for a day? Lucky me!"

Dukas waved a hand at the pile of paper. "My son, one day all this will be yours."

"What's your wife going to say?"

Dukas groaned.

Piat's Ukrainian deal went down without a hitch, and the seller paid up, just like that. He'd been home for ten days, and Mull seemed very far away. Now Piat sat on the precarious balcony of his favorite chocolate shop and drank his second Helenika of the day, closed his laptop with a snap, and contemplated the archaeological report he had bought on Mull about Scottish crannogs. He was bored and he had nothing better to do than read it. He'd glanced through it on the plane—very dry, almost no analysis at all—and now he turned to the color plates of the finds. Most of them were dull, and worse, unsaleable—who would buy a three-thousand-year-old bundle of ferns once used as bedding? But there were valuable items, as well: a single gold bead, a copper axe head, a remarkable slate pendant shaped with sides so well smoothed he could almost feel them under his hands.

Crannogs were late European Bronze Age. And the cold water preserved things very well indeed. Piat sipped coffee and ordered a third. He felt rich.

Lesvos was full of tourists. Piat had avoided them for a year by leaving the island during the height of the season—one of the reasons he'd headed off for Iceland, and devil take the consequences. Now Molyvos was crawling with them, and his chocolate shop perched on the edge of the town with a hundred-foot drop to the old Turkish gate below was filling up. Soon enough, Sergio would give him the eye and suggest that he move along and make room for more customers. Piat looked into the shop. There was a big, dark guy at the counter with a very pretty woman with a baby. Piat admired the woman's backside for a moment, and then—

"Jesus," Piat said, out loud. The man at the counter was Mike Dukas. Again.

Dukas led the woman out on to the balcony. The whole structure moved under their weight—it was sturdy, but it did protrude well out over the cliff. Dukas looked embarrassed.

"Jerry?" he said. His hand was out.

There wasn't anywhere to run. Piat shook hands. "Mike." He gave the woman a smile. She smiled back, and then looked up at Dukas as if exchanging a joke.

Dukas said, "This's my wife, Leslie." Leslie Dukas was twenty years younger than her husband, rather stunningly pretty next to such an ugly man despite the pack full of baby that she carried.

Piat indicated his table and waved through the window for Sergio.

Leslie stood for a moment, shaking hands with Piat. "You guys can just do the guy thing. We'll go have a feed, won't we, kiddo?" A tiny pudgy hand reached out of her baby pack and tweaked one of her nipples. She laughed. "Gotta go, guys."

Piat was left with Dukas. Dukas ordered coffee and a big pastry. He made a joke to Sergio in decent Greek.

"Your wife's lovely," Piat said.

"Yeah," said Dukas. And again, "Yeah."

"That's the small talk, then. What are you doing here?"

Dukas still looked embarrassed. *He doesn't want to be here,* Piat thought.

"Partlow wants you back," Dukas said. He shrugged.

"Dave's already fucked it away?" asked Piat.

Dukas shrugged again, looking as Greek as a local, his arms spread wide on the bench back, his weight slumped a little. "Did you expect it?"

"Phff." Piat's noise was contemptuous. He had realized himself that he was still smarting under the speed with which he'd been tossed aside. "I don't know what Clyde was thinking. The guy couldn't handle a hooker."

Dukas snorted. His eyes were on Piat's book, but they flicked up and met Piat's quickly. Piat was off thinking about Dave and Partlow. "So where do I meet Clyde? Is he hiding in a hotel in Mytilene?"

Dukas passed Piat a slip of paper. Piat disappeared it into his pack with a minimum of fuss. Dukas said, "Not as far as I know."

"Still in Scotland?"

It was the look on Dukas's face that finally warned Piat—a little look of interest, almost triumph, at "Scotland." Dukas had been looking at the book—Dukas hadn't said anything—

"You *don't* know, do you?" Piat said.

Dukas hesitated and then shook his head. "Nope," he said. And then he smiled and said, "But I bet it's in Scotland."

Piat leaned closer to Dukas. "I thought you were in on this." He shoved the crannog book into his pack and glanced at the slip of paper—just a DC telephone number.

"Partlow doesn't know where to find you." Dukas rubbed his nose and his eyes met Piat's. "I thought you might prefer it to stay that way."

It wasn't said as a threat, or at least it didn't sound like a threat to Piat, and he had been threatened by experts. But it did speak volumes. Dukas was saying *I could have fucked you and I didn't, so you owe me.*

"I do. I like it here." Piat glanced out over the cliff to the brilliant blue sea and the black volcanic beach. It all flitted around his brain—Hackbutt and Irene and the birds and Dave and Partlow and the sea trout in the loch. On balance, it didn't look very attractive from here. It looked like work. "How much?"

"I'm just the messenger." Dukas was looking over the balcony. Piat realized that Dukas's wife was directly below them on the street.

They both watched Leslie. Her laugh and the baby's mewl

of delight were easy to hear. Then Dukas said, "Listen, Jerry—Al Craik thinks it's important. You know—"

"I know you two go way back. Everyone in the business knows."

"Okay. That's all I can say, except I've been straight with you, and now I'd like a little payback. I'd like to know what this is about."

Piat sat back. "I don't really know, Mike." He didn't want Dukas to feel he was shutting him out—Piat was gathering his thoughts and trying to decide where his interest lay. And, he admitted to himself, Dukas *had* been straight with him. "Partlow asked me to re-recruit an old agent."

"In Scotland?"

"Mull."

Dukas made a gesture: "Mull" had no meaning.

"Mull's an island. Scotland." Piat shut up. He'd said enough—way too much, probably, but he'd provided plenty of data for a guy like Dukas.

"And?" probed Dukas.

"I signed a piece of paper. Ask Partlow." Piat indicated the backpack, and by extension, the phone number.

Dukas shook his head. "That's the best you can do for me, Jerry?"

Piat sipped the last of his Helenika. He found that he wasn't thinking about what favors he might owe Dukas. He was seeing another angle—his own safety. Something about this operation just didn't smell right. Now it stank more. He felt the pull of the scrap of paper and he thought that he might just tell Partlow to suck eggs—but he suspected Partlow was going to have to make a big offer. After all, Mike Dukas had come all the way here with his pretty wife. So, big money. And Piat reacted to big money.

So, say he did it. Took the money. Dukas might give him an angle. What if the whole thing was *bad*. Piat had seen ops go bad, back in the day.

All that in the blink of an eye and a sip of Helenika. "The guy—my old agent—is a falconer."

They shared a long look.

Piat pushed his cup aside and leaned forward to Dukas. "My turn. I really don't know squat about this, okay? And I just told you everything you'd need to know—right? Okay. So here's my side. Give me your home number and an address. Maybe I'll tell you a thing or two as we go along. Or maybe I'll tell Clyde to fuck off. Okay? And in return—in return, if I do this, and it goes to shit, you get me out. Because, let's face it, I don't like Clyde Partlow."

He certainly had Dukas's attention. "Get you out? Jerry, no offense, but I'm no part of this."

Piat looked him squarely in the eye. "Bullshit. You want the goods on Partlow's op. Frankly, I think Partlow will work overtime to keep me in the dark, but I'm offering you my 'cooperation.' Right? And you give me a nice number on a piece of paper somewhere, and poof! I'm an informer, and you can protect me. Right?"

Dukas shook his head. "I don't hire informers inside the CIA."

Piat laughed. "You would if there were any available. I'm not 'inside the CIA' anymore. I'm some guy, a petty crook, that Partlow wants for the great game. I could even be a pretty decent source on antiquities."

Dukas looked so dubious that Piat laughed, and then they both laughed. Other patrons glanced at them.

Dukas leaned forward and shook his head. "No, Jerry. No protection. I'd like to hear what you have to say. I'd probably go to bat for you if Partlow tries to screw you in the end. But I'm not going to give you a security blanket so that I can find in a year that you left it wrapped around my head while you liberated the contents of the British Museum."

Leslie returned and interrupted them. They were staying in Skala Eressos and she said they had to go. Piat walked them down to the old Turkish gates as if he were their host, pointing out other features they might enjoy, rating the quality of pots in each shop, indicating the good silversmith and the bad one. In the tunnel of the gate, he stopped, and he and Dukas shook hands. Dukas's handshake included a slip of paper.

When he opened it in his house, it had a phone number in Naples and an address. Piat smiled. He realized that he felt reassured. Few things and fewer people had that effect on him anymore.

He went out the door to call Clyde Partlow.

4

Piat's passport was less than a year from expiry. This cost him an hour in UK customs at Glasgow and preyed on his mind as he drove his rental Renault up the A82 along Loch Lomond and into the highlands. Ingrained paranoia and a horde of legal issues prohibited him from simply renewing it.

The Green Welly Stop at the turn for Oban provided him with terrible coffee and a delicious, fat-filled pastry, and fuel for his car as well. He browsed the sporting goods, annoyed as usual by the prices that the English and Scots paid for stuff that would cost a few dollars in a Wal-Mart. He was looking for something to buy for Hackbutt or Irene. Nothing offered—and besides, he didn't have a contract yet. No need to spend his own money.

Oban reminded him of Mytilene—same harbor shape, same stone houses, same odd mixtures of industry, fishing, and tourism. He parked on the high street, checked his time, and whiled away fifteen minutes in a very promising shop that catered to high-end "anglers" and sportsmen in general. The shop carried rifles for stalking and shotguns for pheasant and grouse—not that Piat ever felt the need to have a gun, but always handy to have access. They also had a wide selection of sporting clothes—decent wellies, good boots, shooting coats. In his mind, he was spending

Partlow's money. He thought that he knew what was coming with Partlow. Why else summon him back?

When his watch read three exactly, Piat paid for a tide table for the area and a handful of flies and walked through the door, casually checking his car, the street, and the faces and apparel of passers-by in one sweeping glance. He didn't see anything to alert him and moved off down the high street toward the Oban Hotel. He entered the lobby at four minutes after three and went to the main desk.

In minutes he was on his way to meet Partlow. The opening door revealed a cheerful room with a view of the harbor and two comfortable chairs. One of them was occupied.

"Hello, Clyde," Piat said.

Partlow smiled. It was a rare smile—quite genuine as far as Piat could tell. It told him a great deal. Partlow was genuinely glad to see him. Piat added a zero to his fee.

"Right on time, Jerry. I'm so glad."

Piat considered saying that the ability to be in a place on the dot of a particular minute from half the world away was a matter of basic competence in the profession. He thought about several ways of saying it—snappy, derogatory, modest. *Wrong. Partlow needs me, and this is the time to make a new start.* Because he couldn't decide how to begin, he said nothing.

Partlow didn't seem to know how to begin, either. He cleared his throat, twice. "Good trip, Jerry?"

Piat shrugged. "My passport's almost expired. It cost some time. I'm here." Now he was enjoying it. Partlow was discomfited by the absence of raillery or outburst.

Partlow nodded as if Piat had said something important. He clasped his hands over his knees.

Finally, Piat decided that they might sit that way all day. He *was* curious. "I take it Hackbutt tossed Dave out."

Partlow rubbed his face. He looked short on sleep. Piat couldn't remember seeing Clyde Partlow short on sleep. After a few seconds, he said, "Well, no. I tossed Dave out, Jerry. But in effect, the result is the same."

Piat nodded. "And you want me back, I take it? Or just some advice?"

Partlow had been fed the hook, but he didn't take it immediately. "Where did you leave Dave with the matter of the girlfriend, Jerry?"

Piat narrowed his eyes and slouched. "I told him we had to recruit the girl to get Hackbutt back. He told me to fuck off."

Partlow nodded slowly, as if his fears were confirmed. "No bullshit, now, Jerry. You *told* him to recruit the girl."

Piat was annoyed. He took his time, and then said, "Yes."

"Dave believes you sabotaged him and the operation."

"He'd have to believe that, wouldn't he? Otherwise he'd have to believe he wasn't competent to recruit and run a US national in a friendly country." Piat allowed a little edge to creep in, but otherwise stayed at Partlow's level—remote, professorial, as if the operation were an academic exercise.

Partlow steepled his hands and pursed his lips. "My fault. I should have kept you on board. I did have another CO lined up, but he went to Iraq instead."

Piat spoke quietly, the way he did when he consoled a survivor. "I tried, Clyde. He just played the goon, and I walked away."

"You could have warned me." Partlow held up a hand and winced. "No, forget I said that." He blew out several puffs of breath. "You *did* try to tell me."

Piat raised his eyebrows.

They sat in silence for a while. It finally dawned on Piat that there might not be an operation anymore. Pisser if true. He glanced at Partlow, who was watching a sailboat, a two-masted ketch out in the harbor, as she got her foresail up, the boat and the sail crisp and clear against the blue water and the clear sky. Maybe not a pisser. Back to Greece and shot of the whole thing.

"I could run you directly. That's how I should have done it to begin with. Free hand, Jerry. On an op that matters."

Piat had pretended to be a gentleman for ten minutes, and he found the restraint wearing. "I could make a real difference?" he said with gentle sarcasm. "I've heard this speech a few times, Clyde. Hell, I've made it a few times."

Partlow nodded, or rather his head swayed back and forth as if he were laughing very softly. He said, "Listen, Jerry. As such things are reckoned, you were one of the best of your generation. So good that everyone passed you over for promotion so that they could use your reports and your agents to make their careers."

Piat shrugged. The flattery was an essential part of any recruitment speech, but he couldn't completely resist its allure, as he suspected it was true.

"Now I have an operation with one of your old agents, a prickly man with a bitch of a wife. I need him, Jerry. I don't have another falconer to hand, and Mister Hackbutt gets top grades from some people that matter in the falconry world. And here you are. Will you do it?"

"What, for love?"

Partlow sighed. Piat thought he was secretly pleased to be on familiar ground. "For money, Jerry."

"How long?"

"As long as it takes."

Piat had this part ready. "Fifteen hundred a day. All expenses and no bullshit about them. That's going to be a lot, because Hackbutt's a social basket case and needs clothes, deportment, time eating where rich people eat, all that stuff. No bullshit about any of it."

Partlow looked over his hands. "Jerry, why do you think Hackbutt needs all these things?"

Piat was dismissive. "Falconry is about money and power. You're targeting an Arab right? Somebody rich, somebody with old money and birds."

Partlow deflated very slightly. "Touché," he murmured.

"Ten thousand advance, ten thousand on termination. Success bonus—up to you. Payment monthly. In cash."

Partlow nodded.

"An EU passport for me. And you walk my true-name passport through State and renew it for ten years."

"Not possible, Jerry. I mean, sure, I can get your true-name passport renewed by Friday. You could do it yourself—I know, paranoia reigns supreme—but I don't hand out cover passports to agents, however much I need them. I *can't*, Jerry. The world has changed."

Piat leaned forward. In his head, he was already a case officer again. It was an odd change, to suddenly think like a case officer and not like an agent. "Clyde—you want me? I want to play. I want to do a good job. And I'll still be me. You want to bury me in flattery, Clyde? Look how many ops I lost in my whole career—two, and how many were penetrated—none, and how many of my agents got waxed—one, Clyde, one, and that was the lapse of some dickhead in SOG. I run a tight ship. The tight ship starts with operational security. I'm a petty black-market art dealer. Small-time. But still—by now, somebody has noticed me—the Brits, the Swedes, the Russians. No way am I jogging back and forth from here to Dubai or Riyadh or wherever the fuck you want Hackbutt going without a passport."

Partlow smiled. "I'll pay fifteen hundred a day for *that*," he said. "I'll consider the passport. To be honest, I hadn't imagined you'd travel with the falconer. Tell me why you'd need to."

"I wouldn't send Hackbutt to cross the street on his own. He'll need control all the way. He'll panic the first time he sees the target. He'll suck at border crossing. He'll take Irene as his security blanket, but he'll need a shoulder to cry on—she's hard as rock."

Partlow uncrossed and re-crossed his legs. "The girl?"

"We have to get her on board and keep her happy." Piat was holding Partlow's eyes now.

"Bad operational procedure."

"Yeah, for newbies. If this doesn't matter, Clyde, if this is some petty-ass grab at some two-bit creep, then just walk away. Okay? Hackbutt's a pain in the ass and Irene's going to do something fucked up, and they're a tangle of loves and resentments. On the other hand, Clyde, if this operation *counts,* if this one could *make a difference,* then you need that woman and all the risk and crap and baggage that she'll bring."

Partlow had both hands up in front of his face. "Sold—sold—sold before you told me. We need the woman. If we didn't, Dave would still be here. How do we keep her?"

Piat shrugged. "Money?" he asked. "Works for most people."

"Dave thought she was 'anti-American.' Said she hated everything about the administration—" Partlow gave a little half-smile. "I gather she's Canadian."

"She's sounding better by the second, isn't she? Come *on,* Clyde."

"How much for her?" Partlow asked. The word "soul" lingered invisibly in the air at the end of his sentence.

"Hundred thou?" Piat guessed.

"Christ Jesus!" muttered Partlow, in Anglican agony.

"Let me promise Hackbutt a new bird."

Partlow hesitated, his hand on his chin. Piat drove over his caution.

"You want this guy? Promise him a bird. It'll help both as a control tool and as a bargaining counter. And it can stand in lieu of payment, I'll bet. Promise him a bird at the end and he'll be happy. Besides, we'll need a McGuffin for the Arab."

"I've never said the potential target was an Arab."

"You never said your wife was the daughter of an Anglican minister, either."

"Sometimes I find you just a little scary, Jerry."

He saw the challenges and the roadblocks ahead and he had to swallow a laugh.

"You can work for me, Jerry?"

"Yep." Piat looked around the room. "Got anything here to drink? Yeah, Clyde. As long as I get to write the contract and as long as you let me *consult* on operational issues, I can work for you. Just this once, old times' sake, all that jazz."

"Scotch in the bedroom. Laphroaig and a local—try it. You just added two hundred thousand to my operational budget."

"Air travel. Probably six trips—three for training, three for real. Three contact attempts—he'll fuck up the first one, so I'll plan it for him to fuck up—third one just to have a fall-back." Piat was feeling a little high. The scotch settled him.

"You still don't know what the op is. Aren't you curious?"

Piat spread his hands. "No. Yes. Listen—first I lay out my terms. Then you accept them and we sign something. Then you brief me. Right?" He shrugged and waved his glass. "Or you reject them and I walk away."

Partlow made a moue of distaste. "Not much chance of that, is there, Jerry? Which you bloody well know."

Piat raised his glass to Partlow and drained it. "I think I'm being damned good about the whole thing, *old boy*."

Partlow leaned forward. "That's what worries me."

Piat laughed. One scotch had hit him and his adrenaline high like a hammer. "You know what, Clyde?"

Partlow looked a little pained.

"I think I want to do it. One more time."

Partlow went into the bedroom and poured them both more scotch, and then they raised their glasses and drank.

And then they signed some papers and made a plan to communicate. They discussed Piat's cover and Partlow's role and the nature of the target—"no names yet, Jerry, we're not there yet"—and Piat, despite three glasses of scotch, had no difficulty dictating notes on targeting possible meeting venues.

Partlow handed over ten thousand dollars, mostly in pounds. "All I have. I want hand receipts on that. Deduct your travel here. I'll meet you in a week and we'll see where we are on cover and money."

Piat had a faraway look in his eyes. "Don't come near Scotland again, Clyde."

"Where?" Partlow was in the room's tiny front hall, ready to walk out the door, dapper in light tweeds, and somehow, obviously American. "Jerry—I'll decide the meeting location, okay? Try and remember that I'm your case officer, and not the other way around."

Piat shrugged. "Whatever. Just not Scotland. London, Antwerp, Dublin. Athens would be nice—I could get some stuff from home."

Partlow nodded. "Athens it is. I have business there."

They shook hands. Partlow's jawline moved, but whatever he had to say, the moment passed, and he was out the door.

Piat lay on the bed and started his shopping list.

5

Piat woke next morning in Oban with a hangover and a mix of foreboding and guilt. The operation was all very well when discussed from the safety of an expensive hotel room, but in the chilly gray air of a Scottish morning all he could think about was Hackbutt—and Irene. Partlow had been cagey about what *exactly* had cued him to fire Dave.

Hackbutt had changed from the old days in Southeast, but Piat still felt he knew where his mind would go. *Betrayal.* Personal betrayal of trust by his old friend Jack. From Hackbutt's perspective, good ol' Jack had walked off and abandoned him to the tender mercies of Dave.

Piat considered it from a number of angles while he drank grapefruit juice in the hotel's restaurant. He added to the list in his head—props. Envelopes. Tickets.

On the ferry to Mull he read more about crannogs to keep his mind off his worries.

This wasn't going to be pretty.

The dog greeted him with silent appraisal, its eyes following him from the car to the door while Piat's stomach did back-flips in anticipation of Hackbutt's welcome. He temporized by extending a hand again, letting the dog sniff; and he was about to try petting it again when he heard footsteps and the door opened.

"Look who the dog dragged in," Irene said as she opened the door. Her face had all the expression of a runway model's. The sexual performance was not on offer. Piat guessed she was angry. Over his sudden disappearance, or for her husband's sake? Or was it Dave and whatever he'd botched? Piat had too few cues to do anything but guess wildly, but since he had to guess, he suspected that Hackbutt had told her everything and she had hated it. Not a good start.

He narrowly avoided the trap of asking for Hackbutt. That way lay Dave's disastrous attempt—excluding Irene.

Piat met her eyes. "I want to try again," he said.

Irene's face didn't move. "Can I offer you anything, Jack? Tea?"

Piat nodded—not too eagerly, he hoped. "Tea would be great."

Irene was wearing another shapeless bag. The slight sheen of the material and the coarse beadwork suggested that it was an expensive shapeless bag. She was barefoot, and as she walked off to the kitchen, he saw that she had small feet arched like a ballerina's. Her back remained straight, her shoulders square. Nothing sexual was being shown, and he was grateful.

She put water on. The door to the room she called her "studio" was closed; the photographs were still up in the same places; there was no sign that she was "working" or doing whatever people who thought they were artists did.

"Hackbutt's up on the hillside. He's flying his young birds." She paused, reached into a jar and pulled out a handful of loose tea. "Herbal, or do you run on caffeine?"

Nice to have the right answer made obvious. "I drink coffee when I want caffeine. Herbal, please."

Irene's back remained to him. "Good black tea has more caffeine than coffee and is better for you. I'm sorry Eddie isn't here—but I'm not sure he'd have much to say to you."

"I fired Dave," Piat said. It came out easily, smoothly—the foundation lie on which he intended to build his castle.

She was putting leaves in a tea ball. Her hand paused for a moment. "Really?" she said. Her feigned disinterest was the first hopeful sign Piat had detected. "Jack, I'm not sure that you know Eddie very well. He feels that—that you betrayed him." With her last words, she turned around, teapot in hand.

"I certainly abandoned him. Yeah. I thought it was for the best. Look, can I level with you?"

Irene sat. In one motion, she brushed her shapeless bag under her knees and pulled her legs up under her, so that she sat sideways in a wing-backed armchair. She looked like a yoga master. Her smile was social. "My father told me that the expression 'can I level with you' always means the opposite. He was a capitalist pig of the first water, but he knew people." She poured tea into heavy terracotta mugs.

He was nervous and making mistakes. He shrugged and exhaled hard. "Okay. Point made. I'm done." He swallowed some tea—good tea. Big gamble. *She has to want the money. He must have told her that there's money. Or I'm out the door.*

She smiled again—but it was a different smile. Secret pleasure. "So—why did you fire Dave?"

"He didn't know how to deal with you," Piat said, from the hip.

"And you do?" she asked.

"Irene, I know I *have* to deal with you." He just left it there. She wanted to be in control—being in control was one of the things that made her tick.

She sipped her tea demurely. "What do you want?"

"Digger's help. A contact. It'll require hard work and some lifestyle adjustments for both of you."

"Like what?" She leaned forward.

Piat sensed the intensity of her interest but misplaced it as revulsion. "It's just cosmetic, Irene. Like a costume. Like makeup." She wore a little. Not much, but enough to suggest that she had a human interest in her own looks.

She made a gesture of dismissal with her teacup. "What changes?"

Piat felt a ray of hope—just a single ray, but as bright as the rare Scottish sun. She was bargaining—her body language and intensity said she was bargaining.

"Clothes. Haircut. Table manners. Social interaction. Travel."

She looked at him over her mug of tea. "And me?"

Piat smiled blandly. "What do you want me to say? I suspect you're already pretty good at wearing a string of pearls and chatting with debs. Right?"

She leaned back, put her feet up on the old trunk that did duty as a coffee table. Her soles were dirty. "I shit that life out of me with the last meat I ate," she said in a matter-of-fact voice.

Irene used words like *shit* to shock. It had been one of Piat's first clues to who she was, or might be—that she had grown up with people who *didn't* say shit every third word. Rich people. People with *culture*.

"I need Hackbutt. I need his expertise with these birds. I know he can do this. And Irene—it'll help him. He can help change the world, and he can spend the rest of his life knowing that he did it."

She nodded, but she didn't look very impressed.

"You and the birds—together—have made a more confident, more rounded man than I knew in Southeast. So let him do this. It won't hurt him—far from it." Piat tried to hold her eye as he made his little speech, but she glanced away and then back. She'd looked at her photographs, he knew. She had as much as said, *What's in this for me?*

"And I'll pay both of you, handsomely. I know that you guys don't run on money, but it's what I have. Give it to charity if you want." Most people liked to pretend they didn't want money. He suspected that Irene would pretend pretty hard.

He was wrong.

She swiveled to face him, plunked her bare feet down on the stone floor. "How much money?" she asked directly.

"Fifty thousand dollars," Piat said.

"We'll need more than that. *I'll* need more than that. You pay for my installation—materials, transportation, insurance, *chai*. The works."

Piat shook his head, apparently reluctant. "I'm sorry, Irene. I can't make open-ended financial commitments. I can offer you a lump sum—I can set a payment schedule. I can't just say I'll pay for every expensive hotel you book in Paris—or wherever you get your show."

Irene leaned forward over the table, her breasts visible almost to the nipple under her dress, her well-defined arm muscles in high relief. *She's tense.* "Fifty thousand *each*, then." Her voice was low, a little raspy. "I *love* the irony—the military-industrial complex paying for my installation. I might have to add some new pieces." But the tension remained, and only when it was too late did he realize that she was, perhaps unconsciously, trying to set her price too high. She wanted him to say no. She wanted—what? *She wanted not to have to follow through with her "art."*

But by the time he'd understood, the moment was past. He hadn't flinched at the amount. He'd kept his tone businesslike. "Five thousand each when Hackbutt agrees. Ten thousand each when Hackbutt completes the cosmetic part to my satisfaction. The balance when we're done. Either way, success or failure—but not until we're done."

She looked at the photographs and then at the front door, as if she were looking for an escape, and said, "You have ten thousand dollars *on you*?" she babbled. "This is all happening too fast—my God, we just met you—really, I think you're moving us too fast—"

So.

Piat opened his blazer and took out four envelopes. He

laid them out on the old trunk. Two said "Irene." Two said "Hackbutt." He pointed. "Five thou." He moved his hand. "Tickets to London. For shopping." He waved at the other two. "Ditto, for you."

"I don't get all giggly at the prospect of shopping."

He knew he had to push. "Deal, Irene?"

She rose to her feet. "More tea?"

He drove away from the farm without having seen Hackbutt but with a sense of release from danger. And a little elation. The next part—making up with Hackbutt—would be messy and difficult and emotional, but that was life in the business.

From a roadside phone kiosk, Piat dialed the number he and Partlow had arranged to use for routine communications and left an eight-digit code that he typed out on the stainless steel keypad. Then he spent three hours counting his remaining money and renting a room in Tobermory. The woman at the front desk of the Mishnish remembered him. He told her he was back for the fishing.

"Oh, aye," she said.

Piat believed in living his cover. He spent the rest of the evening on the estuary of the Aros River, fishing.

In the morning, he didn't go straight to the farm. Instead, he put on his boots and first drove, then climbed to his loch. He took a rod, but he didn't set it up. Instead he took a cheap digital camera. Then, from the pub in Craignure, he accessed his "Furman" account online. Furman was the identity he used in Athens to sell antiquities. He uploaded three digital images of the crannog from the cheap camera and sent them to three different addresses; one in Sri Lanka, one in Florida, and one in Ireland. He wasn't sure just what he was meaning to do yet. So he was testing the water.

* * *

As he drove back down the gravel road to the farm, he caught a flash of Hackbutt among the cages behind the house. His stomach rolled over. He pulled around the house, parked, and took a deep breath.

As he got out of the car, Hackbutt came around the house and waved. Hackbutt's wave said it all, he hoped. Piat gave up the idea of trying to make contact with the dog and faced him.

"You really pissed me off," Hackbutt said from thirty feet away. His tone was high, almost falsetto. As he walked toward Piat, he said, "It's not that I can't be your friend. Not that I'm angry—really angry. But it wasn't decent, leaving me like that." He looked like shit. He looked like a beggar in the wilderness—beard uncombed, hair wild.

"No, Digger. No. I abandoned you. It's not the way I meant it to be, but I did it. I'm sorry."

Hackbutt's hands were trembling. He rubbed them together. "Why? Irene says I should forget it. That it's not our business. But I can't—I think you have to tell me."

Piat had forgotten how Hackbutt really was—the pile of insecurities and grandiosities. Piat put an arm on the other man's shoulders. Lies that he might have told other agents wouldn't work on Hackbutt—lies that he had been busy, that he had had to use Dave, that he'd been somewhere else saving the world. Waste of breath. To Hackbutt, there was only Hackbutt—and maybe Irene. Instead, he said, "I needed to get you guys the money. That's all I can say, okay?"

Hackbutt's face was blotchy. "Dave said you weren't coming back. That you didn't give a shit about me or Irene. That you only worked for money and that he was my real friend." He was almost crying. He was very much the Hackbutt that Piat had run in Malaysia.

Piat nodded, hugged Hackbutt a little harder. He could imagine the vitriol that Dave must have spewed. He could see how a fool like Dave would think that he could achieve control that way.

"But I came back, Digger." Piat didn't care that he could see Irene at the window, that he was practically hugging her man on the driveway. "I came back. I should never have left."

"And you won't leave again?"

"Not until the end." Piat believed in being prepared for the end, right from the beginning. "And then we'll just go back to being friends."

Hackbutt was crying now. But he was returning the hug. Piat was patient, almost tender.

"Irene will think we're making out," Hackbutt said after a full minute. He giggled.

That laugh's got to go, Piat thought.

Irene had made tea. The door to her studio was still closed, but a third of the photographs had been taken down, and some lay in untidy piles on the furniture. Irene was taciturn, seemingly nervous. Regretting it?

Piat cleared a space on the couch and sat, opening his backpack.

"Okay, folks. Today we start working. First, anybody have something on their schedule for the next two months? Weddings? Funerals? Spill it now, because the moment I'm paying, you're on my calendar. Okay?"

"He's always like this at the start," Hackbutt said to Irene.

Irene stared at him.

"Good. Digger, you remember these forms?" The forms themselves were creations from Piat's laptop, but they were enough like CIA documents to pass muster with an agent. "You pay US taxes?"

"No," they said together.

"Then we don't need this one." Piat crumpled a W-2 invoice form he'd downloaded. He'd always thought it funny that US agents paid income tax on black ops money, but they did. "Contract. Security agreement. Confidentiality. These don't constitute a security clearance, just an arrangement. Okay?"

"We have to sign," Hackbutt said to Irene. "It's okay." He was reassuring her from his years of experience as an agent, and he sounded fatuous. She, however, was reading the whole document and not listening to him. *Looking for a reason not to sign,* he thought, but there was a resignation about her that suggested that she was simply going through the motions. If the idea of actually putting her art on display frightened her, another part of her very much wanted to do it. That part, he guessed, had already won.

Piat had looked at her website. She actually had a small reputation, had done "installations" in Auckland and Ontario and Eastern Europe. But the website hadn't been updated in three years, and he wondered if she really was an "artist"—he couldn't think of the word without the quotation marks—who'd run out of ideas. Or whatever it was that "artists" had in their heads.

At any rate, she signed. Looking unhappy. But sexually interesting.

When they had both signed, Piat handed out envelopes. "Five thousand each. Okay?"

He'd made a mistake, and he saw it too late. Hackbutt's face froze and his skin got blotchy again. He followed Hackbutt's eyes and saw that Hackbutt only now realized that Piat was paying both of them, and that as much as that made sense to him and to Partlow, it wasn't the right move for Hackbutt, who wanted to give her the money himself. Without much of a pause, he turned to Irene. "Hackbutt wanted you to have this money for yourself. The contract's with him—but he wouldn't do it without you. And I'm sorry to be so crass with both of you but, Digger, you remember that we have to play for the bureaucrats with money. I can get you more for both than I can get just for you, Digger." He said it all so smoothly that Hackbutt's face was calm again before he was done.

Hackbutt smiled shakily at Irene. "I thought I'd get to give it to you myself," he began, but she launched herself out of her chair and embraced him. In seconds they were locked together, kissing like teenagers.

Piat busied himself collecting the documents. After ten seconds he said, "Okay, kids. Really."

Irene pulled herself free and shook out her hair, laughing. Hackbutt laughed, too—a real laugh, not a giggle.

Piat smiled with them and opened a calendar. "Digger—you first. You need clothes."

Hackbutt nodded. "Irene's been telling me that for a year."

"Now Uncle Sam's paying. Irene may need some too. It's too early to tell you the whole ball of wax—you know the rules, Digger. But let's just say you're going to meet some rich, powerful people. You have to be ready to be *with* them. Okay? I don't expect you to become James Bond, but I need you to look the part and act the part."

Hackbutt crossed his arms, his scrawny elbows showing through rents in his ancient sweater. "Jeez, Jack. I'm not good at social stuff."

Piat looked at him without mercy. "If this were easy, we wouldn't be paying so much money for it. Okay? This is go-no-go stuff, Digger. You have to do the social stuff. We'll have training for it—practice, role-play. Just like in Jakarta. Okay? Same for Irene." He tossed the last in because he wanted Hackbutt to feel that he wasn't alone in being targeted.

Irene's frown caused her eyebrows to make a single, solid line on her face. Piat didn't know her facial expressions yet. Tension? Anger? Hard to know.

His eyes roved down his list. "Right now I'm mostly focused on clothes. Digger, can you wear some real clothes?"

"Like what?" Hackbutt sounded suspicious.

"Wool trousers, for a start," said Irene. "Green like your eyes, Eddie."

Piat felt as if Irene were speaking lines he'd written for her, except that he hadn't. What a fool Dave had been to ignore her. "Exactly. Clothes. I don't want to overdo it—you're an American, you'd look silly in breeks—but the Arab idea of a Western gentleman is an Englishman. I need you to look the part."

"What're breeks?" Hackbutt asked.

"Knee breeches. For shooting." Piat paused to see if Hackbutt would respond.

"Sounds kind of faggy," Hackbutt muttered. He clearly thought Piat was making fun of him.

"You both have to eat meat. Not all the time. Okay? But enough so your systems don't reject it."

"No way," Hackbutt said. "I've given all that shit up." He looked at Irene for confirmation.

She gave Piat a considering look. "I won't eat pork. Lamb or beef I can probably hack."

Hackbutt stared at her.

Piat nodded. "Fair enough. Okay. I won't hide from you that our target is Arab. He won't eat pork, either. It'll probably actually help his subconscious cues with you two if you don't eat pork. Fine. Pork's off the training menu. Anyway—you're game for the clothes and food. Right? Okay. Conversation."

Hackbutt all but cringed. Irene put a hand on his knee.

"Here's the plan. We three eat together three nights a week. Okay? At dinner we play a game. It goes like this. Irene and I speak only when we're spoken to. Understand, Digger? We'll answer questions. If encouraged, we can respond and ask questions of our own, but otherwise, we just sit there. Boring dinners, Dig, unless you come to them with some prepared topics and you get them started."

Hackbutt looked back and forth between them. "Why you and Irene? I mean—when does Irene get the training? You're not helping her." He trailed off.

Piat nodded, wondering just what to say.

Irene picked up the ball immediately. "Sweetie—I know

how to make conversation. How the hell do you think I deal with agents and gallery owners and buyers? It's you, dear man, who can't make small talk with a telemarketer."

Hackbutt nodded. "Why would anyone want to make small talk with a telemarketer?"

"And three days a week you give me some training with the birds," Piat said.

Hackbutt sat up. "Really? That's great, Jack. I didn't know you were interested!" Then more slowly, "Oh, for the op, you mean."

"I have to travel with you. I'll be with you most of the time. So I need to know enough to pass."

Hackbutt frowned. "The birds'll know in a second if you don't want to be with them, Jack. If you're—afraid. Or fake." He realized what he'd said. "Oh, Jack—sorry."

"Why? Why be sorry? You're right. But let me have a go at it. They're beautiful and I imagine I can make my way." In fact, Piat was not at all sure he'd be steady with those killers flashing their beaks a few inches from his nose, but he had to try, and he'd done worse in the line of service.

Later at the car, Piat nodded toward the dog and said, "Why's he so unfriendly?"

"Is he unfriendly?" Hackbutt looked at the dog as if he'd never thought about it. "He's a nasty animal."

"Well, shy."

"Before I knew what he was like, I left the gate open and he got in with the birds and scared them. He went crazy—running around and barking and stressing them. I kicked his butt right out of there." He was proud of himself. "I mean I *kicked* him." He thought about that, apparently with satisfaction, and then said, "Then I chained him up."

"Do you walk him?"

"Annie does. Sometimes."

"Who's Annie?"

"Oh—a kid who helps with the birds sometimes. Sort of

an apprentice. She *likes* the dog. I've told her, if that dog gets in with the birds again, I'll take my shotgun to it. I won't have the birds stressed."

Piat suppressed the things he might have said.

Over the next couple of weeks, Piat, coming every other day to the farm, made more progress with the dog than he did with Hackbutt or Irene. The falconer didn't want to become a social creature, it turned out, and he dug in his heels; Irene didn't want to be an agent and stayed in her "studio;" the dog, on the other hand, wanted to be a real dog, and he accepted Piat's fingers, then his hand on his head, and then a caressing of his ears. After several days of it, Piat took him off the chain and opened the derelict iron sheep fence and let them both through and up the hill. To his surprise, the dog stayed at his left knee.

"Don't you want to run?" Piat said. The dog looked up at him. The dog expected something but couldn't tell him what.

"Run," Piat said. "Get some exercise."

The dog looked at him.

"Run!" Piat said. He made a sweep with his arm to suggest the openness of the world, and to his surprise the dog took off. Later experiments showed that it was the gesture. All he really had to do was point ahead, and the dog went; if it went too far, he found he could whistle it back—it would dash to his feet and then sit, head up, ears alert.

"What does he want?" Piat said to his new friend, the owner of the tackle-and-book shop. He'd made the shop part of his off-duty routine, cruising the books every few days and usually buying something. "The dog comes back and sits and looks at me and I don't know what to do."

"It sounds like quite a good dog. Probably a herder: you get a lot of those here. They'll herd anything—sheep, children, ducks. Quite smart, is he?"

"Well, he sure seems to know things I don't."

"Ye-e-e-s." The man stroked his long, unshaven chin. "Sounds as if he's been trained and expects you to know the signs. Or partly trained, perhaps—young dog, is he? Tell you what, carry a few treats in your pocket; try one on him when he sits down like that. He may be used to the odd reward for coming back. Not every time, mind—if you do it every time, he'll use it as a dodge to gorge—but often enough." He talked about hand signals that the dog might know. "Friend's dog, is he?"

"They neglect him."

The shop owner laughed. "Mind he doesn't become *your* dog, then." He grinned. "You know what Kipling said." He waited. Then: "'Don't give your heart to a dog.'"

"Kipling also said, 'He travels the fastest who travels alone.' I travel fast."

But he bought a packet of something called Bow Wowzers, and when he gave the sitting dog one, a new relationship was forged. He became the replacement for some earlier man, the trainer, the giver of treats, the divinity. The dog ran for him, returned for him, herded for him, waited for him. Every day.

It was Annie who gave him a name. "I call him Ralph," she said, "because it's what his bark sounds like—Ralf! Ralf!" Annie was perhaps sixteen, not pretty, but, despite her big shoulders and heavy hips, she had the kind of complexion that was imitated in decorating china figurines and postcards. She also appeared to be as strong as an ox, and her handshake was firm. She was more or less Hackbutt's apprentice, apparently as daft about falcons as he was. If she felt any jealousy of Piat over the dog, she certainly didn't show it. She was basically a good kid who liked animals.

"Ralph," Piat said. The dog wagged his tail. What the hell, he'd be Ralph or Emily or Algernon if this man would just be his human being.

Piat bought Ralph a green tennis ball. And then a chewing toy.

Irene was sardonic about Piat and the dog. Amused, but sardonic. In fact, he didn't see her as much as he'd expected to, as much as in fact he'd hoped. He found himself responding to that tall body, the more so as she toned down her sexual advertising—the shock words, the wet kisses with Hackbutt—as Piat became part of her landscape. Whatever her fears of her "art" were, she'd grasped the nettle. Every day he came to the farm now, she was "working." Mostly, she was shut away in her "studio" and he didn't see her, and he increasingly found he wanted to. He sensed that increasingly she *didn't* want to see him.

In his hindbrain, he wanted to see more of her. In his professional brain, he was satisfied that she kept her distance. When he was bringing Hackbutt in to Partlow as a one shot, the thought of fucking her had been exciting, but Piat had rules, and one of them was that sex and operations didn't mix. This was his operation now.

The rules didn't always penetrate his hindbrain.

When she came out of her isolation, it was to cook and take part in the training sessions, which started by not going very well and then got worse.

"I don't know *how*!" Hackbutt's voice would quaver like the whine of a housefly. "Why won't you *talk* to me?"

Piat, Irene, and Hackbutt were silently eating their way through a curry with some shreds of lamb, Irene's first attempt to add meat to their diet. The food was simple but good. The conversation was nonexistent. So far, Piat had managed only three kinds of interaction: silence, a harangue from Hackbutt about falconry, and a harangue from Irene about overwork.

Piat kept eating. Irene looked at Hackbutt for a few seconds, flashed him a smile, and went back to her food.

"You're both *picking on me.*"

Piat smiled. "Nope. This is training. Listen up, Digger. First, a pep talk. Okay? We'll get one shot at this guy. Think about that. We're going to spend a *fuck* of a lot of money and time to get you near this guy *one time*. You're going to have to get through to him. One time. In about fifteen seconds. Okay? It might be at dinner. It might be in a parking garage. It might be a line at an airport. One time. Okay?"

"I can't!" Hackbutt's voice had a whiney tone that Piat realized had been absent on the hillside with the birds, but it was familiar from the old days.

"You can. Okay? Now, a demonstration. Irene, may I have some wine?"

Irene picked up the bottle, a French white, and filled Piat's glass.

"Thanks. Pretty good wine."

"Better than anything we ever saw in the States," Hackbutt replied.

"It's the European Union," said Piat. "In Greece, in Scotland, wherever—French wines, German wines, Greek wines even. Look at that little store in Salen—the whole thing is smaller than a corner store in Manhattan, and it has a selection of wine you'd have to go to some ritzy liquor store to buy."

"At French prices, too," Irene said.

Piat turned to Hackbutt. "I could branch out now. I could easily turn my bottle of wine into a rant against the agricultural policies of the EU. Or in favor of the no-borders policies of the EU. A rant against the Bush administration. A harangue about wine. A dissertation on grape cultivation. Those are all monologues—sometimes good to start a conversation, but not really social—not nice. So what I really want to do is pimp you guys to talk. So I say—to Irene." Piat turned away from Hackbutt. "Have you been to France?"

"I was at the fucking Sorbonne," she said. She smiled bitterly. "For a little while, anyway."

Piat wondered what they talked about when he wasn't there. "The Sorbonne?" he asked. "Where's the Sorbonne?"

"It's a university in Paris. I studied art—Medieval art, modern art. You've never heard of the Sorbonne?" Irene's eyes narrowed as she realized that Piat was mocking her. "Fuck you."

"No—no, really." Piat laughed and shook his head. "Digger, it's better to ask questions than to know the answers. It makes for better conversation. Okay? You see?"

Irene's hands were in her lap—she looked angry, and Hackbutt's eyes were on her, worried and annoyed.

Hackbutt said, "Yeah, I see that you're making connections. With whatever she says. Whatever. Except you're pissing Irene off, which pisses me off."

Piat decided that he had drunk too much wine and was trying to move too fast.

He leaned forward. "It's a game, Digger—but it's a game you play with the other people, not against them. You have to *listen* to play. It's not about dominance. Not about winning. Just about being there."

Hackbutt nodded without understanding. "Sure," he said.

Piat ran a hand through his hair. Irene was sullen, as if she'd been wounded by a single shot. A stupid mistake on his part. "Digger, do you feel different when you're with your birds?" he asked.

"Sure," Hackbutt replied. The "sure" had a whole different content.

"Maybe you should treat us as if we're birds," Piat said.

Him and his birds. Maybe he'll do better when we get to London, away from the goddam birds and all this gloom. He saw that he'd made a mistake by not taking them to London as soon as they'd signed on. New clothes, a haircut, a new environment, and Hackbutt would see a new self.

But Irene's "art," which should have solved a problem by pleasing her, became a problem because it took so much of her time. Because she *made* it take so much her time.

"I'm not allowed in there," Hackbutt said one day, nodding toward the closed door of the room she called her studio. He gave a perfunctory guffaw for machismo's sake, but the truth was that he adored Irene and thought her creative life was an overawing mystery. "Something I couldn't do in a million years, Jack! And all out of her head. Like a frequency she hears and I don't."

"Do you understand the stuff she does?"

"Understand? Oh, no. Well, not really. I don't have the—I'm not artistic."

Then one day Piat let himself in the front door and walked through the house, expecting Hackbutt but not finding him. For the first time, Irene's door was open, a sound like a blender coming from it. Piat moved down the corridor on tiptoe (why? was he afraid of her?) and peeked in.

She was drilling holes with a battery-powered drill. She had on a man's cargo pants and a checked flannel shirt and a tool belt, and she was leaning into the drill to push it through a sheet of metal held in a big vice on a workbench that took up the whole end of what had once been the cottage's parlor.

Piat looked the room over. No furniture. The wall above the bench was hung with tools on nails and hooks; another wall had a dozen sketches taped to it; the floor was littered with heterogeneous junk, although even a glance suggested that some sort of order might be possible. He saw animal bones, a dead seagull, part of a baby carriage, greasy parts of what had once been a car engine. A puddle of what looked at first to be dog turds, then finally made sense as condoms, not necessarily unused. In the midst of this, a bulbous something heaved up from the floor like a mound of jelly, shining, repellent, monstrous. He focused on it and saw that it was fiberglass, the stuff they make boats out of.

At that point, she became aware of him. She pushed a clear plastic face guard up on her forehead. "Can't you see I'm working?"

"Yes, I— Yes, of course." It was humiliating to be flustered by her. How had she put him in the wrong? "I didn't know."

"Now you do. This room is off-limits, Jack. I got so fucking hot I had to open the door. It's not an invitation."

"I'm sorry. Really."

She came toward him, still carrying the drill. She brushed hair away with the back of her left hand, blew air out in a way that made her lips bulge and shake. "Fucking hot." She looked around the room. "Yes, this is mine. This is it. Surprised?"

"I didn't know what to expect."

"You expected to find me in here reading magazines and eating chocolates, right?" She breathed out again, then began pumping the front of her shirt in and out to make a breeze. He saw parts of a no-nonsense brassiere. "That fucking Paris agent got me a date for a show that's *months* ahead of what I told her, Jesus Christ, I'm running around in here like a chicken with its head cut off trying to make stuff."

"Hey, that's great! A real show?"

"Yeah, a real show. If you call a two-bit gallery in a two-bit French town a show. She promised me Paris, she delivers a provincial burg called Arras. But the truth is, I either take what I can get or I give it up. It's no secret I'm not exactly a household name, right? You looked at the website? I thought you would. Not too impressive. I need them more than they need me. But Jesus Christ, she's got me on a schedule that's a real bitch."

Piat said nothing. He didn't know what to say. He wasn't sure whether he was impressed or repulsed—or what his reaction was. He could tell she wanted one. And that it was important to her.

"Don't think this all happened because of your money, either. Don't flatter yourself." She walked into the middle of the room and looked down at the plastic mound. "This is fiberglass," she said. "It's going to take me weeks to finish, no matter what." She looked at him. "What do you think art is, Jack?" The question wasn't flirtatious, but at the same time it was a question, a prolonging of his being there, so he knew she wanted him to stay. Then he knew that she was as divided as he—wanting him, just as he wanted her, but held back, she by Hackbutt, he by the operation.

"The creation of beauty," he said slowly, knowing it was the wrong answer. Irene, of course, knew nothing of his other life as a dealer in antiquities, and he wasn't going to tell her.

"Bullshit. Art has nothing to do with beauty." Irene smiled, as if the apparent ignorance of his answer satisfied her. She looked around. "This is art. This is the bust-your-ass part of art." She gave him the same look. "You think art's some kind of fake, don't you, Jack? You think it's a way of gaming life—right? Art is some woman pouring a can of beans over her naked ass, right? Art is some weirdo wrapping Canary Wharf in pink plastic, right? It's all bullshit and hype, stuff that fags and women make up because they can't cut it in the real world, right?" She aimed the drill at him and pulled the trigger, got an angry whir.

Piat raised an eyebrow. "No," he said.

She glared at him and pulled the trigger on the drill again. "No? Just no?"

Piat took a deep breath and let it out. She wanted a quarrel. And behind that was something else—maybe sex, maybe something deeper or older, some kind of scar. Something about art.

Piat knew something about bullshit and hype and art, but he kept his mouth shut. After a moment that went on too long, he said, "Just plain no."

Irene snorted. "Next time, try to remember that not every open door is an invitation." She came back, put her free hand on the knob. "I'll come out in a few hours and be nice Irene and play Miss Manners with you and Edgar." She leaned in to him, making closing the door part of the motion. "But I'm feeling a lot of pressure, and you're part of it."

And she closed the door.

The dog was a relief after that.

Then there were the sessions when he and Hackbutt reversed roles and Hackbutt tried to train him—about the birds.

"Don't flinch like that, Jack. Sheila, stop!" Hackbutt reached over the head of the angry bird he called Sheila and stroked her plumes, despite the fact that she had just taken a few grams of skin from Piat's arm and looked mad as hell. Hackbutt's tone was imperative.

Piat tried to support the weight of the bird on his fist and remain nonchalant while watching a stream of blood flow down his arm. He *had* flinched—no point in denying it. And at another level, he marveled at the Hackbutt he had just seen—Hackbutt the commander of birds and men.

Patiently, Hackbutt stroked her, fed her a morsel of red meat from his pocket. "She knows you're afraid, Jack." He smiled out at the endless rolling gray beyond the dripping moor. "I was afraid myself. Sometimes I still am. Can't let them see it, okay? It'll take time. Just get used to her—the weight of her, the smell." His voice was gentle, soothing—not like his usual voice at all. "Here, pass her over. That's a good bird. What a pretty lady. See? She's back in the zone, Jack. Just like that. Now you take her again."

Sheila had hopped on Hackbutt's hand quite willingly, but no amount of Hackbutt's moving and rolling his wrist would get her to step back to Piat's glove; in fact, she clung to Hackbutt, constantly reorienting herself on the moving comfort of his wrist and arm.

"Jack!" Hackbutt said carefully. "You have to participate! Put your fist next to mine. Now push the bones of your wrist against her feet. *Don't flinch*. There. *There*. Well done."

Once again, Piat had the weight of the heavy falcon on his arm. He took a deep breath. Sheila raised her wings a few inches, rocked her head back and forth. *Yeah, I don't like it any more than you do, honey.* Piat let out his breath, realized that he was full of adrenaline.

"Just walk around, Jack. Just walk over to the wall and back a few times. I'm going to get the other haggards. Okay? Just walk." Hackbutt turned and walked down the hill toward the farm.

Piat started to walk. The bird had a hood on, but somehow she still managed to track Hackbutt's retreat. Suddenly she raised her wings to almost full extension and gave a scream.

Piat kept walking. The bracken had been knocked back here by generations of human feet and some cattle, and the grass was as short as a lawn and far finer. Just beyond the wall of loose stones a stream poured water down the hillside and a white rush to the loch at the bottom of the hill. Piat concentrated on the middle distance and walked. Sheila folded her wings and sat.

He turned at the wall and started back, the weight of the bird tugging at his arm. She was starting to preen, her wings safely in. His pulse slowed. He could just see losing one of Hackbutt's precious birds—he *said* they wouldn't fly while they wore a hood and jesses, but Piat wasn't sure—and then he found that he'd made another circuit and she was still preening.

"Pretty lady," he said.

He decided it was time to get them all to London and see if that would work.

6

Two weeks after he had asked Mike Dukas to find Piat for the second time, Alan Craik, in civilian clothes, finished a meeting at the FBI and rode the Metro around to the Anacostia station. He'd left his car there, now drove down to Bolling Air Force Base. Once he was free of the parking lot there, he found it a pleasure to walk: the day was warm but not hot, not too humid as Washington days went. Women were still in summer clothes—always a plus. He walked fast out of habit; even if he'd been going nowhere, he'd have looked like a man with a mission. In the elevator of DIA's building, he rode up with a woman from counterterrorism, a three-striper but in civvies, as he was. Their chat was short, meaningless, not unpleasant. *You never knew who would have something useful.*

Craik was the collections officer for the Defense Intelligence Agency. A collections officer deals with numbers and ideas; he is a bureaucrat with one foot in the world of operations—not because he will be operational but because he has been—and one foot in desk work. What a collections officer does, in four words, is say yes or no. Or at least convey messages of yes or no, because he sits on several committees and belongs to several working groups, at which people from the entire intelligence community decide whether proposed intel operations should be allowed to go forward. You want to plant a bug in Osama bin Laden's drawers? Find an intelligence task in what is called the Green Book and make sure your proposed operation fits within it, no crowding, nothing left over, and then justify it with references and persuasive prose and recommendations from heavy hitters, if not in writing then on the jungle telegraph.

The Green Book is the bible of the collections officer's religion. It is the same book for the entire community; any notion that the individual agencies work independently is nonsense, at least at this stage. They all see the proposals; they all review the proposals; they all pass on the proposals. Afterward, there may be some fudging and some lying, but at the collections phase, everybody is on board.

An intelligence task is like a template. Your idea has to fit into the template. Will the bug in bin Laden's drawers fit under 57L9-3, "Acquisition of East German intelligence through electronic means?" Obviously not. Will it fit under 98K147-13, "Recruitment of key Islamic persons in nuclear technology?" Probably not, no matter what you've heard about bin Laden and the bomb. But there are thousands and thousands of tasks, dating back to the end of World War II, so somewhere in there you'll find one into which your idea will fit.

Except that sometimes the idea won't fit, and then you need to go to the collections officer and write a new requirement. And that requirement has to be approved by the community, by the collectors, by politicians—in some cases, by the General Accountability Office. Because really, collections management usually comes down to one limiting factor—money. The taxpayers only provide so much. And the collections officer and his staff are, at the simplest level, deciding where that money will be focused.

And then at a meeting, somebody from an agency's ops will say, "Bin Laden doesn't wear drawers," and everybody will vote no, and the affected collections officer will have to go back to the person who proposed it and say, "No dice." Which is why collections officers get quickly unpopular with their constituencies, because everybody hates the messenger, no matter what logic says. And the hatred will be deep and long, because what depended on approval of your idea was next year's budget and the chance for looking good.

It was in this job that Craik now found himself. It was a hot billet—so long as you did it well and didn't piss off the wrong people. You could springboard from it to higher rank. Or you could end your career if you screwed up. Sometimes even if you didn't screw up. But it was interesting.

Now, in his own office overlooking a vast room full of people who worked for him, Craik hung his coat over a chair and sat in front of his computer, clicking the mouse and eyeballing his desk for message slips. Only four, none urgent. In his inter-office mail were three draft tasking orders from other agencies; glanced at, they told him little except what he'd already heard about them in a working group. *Iraqi education system, penetration and utilization of; HUMINT in Northern Iran, expansion of; Vatican assets in East Asia, cooperation with.* Yeah, yeah, yeah.

He called up a subroutine he'd written when he'd first made captain and taken this job. It allowed him to search such intelligence traffic as he was allowed to see—a lot—for terms that he defined. It wasn't illegal, but it wasn't necessarily something he should be doing, either. Its advantage was that it allowed him to pull items of information together in clusters that hadn't been intended when the information was disseminated. Occasionally, this produced something that gave him a leg up in one of the working groups and allowed him to beat the drum louder for DIA. Knowledge is power.

Now he added as a search term the collection management number of Clyde Partlow's operation (more numbers—he worked with more numbers than Albert Einstein). He clicked the mouse, and the subroutine put its snout into the classified traffic of the intelligence community and began to root. Specifically, it was looking for subsidiary taskings—those items that would show that Partlow was moving to a second phase, data gathering—of his operation. All that Craik knew of the operation so far was what he had told Dukas and what they had approved in the working group, a specific but undescribed operation under a counterterrorism task titled "Penetration of al-Qaeda Financial Resources." All that Partlow had said in the meeting was that they "were going in through the target's hobby." Sounded good. Go for it, Clyde. (What hobby? Stamps? Golf? Macramé?) Brilliant.

Without so much as a grunt, the subroutine found a truffle.

The computer dumped three subsidiary taskings on the screen. He was about to learn some details of Partlow's operation:

One tasking was directed to collection officers and attachés, Middle East, asking for "ongoing data concerning individual named Bandar Muhad al-Hauq in the specific areas of (1) falconry (2) collection and display of Islamic art, including donations to museums, funding of art exhibits, and similar activity (3) financial transactions, including via Grandwell and Forstone Bank of Grenada, which individual is believed to have taken over two years ago (lengthy citation here of two classified reports).

One was directed to active intelligence-gathering operatives and their superiors in Southeast Asia and the Middle East, asking for data on travel within the last five years by individual named Prince Bandar Muhad al-Hauq and for data on planned or rumored travel by this individual.

One was directed to the National Security Agency and to the signals office of the Defense Intelligence Agency, asking for data on international intercepts of telephone and computer contacts with or about an individual named Prince Bandar Muhad al-Hauq within the last five years. *Oops,* thought Alan. *I shouldn't have been able to see that.*

Taken together, the three taskings meant that Partlow was planning a move against a Saudi named Bandar Muhad al-Hauq, who might be an al-Qaeda bagman (the banking), and that he was looking for a place to do it (the travel stuff). Either falconry or art would be the means of contact (the hobby), which must have meant finding an agent with knowledge in one of the areas so that he or she could show a common interest. In fact, Partlow must have had an agent already in his sights, because pretty clearly he had needed Piat to make the agent contact. At least Craik couldn't see any other reason for wanting Piat right there at the beginning of the operation. And that meant that Piat knew the prospective agent, knew him well, maybe even—the ploy would hardly be new—had run him before. But falconry? Or art?

Interesting. Very interesting.

But Craik wasn't going through the taskings to find what was interesting. He wanted to make sure that he wasn't connected, even remotely, with a turkey. (There had been a set of orders, money spent, time used, to go to Iceland.) Such was Partlow's reputation that, in the plainest terms, he wanted to cover his ass.

Craik read the taskings again, glanced over the headers, pursed his lips over the references. There were five in all, used in various combinations in the three taskings. Presumably, they bolstered the cases for gathering data on the Saudi. One he recognized as a defector report from before the Iraq war, probably not worth a crap. One he remembered from the working group as a CIA paper on the al-Qaeda money-laundering and money-moving operation. He drew a blank on the others.

He glanced at his watch. He was running behind already, and it was still morning. He isolated the three unknown references and then sent them to a Marine sergeant sitting against the far wall of the room beyond. He typed in,

"Sergeant Swaricki: Please locate these and send to me. Not urgent."

He squeezed as much work as he could into an hour, then walked through the big space where his people were working, checking with some, nodding to anybody who met his eyes. Showing the flag, checking with the troops.

He went to another floor for a briefing, stopped to report quickly to his immediate superior on the meeting at the FBI ("the usual crap from Justice—'trust us, it's legal'—but no underpinnings") and had a quick and not very good lunch in the basement cafeteria. He had a limited appetite for boiled greens and black-eye peas. The banana custard with vanilla wafers was good, though. The place was full of people he knew, lots of waving and smiling, but there were also civilians he didn't know, including, somebody told him, a congressman.

"What's he want?"

"Who the hell would know? Just hold on to your wallet."

Craik had forty people working for him, mostly analysts, both civilian and military from all the services. He had started them on a big push to update the Green Book, get rid of the chaff left over from decades ago and give attention to new tasks that would put collection right where breaking news was. It wasn't an easy job. There was a big constituency of the lazy and the fearful for the oldest and least pertinent tasks: to the people who gave out money and medals, a task was a task, and if you managed to get an operation going under one and brought it home successfully, up went your budget and your reputation. Should anybody care that the task had been written in 1947 and had to do with assessing the threat level posed by radical Buddhists in the old Siam? Not the people who gave out the money and the medals, certainly; to them, a task was a task, so don't waste your sweat on the hard ones, boys.

On his way back from lunch, he went through the big room again, but this time managed to pass all the cubicles and have at least a word or two with half the people. He was really focusing on the seven who were leading the internal Green Book review groups. Clustered by geographical area, the groups were each reading all the old documentation from when the tasks were first created. Boring, sometimes laughable—the early Cold War had some people in stitches—but essential. He touched base with all of them, not necessarily happy with himself for doing it but knowing it should be done. *My God,* he thought, *I'm shmoozing*. He remembered a day with his father, who had been a Navy squadron CO—the same glad-handing, the same constant greetings, the jokey tone.

"Sir!" The voice was female, every word coated with the thick syrup of the Deep South. He knew who it was before he turned around. "You're about the fastest walker I ever tried to follow!"

She was middle-aged, somewhat overweight, brilliant. She was also, in the absence of an assistant (the post was supposed to have been filled weeks before—some screwup) the closest thing he had to a right hand. Her name was Rhonda (after a fifties movie star) Hope Stillman, and she used all three because she was Southern. She had a hefty frontage and tiny ankles, and she gave off emanations of a demure and muted womanliness—Mother Earth with a Georgia accent.

"Mrs Stillman," he said.

"Captain, you are a *walker*!" Presumably, she liked him, too. She had been there for thirteen years, counted as a kind of senior eminence among the analysts. Now, she wanted to take him aside and tell him that people were feeling overworked, and could he lay back a little and relax just the teeniest bit the deadline for the Green Book review? Could he?

She made him smile. She was so serious and yet so nice.

Like a shop steward without attitude. He said, "Send me what you have in mind and we'll talk about it." He suspected she had been a cheerleader. Still was, in a sense. He said, "But if you can do something about the mid-afternoon gabfests when the coffee truck comes around, I'd appreciate it."

"People need their recreation."

"Not forty minutes of it on my time. See what you can do."

He passed on along the line of cubicles, came to Sergeant Swaricki's, put his head in and said hello and would have passed on, but Swaricki said, "They're on your computer."

Alan remembered in time. "Oh, the references on the CIA operation."

"Yessir." Swaricki was in his late thirties, one of the Marine Corps' tactical intel specialists, rotating through on a shore tour. He didn't think a lot of paperwork, had at first been irritated by the Green Book review, then had come around when he began to see it as clearing the crap out of a complex system. He was about six feet, lean, big-handed, like a basketball player from those long-gone days when six feet was tall and the pros wore short shorts and neat haircuts. Now he said, "Problem with one reference."

"You couldn't find it?" That would be odd, and bad for Clyde Partlow.

"Found it, sir, but no headers or footers. Can't tell much about it that way."

Craik wasn't sure he saw the problem; what he thought he wanted would be in the text, not the frame. Still, because he respected Swaricki, he said, "Why?"

"You read it, you'll see."

Craik moved into the cubicle and stationed himself behind the Marine. "Bring it up here and show me."

Swaricki brought up a document that was almost entirely blank. Two-thirds of the way down the screen it said, "after twenty-five minutes, subject alluded to individual named Mohad al-Hack and told this interrogator particular individual is financier for al-Qaeda."

"That's it?"

"Well, you get this—" Swaricki scrolled up to what would have been the beginning of the document if there had been one. After a space, it said, "8 A.M. in the morning. Subject sleep-deprivationed previous 24. This interrogator entered the space and". Three inches below that, it said, "broke for lunch and", and another four inches down, "decided not to break for dinner and". Swaricki scrolled to the end of the document, which said, "subject's condition not conducive to further interrogation, so called [deleted] to [deleted] subject back to his [deleted] and ended interrogation for then. Instructed [deleted] to continue with [deleted]."

"Not real helpful," Craik said.

"Fucking disgrace, excuse me, sir. They got no more business referring to this pile of shit than I got playing on the Pittsburgh Steelers."

Craik read the scattered words again and said, "What do you make of it?" He thought he knew, but he wanted the Marine's opinion.

"Torture, sir. Sleep deprivation followed by something worse. 'Condition not conducive to blank'—that's *torture*." Swaricki said it with disgust. He was a rigidly moral, maybe self-righteous man, a Roman Catholic who might as easily have been a priest, the type not unknown in the military.

"Depends on what 'blank' means, doesn't it?"

"I read 'blank' to mean 'further interrogation.'"

"Could mean 'persuasion' or 'a liking for jelly beans.'"

"'Called blank to blank subject back to his blank'—'called *guards* to *carry* subject back to his *cell*.'"

The Marines had their rules. If it wasn't in the Code of Military Justice or the Geneva Conventions, they were against it. The Marines had enough trouble in Iraq as it was. Still, he said, "That's one reading, Sergeant. But not the only one."

"Why all the deletions? He's describing what he did, is why. Brass can't allow that. Deleted it. Cleaned it up."

"Then why leave the little that's there?"

"You can't put one sentence in the middle of a page, which is the sentence they needed for the reference, and cut *everything* else. See, the stuff they left in gives it a sort of reality. Authentication. Like, 'This really happened and this is the straight skinny.'"

Alan looked at it again, then took the mouse and scrolled up to where the header should have been. Above that was nothing but the reference, a date-time group that showed that the report dated from the very end of 2001. "Damned early," he said.

"Afghanistan."

Alan nodded. "December Oh-One's damned early for torture, too, if that's what's in there. There weren't any findings on torture until a littler later." He leaned back against a desk that stood at right angles to the computer table. "Anyway, that's a different story. *This* thing—" he stabbed a finger toward the screen—"may be about torture and maybe it's not. But it's a lousy reference to support an operation. Print me out a copy of it and I'll take it with me."

"Mostly blank paper," Swaricki grumbled.

"Yeah, but not entirely. Maybe there's enough words to take it another step."

7

London was just as wet as Scotland, without the vistas or the fish. Piat didn't know London very well—to him, it was a city he flew through, not a city he flew to. But it met his criteria—far enough from Mull to be foreign and secure, close enough to save money and time.

He landed them at a small tourist hotel off Russell Square. It was simple and spare and didn't cost much by London standards. They were in their rooms as soon as the concierge let them—noon—and out the door again. Irene looked like a certain kind of American tourist. Piat looked like another. Hackbutt looked like a refugee. The three of them were incongruous together and that worried Piat. Hackbutt looked so odd that he was going to be memorable—too tall, too scraggly, too ill dressed. And he looked odder for having Irene and Piat in tow.

Irene hadn't wanted to come. She was going to lose two days of work. Piat thought she was complaining too much—maybe was setting herself up to be able to back out of the art show and say it was his and Hackbutt's fault. He'd insisted she be there. He knew that Hackbutt wouldn't go along with everything unless she was there. Hackbutt had to be transformed.

The process was a simple one, and one that Piat had used before. First, dress Hackbutt like a human being. Then take him shopping for real—once he wouldn't stick out like a clown from a circus. And in between times, try to get him to make small talk on some subject other than birds.

Spitalfields had a sporting goods store that catered to a twenty-something clientele of up-and-comers who did things like rock climbing and mountain biking. In thirty minutes, Piat piled the counter with three shirts (colors chosen by Irene, neutral, microfiber, expensive), a single pair of hard-wearing hiking trousers with a minimum of cargo-pockets, a Gore-Tex windbreaker. Shoes were a problem.

Hackbutt didn't resist the shirts or the trousers, but he wasn't really interested until Irene started moving him through the shoes. He had on his feet a pair of "running" shoes so ancient that the nylon mesh fabric had ripped away, and the logo, the most prominent part of the design, was unrecognizable. The rubber internals had broken down and the shoes didn't sit right on his feet. Their color was somewhere between that of mud and that of pigeon blood. Even Hackbutt recognized that his shoes were disgusting. Piat suspected that they were the only pair he owned.

Hackbutt, suddenly enthusiastic, cruised the racks of waiting shoes and boots with an air of childlike wonder. Irene prattled at him, fussed while he tried boots on, chided him when he was attracted by colored laces. But in the end, it was Piat who made the choice for a pair of Vasque shoes, built like running shoes but with heavier, leather uppers. Hackbutt was so delighted that he put them on immediately. Piat threw his old shoes into the box as soon as he paid and tossed the box in the first dumpster they passed when they left.

Hackbutt walked through Spitalfields with his eyes on his new shoes. "They're so comfortable!" he said. For the third time.

Irene smiled. "That was easier than I expected," she said quietly.

"That was the easy part," answered Piat.

* * *

The contact report was on Craik's computer when he got to his office in the morning. With it, however, was a note from Swaricki that the Marine hadn't bothered to tell him about the day before—Swaricki apparently didn't like to repeat himself. It had the same charge of torture and the Marine's disgust with the heavy censoring, but it also had something new. "This material was not in our system before about two months ago. It appears to have been part of a big take from Mossad that included all that stuff on Shiite politics, but this is sort of off the wall—different subject. But it comes with the routing number of the Mossad take. Maybe they swept up a lot of stuff to pad the take, give us a thrill. My question would be, is it an Israeli report? I thought it was US."

Mossad cleaning house? A small voice said, *Well, the Israelis use torture. Even though their supreme court said it's illegal.*

Or somebody screwing up? Not screwing up big-time, but making one of those little mistakes that everybody does. And saying when it was discovered, "What the hell difference does it make? It's a nothing."

Except that this nothing was supposed to be an *American* intel report. Partlow hadn't given any indication that it was otherwise. And it sounded American—American jargon, written by somebody who'd been at it long enough to write in army-speak. But if it was American, it must have been sent *to* Israel in the first place. Which was not at all unusual—allies trade intelligence. But getting it sent back was.

Craik put his hand on his internal phone and called Swaricki. "Did you get *any* indication that that document had been in our system before two months ago?"

"No, sir. If we had the headers, we might pick up a number we could look under, though. It could have been here all the time that way."

Craik put the phone down and tried to walk the cat back: Partlow would have been looking for a target to match an existing antiterrorism task. Maybe he had already had some names, had pinged on the one in this document because it connected to al-Qaeda—a great selling point. Partlow was being a good bureaucrat. Looking for an operation that would support a task and bring in money and medals.

Except that it was awfully convenient that the document had turned up just in time to serve Partlow's purpose. Unless Partlow had known another way to access it in the system—a way he hadn't indicated in referring to it.

"I don't have time for this shit," Craik said out loud. He had E-6 fitness reports coming up. He jotted some notes on a yellow sticky and stuck it to his screen amid a forest of other such notes. The process of writing made him uneasy. The note said only:

> *Partlow*
> *Israel*
> *Access?*

But the words hung there. That was when he knew in his gut that he was looking at something bad.

A London hairdresser was a more difficult proposition altogether for Hackbutt than clothes or shoes. He couldn't explain *why* he was so resistant, but he was. Because he had no rational reason to resist, it was almost impossible for Piat—or Irene—to convince him to go.

Piat resorted to force. He called the salon he had selected and made an appointment—a late appointment.

Hackbutt wouldn't look up. "I don't want to," he said. He was pleading.

"Too bad," Piat said. "The appointment's made, Digger. Here's the deal. If we miss it, the op's off. That simple."

"You're trying to make me into somebody else!" Hackbutt said. *Point for Hackbutt. Maybe game, set, and match, too.*

Irene brushed Hackbutt's lips with a finger. "He's trying to make you into *yourself,*" she said.

Once again, Piat had the feeling that she was speaking lines he'd written for her. Case-officer lines.

Hackbutt looked up at her, and they hugged. He looked miserable, but he hugged.

They made the salon on time.

The difference afterward was so remarkable that Piat had to keep himself from looking at Hackbutt the way that Hackbutt had looked at his new shoes. His beard was trimmed now, neat; his moustache was full and dark, his hair groomed—still a little wild, but disciplined. The man with the scissors had been gifted. He'd cut like a sculptor, revealing rather than excising. Going into the salon, Hackbutt had looked like a street person in expensive shoes. Coming out. he looked like a retired U-boat commander.

Irene glanced at Piat. "How did you find that place?"

"I liked the sound of the guy's voice and the style of his website. He never used the word *art.*" Piat shrugged again.

"As if you'd know art," Irene said. Then she ran her fingers through her hair and raised her eyebrows.

"Of course," Piat said.

Near the end of the Washington work day, not too long before most people would leave (but Craik wouldn't; he'd be there until eight or nine), he headed downstairs, down past the ground floor and the nominal basement to the B-2 level. Two floors below ground. The burrows of the computer geeks, the real masters of the intel universe.

Down here were IT support people from all the services. The Navy specialists were DPs—data processing ratings. Craik made a point of spending time down there, both to understand how things were done and to get to know a few of the people. One, a DP second class named Brakhage, had proven to be a familiar face, a young black guy who had spent six weeks on his team prepping an exercise in India several years before. Now, Craik headed for the big room where Brakhage and fifteen other people sat all day at computer monitors.

"Hey, Captain."

"Hey, Brakhage, how you doing?"

"Not as much fun as planning that war game. But sort of fun."

"If your work is fun, you've got it made." Alan pulled a rolling chair over from an empty station and sat down. Brakhage was inputting data from what looked like hand-written notes. Rather a contradiction, that anybody worked by hand to give stuff to a computer. Some old-timer. Brakhage kept working, but he said, "Do something for you, sir?"

"I've got a sort of peculiar problem."

"Just give me a minute, sir." Brakhage tapped the keyboard, turned a page, tapped some more. What appeared on the screen was gobbledygook to Alan Craik.

"Encrypted?" Alan said.

"Yessir."

Brakhage stopped typing and studied the screen, his eyes screwed up as if he needed glasses. Craik thought of asking him if he did, decided it was none of his business. Then Brakhage swung around to face him. "Yessir, what can I do for you?"

Alan took the folded printout of the contact report. Unfolding it, he said, "This is kind of strange." He handed the paper over.

Brakhage eyeballed it and looked up. It didn't take long to read the almost blank page. Craik explained. "It's the contact report on an operation I signed off on. I'm just dotting the i's now." He leaned back. He wanted to seem casual but assured that what he was asking was okay. "It's got no headers or footers, so I don't know where it's from or who did it. I thought maybe you could do a search on the text and find the original."

"Been really redacted."

"Sure has. Can you search on the sentence that has the Arabic name in it?"

"Might do that," Brakhage muttered.

"Not much to choose from."

"Any unique string'll do."

"Can you do it?"

"You're gonna authorize it?"

"You want it in writing?"

Brakhage sucked air through the space between his front teeth and said he guessed not. The implication was that Craik was asking for something that was probably not quite legit but that would pass muster if anybody ever checked. Which was exactly the way Alan saw it. It didn't hurt that they'd worked together before and that Brakhage had seen then that Craik was a straight shooter.

"Shall I come back?"

Brakhage shook his head. He clicked his mouse, and the current screen disappeared; he clicked some more and apparently got out of the encryption program, and then he called up a vivid screen with the DIA seal in the middle. From that, he progressed to one with the Department of Defense seal, and finally to a fairly drab one on which Craik was able to read only "CETIX Search" and a multiple password window.

"Don't look," Brakhage said with a grin. He began to tap the keyboard. He muttered, "Short string." He clicked his mouse and fell back in his chair and watched the screen. So did Alan.

It took an uncomfortably long time. Brakhage didn't say whether it was traffic or the age of the program or just density of data in the system. But they had time to talk about baseball and who would make the playoffs and who would win. Brakhage looked at his watch. So did Alan, and he saw that it was quarter to five and Brakhage could have left fifteen minutes ago.

"I'm sorry, Brakhage."

"No biggie, sir." Maybe Brakhage figured that now Alan owed him.

"Jesus, at last."

The screen was blank except for an unglamorous, unboxed message in the upper right corner that looked as if it had been typed on a manual typewriter that needed a new ribbon. It said, "Access denied. 711140095737. 14-3. 52189702. PERPETUAL JUSTICE code-classified."

"What the hell?"

"Yeah, I was sort of afraid of that."

"Security classification?"

"Yessir. That's the 7111—means it's got a special classification above the level of the clearance of the search engine. That's not so unusual, but I usually run into it with stuff out of National Security Council or parts of Defense, like that. CIA not so much. DIA hardly ever, but there it is."

It took a while for Alan to digest what he meant. "This is a *DIA* document?"

"Yessir—that's the 737. That's us."

Us. The Defense Intelligence Agency. His own outfit. He said, "The date-time group that was referenced was for December, 2001. So this is a DIA document from 2001?"

"Yessir, I expect it is. It'd be really rare to change the code in the system, even if another outfit got the document and let's say incorporated it into something else—they'd still have to classify all of it up to this level, and they'd use the same number." He looked at the hard copy Alan had given him. "I guess a lot's been stricken out from it, because what you got here isn't classified that high."

"If you searched on just the Saudi guy's name, would it come up with the document you just found?"

"Yessir, if I go into this system. But in the general system, no, sir."

But the Saudi name, Alan knew, was misspelled. In the

other documents, it was al-Hauq, not al-Hack. You'd have to know about the misspelling to find this document.

He thanked Brakhage and went back to his office. Had he learned anything that he hadn't known before? Yes, he thought, he had: he knew now that there was information in Partlow's reference that was—or had been, because stuff kept its classification for decades after the reason for it was dead—so important that DIA wouldn't let the intelligence community see it. And what had to be in there, besides possible references to torture, were the headers and footers: the task number, the operation number, the identity of the originating office, the number of the operative who had written the report, and the authorization under which they had done what they did.

Very interesting.

The first night in London, Piat found it hard to sleep through the sounds (love-making? certainly not the telly) coming from the room next door, and he went out and walked, ranging as far as the BBC complex. He sat in a pub and had a beer and tried not to over-analyze why their fucking bugged him. Then he thought about how little he knew about the target of the operation. It was one thing to hit a target overseas—another to turn that meeting into a contact. He tried to imagine a rich Arab falconer—were they all like Hackbutt? Driven? Whacked?

He needed Partlow. He needed information, money, targeting data.

He found that he was thinking about Irene. And the sounds from their room.

Craik called Dukas at home in Naples. Dukas, he knew, went to bed late, but Dukas let him know that Craik was pushing the envelope.

"It's the price you pay for having a secure phone at home."

"What is it now? You want me to go find Jimmy Hoffa?"

"I think there's something interesting about Partlow's operation," Craik said.

"Interesting how?"

Craik told him about the contact report.

Dukas's reaction suggested that "interesting" wasn't the word he'd have used. When they'd talked it over and had an idea of what came next, Craik said, "I'm going to have to talk to Partlow, and when I do, I'm going to have to take your name in vain. I'm going to tell him you're a very unhappy special agent."

"Not far from the truth."

The first full day in London, Piat was ready to take Hackbutt to the big time—Pall Mall, the Arcades. Burberry and Aquascutum. Farlow's.

The change wrought by the haircut was profound—perhaps the shoes helped. Hackbutt stood straighter, walked better. Irene fussed while she dressed him. Piat worked to keep him enthusiastic for another day of shopping.

Before they walked out the door of the hotel, Hackbutt told them he needed to take a piss. Irene pulled Piat aside.

"I want to know what you're going to make him into, Jack," she said. She shrugged. "He can't do power businessman. You know?"

"Eccentric rich falconer. Old money. I think it's the best we can do."

She considered for a few seconds. "And me?"

He gave her an envelope.

"Thousand pounds," he said. He shrugged. "All I have right now." He already needed the extra funds Partlow would bring to their next meeting. In fact, he was spending his own money on the op. Good case officers always did.

She raised an eyebrow. "What for?"

"You. Clothes. I can guess at what he ought to wear but I can't even pretend to know what you ought to wear. Okay? I need receipts."

She took the money but she sounded impatient. "Tell me exactly what you want me to look like," she said. "Don't give me a lot of shit. Just lay it out. Who am I?"

Hackbutt was coming out of the washroom. "You guys have a secret?" he asked happily.

"No," they said together. All three laughed.

"Irene needs some new things, too," Piat said.

"That's great!" said Hackbutt. "I can help, too."

Perish the thought. Piat nodded. He wondered how fragile Irene's cooperation was. He had the feeling she had an edge of resentment under the surface—resentment that he was changing Hackbutt? Or was that too facile?

"I don't know," Piat said. He stood appraising Irene. Was the target gay? Straight? If the target was hetero, Irene could be a bonus. He shrugged. Or not. He moved his eyes off her.

Irene laughed nastily. "Always a pleasure to hear a man say that out loud. Listen, Jack—just point to women on the street. Tell me what you're looking for."

Piat went back to looking at her carefully. "Skirts? Stockings?" he said tentatively.

She rolled her eyes.

They walked out into the rain.

In the richest part of one of the richest cities in the world, it was Irene who stuck out. Piat was invisible—ancient tweed jacket, serviceable shoes. Hackbutt looked—well, he looked like an actor learning a role, but the role fit. It was Irene who missed the mark. Sack-like dresses and heavy wool bags were oddly appropriate on Mull, or even in Spitalfields. A statement. In the Burlington Arcade, two hundred years of snobbery shed her statement like water off an Aquascutum slicker and left her a past-sell-by-date hippie in an ugly, baggy dress.

While a smooth shopgirl plied Hackbutt with ties, Irene squirmed. "I could spend all this on one coat." She shrugged in disgust.

Piat agreed. He wasn't mentally prepared for the jump in prices. He didn't have the funds to support both of them, even if he spent every dime in his own accounts.

"Get cards. Pick your items—color, detail, size. We'll do the ordering by phone next week."

She smiled mockingly. "Promise?" she said. Her eyes did something—Piat couldn't decide what it was—something derisive.

Hackbutt loved Farlow's. He loved the staff and the vast range of green clothes. He loved the fishing flies and the shooting socks and the flasks and the hats. Especially the hats.

"Why do nerds always love hats?" Piat asked Irene.

She just laughed. "He likes it here. You're on your own."

They got him fitted for trousers, a decent jacket, some shirts. The unavoidable hat, an expensive, heavy felt hat with a broad brim and a puggaree band. The rest Piat decided to order from the catalogue. He wrote down items, including a number of things for himself. He paid cash for the trousers and jacket and gave the address of the farm on Mull. By the time they were done they'd attracted a lot of notice from the store staff. Piat didn't like it, but what he did like was the way Hackbutt was beginning to react.

He seemed to take it as his due.

In another store in the East End, Piat got similar quality items—the most expensive items on his mental list: two pairs of heavy walking shoes, an Aquascutum oilskin, a chance-found tropical-weight suit that fit Hackbutt as if made for him. These items were all used, which was an advantage in itself. Piat wondered idly how many spies shopped there.

He also bought two sets of evening clothes, black and black, no vests, no color. They were cheap, and rich people wore such stuff. He dropped the whole bundle of used clothing with a Greek tailor to be altered to fit and paid the man with the last of his money.

Back in Mull next day, Piat picked up the answers to his emails. They made him smile. One even made him laugh aloud. He replied to all three, located a place on the main-land to get long-term rentals of diving equipment, and fired off a stream of requests.

Then he caught the ferry to Oban, drove to Glasgow, and flew to Athens.

8

On a Monday, Alan Craik telephoned Clyde Partlow. There was some falsely jocular give and take, then the requisite short pause, and then Craik said, "You going to have a minute sometime? I need a little help on something." He'd started to say "clarification," but he knew that the word would put Partlow off. Even as it was, Partlow's voice was guarded when he said, "What kind of help?"

"Oh, a common interest. Not for the phone."

"Well, I'm always glad to share with another member of the community, Al. Delighted to have you drop by and try our coffee. Kind of special—a dark roast from Uganda that'll curl your toes."

"Sounds great. Want to name a time?"

So it went for another minute, a form of delicate fencing with foils so thin they were invisible. At last Partlow, no longer able to put it off, named a time that day, his office, Langley. They parted the best of friends.

"It's a little hard to talk about, Clyde." Craik sipped the really excellent coffee—china cups, a real sugar bowl, a silver goddam spoon—and smiled and said, "An intelligence officer never likes to admit he's confused."

"Is this the Navy asking the CIA for help?" Partlow smiled, too, checked his watch, and glanced at the suitcase that stood against a chair, a Burberry raincoat tossed over it.

"Practically throwing myself at your feet."

Both men laughed.

"You remember Mike Dukas." Craik kept his face as innocent as a reality-TV contestant's. "What he did for one of your operations."

"Oh, the fellow who got the, mmm, that guy I asked you to— That one?"

"Mike Dukas, right. Head of NCIS, Naples. He brought in the guy named Piat for you." Alan smiled. "Twice."

"Oh, right, yes, I remember now." Partlow, every bit as guileless as Craik, said blandly, "How is he?"

"I guess he's fine, but he's got this problem about that operation. I felt that I had to share it with him, him being so close to it. So useful to you on it." Partlow's smooth face allowed itself a frown. Alan said, "It's probably nothing, Clyde, but there's a reference in your plan that doesn't seem to pay out. Could I have some more coffee, please?"

"Pay out?" It was as if Partlow couldn't grasp the concept of paying out. "What reference? Cream? Sugar?"

"Black. There's a reference that's meant to support an al-Qaeda financing link, but when you check it, there's almost nothing there."

"You checked it?"

"That's my job." Not quite true, but close enough.

"Obviously we thought that there was plenty there, or we wouldn't have used it."

"Well, have a look at it. Maybe somebody else did the leg work, didn't understand how important it is. But if you look at it, you'll see that it's pretty much a pig in a poke. Not even clear what *country* it came from."

"It's perfectly obvious it's ours," Partlow snapped.

Craik made a *Gee-I'm-sorry* bob of the head, eyebrows raised. "Maybe it's in the eye of the beholder. I see an Israeli routing number, I think, whoa! What have we here?"

"I don't remember any Israeli routing number."

"It's not in your reference; it's if you go into the system for the document."

"Anyway, if it was Israeli, it'd be rock-solid. They're as good as we are."

"Yeah, sure, but—mmm, well—There's a question whether the information was got with torture. We both know that the data you get with torture isn't worth spit."

"Anything I referenced is solid. Rock-solid. What's the document?" Partlow swung around to a computer.

"You reffed it by a date-time group in 2001." Alan read off the numbers from a slip he had ready in a pocket. Partlow, head tilted back so he could look through the lower half of his glasses, tapped on the keys. He looked quite professorial, somehow, perhaps the tilted head. His clothes, however, were far more those of a Washington heavy hitter—expensive suit, the jacket currently off; striped shirt; power suspenders in a dark red silk; a tie in a fabric heavy enough to have provided the Medici with drapes. Probably eight-hundred-dollar shoes, although Alan couldn't see those.

"It looks perfectly fine to me," Partlow said.

"May I look?"

Partlow swung the flat-screen monitor around to him. Craik saw exactly what he had seen on Sergeant Swaricki's computer. "But, see, Clyde, there's the problem—I mean, *look* at it. No headers, no footers, almost everything censored out."

"The name's there. The al-Qaeda link's there. 'That's all ye know and all ye need to know.'"

Alan made a face. "That's not how Dukas sees it. He used the word 'bullshit' several times."

"Dukas doesn't need to know a thing about this operation. It isn't your job to tell him about it."

"Well— See, Clyde, Dukas sort of feels he's been had. He went out on a limb for you—*twice*. He's not going to feel very cooperative if you ask him for a favor again."

"It wasn't a favor. He had orders."

"Oh, come on, Clyde—it was a favor. He did you a favor; I did you a favor. I was glad to do it. All Dukas is asking is that this point be cleared up a little."

"What the hell does 'cleared up a little' mean?"

"I guess it means that the whole document ought to be available. It's a reference, after all."

"Not possible. Negative. No can do."

"But *you* must have seen the whole document when you were putting the plan together." Alan smiled. Partlow was looking for a way out. Alan said, "You'd never accept information from a document you didn't trust, Clyde. You're too good for that."

Partlow settled himself in his custom-made chair. He studied a pencil. "I suggest you tell Dukas to have some faith in me."

Craik sighed. "Clyde, Dukas is two steps away from being the head of NCIS. He didn't get there by trusting people. He's a hardnose."

Partlow would be calculating what the cost might be if Dukas was unhappy, Alan thought. What could Dukas do to him? Not so much because of Piat, maybe, although Partlow wouldn't be sure just how close Dukas and Piat were. But if Dukas really got to be head of NCIS, and if he held a grudge against Partlow—yes, that could present difficulties.

Partlow finished his calculations and didn't like the total. He said, "How much do you need to know?"

"The whole document."

Partlow shook his head. "Out of my hands. I can't release it."

"Headers and footers."

Partlow shook his head again.

"Task number."

Partlow creased the smooth skin between his eyebrows a fraction of a millimeter, then, to Alan's surprise, allowed a small crease to form at each end of his mouth. A mini-smile.

Not meant for Alan, for Partlow was still looking at his pencil, but perhaps a smile over someone else's discomfiture. The mini-smile of *schadenfreude*? Partlow spun the monitor back toward himself and studied it, then tapped on the keyboard and waited. Alan watched Partlow's shirtfront in the reflected light of the screen: it turned mostly blue, then gold, then gray, the first two with a suggestion of brass in the center. Exactly the sequence that Brakhage's computer had gone through when he was trying to recover the document with a word string. And had got a firm no at the end.

But Partlow didn't get a no. He got a pale green shirt. "Task number?" he said.

"You bet."

Partlow was beside himself with satisfaction. "There isn't one you'd recognize."

"There has to be one. They'd never have got past the preliminary vetting without one."

Partlow smiled quite broadly now. "I'd let you look, but I can't."

"So we're back to me taking what you say on faith."

Partlow was back to playing with his pencil. He tossed it on the desk and stood up. "I have to excuse myself, Al. I'm getting to that age where the prostate doesn't do its job so well anymore. Right back." He walked deliberately the length of the office to his private bathroom and closed the door. No wink, no nod. His way of saying, *If you do it, it's on your head.*

Alan reached over the desk and swiveled the monitor toward him. He glanced over the document on the screen, saw that it was unedited, saw that the Saudi's name was properly misspelled, checked out the last line for the stuff about "subject's condition not conducive to further interrogation," and saw that Swaricki had not been too far wrong: "subject's condition not conducive to further interrogation, so called guards to take subject back to his detention facility and ended interrogation for then. Instructed guards to continue with sexual stuff." The rest of the document made it clear enough that the subject had been hooded and that water had been used.

He looked at the header. Partlow had told him the truth, but not the whole truth: in the space for the task number, there was, indeed, no task number as he knew them, but there were actually *two* numbers: PJ12 and 11X97-02 and a superscript annotation, "superseded." He thought that 11X97-02 looked like a legitimate task number, but PJ12 didn't. And which one was superseded—and how?

The toilet flushed in Partlow's john, a discreet sound rather like the clearing of a throat. Alan glanced over the rest of the header, saw nothing that was going to help him—an acronym, OIA, in the slot where the controlling entity was supposed to be listed; a November, 2001 date; no references whatsoever; a subject number that meant nothing to him; and a number for the writer of the report that he just had time to write on a cuff with Partlow's pencil before the man himself came out of the bathroom.

"Sorry to have been so long," Partlow said. His shoes did, indeed, look expensive.

"No problem."

"Can you put our friend Dukas's mind at ease now?"

"I think I can make him see that you've done the best you could."

Partlow smiled. The smile looked genuine, but who could tell? He put out a hand. "Any time."

Craik got up and shook the hand. They parted, if not friends, at least allies. Or non-belligerents. Alan went out wondering whose ass Partlow was biting by letting him see the document. It was actually as intriguing a question as what those numbers meant.

The lobby of Athens's Attalos Hotel was done in marble and mirrors that failed to hide that it was small. Very small. Ten guests could pack the lobby to discomfort. In effect, the lobby was just a front hall. But the rest of the hotel was vast, with a web of corridors opening off the minute and cranky elevator, so that every level represented another adventure in mapping, and the infrequent visitor or yearly tourist could discover new territory on every visit. Different floors were in different stages of reconstruction, each started in a different époque of hotel decoration—mirrors, paint, wallpaper; quaint, moderne, baroque. The process never seemed to end.

Piat liked the Attalos. He liked the rooms, both small and large, and the lobby, and the staff. Most of all he liked to sit in the roof garden and stare at the marvels of the Acropolis towering in the distance, filling the sky at night with the reflected white of two-and-a-half-millennia-old marble. He didn't use the hotel too often—native caution—but this seemed the right time.

"You take me to the oddest places, Jerry," Partlow said as he sipped his scotch. Aside from the bartender, out of earshot in the roof bar, they were the only tenants on the roof.

Jerry drank ouzo. He watched the clear alcohol cloud as the water and the impurities mixed, a swirling white that suddenly filled the glass. Some sort of a moral lesson there, he thought. "Good to see you, too, Clyde."

Partlow looked at the Acropolis. It was evening, and the sun's glow was just dying away in the west, and the Acropolis stood in splendor against a dark pink sky. Partlow watched the colors change for five minutes.

Piat drank a second ouzo. He'd become abstentious in Scotland—avoiding drink because his agents didn't drink much. It was that simple. But Athens was a different world, and here, Piat wanted to drink.

Finally, Partlow tore his gaze away from the Parthenon and turned to the matter at hand. "First, Jerry, please give me your passport."

Piat reached into his pocket and took it out. He caught

himself hesitating, calculating—just what Partlow no doubt intended and was now watching. He forced himself to slide it across the glass top of the table as nonchalantly as he could manage.

Partlow collected it and put it in his pocket. Then he produced another and slid it back. "Bona fides, Jerry."

It was a new passport in Piat's real name, with an expiration date ten years hence. Piat knew that Partlow would have had to walk that through at State Department himself, using up favors. He hadn't done anything illegal, of course—just something tedious and difficult. How unlike him, Piat thought.

"Thanks, Clyde," Piat said. He was smiling like an idiot.

"Don't mention it, Jerry. May we move on to business? Perhaps we should go to your room?" Partlow looked at the bar and the door from the elevator significantly.

Piat shook his head. "This is better. Trust me, Clyde. Look around you. Unless we're unlucky, we won't be interrupted until the after-dinner rush. Nobody can listen. No lasers on windows, none of that shit. Okay?"

Partlow looked around him, his head bobbing to acknowledge the truth he now perceived. "Okay," he said after a minute's reflection. "So—how are they doing?"

Piat sat back, wondering if his current state of mental and physical fitness could stand a cigar, even a small one. "They're fine. Better than fine. The woman is working so well that I have to expect there's a control fight coming—she's so cooperative she'll have to revolt soon. You know?" he said, making a hand gesture to indicate the way agents had to be.

Partlow nodded. "What does she want?"

Piat shrugged. "Money? Power? Her show to be a success in the art world? I don't know what she wants because she doesn't know herself. She needs to be motivated, and I don't have the handle yet."

"And the falconer?" he asked.

Piat slid a digital photo across the table—a snapshot he'd taken after London. It showed Hackbutt in his new guise as retired U-boat commander—in a heavy turtleneck, a gold signet ring from Bermondsey Market glinting on his ring finger.

Partlow whistled—and pocketed the photo. He gave Piat the same smile that he'd had when he greeted him back in Oban—a real smile of happiness. "Well done, Jerry."

Piat drank off the rest of his ouzo. "Don't cheer yet. Too much could fuck up now—as ever. I have a pile of requests, and the top one is money."

Partlow nodded. "I have money now."

Piat let out a sigh of relief. "That's good to hear, Clyde, because I've been spending my own. Here's the receipts." Piat handed over the whole batch—the "contracts" for both of his charges, the receipts for every dime spent in London. On another sheet he had his anticipated expenses for the next phase, all typed out neatly with bland line items, no dates or names. And some serious padding.

Partlow flipped through the receipts, nodding, then glanced at the expenses. He stopped at the cost of the hairdresser in London. "That's quite a lot of money for a haircut," he said carefully.

Piat shrugged. "Look at the picture again and tell me I wasted the money."

Partlow straightened in his chair. "Point taken." His finger was running down the anticipated expenses. "I'm not made of money, Jerry."

Piat shrugged. "I'll be right back," he said, and walked up to the bar. The Greek woman behind the bar was forty, handsome, oddly at home in a white evening shirt and a man's black vest. Piat got two more drinks and a small Dutch cigar. He over-tipped her. She was apparently unimpressed by his Greek or his tip, but one corner of her lip unbent just enough to signal him that he was not totally wasting his time.

When he came back to the table, Partlow had put all the

receipts away and had the expenses in front of him. He had glasses on his nose. Piat had never seen Partlow with glasses before and had to fight an atavistic urge to needle Partlow, but this was a new age and he kept to his intention. The good agent. He put another scotch by Partlow's hand.

"This is all rather high-end, Jerry."

"Clyde, I could argue money item by item, okay? And you could play the good manager. Let's just skip that part. Tell me about the target, and *then* let's talk money."

Partlow sat back with his new scotch. His eyes moved around the roof garden—one last check to see who could hear them. "We're just not there yet, Jerry."

Piat fought with a quick flare of anger. He didn't completely win. "Fine. Play spy games. Let me lay this out as I see it, Clyde. Either you're going for some two-bit creep, in which case this whole op is a waste of time and money, or you're going for a big shot, a serious player, in which case—let's face it, Clyde, you wouldn't waste your own time on a cheap trick. Right? So this guy is somebody who matters. Arab. Falcons. Rich. Right? Do I have to lay this all out? I lived with those people out East, Clyde. They don't stand around in airports. They don't go out on the town. In fact, they don't do *anything* that Americans or Russians or even Chinese would do. They rent whole hotels. They surround themselves with layers of flunkies and courtiers. They have their own planes and their own staffs."

Partlow was looking around the roof again. "Make your point."

Piat leaned forward. "The falconer has to look rich. He has to mix rich. He has to taste rich. Even then—even if I do this perfectly, Clyde—getting alongside the target you are so busy keeping from me is going to take a *fucking miracle*."

"Keep your voice down."

"Don't be a prig, Clyde." Piat stayed forward, his elbows on the table.

Partlow looked at the Parthenon and then back into Piat's eyes. "Again, point taken, Jerry. Your surmises are, as usual, eerily accurate. But that's as far as I can go right now."

Piat blew out a gust of breath in frustration. "Have you got venues? A schedule?"

Partlow opened his briefcase and withdrew a day planner. It was a plain black book, without gold edge or affectation. Piat flipped through it. Someone—probably Partlow—had copied dates and places in careful block letters. It spoke volumes for Partlow's level of commitment to the operation that he'd gone to the trouble of creating such an artifact. "He only leaves his home infrequently. You'll find the dates and times."

Piat already had found one. "Monaco? You're fucking kidding me. You want me to try Digger at Monaco?"

Partlow shrugged. "We don't have much choice."

Piat flipped forward. The Derby in England. A date in Mombasa—that caught Piat's eye. He couldn't think of a reason for a member of the ultra-rich to go to Mombasa. A date in Barcelona, ten months away.

Piat looked up. "Jesus, Clyde, how long do you think this thing's going to go on?"

Partlow rubbed the corners of his mouth. "Until it's done."

Piat leaned all the way forward, until he was almost touching Partlow's nose. He spoke quietly. "What the fuck, Clyde? What's the goal?"

Partlow leaned away from Piat. He was back to watching the Parthenon, now silhouetted against darkness. "Need to know, Jerry."

Piat leaned back. He sipped his third ouzo and lit his cigar. The nicotine hit him. "Okay, Clyde," he said, drawling the words. "I'm a mushroom."

Partlow was still looking at the Parthenon. "Don't be like that, Jerry."

Piat shrugged. "You want me to prepare two fucking

unstable twits to meet a heavy hitter with no prior dope, no research. You want me to pull this off with venues that would challenge a fucking professional to make the contact. The Derby!" Piat's snort was contemptuous.

"Keep your voice down, Jerry."

"Think it through, Clyde. What are we going to do, put him out there with a fucking bird on his wrist and hope this rich fuck waltzes up and initiates?" Piat took a quick swig of his ouzo and subsided. He changed his posture, climbed off his mental high horse, checked his temper. He leaned forward again. "Clyde, have you ever done a contact on a big shot?"

Clyde was obviously stung. He put both hands on the table. "This isn't really about my credentials—"

"No, fuck that," said Piat. "I'm not challenging your authority. This is not a control fight. I want you to think about it, Clyde. Have you ever done a contact op with a heavy hitter? The kind that comes with a mistress and a dozen bodyguards and fifty flunkies?"

Partlow considered. He rubbed at the corners of his mouth again, and then ran his hand back over his hair. "No. I have not."

Piat sighed. "Okay. Forget my tone and my three drinks and all that shit. Just put yourself *there*. Forget the falconer and his total lack of social graces. Picture it was you. You against a wall of bodyguards and courtiers, just to get—unnoticed, of course—next to the target. And then you have what, three seconds? To turn him on."

Partlow straightened his tie, a gesture Piat hadn't seen him make in ten years. Partlow took a drink of his scotch, swirled the ice in the glass. "I see," he said. And it was obvious that he did. He met Piat's eyes. "So do we forget it?"

"Your call, Clyde."

"Can it be done at all?" Partlow asked.

Piat looked into the cloud of the ouzo. "With luck? A little daring? Yeah." He smiled. Piat believed in luck. You made it with work, you earned it, you courted it. Sometimes, you even got it.

Partlow took a deep breath and let it out. "I need to think."

"Sure."

"Can you do tomorrow?"

He meant a meeting, another meeting. Piat looked at his watch and then, rather ostentatiously, at his airline ticket. "Has to be breakfast."

"Done. I'm sorry, Jerry. Really sorry. I think I misjudged—something."

"Don't confuse me by being a good boss, Clyde."

Partlow gave a cautious smile and offered his hand. They rattled though the tedious formalities required for the next day's meeting codes, and Partlow took his briefcase and left.

Piat, who had let two of his vices off the leash for the evening, decided to tickle the third. He went and sat in the bar.

Despite a late night, Piat was up early. He ran through the deserted Plaka, climbed the hill of the Acropolis, fought the hill and the gas fumes and last night's various sins to the top, then ran around the theaters and back down to a shower. By the time he checked Partlow's signals and walked into his hotel, he felt great.

Partlow looked great, too. He had on a superb suit and a pair of very expensive shoes. An equally expensive suitcase, a Burberry tossed over it, stood waiting. His room was immaculate—in fact, a cursory glance showed Piat that Partlow hadn't slept here. A few seconds with Partlow suggested that he hadn't slept anywhere. He looked a little fuzzy around the edges.

"Here we all are, then," Piat said.

Partlow indicated a chair and sat himself. The chairs were carefully arranged, with a table to the side—not between, just available. "Okay, Jerry. Let's go over this again. Let's assume for a moment that all of your surmises are correct, shall we? The target is a rich, powerful Arab, with all those people around him. His own plane, all those things. Yes?"

"Sure, Clyde."

"The venues as noted." Partlow tapped the little day book.

"Sure."

"Can the falconer do it?"

"Maybe. No, don't get like that, Clyde. Maybe's all you get. It'll take ferocious planning and *then* it'll take luck." Piat wanted to say *Jeez, Clyde, it's all luck—where have you been?* But that would have been counterproductive.

"So we'll go forward." Partlow tapped an expensive mechanical pencil on the day book, then slid it over the table. "Yours."

"Good." Piat took the day planner.

"I'll give you a briefing on the target before you hit the first venue."

Piat shrugged. "Spy games."

Partlow bore the shrug without reaction. "Need to know."

Piat said, "Okay. Let me try this on you. Monaco, then Mombasa. Monaco for a look—check his entourage, check his situation. Frankly, give our boy an outing to fuck up, without letting the target see him."

Partlow put his hand on his chin. "Sounds risky." He poured coffee from a thermos for both of them, held out a bagel which Piat refused in favor of a scone. "I could quote chapter and verse from the ops manual."

Piat waved that away. "Yeah, yeah, whatever. Without a look at the target's lifestyle and his people, I won't have a clue."

Partlow took a bite of the bagel, chewed, swallowed. "Let's work toward that. I'm not saying yes or no, Jerry. I need to think it through. But yes—scouting was always your métier, wasn't it? I can see the logic. And Mombasa? Why Mombasa?"

Piat was in mid-scone. He gave a big shrug, swallowed, and followed the shrug with another. "Woman's intuition? It's out of the way, and there's not much cover for the rich. I guess my gut feeling is that the target won't have anywhere to hide in a town that poor. Even out at the beaches."

Partlow sipped coffee.

"Can I ask you to get me all you can on those venues, Clyde? Monaco and Mombasa? Like, why? And where the guy stays? And who he fucks while he's there?"

"Not that kind of Arab, Jerry."

"Whatever. Tell me when you're ready to tell me. Okay. Let's talk money."

"Jerry, I always have the feeling you're not sure which of us is the case officer."

Piat looked at his watch. "Fair enough, Clyde, but I have to get my bag and get on a plane."

Partlow opened his brief case and slid a credit card across the table. "Fifty thousand for future ops expenses. Sign."

Piat signed. The card was in his true name. A two-edged sword—every payment on the card would allow Partlow to watch him, track the op, ticket the expenses. On the other hand, it was a damned convenient way to keep the money.

"Here's a month's pay for you—forty-five thousand dollars. Sign." An envelope, thick with cash.

Piat signed. Piat could make that much money last two or three years.

"Repayment of personal funds spent on operational expenses to date. Seven thousand, two hundred and five dollars and sixteen cents. Cash and hand receipt. Sign."

Piat signed. This envelope jingled—Partlow had actually included the sixteen cents.

"We're square?" Partlow asked.

Piat wished that he'd asked for even more money, but what the hell. "Square. Can we talk Opsec? Or do I have to wait for you to bring it up?"

Partlow shook his head. "Not yet."

"You're going to leave me wandering Europe in my true name?"

"Yes." Partlow looked confident in his decision. "Until you go operational. I'll have an identity prepared for that."

"Lived in? Ready to take a scrutiny?"

"Yes."

Partlow looked determined. Piat had serious doubts. He'd never have run it that way himself—left to his own devices, he'd have covered his principal agent and *both* the sub-agents from the git-go, just to hide any little traces left in purchasing and training.

He looked at his watch again and decided he didn't have time to argue. "Next meeting?"

"You call it," Partlow said, getting up. "When he's ready."

Piat nodded. "Clyde?"

Partlow had the Burberry over his arm and the suitcase in his hand. He was already mentally on his way to his next meeting. He snapped back. "Yes?"

"Clyde, we don't have any recognition signals. No serious fallbacks. What happens if you get hit by a car?"

Partlow put his hand on the doorknob. "You get to spend all that money, and everybody goes home."

And Piat thought, *Jesus, Clyde, what are you up to?* But what he said was, "See you next time, then. Keep an eye on the traffic."

Partlow said, "Thanks, Jerry."

Piat started to say something further, but Partlow had closed the door.

Piat stopped at a bank and used his new passport to open an account. He called the airport and changed his flight and made a few arrangements that included wiring money to two email addresses and visiting a friend in the Plaka who sometimes made antiquities for old friends. Piat showed him some pictures of northern European Bronze Age pieces. Piat had the glimmerings of an idea that might make him enough money so that he would never have to worry about money again.

He paid for his house on Lesvos for another year, in cash. Then he sat in a café at the base of the Plaka and doodled on a napkin. He was trying to figure Partlow's operational cycle. Partlow had identified the target and the possible agent—Hackbutt—at least two months ago. But he only had the money now. So he'd lined up his players before he got his approvals.

Piat crumpled his doodles and put them in his pocket, stood and finished the last dregs of his Helenika. Partlow had started his operational activity before he had his approvals. Piat was sure of it.

Not a good sign.

He left a decent tip on the cup. And then he collected his bag and headed for Scotland.

9

Alan Craik was sitting at his desk, coat off, sleeves rolled up. He was in civilian clothes—chinos; white button-down shirt; rather nifty raw silk tie his wife had given him, a sort of dusty orange and olive. A black blazer was draped over the back of the chair. Allen-Edmonds loafers, whose name he wouldn't have ever heard of except for Dick Triffler, protected the feet that were perched on an open drawer.

He was working through a stack of roughed-out fitness reports, going fast but thinking about each person, picturing the face, remembering what the man or woman did. At the same time, his mind was flicking back and forth over Partlow's operation and the unexplained contact report. It rankled.

He wanted to talk to somebody about it at length. If Dukas had been in Washington, he'd have talked to Dukas. But not over a STU. Not at a three-thousand-miles remove.

He finished a fitness report for Meserve, Geraldine, USA, and initialed the rough and tossed it on a different pile. Then, instead of picking up another, he reached for his outside phone and dialed a number from memory.

"Pearsall, Hench, Rostoff and Gallaher, good morning how may I help you can you hold?"

"No."

"What?"

"I can't hold. Please give me Mister Peretz."

"Oh—really—!" The phone disgorged music but didn't tell him that his call was valuable and would he please stay on the line. The firm was too classy for that. The music was vaguely classical, too, suggesting that they were serious lawyers.

"Peretz."

"Abe, Al Craik."

"Hey, my God, good to hear from you." Peretz was an old, *old* friend, first his father's friend and then a mentor to Alan himself. He wasn't a lawyer but, nowadays, a security specialist.

"How about we get together for a drink?"

It wasn't code, but since his injury, Peretz believed that he was surrounded by enemies, and he insisted on caution. Craik, in fact, wondered if something in his old friend had been pushed over the edge of caution into paranoia.

Peretz said that a drink would be great. "Sixish?"

"How's that place that used to serve the great whitefish?" This wasn't code, either, but nobody listening would know that it referred to a neighborhood bar and grill in Northwest.

Peretz okayed that, and they chatted about Craik's wife but not about Peretz's wife or daughters. Then Craik hung up and spent the rest of the day writing fitness reports and doing other things that collections officers do, which is mostly stuff that makes other people dislike them.

It was cold in Mull, and the rain was falling in sheets instead of the usual heavy drizzle. Piat parked his car and walked down the gravel slope to the cottage. The dog was always happy to see him now, but today it stayed in the shelter of the tarpaulin, its pleasure made evident by its tail and the posture of its head. Piat detoured to greet him, crouching in the rain to ruffle the hair behind his ears. Then he paid a visit to Bella, the sea eagle, who glared at him through the wire mesh of her cage in the way only a big predator can do—in other words, she looked at him as potential food.

Piat stood bare-headed in the torrent, still stunned by her size. She had easily four times the mass of any of the other birds, twice the wingspan, more than twice the height, with long white feathers sticking straight down from her back, and a pale golden head. Beautiful, in a scary way.

Piat had done some reading. There were fewer than four hundred sea eagles left in the world.

Nice bait.

They gazed on one another with much the same look.

The packages from Farlow's had come that morning. Hackbutt was trying everything on.

"I never knew," Irene said.

"Me either," Piat replied.

They spent an hour watching Hackbutt preen. Irene was on edge—perhaps because Hackbutt had center stage. To jolly her, Piat went through her cards from the shops, going through the motions of being the man in charge of the money, secretly appalled by the cost of every garment she had chosen. He wondered fleetingly if this was the feeling he had given Partlow. Or whether she was looking for his refusal.

"Three hundred pounds for a *skirt*?" he asked and instantly wished he hadn't.

"Fine." She snatched at the card he was holding. "I don't need this shit at all. I gave this shit up. I feel like I'm working for my fucking *mother*."

Piat noted that with two shits and a fuck, it was *mother* that sounded like the curse.

Hackbutt peered out from the bedroom. "Honey? What's wrong?" he asked. "Do you know what I did with my new hat?"

Irene's face had the puffy look of someone about to cry. "On the bed!" she shouted, and fled to the kitchen, where she began to take out her aggression on some dough.

"What did you say to her?" Hackbutt asked. He was wearing

a pair of tweed trousers and his new boots with his ancient sweater. It had once been a good sweater, and Piat noted that he looked *just right* for a flaky American, which Piat had decided was the best they were going to do, anyway.

Piat let out a long sigh. "Irene," he started.

"Don't try to sweet-talk me, you pompous shit," she said while pounding the dough. She now had her runway model face on. Piat suspected that from a woman, most people found this pretty intimidating. He found it interesting.

Hackbutt looked back and forth between them. "What?" he asked. "Irene, I really like the clothes. It's okay." He smiled hesitantly at Piat. "The pants are warm." The new tweed pants, part of a suit that had cost four hundred pounds used, had pigeon blood on them. "She's mad because she thinks you're making me do this, you know?" and to Irene, "It's okay, honey."

In the kitchen, Irene cut a wodge of dough in two with a cleaver. The sound echoed like a pistol shot. Hackbutt headed for the bedroom again, muttering something about a jacket.

Piat walked into the kitchen. "I'm sorry. Really. I've never spent six hundred bucks on a skirt before as an ops expense."

Her back was to him. "Fuck yourself. I'm not your fucking agent and don't you forget it."

He sighed again. "Wrong," he said. "You are my fucking agent and you can sink this thing as fast as Digger can—no, faster. Okay?"

She whirled on him. Her face was flushed but set, her knuckles white where she was clutching the counter behind her. "Don't imagine that your money gives you the right to talk to me like that," she said. "You and your money and your planning—you're driving me off my center. Robbing me of my energy. You are making me a thing, not a person."

No swear words at all—different attack altogether. Piat thought she had a few people running around in her head—

rich girl, tough girl, artist. He didn't flinch. "Okay," he said. "So you're out. Game over?"

"That's what you do when you're threatened?" she asked. "Just give up? I thought you were the trained tough guy." Her voice was low, with the clear intention of hiding the quarrel from Hackbutt. Maybe, then, she wasn't serious.

He shrugged. "Whatever. Irene, I like you fine. We can work together. *But there's room for just one touchy, insecure dick on this case, and that role's taken.* Okay?"

"How dare you speak about Eddie that way?" She was truly interesting when angry—positive that she could use it to get her way, even when most of it was a put-on. And sex was the bass accompaniment.

"Who said I meant Digger?" Piat laughed. "Now, are we ordering some clothes, or not?"

"Fuck yourself," she said. But the tone said she was ready to back off, if he would.

He spent four thousand dollars of ops funds off the credit card in five phone calls while she made witticisms from the kitchen and Hackbutt fed the birds. It was too wet for flying. When Hackbutt was done, Piat helped him rig the outdoor heaters that would keep the birds warm if the temperature dropped any more.

The encounter in the kitchen had rattled him. He didn't think about it while he nailed an extension cord into the rafters of the shed, and he didn't think about it while he rewired an ancient space heater with ceramic coils that had been new when Hitler was the chancellor of Germany, and he was still not thinking about it when he left the cottage late in the day.

Northwest Washington's Park View Grill didn't have a view of Rock Creek Park but was close enough that you could walk there in three minutes if that was important to you. Craik arrived first, bought himself a beer, and went to a booth near the back. When Peretz came in, Craik winced, as he did every time he saw this old friend who was no longer quite like the old friend he used to know. It wasn't age that had changed Peretz but a bullet, which had gone through somebody else first and then fragmented in Peretz's abdomen, destroying his spleen, reducing his bladder to the size of an orange and leaving him with a bent back and a permanent drag to his left foot. And a conviction that the world was made up of enemies.

"Abe! Back here."

Peretz came back—more slowly now than he used to—an old man's uncertain smile on his face. When beer had appeared, and when they had both shut up until the waitress had gone, Peretz said, "We've got to stop meeting like this." He smiled. But it was a joke wrapped around a sadness. "I feel like the other woman." He waited for Craik to laugh, but Craik didn't get it. "Meeting in holes-in-the-wall so the wife won't find out."

Craik smiled. "Not my wife, but your uncle." Peretz didn't laugh at the reference to Uncle Sam, the implication of his fear of his own government. Craik didn't want to launch into his problem straight away; he didn't want to seem indifferent to Peretz's situation, to the sadness inside the jokes. He said, "Anything new on the family?"

Peretz's face contracted. "I got a message from Leah." Leah was the younger of his daughters—now, Craik thought, about eighteen. She had vanished in Israel with her sister and mother, presumably into the arms of Mossad, when she was fifteen. Her mother had been passing classified material that she had found on Abe's desk at home—a double whammy for him because, like everybody else, he had violated a rule by taking stuff home, and, unlike everybody else, his wife was a traitor.

Abe talked about his daughter's message. "This stuff they do with cell phones. Like email only without spelling."

"Text-messaging."

"She wants to come home." His voice broke on the last word. Like some men who have been tortured, Peretz didn't have the tight control he'd had before he'd been shot. Or before his wife had committed treason. "It started—" now he was writing with a finger on the table—"p-l-z, p-l-z, p-l-z. It took me a while to see she meant 'please, please, please.' Then—no caps—i w-n-t numeral 2 c-m h-o-m. 'I want to come home.' And it ended with please, please, please again." Tears shone in his eyes.

"How did she get it to you?"

"She sent it to somebody. They sent it on. Maybe somebody she met over there." A bitter look passed over his face. "Or maybe Mossad." Peretz chewed on his upper lip and looked away before he said, "Now she'll be on a list. So will whoever forwarded it. So will I. Everything any of us sends will get read."

Craik wondered how sane his friend was. "Not legal," he said, although he knew how often legality was ignored.

Peretz shot a finger into the air. "These people make up their own definition of legal!" He bent forward, lowered his voice. "Anybody give you grief because you called me today?"

"No, no, no. We're old friends. I've been over it with my security officer. Oh, yeah—don't look so shocked, Abe—you were one of the people I made a point of telling her about. And you know why. You took a bullet for all of us, and so you're a great guy and you got three medals and a swell medical retirement package, but you have a wife who did a Pollard, so you're a suspect guy and a possible security risk. Come on, you know all that."

Peretz was quiet, and then he smiled. "If I weren't a goddam socialistic, secular-humanist, fallen-away Jew, I'd be the darling of the right."

Alan let a little silence fall to mark a change of subject. He said, ready now to talk about his own problems, "A funny thing's happened."

"Funny peculiar or funny ha-ha?"

"Not very ha-ha."

"Too bad. I could use a shot of ha-ha. What's up?"

Alan told him—the heavily edited contact report, the visit to Partlow, the existence of a classified version he wasn't allowed to see. He emphasized the strange task number. "That's a real red flag, Abe. An operation can't go through the process without a task number. I looked up the task number that was on Partlow's computer. It wasn't generated until six months after the contact report was written—that's what 'superseded' meant. Somebody ran an operation and *then* made it legal."

"Who says it went through the process? You say it was the end of 2001—that was a dumbnuts carnival. Washington was a very dicked-up place."

"Even so. My computer geek says the classified version has a DIA code blocking it. DIA wouldn't have honchoed something without a task number."

"Maybe it isn't theirs. Maybe it just has their code on it."

"What're you saying?"

"I don't know. I'm offering options—isn't that what you want me to do? I'd ask the question differently, Al. Is anybody dumb enough to have got an operation going without a task number, meaning without going through the process?"

"Nobody."

"But maybe somebody. Somebody who's never done it before." Peretz got a new expression on his face, something approaching a fanatic's gleam. "Somebody who doesn't even know there *is* a process. Somebody who never heard of task numbers. Somebody who doesn't know dick-all about intel but thinks he knows everything!" He poured more beer into his glass, sipped, licked his lips. "Take that kid who got me shot."

"Spinner?" Craik hadn't been there, but he'd heard the story from Dukas, later from Peretz. "He isn't a kid, and he didn't get you shot, Abe. He got suckered by Mossad because he was too dumb to walk and chew gum at the same time, and your shooting was an accident."

Peretz checked himself, then apparently thought better of getting angry. "My point is, he got sent to Tel Aviv to gather intel and he sure as hell didn't go under any task number."

"Yeah, but—" Craik thought about it. "You think?"

The fanatic's face returned. "The DIY Intelligence Agency, aka the Department of Defense Office of Information Analysis. The brilliant stars of the new regime. Those guys were so smart they sent Little Running Dumb-Fuck off to Tel Aviv with no cover, no country clearance, no nothing. And I got shot."

"You're a little bitter."

"More than a little." Peretz got up. "I shouldn't drink beer. I have to change my Pampers." He'd had about a quarter of the bottle.

While he was gone, Craik ordered a second beer and thought about the possibility of the contact report's having come out of a rogue Defense Department operation. In that case, why would it be classified under a DIA code? And did "OIA" on the version he'd seen in Partlow's office really mean Office of Information Analysis? He was still worrying over it when Peretz came back.

Abe said, "Al, a lot of stupid stuff was done right after Nine-Eleven. People were scared shitless. They were also in shock. There was a feeling of, 'Forget dotting the i's and crossing the t's; forget the fine print—go for it!' A missing task number wouldn't touch some of it."

"The contact report sounds like there was torture."

"Tell me about it! There was also a feeling of 'No more Mister Nice Guy.' International law was out—batten down the hatches, do it ourselves, get tough. And they had clout."

"Not enough clout to ride roughshod over the whole intel community."

"Oh, really? Al, sweetheart, look around you! Who's been blamed for Nine-Eleven? The intelligence community. Who wasn't defending America until the current administration came along? The intelligence community. Who favored criminal prosecution of terrorists instead of military action? The intelligence community. Who needed reforming and got a new Galactic Intercontinental All-Powerful Czar to clean things up? The intelligence community!" Peretz's voice had risen; the waitress looked over at them. "By contrast, the geniuses in the White House and DoD were white hats—never committed intelligence in their lives! Virgins! *And* true believers."

"Off-the-books operations cost a lot of money."

"This administration has money up the wazoo."

"But no professionals. Even the DIY Detective Agency wouldn't send an amateur like Spinner to *torture* somebody. Or to shoot you. They sent him to Tel Aviv on a collection mission—okay, that was stupid. But a black op would be something else."

Peretz tapped the table with a fingertip. "I wouldn't put anything past them! If you offer a thousand bucks a day, you'd be amazed how many private contractors there are just waiting to rip somebody's fingernails out."

Craik said nothing, not wanting to provoke a tirade.

Peretz said, "If we were playing Let's Pretend, I'd look for a private company that's got a lot of traction with the administration. Probably one that's post-Nine-Eleven."

"That'd take big bucks."

"What did I just say?"

Craik stared at the bar without seeing it. He raised his eyebrows as if to say that even stranger things were possible. He tried to make it a joke. "Well, I wanted to talk to you because I knew your take on it would be cynical. I didn't know just how cynical."

Peretz tapped the Formica tabletop again. "Look to see

where the hotshots went for their payoff after the second term started. First term, you do the service; second term, you leave government and make big bucks. These people believe that patriotism is everything, but it should pay well."

Craik was silent. He didn't want to listen to another tirade. He said, "Let's stop talking about it for now. What are you going to do about Leah?"

"What can I do? I don't know how much freedom she has. I doubt she can leave Israel."

"I thought you said it came from Mossad."

"I don't *know*. If I knew—" His face got the bitter look again. "I can't trust them." He didn't say who "them" was.

They left the bar separately.

Piat started Hackbutt on role-playing. Piat played various targets, sometimes with Irene to help him, sometimes with Irene as Hackbutt's other half. They played at being in airport bars and dinner parties, both equally hard to imagine in the slovenly confines of the cottage. Hackbutt's attempts to make a contact were forced. Transparent. Laughable. And they made his hands shake. The more he screwed it up, the more impatient Irene got. She drummed her fingers on the arm of her chair. She fidgeted. One afternoon, she got up and went into her studio, slamming the door.

The only subject that Hackbutt could start and maintain was falconry. He used it on them at dinner, at breakfast, in pretend ticket lines and in make-believe rail stations. He had assimilated only enough of Piat's teaching to be able to turn any subject, any hint, into a conversation about falconry. He could talk about raising young birds when children were mentioned; he could discuss Frederick of Hohenstaufen's manual of falconry when the Middle Ages surfaced. Food, wine, sex, music—all led him to falconry.

Piat decided that it would have to do. But it certainly was boring.

Then Piat began to give them some basic understanding of the methods and means of espionage. It wasn't an obviously important part of the training; Piat couldn't imagine either one of them engaging in lengthy counter-surveillance routes, making carefully timed meetings, or servicing dead drops in dangerous foreign countries. The importance of the training was to remind them of the real purpose of the clothes and the conversation, to focus them both on the target and the goal.

With most agents—like Hackbutt—the espionage training served both to sober them up and to understand the depth of the commitment they had made. It was a trick of the trade.

It had the opposite effect on Irene. The professional paranoia and counterintuitive nature of routine tradecraft made her laugh. It wasn't her fake, self-conscious laugh, but a genuine amusement that angered Piat and raised resentment in Hackbutt.

She and Hackbutt scrapped about it, and then she became bored. After that, she got tense and impatient and said she could be spending her time better at her own work.

They drove around the island, crammed into Piat's Renault, as he pointed out the possibilities of landscape and road layout—where a meeting could be held, the turn that would allow them to see a potential surveillant, another set of turns that would sort a real pursuer from a random encounter. The training irritated Irene (stupid games, sweetie, and don't you forget it, and I'm a busy woman now, and don't forget *that*, sweetie). Hackbutt loved it, of course.

10

Tension, irritation, bickering—Piat wasn't sure what to call it, but it began to run through the little house like some low-voltage, barely felt current. At first, he blamed Irene, thought it was her "work," her "art," her self-induced stress. Then he saw that some of it came from Hackbutt, as well. One evening, he and Hackbutt came in from dicking about with the birds; Hackbutt went into the kitchen, and abruptly there was a slamming of cupboard doors, and Hackbutt was screaming Irene's name. It was unusual enough that her studio door popped open and she looked out, her eyes wide.

"Goddamit, where's my cup? I can't find my cup!" He had a favorite cup with a hawk on it.

"Oh, Eddie, I'm sure it's around—"

"Jesus Christ, is it asking too much that my fucking cup be put back in the same place? For Christ's sake!"

"Eddie, please—"

"Don't Eddie *ple-e-e-ze* me! Find my fucking cup!"

It was a childish tantrum. Rare—in fact to Piat unique. Even he was infected by its violence; he got up and went into the kitchen, hands spread. "Jeez, it's my fault, Digger, I helped put the dishes away last night. My fault." He tried to make a joke of it. "'New girl, new ways.'"

Hackbutt's voice changed to a whine. "Well, where *is* it?"

Piat found it in the cupboard with the plates and saucers. He remembered putting it there. He apologized again; Hackbutt poured himself tea, then went into the sitting room and sulked, his silence extending into the evening as embarrassment at what he must have known was childishness.

Then Piat saw that the tension came from him, or from him and Irene and their mutual attraction-avoidance. By then, he had begun unwittingly to merge into their lives. Trying at least to seem sympathetic with Irene's work (to keep her happy as the agent's girl, but also to keep her happy), he had offered to cook one night. He wasn't a very good cook, mostly man-who-lives-alone stuff, but he could manage by multiplying the quantities by three. Then he did it again; then he was helping with the dishes, then the shopping. Irene didn't seem particularly grateful: "Well, you're the one that gets every other day off. It wouldn't kill you to drop by a shop now and then."

Three days a week should have been enough to train them as agents. He found himself coming more often, however—for Irene and for the dog. Coming for a woman was understandable; coming for a dog was laughable. He took it with him to the loch one day, let it sit on the bank while he fished. It had taught him the flat palm out gesture that meant "stay," and when he used it, Ralph stayed—sitting or lying down with his head on his paws, alert to the bend of the rod, ecstatic when a fish flopped on the bank.

A woman and a dog. It was bad practice to have a relationship with your agent, but nothing was said about her dog.

But the more he was there, the more uneasy he found the atmosphere. Something was happening to them—to *them,* he thought, not to himself—some process that was changing them. He thought he was the catalyst, not himself one of the reagents.

* * *

He came in one day and smelled coffee. An old-fashioned percolator sat on the stove, half full. He had a cup, found it not bad, later saw Irene pour herself some. She looked at him, shrugged. Maybe it was the meat she was eating now, changing her metabolism. Something, certainly, was changing.

The house had a covered porch that protected the front door from the local climate. Stone-floored, the porch was a last clutch at dryness before you plunged into the rain to make the sprint to your car. The coal box sat out there; so did mops and a shovel and an axe with a broken handle.

He found Irene there one day. She was in her work clothes. Smoking a cigarette—another change. Seeing him, she blew smoke sideways and said, "All my bad habits are coming back. Soon I'll start fucking strange men."

He smiled, took the cigarette and puffed and gave it back. "You're not a stranger. Would that you were."

"That one hurt."

"Everything's different since you came." She took a pack out of a front pocket of her jeans. It was already half empty. She took one out, lit it, put it back, then remembered to offer him one.

"I'll just puff on yours. Next best thing to kissing."

She looked at him, puffed, blew smoke to the side. "We're doing all this stuff. All this shit. Eddie goes to his goddam birds every day like he's running away from home; I go into that room and work my ass off." She shook her head. "Changes."

"You were working before I got here. All those photos."

"Those photos had been up there for a year. Eddie and Irene's little fantasy—Irene's an artist; Irene's going to be a household word! I hadn't done squat for a year, two years, three, Jesus, until you— I'd lost it. What do jocks call it? My drive, my edge. Now look at me."

"You should thank me, then." As soon as he said the words, he wished them unsaid.

She shook her head. "Change scares me."

"It's only temporary."

She dropped the cigarette on the stone and ground it out with a toe. "Everything's temporary, isn't it?"

She went inside; he went to walk the dog.

Hackbutt was beginning to learn—maybe it was the clothes—but had another tantrum, this one aimed at Annie—maybe that was the clothes, too, the squire and the slavey. Piat wasn't there but heard about it when he found that the dog hadn't been fed. Irene and Hackbutt had forgotten. Annie, it appeared, hadn't been back for two days.

"She upset Bella," Hackbutt said. "She's a stupid little bitch. I don't want her around anymore."

But Hackbutt found he couldn't really get along now without Annie, who, as well as helping with the birds, fed and watered and walked the dog when Piat wasn't there and did the washing-up when Irene or Piat didn't have the time or the inclination.

Annie came back after Hackbutt drove to her father's farm and apologized to the entire family, but she wasn't the same. Like the rest of them, she was altered by whatever Piat had brought to the house.

One day, she said to him, "Are you taking the dog for your own, then?"

"You mean, home with me? No, Annie, of course not."

"It's fair cruel to lead him on then, isn't it?"

"I'm not leading him on." He laughed. "I'm giving him some attention."

"I saw you and him on the road, he was sitting up in your car with you like he was a ship's captain or something. You take him about with you everywhere. He'll be that broken-hearted when you go away."

"Why don't you take him, then, Annie? He likes you."

"I'm not staying one day after I leave school. Next day, I'm off to Glasgow."

"I thought you were daft about the birds!"

"There's birds in Glasgow. And *people*!"

"No dogs?"

"Poor tyke." She tossed her hair back and looked him in the eye to say, "I've as much right to go my way as you, Mister Michaels. And it isn't me will be breaking the doggie's heart."

Then Irene was drinking more. It was part of the smoking and the coffee-drinking, he supposed, a return to an old, perhaps more genuine pattern. He cooked two or three nights a week now; she helped sometimes, a glass of wine always close by. When they touched, she didn't jump away; sometimes she responded with a light bump or an elbow. But nothing more. One night, they were cleaning up; Hackbutt was in the sitting room; they passed each other close, both with dishes in their hands; neither could have grabbed the other even if grabbing had been on the menu. She looked at him. He looked at her. She chuckled. "You, too?" She was a little drunk.

They put their dishes down and he turned toward her and she half-dodged away, a move like the overtly sexy Irene of the first time he'd seen her. She giggled, kept her voice low. "When you first got here, I thought you were going to be the Zipless Fuck. You know that book? I read it—a woman author— Anyway, the Zipless Fuck. Then we didn't, and now everything's complicated." She took out a cigarette. "And now you can't because it'll ruin your operation, and I can't because—" She jerked her head toward the room where Hackbutt was still sitting. "Why can't things ever be simple, eh?" She laughed at having used the Canadian "eh?" and ran out of the room.

* * *

Then, briefly, Irene gave up her "art." She said she couldn't make the deadline she'd been given. The agent and the show could go fuck themselves. She wasn't going to be their gallery slave.

For a day, she sat around in one of her baggy dresses and read an old book that had come with the house. Then, a couple of days later, her door was closed and Piat heard hammering, and everything went on as before.

One afternoon there was a fierce thunderstorm. Hackbutt dragged Piat out to help him comfort the birds; Piat didn't know what "comfort" meant, so he went and held the dog and nuzzled him because the dog was frightened. After the storm came cold and brilliant sunshine; when they went inside, new sounds were coming from the studio. Mostly, an almost rhythmic groaning; then a throaty scream, drawn out and guttural. The moans might have been sexual but suggested pain, too, even death. Then another scream would come, and he thought of rape, but the pitch was wrong.

"Irene's music," Hackbutt said. He knew all about it. She had recorded hours of the waves on the rocks where the Atlantic broke against the island, then had paid somebody in Glasgow to re-record and overlap and slow everything down.

"The screams were gulls," Hackbutt said.

"Sounds like the track for a horror movie." But he didn't say that to her.

It was late morning in Naples, a brilliant day that felt as if it had been washed overnight and laid out in the sun to dry. Dukas had for once got seven hours of sleep. He was sitting a leg-length away from his desk with both feet on the desktop, a six-cup Moka Express perched within reach and a cup in his hand. On the computer table were the remains of a box of honey-covered fried dough. Without looking, Dukas took one and brought it to his mouth, still reading.

"You should have a bed moved in," Dick Triffler said from the door. He crossed to the far side of the desk from Dukas and leaned over to look into the pastry box. "Those things will kill you."

"Promises, promises."

"You eat too many of them."

"I'm an addict and I'm not responsible for my actions."

Triffler was munching one as they talked. Dukas scowled at him, looked into the box, and took the last one. "Did you come in here just to steal my last zeppole?"

"No, I came to ask why Al Craik wants me to stand by a secure phone at eleven-thirty."

"Because I told him you're the world authority on the Office of Information Analysis."

"They're out of business."

"Al's interest is historical. Post-Nine-Eleven. I told him you'd got me an OIA personnel roster when I was having my adventure with their jerk-off in Tel Aviv."

"Aha." Triffler leaned over and looked in the box again. Finding crumbs, he tipped them into a corner and then dumped them into his palm. "Italian food *is* addictive. What's A's interest in OIA?"

"Can you see that I'm reading?"

"Yes. Are you worried about my eyesight?"

"I'm worried that I got a week's work on my desk and you're keeping me from doing it!"

"Anybody who can't read and talk at the same time doesn't deserve to be in NCIS. Some of us can read, talk, and *think* all at the same time. My theory is you should be promoted out of this busy posting and let me take over. You go to DC, I stay here, and we'll mail you care packages of Neapolitan pastry."

"Al will want the OIA personnel list. You still got it?"

"Nothing is ever created or destroyed."

A woman poked her head in the door and said that Triffler had a secure phone call. Dukas said, "Thanks, Jesus." Triffler said he was a blasphemer but likable and went out and along the corridor to his own office. "Triffler," he said into the STU.

"Hey, Dick—Al Craik." It didn't sound like Craik, but that was the effect of the STU.

Triffler said, "The great man just told me what you want. I got an OIA personnel list as of the end of 2001. That do you?"

"Just what I want."

"This didn't come to me exactly through channels, Al, so don't put it on CNN, okay? A couple people did me favors."

"This is just for me. Can you secure-fax it to me?" He gave Triffler a number. "What else have you got on OIA?"

"Only open-source stuff. It was in a few papers, couple of magazines for a while, then the story died. Nobody was getting his jockey shorts wet over it back then. From what I read, it was a small bunch of people in DoD who agreed with like-minded folks elsewhere in the administration that intelligence was not something that should be left to people who spend their lives at it. They were going to be a fresh eye, a fresh voice. Welcome to Iraq."

"Anything about them ever being operational?"

"Never heard that. People who wrote about it said it was into 'purifying' what the White House saw. And I can understand where they were coming from—after Nine-Eleven, the intel community wasn't looking too good. I'd have voted for something new, myself."

"Yeah, but we're still all here. And I understand they aren't—they went away after Bush's first term?"

"You know the suicide note that George Eastman left behind—'My work is done, why wait?' And my hat is off to them—a government office that puts itself out of business gets a gold star!"

Craik grunted. Or the STU hiccupped. Craik said, "I'm not

ready to do that yet. Fax me the roster and I'll take it from there."

When the roster came some hours later, he saved it to his computer and printed out a single hard copy, which he sent by snail mail to Abe Peretz at home.

11

Piat's interest in the crannog was more than academic now. He had plans for it, and he brought them toward fruition with the same thoroughness that he ran an operation—indeed, in his mind, it was an operation, even if an operation subordinate to the one he was running for Partlow.

It certainly ran on Partlow's money.

On a Saturday, Piat rented a cottage in Dervaig. It had two beds and could hold a third on a fold-out sofa. He paid cash and called himself Jack. Risky, but allowable. He caught the midday ferry to the mainland and drove around Oban, claiming various packages—a generator, an air pump, a surprising number of air tanks. He rented a second vehicle and put it on Partlow's credit card, the riskiest part of the whole game, but he had no other source of funds.

At two in the afternoon, he walked into the bar of the Saint Columba Hotel. Any splendor the Saint Columba might have had—and it had had plenty in its day—was long gone. The same might have been said of the three men waiting for him in the gloomy bar. They had a certain sameness about them—short hair, tired polo shirts, khaki trousers, heavy sunglasses, muscles, tattoos. Like dangerous, superannuated beach boys. Two of them were dirty blonds with identical moustaches. The third was black.

"Sweet Jesus fuck, Jack," one hailed Piat as he walked

in. Lots of back-slapping. Then handshakes all around.

"You all know each other already?"

The black man leaned forward over his beer. "We're already fuckin' blood brothers, man. Leastways, that guy bought me a beer." He indicated the thinner white man.

The thinner of the blonds nodded. "Didn't take a fockin' rocket scientist to guess we was all here for you, Jack."

Piat nodded. "Introductions all complete?"

"Never fockin' came up," said the thinner man. "Ken Howse." He shook hands all around, again. His accent was peculiar—Irish, then cockney, then Irish again. Howse had been born in Belfast and spent twenty years in the SBS.

The black man smiled. "Leamon Dykes. Just call me Dawg." His hands were so big they covered the beer. By contrast to Howse, Dykes barely had a trace of an accent—the result of spending twenty years as one of the few black NCOs in one of the most elite—and white—units in Joint Special Operations Command.

"Tony Dalepo," the third man said. "Glad to meet you gents. Now, Jack. There was some mention of money." Dalepo had put in his time on SEAL Team Two. Piat had worked with him twice.

"Just fer showing up," Howse put in.

Piat handed out envelopes. He gave them a cursory brief on what he had in mind.

"Shares?" Dalepo asked. His Alabama accent was so thick that "shares" had an uncountable number of syllables and two diphthongs.

"No. Straight cash, payments weekly. Bonus if we find something worthwhile. Otherwise, payment for services rendered."

All three men nodded. They nursed their beers. Howse and Dalepo smoked. Piat waited. The money was good, and the idea was fine. Men like these—mercenaries, for want of a better word—had superstitions and beliefs that went beyond the simple realities of money and danger.

Finally, Dykes drained his beer. "I'm in. Sounds like fun. Anyway, my daughter's going to college—this's a safer bet than robbing banks. Or playing rent-a-gun in Iraq."

Dalepo crushed out his second cigarette, picked up his envelope, and pushed it into the back pocket of his chinos. "Fuck, Jack. Ya' know I hate divin' in cold water. Long trip ta' tell you that. Ya'all pissed at me?"

Piat shook his head. "Catch you next time, Tony."

Dalepo picked up an old Navy flight jacket and walked out.

Howse was terse. "Too fockin' close to home, mate," he said with a shrug. "I don't do nothin' UK. Okay?"

"If you say so," Piat answered. He was disappointed. He knew the job required two men. He preferred to use men he knew.

Dykes watched Howse through the door and then turned back to Piat. "You don't want no part of that one," he said.

Piat raised his eyebrows.

"Just something I heard." Whatever he had heard had thoroughly convinced him, though; Piat could read it on his face.

Piat shrugged. "Either way, I don't think you can do this on your own."

Dykes put his hand up. "Hey, man—I know a couple of guys over here. Good guys. I did a cross-training thing. Let me a make a call. Okay?"

Dykes's friend proved to be a retired rescue diver from Royal Navy Fleet Air Arm. He lived in Manchester, drove himself up and arrived in time to make the ferry. He looked more like a pirate than a retired British officer, with a bone-crushing grip, a heavy beard, and a striped shirt. Piat thought that all he needed was a parrot and an eyepatch. His name was Tancred McLean, aka Tank. He and Dykes seemed to get on like a house afire, and he needed the money.

They caught the last ferry for Mull, Piat in his own car and Tank driving Dawg in the new rental with the equipment. By nightfall he had them settled in the cottage in Dervaig. He drove them over to the windswept road where the hillside rose to the slope of the caldera above the crannog. In the moonlight, it looked even steeper than it was.

Dykes shook his head. "We're going to carry a *compressor* and a *generator* up that shit?"

McLean was filling his pipe. "Looks tough."

Piat said, "It *is* tough. I've been up and down three times carrying nothing but a pack."

The three men sat and watched the hillside.

"What's the plan, then?" asked McLean.

"Later tonight, we come up here and unload the whole kit. See that shingle at the base of the glen? No, right here. Solid rock, screened from the road. Everything goes there. We make two trips a day until we get it up. Either of you guys know how to strip and reassemble a compressor?"

Both men looked at him as if he was an idiot.

"So we strip it and take it up in pieces."

"Fair enough," said McLean.

Dykes rolled his eyes. "You better be payin' on time, Jack."

Piat put a colored square of pasteboard in the windshield. "Cover. We're fishing. For the next three weeks."

Dykes brightened. "Hey, I like fishing."

Piat smiled. "Good."

They spent two hours unloading the rental van into the ravine. Every part of Piat's body from the abdomen down ached after the first climb, and the repeated trips up and down the wet rock of the ravine sides turned the ache into a raging fire. Nonetheless, the three men worked well together. Jokes were made. War stories told.

In the end, it was done.

Dykes looked pointedly at Piat when Piat was ready to leave. "You better be around for some of this, boss-man."

Piat waved. "Until it's done," he said.

He dropped in on them on a Sunday at the self-catering place he'd found for them. Dykes and McLean were eating breakfast together in their shared kitchen. After a round of greetings, Dykes set to work making a stack of American pancakes for Piat. Piat watched the big man cook. Dykes laid everything he needed out on the counter with military precision and cleaned his dishes as they were made, every movement planned and executed with precision. It was not Piat's method of cooking by a long shot, and Piat wondered what the man was like as a husband or a father. Rigid? Authoritarian?

McLean drank coffee and read the Oban paper.

"I thought we'd have a go today," Piat said.

Dykes's back indicated a shrug. He flipped a pancake. "Thought we were doing the moving at night."

Piat glanced at McLean. "No one drives down that road. No one much, anyway. I thought we'd take turns watching and climbing."

McLean turned a page in the paper. "Mind if I smoke?" he asked.

Piat shook his head. McLean began stuffing his pipe. Dykes whirled and delivered a plate of pancakes with a flourish. "Better than sittin' here all day," he said as the first pancake disappeared into Piat. He glared at McLean. "Smoking an' food don't go together."

The first trip was the worst. Piat climbed with McLean, wearing two tanks as a pack, while McLean carried the frame of the generator and Dykes watched the road. The rain, though light, had soaked the turf under the grass, and every step was like walking in a marsh. The higher they got on the slope of the caldera, the heavier the tanks were on Piat's back, the straps cutting into his shoulders, the tops of his thighs reliving every effort of the last seventy-two hours.

McLean didn't like it any better, but his response was humor, some of it dark, a lot of it funny. McLean had no notion of a race to the top, however. He stopped twice to smoke, and once, just at the rim, to admire the view. The weight of the generator didn't seem to trouble him, nonetheless, and Piat realized that the pauses had been for him. McLean surprised him by being Canadian, not British, with a wealth of outdoor experience in places whose names were familiar but whose terrain was unknown—Northern Quebec, various ice stations north of the Arctic Circle, the Middle East and East Africa. He spoke easily of his career and past postings—probably the result of having been a rescue diver and not a special operations guy, Piat thought. He didn't have to be cagey. By the time they built a hide on the loch, Piat liked him. They stowed their loads and started back.

"You don't strike me as one of Dawg's hard men," McLean said.

Piat smiled. "No," he said.

McLean turned and looked at him, then smiled. "Oh—got it." He was chuckling as he climbed down. "You're a spook."

"Mmm," Piat said, noncommittally.

McLean raised an eyebrow. "What's the angle?" he asked.

Piat shrugged. "Angle?"

McLean pointed at the hide. "Dawg doesn't seem to care. I do. I know people who dive crannogs. The stuff inside them isn't worth a shit on the market."

Piat shook his head. "Wrong. Northern Bronze Age is the hottest stuff on the market. One piece—one decent piece—will pay for this whole thing and some bonus money."

McLean gave him a long, steady stare. Then he shrugged and started down the hill.

Dykes and McLean took the next load, and Piat lay on the grass and watched the road and the mountains, aware that the landowner might just as easily come across the moorland from the west on an ATV. He wanted to smoke. McLean's pipe smoke was scratching at the door of his old addiction.

The two men got up the hill in a little more than half the time Piat had taken with McLean, and they were back sooner, too, but by the time they came back, Piat felt better. He took the last two air tanks; Dykes took a pack full of machine parts. McLean was to follow them with the last load as soon as they were out of sight.

Piat's back still hurt, but his legs were surrendering to the exercise. He was still trying to find a way to make small talk with Dykes when he found that they were over the top of the caldera and on their way to the hide.

"So pretty here, I'm 'mazed you're paying me to come," Dykes said with a big smile. His head was swiveling in all directions, as if he was trying to get everything in a single sweep. Then he pointed at the loch. "Got fish?"

Piat was sitting in a heap on the shingle, just breathing. But he had carried his rod up snapped to the harness that held the bottles, and he pushed himself to his feet.

"I'll show you," he said. Still trying to control his breathing.

He stayed on the shingle and cast a heavy red fly into the mouth of the underwater vent. The second cast got a swirl of movement and the third cast hooked a good brown trout—possibly the same one he'd caught the last time, possibly not. Piat landed the fish with care.

Dykes whistled. "I seen guys out west—Marine Mountain Warfare School, you know it? Anyway, I watched 'em fly-fish, and I thought, shit, I gotta learn to do that, it's slick. But the stuff's all so frickin' expensive, and—"

Piat got the hook clear of the fish. "Shall I kill it? You want to eat it?"

Dykes said, "Shit, yes!"

Piat whacked it in the head and moved along the shingle to clean it. "It's not rocket science, Dawg. People are always adding mysticism to it. Nothing to it. Hand-eye coordination you got—the rest is just practice. And fishing is your cover here, starting today."

Dykes smiled from ear to ear. "You *sure* this ain't a vacation?" Then he put the smile away. "Hey, Jack. About that Howse guy. He's gonna talk."

Piat smiled. "I expect he will."

Dykes nodded, having confirmed something. "So you got that covered."

"Unless he talks to the cops. I don't have *that* covered." Piat tossed another cast into the vent. "Your friend McLean wanted to know the angle. I don't know him. I know you. So here's the angle."

"I'm all ears," Dykes said.

"Conditions are pretty much ideal for a lesson, Dawg. Nothing to hit on the back cast, fish to catch in front. Take the rod."

Dykes hesitated, an odd look on his face. Embarrassment. Fear. "My spin rig'll come up with Tank," he said defensively.

Piat forced the cork grip into his hand. "Dawg. It won't bite. The line's on the water. When you want to re-cast, just pick it up and flick it again. Never mind—you've got a fish on." Without changing his tone, he said, "I doubt you'll find anything in the water here, Dawg. But that's not a problem. I'm going to supply a few artifacts."

Dykes's hesitant movements of the rod tip had apparently lured a small brown trout. Dykes got it ashore. It was ten inches long and worth eating.

"And we'll just find them," Dykes said. He killed the fish.

"And I'll sell them. If Howse runs his mouth, it'll just help sell the idea that we've found a site." Piat took the dead fish and put it in a mesh bag in the cold water of the loch.

Dykes was casting when McLean walked up, dropped his pack, and lit his pipe.

"I caught a trout," Dykes said.

Piat had to hide a smile. Dykes had done HALO jumps and desperate missions, and he was beaming at having landed a ten-inch trout on a borrowed rod. It was one of the things that made Dykes so easy to like.

McLean spoke around his pipe. "We've got the fishing?"

Piat said, "Yeah. For two weeks."

McLean nodded, took in a lungful of smoke and exhaled slowly. "You going to stand there with that rod, or you going to fish?"

That night, they went over the possibilities. McLean and Dykes had made a single dive in the last good light, swum all the way around the foundation of the crannog, lifted the silt a little.

McLean had another bite of fish, chewed, swallowed. "No way we can shift the foundation of that thing. The base timbers must weigh a ton."

Dykes shook his head. "Maybe a tackle from the shore. But it'd show, Jack."

McLean said, "And it'd wreck the fishing."

Piat ate more fish, drank some wine. "Okay. Let's just sift the silt around the edge. With the blower. Can we do that?"

Both men thought that they could. They all clinked their glasses.

Piat relaxed and enjoyed himself. He had too much wine, but he still managed to issue them a communications plan, pay them for two weeks, and work out a schedule.

McLean looked inside his envelope and frowned. "This is spy shit."

Piat shrugged.

Dykes put a hand on McLean's shoulder. "I told you how it would be."

McLean looked from one to the other. "I went out of my way to avoid this kind of shit in the RN. Dykes said cash for some cold water dives and no questions, eh? That's good. But the rest of this shit. Comms plan? Fallback? Who are we fooling, the KGB? Eh?"

"Humor me," Piat said quietly. "Old habits die hard."

McLean stared at him for a long ten seconds. Then he gave a quick smile. "Okay. Just don't push me. I always thought James Bond was a twat."

Piat knocked back the rest of his wine. "Me, too."

The next time he went to the farm, Hackbutt wasn't there. He didn't know that when he pulled in, scratched the dog, and looked up to find Irene leaning in the doorway with a peculiar smile on her face. "Well," she said. She leaned against the door sill. "Edgar isn't here. I tried to call you."

"You want to offer me a cup of tea?" he asked. He wondered if in fact it was a good idea.

"Of course. Come on in." She was wearing lavender track pants and an old T-shirt. A yoga mat stood rolled up against the fireplace. She had incense burning in the grate and a single candle on the old trunk that served as a coffee table. The smell of incense caught at Piat's throat, as did the smell of pot. Music with a heavy beat played in the background.

"Did I interrupt?" Piat asked.

"No. No, I did a little meditation, and then—"

And then you smoked a bit. "Sure," said Piat. He was a little off balance, just looking at her.

She stepped past him, headed for the kitchen. Her trailing

hand touched his cheek, just for a moment, and moved, feather-light, along the line of his jaw.

He sat down quickly.

"Herbal or caffeine?" she called.

"Caffeine."

She brought him a pint glass of water. "You need this more than caffeine, sweetie." She folded her legs under her on the floor and flipped her hair over her shoulder.

"How's Annie now? She's forgiven Hackbutt?"

"Ach, who cares?" Irene laughed, her accent a fair mimicry of Annie's. Her laugh had a contemptuous edge to it.

She *was* high.

The kettle started to whistle, and she rose to her feet and went to the kitchen. Piat watched her straight back and her legs and he wanted her. Just that simple. But he wouldn't do it, because he wanted the operation more. His brain, like all human brains (like hers, if he'd thought about it) was a curious place, full of contradictions and rooms with closed doors. Even as he slammed down the blast doors against the notion of fucking Digger's girl, he was planning a different kind of operation, this time involving Bella.

"She seems good with Bella. Not afraid of her."

"*I'm* not afraid of Bella, Jack." Irene's voice was almost girlish. "I just don't like her."

Piat felt as if he were interrogating a prisoner on truth drugs—a babbler. "You don't like Bella?" he asked.

"Bella, Bella, Bella." Irene came back with a teapot and two ugly cups. "She's a dumb, mindless killer. She throws me off my center. You going to try to fuck me? It's the best chance we'll get, if you don't mind fucking somebody's girl in his own house." She smiled.

He shook his head.

She smiled some more and nodded. "I told you it had got complicated." She giggled.

She poured tea. "Could we at least talk about something different for a change? I hear enough about birds—"

Piat took the tea. "I just wonder if Digger knows what she's worth," he said.

Irene spilled tea on the floor. She gave him a false smile and went back to the kitchen and returned with a rag. The area she wiped became the cleanest spot on the floor. "He'd never sell her," she said. "I don't want to talk about money or birds. Understand?"

Piat sipped his tea. He couldn't help looking at her. She looked at him. The silence lengthened and Piat thought of how much she had aroused him at first. Forbidden now because she was Digger's, forbidden because only an idiot fucked an agent, with all the consequent messiness. In those first two days, when he thought he was in and out—in and out. He grimaced at the turn of his own mind.

Irene got up. "You're boring."

"And you're just bored," Piat said.

She laughed, a long, girlish peal. "With everything. *Everything.*" She lit the butt of a joint from the candle, took a deep drag, offered Piat the smoke. He shook his head. She said, "I think I'll go do some work."

Piat finished his tea. "I don't want Digger to be unhappy," he said. It was weak, but he wasn't thinking very well.

"Not until you have what you want from him, anyway." She took another hit, flinched as the coal burned her fingers.

Piat winced at her tone and the truth behind it. "I like Digger a little better than you think."

She raised an eyebrow and ground the butt of her joint out in the ashtray. "Eddie saved me from a stupid, bad relationship with a stupid, bad man. I owe him for that. I reckon I've paid. Eddie's a nice boy. He's growing up now."

Piat thought about Digger with Bella. "He's grown up quite a bit."

Irene shrugged, her breasts rising and falling under the

T-shirt. "Sure. I like him. I like him better since you came. Isn't that funny?" She giggled. "How much is the stupid bird worth, Jack?"

Piat wondered if the fumes from the pot were getting to him. "Bird?" he asked dully. "Oh—Bella." He paused, trying to sort out which operation he was working. "Half a million dollars? More?"

She started, and her head snapped around. Her eyes locked on his. "What?" she asked. "That stupid killing machine is worth half a *million dollars*?"

Piat got out and walked the dog.

12

Piat told them fairly abruptly that they were going to Monaco for the first phase of the operation. He laid out the rules and the objectives of the Monaco part, every word and every distinct operational phase another brick in a wall he was building between himself and Irene.

Hackbutt didn't see the undercurrents. But he asked questions—good questions. And while the possible pitfalls of a foreign city made him uneasy, they did not make him childish.

Again, Piat was impressed.

"So I'm not going to approach him directly," Hackbutt said. It was Hackbutt's third version of the question.

"No," said Piat. "I'm going to look at him and his entourage. Maybe—if something breaks just right—maybe we'll go for it. I don't know. But I doubt it. I'm going to look at the target and you guys are going to practice being the people you have to be."

Irene pursed her lips. "We won't know anyone."

Piat missed her point and smiled. "Better that way."

Irene shook her head, annoyed. "No, honey. I mean, we won't know *anyone*. People—the kind of people we're pretending to be—they don't travel that way. They go where people know them. Strangers stick out like a sore thumb. And rich people don't like feeling alone. They like to feel that they're at the center."

Piat rubbed his jaw, staring off into space. She had a point. It was not a problem he had anticipated. He hadn't had a lot of problems mixing with such people—he just aimed at his target and barged in.

Might be different for Irene. Definitely different for Hackbutt.

"We need to *do* something," Irene said.

"You guys play roulette?"

On Wednesday, they went to a restaurant in Tobermory, dressed in thousands of pounds' worth of "casual" clothing. Irene appeared in slacks and a tailored jacket over a heavy cream silk blouse that shouted of taste and extravagance. She also wore a string of pearls and a ring that Piat instantly priced as worth more than her clothes and that he hadn't bought her with Partlow's money. Another care package from Mama?

"I didn't know you had jewelry," Piat said.

"You never asked." She smiled. "Just things somebody gave me."

Hackbutt wore a cashmere pullover and light wool slacks. In the car, he talked about birding on Mull. Over dinner, he talked about birding in Malaysia—all the references to his work and life excised, it sounded as if he'd gone to Southeast Asia for the birds. He talked about New Zealand, a whole environment where birds had replaced mammals. He talked about Java. And birds.

He sounded nutty. But he sounded knowledgeable, authoritative—passionate but eccentric.

He wasn't bad.

After dinner, they drank in the bar with twenty other couples, all tourists.

Without warning, Piat got up, stepped past Irene, and bent next to Hackbutt.

"See that guy at the bar? Suit jacket? Overweight?"

"Sure, Jack."

Piat squeezed Hackbutt's shoulder. "Go talk to him."

Hackbutt's shoulder froze under Piat's hand. "What?"

Piat spoke softly. "I want his name, his business, and where he's from. Do it, Digger. We've practiced this a hundred times. Just do it."

Hackbutt turned his head slowly, like a raptor scanning for prey, and looked at Piat. "I don't want to," he said flatly.

Piat frowned. "Digger—"

Hackbutt looked at his target. "I don't like him. I don't like the way he looks at Irene and all the other women here."

Piat hadn't observed the man all that closely. Apparently Hackbutt had. A good thing all by itself. But— "I didn't say you should go become his friend. Digger—please. Have a go. Okay?"

"I assume this is a test?" Hackbutt said a little too loudly. He put his drink down on the table and got to his feet, straightening his trousers.

Irene glared at Piat.

Piat watched.

Hackbutt walked up to the other man. To Piat, his hesitation was obvious, and so was his lack of purpose. Hackbutt didn't seem to know why he was going to the bar—nor did he take a direct path. More like a mating flight.

He got there. He said something. Beckoned to the bartender. And pointed back at Piat.

Piat didn't like that.

The fat man responded. Looked at Piat and at Irene, shrugged, said a few words and laughed.

Irene whirled on Piat. "This isn't fair. Jack—listen to me, Jack. Eddie can't do this sort of thing. With the birds—that's different. Jesus *fuck*, Jack! Listen to me."

Piat didn't meet her eyes. "Keep your voice down."

Hackbutt was laughing with the other man, bought them both a drink when the waiter arrived. Shook hands.

"Jesus—he's doing it. You are a *cunt*, Jack." Irene was not used to hard liquor, something Jack noted for Monaco.

"Keep your voice down." Heads had turned at the word *cunt*.

Hackbutt pushed away from the bar, now at a loss as to how to escape. The fat man was talking to him, gesturing with one hand while the other held his glass. He gestured at Irene, leaned close and said something that caused Hackbutt's face to change. Hackbutt got red. He reared back like an angry horse. The big man laughed. Quite clearly over the din of the bar, he said, "Don't be a touchy bastard. Here, I'll buy this one."

But Hackbutt had had enough. He came back toward them, his back stiff, his face closed.

"Name's Ken. From Manchester. Sells insurance." Hackbutt hissed at Piat. In fact, he looked disgusted. He stayed standing. Ignoring the chair Piat held out for him. "I want to leave, right now."

"What'd you say?"

Hackbutt raised an eyebrow. "I told him you'd dared me to ask him. Made it a bet." Hackbutt's shoulders sagged. "He was—not somebody I'd want to talk to. Said something about you and Irene. I want to go home, now."

And in the car, "I was having a good time, Jack. Why'd you have to make me do that? I don't talk to people like that."

Piat was driving. "We don't get to pick who we talk to, Digger. I just wanted to build your confidence, show you that you could do it."

Hackbutt said, "I hate that kind of crap, Jack." He looked away. "I don't like it, and I don't like the way you made me do it."

Piat took a deep breath. He wondered if Irene was smiling or frowning. To Hackbutt, he said, "Digger, this is what we do. We talk to people. The guy you're going to meet—he won't be somebody you'd want to take home for dinner. This isn't Malaysian oil, Digger. This is terrorism."

Hackbutt nodded. And he didn't say another word until he said goodnight at his farmhouse door.

Piat used a set of pagers and an email account to stay in touch with the two divers working the crannog. Despite the lure of Dykes's pancakes and the uncomplicated *work* and camaraderie involved, Piat was too conscious of the security of both operations to risk spending time with them. And anyway, they were on night schedules. Piat couldn't imagine making night dives in the Loch—cold water, total sensory deprivation. But the two men seemed satisfied that the job could be done.

Piat left them to it. He checked the pager and his email Friday morning and assumed that no news was good news.

An email from Athens told him that his first shipment of faked antiquities was ready to be picked up. He arranged to have them sent by DHL to a hotel in northern Italy. And then he packed for Monaco.

At the farm, Irene had their new luggage out on the floor and was trying to pack what she called "the costumes" into the space provided.

"Don't mind me, I'm just the fucking maid," she said. Piat moved on.

Hackbutt was outside with his birds. "I don't think I have time to go to Monaco right now. Bella's grown another centimeter, Jack. She must be close to full growth. I need to get her in top shape before I—let her go."

"Let her go?" asked Piat. He ducked Hackbutt's assertion about Monaco.

"When she's fully grown—she goes back to the wild. Haven't I told you that?" Hackbutt sounded petulant. "I've explained the whole breeding program to you—don't you *listen*?"

Perhaps it was her new growth, or the pale golden light of the Scottish winter, but she looked more magnificent than ever. She was calm, her head turning back and forth between Piat and Hackbutt in rapid, perfectly controlled flicks—Hackbutt, Piat, Hackbutt.

Piat shrugged, watching the bird. "Maybe I didn't listen, Digger. Tell me again."

Hackbutt frowned. He walked over to a standing perch and set Bella on it carefully. "You should have listened."

Piat nodded. "Okay. Yes, Digger, I should have listened. I don't always pay as much attention to people as I ought to. So tell me."

Hackbutt kept his eyes on Bella. "You know how raptors are, right? They usually have two chicks?"

"Yes," said Piat.

"They only keep the better chick, you know what I mean?" The whining tone left Hackbutt's voice as soon as he started to warm to his subject.

Piat watched Bella. Her eyes were fixed on Hackbutt, who was fussing with her jesses. Piat said, "No. I don't know what you mean, Digger. You were always hotter on this stuff than me."

"I need to make her new jesses. Maybe with bells—bells for Bella! Okay, listen this time. Eagles tend to have two eggs, but that's not to rear two young—it's like a survival mechanism, right? And insurance policy? So if something happens to one, they've got the other. And then, if both hatch and are healthy—well, it sounds cruel, but they only keep the bigger one, the more aggressive one. The other gets tossed."

Hackbutt was boring Piat, but listening to Hackbutt was part of the game. And he apparently hadn't done his job well here, either. Listening, being interested, being involved. "That sounds pretty harsh, Digger."

"Good for breeding—helps the species grow larger, more aggressive. But not so good for replacing numbers."

"Right."

"So there's this program—I'm in it, they picked me as soon as I moved here, they actually wanted me to help—where we watch the nests, and when a pair has two live chicks, we wait until the female is ready to toss the smaller one and then we try and save it. We rear the chick—teach it to hunt—put it back in the wild. See? That's how I have Bella."

"Jesus, you mean Bella is the *small* one of her family?"

"The runt of the litter, Jack."

Piat tried to imagine how big the other bird might be. "I'm pretty sure you didn't tell me this before," he said. "I think I'd remember if you'd said Bella was the runt of the litter."

"Maybe it's just that you act as if you already know everything." Hackbutt shook his head. "Anyway—in the spring, when the birds hatch, I'm up on the hill every day, rain or shine—if you miss your moment, then all you have for a year's work is a dead chick. In the spring, I'll watch every day. If you'd come in the spring, I'd have had to say no—you see that, right?"

Piat nodded. "But it's not the spring, is it, Digger?"

Hackbutt shook his head.

Piat said, "The guy in Monaco is no different from your chicks on the hillside, Digger. He's only going to be there one time. It's now or never."

Hackbutt scratched Bella's neck. "Why don't you hold her a little?" Hackbutt asked.

He offered her to Piat, who took her, trying not to flinch or react to her weight on his arm. She tolerated him. He reached up cautiously to the feathers on her back and her head came around, an inhuman posture where she was looking up and straight back at him.

"She's remarkable," Piat said, and meant it.

"I don't want to give her up, and that's no lie." Hackbutt shook his head, ashamed of himself. "I look at her, and I think—this is the best thing I've ever done in my life. I found her ready to die and I helped her become—this." He flipped her a piece of chicken neck and she whirled, her head turning a hundred and eighty degrees to snap the meat out of the air. He smiled happily. "Falcons never say thank you. It's one of the first things you learn. You can break your heart loving one and all they do in return is demand more attention and more food. You know what I mean?"

Piat nodded.

"But sometimes I think maybe she knows. And anyway—I saved her, whether she knows or cares. I will have put one more good bird back in the wild." Hackbutt tossed her another glistening red chunk. "Only worthwhile thing I've ever done."

Piat knew that he had to make some sort of patriotic gesture. The thought fatigued him. But he marshaled his forces and said, "You've done a lot of good work for me, Digger. For our country."

Hackbutt shrugged. "Sure," he said, the syllable utterly without meaning.

Piat gave them their tickets and their reservations. Their travel was simple—train, train, train all the way to Monaco. First class, overnight. Time to work into their roles on the train.

Hackbutt lit up. "I love trains," he said.

Irene was somewhere else. Piat suspected that she'd already had something to drink, maybe a couple of somethings. She answered absently, used her hands too freely.

Piat realized she was more on edge than Hackbutt.

He gave them a simple comms plan in case something went wrong, gave them a meeting site in Monaco and a time. Hackbutt listened; Irene paid no attention.

Piat saw disasters looming around every curve, but his course was set and it was too late to back out. So he walked them through the plans one more time and said his good-byes. Irene didn't kiss him. She was angry—or jealous. Or high. Distant and angry and working to transmit those signals.

"See you Sunday," Hackbutt said.

"Play some cards, Digger," Piat said from the doorway. Irene was in the kitchen, standing at the sink, doing nothing.

I've fucked this up, Piat thought. But there was nothing to be done right here, right now, so he got in his car and drove for the ferry.

"I like this place, Jerry," Partlow said as he took Piat's hand. "This place" was north of Torino, Italy.

"We aim to please," Piat said.

They were standing in the stone-flagged courtyard of a Renaissance chateau that was in the process of being converted to a very expensive hotel. The ornate building and its more pragmatic defenses occupied the top of a mountain that looked out over the Piedmont. The Dukes of Savoy had used it as a hunting lodge, and now the Italian government was rebuilding it to house the elite of the thousands of tourists who would descend on northern Italy for the 2006 Winter Olympics.

Most of the work was done. The courtyard was immaculate, from the bronze sculptures in alcoves along the walls to the perfect herringbone of the brick and stone underfoot. Only the strong smells of paint and new masonry indicated that all might not yet be ready.

Light snow was falling.

They walked up to Partlow's room together, unnoticed among the bustle of workers and arriving guests. Partlow had a suite, and the sitting room already had his stamp on it—the furniture moved into the approved arrangement, the suitcase standing ready. All nicely by the book. He had a stone balcony that looked out over a three-hundred-foot drop. Piat thought Partlow looked tense. Worse than tense.

"Scotch?" Partlow asked.

"Please."

"Tell me about the falconer," Partlow said as he sank into a leather armchair.

Piat toyed with his scotch. "He's in good shape. He can do the job—if we get a little luck."

"Something you're not telling me, Jerry."

"Irene—the woman."

Partlow nodded. "You always said she'd be a problem. Are you in control?"

Piat shrugged. "Most days."

Partlow leaned forward. "How bad is it?"

Piat looked out over the drop. "I really don't know, Clyde, and that's no bullshit."

"I can't remember seeing you this tired—this down." Partlow put his glass down and clasped his hands over his knee. "You're worrying me."

Piat nodded. "I need a rest, and there's no rest in sight. It's fucking exhausting, Clyde. His issues, her issues, their issues. It's like herding cats. Training them is like training cats."

"They sound like agents," Partlow said with a smile.

Piat was thinking about Hackbutt and Bella. "It's pretty thankless."

Partlow poured them another scotch. "You want my thanks? You have them."

"Spare me."

"That's rather what I thought you'd say." He handed Piat his glass, refilled to the brim. "Are they ready for Monaco? Are you?"

Piat nodded. "Yeah. They're ready. Hackbutt's okay—better than okay. He can do a cold meeting. All he can talk about is fucking birds, but what the hell. That's what we wanted him for. And he's smoother than he used to be—more mature. It's deeper than the haircut."

"You give him a good role model." Partlow smiled.

Piat rubbed his jaw. "You know, Clyde, just when I think you and I must have hit it off all wrong, you say something so fucked up that I know I was right all along. Role model? What the fuck, Clyde!"

Partlow didn't back down. "You're a man of action. An individual. I've read every report you've written on the falconer, Jerry. I made the time. He wants to *be* you."

Piat waved his glass dismissively. "Can we cut the pop psychology?"

Partlow shrugged. "If you insist. I thought we were being professionals, analyzing the tools of our operation."

Piat thought about that for a few seconds and reminded himself of his new role vis-à-vis Partlow. He was in danger of slipping into the old role. *Role model.* That stung.

He took a deep breath. "Sorry, Clyde. I'm too into it, okay? Too fucking close for analysis. What I need right now is money and the target. I'll settle for the target."

Partlow had a briefcase. He'd had the briefcase outside in the snow, and it hadn't left his hand. He opened it, and produced three sheets of paper, a passport, and some credit cards.

"Your cover. I took the liberty of keeping the name Jack."

Piat leafed through the passport. It was a superb job—Macedonian, with cachets for twenty countries. It claimed to be three years old. "I can't pass for native," he said.

"Lots of semi-stateless persons have Albanian and Macedonian passports."

Piat nodded. "Cover?"

"Two layers. Outward, you're a petty antique dealer. That way, if anyone knows you, you're covered. Shady character like you—of course you have two passports. Right?"

Piat nodded.

"Second level, I've put a code out that this passport is held by an undercover cop. Stolen art—Interpol. You won't ever have to live that cover, but it's there to backstop you if you get picked up in an airport."

Piat smiled. "Interpol thing sounds like a great job."

Partlow laughed. "Maybe for your next lifetime. Will it do?"

"I like it. Nice job, Clyde. I have some concerns about flying into the Middle East, but we'll cross that bridge when we get to it. Cash on the cards?"

"Fifty thousand dollars."

Piat smiled. "That'll have to do."

Partlow raised his glass. "I need you to read the target information. No notes, no takeaways."

Piat was already reading.

The three pages were clearly an assembly of paragraphs cut and pasted from other documents. There were no headers or footers, no identifying data, but Piat could detect the work of three or perhaps four authors. What he read stopped his breath. It almost stopped his heart.

"He's a fucking royal, Clyde." Piat flipped back to the start and began memorizing. He didn't intend to have any connections to these documents, and the vague sense of unease he had felt since his first contact with the operation now crystallized into a solid mass sitting in the bottom of his stomach.

"Not precisely a royal, no." Partlow had his fingers steepled. "His family have historic connections to the Saudi family."

"Could the fucking president tell the difference? Clyde, isn't there a fucking *executive order* from the *President of the United States* that puts all of these guys out of bounds?" Piat took a hit of scotch.

"Not precisely. No." Partlow leaned back and looked out into the snow. More quietly, he whispered, "Not precisely."

"This is what we call a 'gray area?'"

"Exactly."

"Just how fucking gray is it, exactly?" Piat asked and then he started rolling his neck and stretching his back. *Calm down. Be the good agent. Don't go back to old roles.* He told himself that while another, older, more paranoid part of his mind screamed *fall guy. Clyde is trying to run an illegal op against a member of the Saudi royal family and he's going to leave me holding the bag.*

"Somewhat gray," Partlow conceded. He shrugged. "They

want to penetrate terrorism. At the highest levels, they talk about it all the time. At my level, there's a pressure—you know what I mean, Jerry? A relentless pressure to *produce*. As if we can press a button and make a loyal, dependable source appear inside al-Qaeda."

Piat nodded to indicate that he knew what Partlow was talking about. He did. He also knew that most of the real loser ideas in intelligence were generated from just that political pressure.

Partlow continued as if he were addressing a class. "Since Nine-Eleven, the pressure has become immense. People in the business know where the money comes from. It comes from Saudi. I've decided to find a way to follow the money."

"Sure," Piat said, meaning the opposite. "Except that this is outside the box, Clyde. I mean, even for me, this is outside the box. We're going to try and recruit a member of the Saudi family."

"He is not, strictly speaking, a member." Partlow spoke primly.

"Right."

"Are you asking for more money, Jerry?" Partlow said. He smiled.

Piat had noticed Partlow's stress, but now he read the signs differently. He had lines around his eyes and around his mouth, and his left hand, where it rested on the arm of the hotel chair, was white with tension. He poured himself—both of them—more scotch. His hand shook a little.

Piat examined Partlow's statement. "If you're offering more money, I'll be happy to take it," he said. 'But—no. Not money." He flipped through the three pages on the target. "His uncle rules the Eastern Province. The oil. And all the angry Shia."

"That's right. A gold star to you, Jerry."

"You want me to put my guy next to him. Okay. Can do." Partlow nodded. Piat took a swig of scotch and then took a deep breath. "Then what?"

"Need to know, Jerry." Partlow waved a finger to indicate that Piat did not, in fact, need to know.

Piat nodded. "Okay." He took another breath. "What shall I tell the inspector general when he comes around?"

"It won't come to that. It's all Nelsonian, Jerry. If we win, no one will ask how. If we lose, no one will even know we tried." Partlow's strain showed even in his voice.

"Fuck, that's reassuring," Piat said. "I've changed my mind. I want more money."

Hours passed. Piat studied the three pages until he had them memorized. Partlow was patient. He knew what was involved.

In the end, Piat simply nodded. "Want to burn them yourself?"

"Yes," said Partlow. He took each page and folded it in half-inch accordion pleats, placed it in the hotel sink, and set fire to it. Each page burned to ash. Not a scrap was left and the smoke detector missed the whole event.

Piat watched the first page go and then went and stood facing the windows to the balcony, his eyes resting on the snowflakes as he tested his new knowledge. It was all there. Names, dates, places, a biography, some leads. Falconry. He was nodding to himself when Partlow emerged from the bathroom.

"You're ready, then?" Partlow asked. His voice betrayed his eagerness.

"I'll look at him in Monaco. I'll send you a simple signal—go or no go, after I look at his arrangements. One or zero. If it's a go, I think we'll try Mombasa. I take it you didn't get me anything on his itinerary there?"

"Not much," Partlow admitted. "His uncle goes to the game parks and shoots animals. He pays an enormous bribe to do it, which is why we know. As to the target—nothing."

"I'll bet he'll fly his birds there, then." Piat tried to imagine the mind of the Saudi falconer. A Saudi Hackbutt. What would Hackbutt do with unlimited power and money? He'd fly his birds every day in the most interesting environments he could reach. "Ask about it. There ought to be people in Kenya who know."

Partlow made a one-word note in his day book. He handed Piat an envelope with money in it. They both counted the money and Piat signed. Then Piat rose to go.

Partlow stayed in his chair. "Good luck in Monaco," he said. His words were faintly slurred. They'd finished half the bottle of scotch.

Piat shrugged. "Luck's what we need," he said from the door. And then he drove through the snow to Monaco, with a box in his trunk from Athens.

13

Monte Carlo had no snow and was merely chilly. The jagged rocks of the coast stuck out into the iron sea, and the overcast sky made the doll's town of pastel buildings look gaudy.

Not cheap, though. Nothing in Monte Carlo was cheap.

Piat left his new rental car with the valet service at the Hermitage and carried his single bag into the desk. He signed in with his new passport. The system worked as it should have, and in ten minutes he was in a room. Eleven hundred euros a night. Piat's meager belongings couldn't begin to fill its empty luxury. It depressed him, and rather than drink, he changed into jeans and a heavy sweater and went out to walk.

Piat walked around Monte Carlo for three hours. The city had the same effect on him as the room. The obvious wealth, the heavy security, and the lack of taste all oppressed him together.

Worse, it was a dreadful operational venue. Every building had cameras. The casinos had more security than the headquarters of the CIA. The restaurants had both automated and human security. There were no back alleys, few blind avenues, and most of the walkways, however secretive they appeared, had cameras *and* human security.

The target was supposed to arrive later that evening at the Hotel Metropole. Piat walked into the Metropole's lobby via the shopping center, sat in an alcove, and read the *Herald Tribune*. He watched the movement of the lobby. He walked out to the street and back to the bar, taking his time, counting his paces. Then he went to the concierge and did his job, asking a handful of questions. He got the concierge to let him look at a room. His worst suspicions confirmed, he went to the bar and drank a scotch that cost Partlow thirty-six dollars. Then he had another.

All the other people in the bar seemed to be on display. Women, regardless of age, were dressed and made up as if for a movie set. Most of the men were trying to look too young. None of them was particularly attractive, despite their best efforts, and Piat christened them the Pretty People—not quite good enough to be beautiful.

They had conversations without looking at each other, their eyes wandering the room to see if they had attracted the regard of someone new. At a center table, a French couple had an argument that lasted through both of Piat's scotches. Between shots of vitriol, the woman looked at Piat. She wasn't the only one, and after too many seconds spent staring at the bottom of his tumbler, Piat picked up his jacket and walked out.

Tough operational environment.

He had to use his passport to get into the casino. The attractive Indian woman at the counter looked at it and at him for too long before pressing it to a scanner and wishing him *bonne chance*. He found Hackbutt and Irene inside, almost where they were supposed to be. He watched them and their environment for ten minutes. They were doing a fair job of imitating people who were having a good time. Irene chatted with another woman while she played cards. Hackbutt placed very small bets.

It was off-season, and they had the place mostly to themselves. Middle-aged Brits were playing bridge for serious stakes at a central table, and the wheels were going. A handful of Pretty People were playing games to show that they could. Otherwise, the casino was quiet.

He went and stood behind Irene. She was playing chemin de fer with complete concentration.

He waited until she had finished a hand, casually brushing her winnings into the chip holder set into the table, and then he sat down.

"Why, Jack!" she said. "You didn't say you were coming to *Monaco*!"

It was a nice little performance. The only audience were the dealer and the younger woman seated to her left, but the line was delivered very well.

Piat put some chips on the table. "Plans changed. Here I am."

Irene introduced him to Michelle, the young woman to her left, who was going to school in Paris and had come down to collect some cash from her father. Piat nodded as often as required, lost two hundred dollars while they chatted, and left her to find Hackbutt.

Hackbutt was standing at a roulette table now, watching the spins of the wheel and paying attention to the board marked by the croupier indicating the last forty spins on the wheel. He bet very little.

"Digger—you're not trying to play a system?" Piat asked, putting his hand on Hackbutt's shoulders.

Hackbutt looked around. "Shhh!" he said.

Piat smiled. "Digger, they only care if your system *wins*."

Hackbutt smiled back. "I'd just like to win a few times. Irene is—well, she's won quite a bit of money."

Funny how she hadn't mentioned that at all. "How much money?"

Hackbutt shrugged. "I don't know, really. Two thousand euros?"

Piat whistled. "I think we should all go out and have dinner."

Irene materialized at his elbow. "I'd like that," she said. "My treat."

Piat hadn't been to Monaco in twenty years, but he remembered a cluster of decent little restaurants in the streets above the casino. They were still there, some closed for the winter. A few were open, featuring prix-fixe menus and at most three tables for service. The prices were on par with everything else in the town, but what Piat was looking to buy was privacy.

"I'm bored," Hackbutt said as soon as they were seated. "I want to get back to my birds."

Piat nodded. "I don't like this town, either," he said. He meant it, but he also said it to show some empathy for Hackbutt.

Irene said, "It's like a temple built to money. It makes me sick—makes me remember each and every reason I turned my back on this. And these people. Fuck—it's hard to find my center here. It's like they have a machine to suck souls built under the Metropole's mall."

"Okay, we all hate Monaco. Let's do our jobs and get the hell out of here," Piat said.

His agents both nodded.

"Our guy arrives tonight." Piat leaned forward and kept his voice low. He spoke rapidly. It was the only defense he could muster against eavesdropping, and it would have to pass, because he preferred the privacy of the restaurant to the professional eavesdropping in the hotels. "His name is Prince Bandar Muhad al-Hauq. His uncle is the governor of a Saudi Province. He'll be staying at the Metropole and he'll have most of a floor, exclusive access to an elevator, and his own security arrangements."

Hackbutt shrugged. "How do people live like this?"

Irene squeezed his shoulder. "They think they like it," she said. "Okay, Jack. What are we doing?" She was playing a game, and Piat didn't have the energy.

"I want to go back to my birds," Hackbutt said again.

Irene nodded. "What are we doing?"

Piat leaned forward again. "Okay. Irene and I are going to go play in the casino for a little while. We'll walk up into the lobby around eight-thirty, which is my best guess of our guy's earliest arrival time, and we'll have a drink in the bar—maybe two, if we have to waste the time. All we're doing is looking at his entourage—his uncle's entourage, actually. That may be it. Or I may see something. Digger, you've got to stick by the phone in your room. You have something to read?"

Hackbutt shrugged. "I brought Glasier's *Falconry*." He crossed his arms. "But I'm not sure I see why you and Irene are swanning around while I sit in a hotel room."

"I can't let the target see you, Digger. And without Irene, I'll stick out like a sore thumb."

A waitress—probably the owner—appeared and put a wine list in his hand. He glanced at it and handed it to Irene. "You choose—I think you said you were buying." The cheapest bottle was seventy dollars.

The wine list stopped her and Piat rescued her. "Let me. Keep the money for your show." He ordered two bottles of a decent red—actually a pretty good red, ridiculously over priced, paid for by Clyde Partlow. They all ordered simple variations on the prix fixe. And then they were alone again.

Hackbutt kept his arms crossed. "Fine," he said. It wasn't fine. He was on the edge of a tantrum—a tantrum about his need to be with Bella. And, as far as Piat could see, a tantrum about how easily Irene could deal with Monaco.

"Digger, do you guys need some alone time? That's cool. No problem," Piat said.

"Really?" Hackbutt asked, sitting up and uncrossing his arms. "I know you need her help—"

"I can handle it," he said.

Hackbutt smiled. "If you only need her as a cover—well,

unless you've changed from out-East days, you can find one yourself in five minutes."

"Find one *what*? How much sexist crap do I have to take from you two?" She was pulling at the rope of pearls around her neck, tugging so hard that the pearls at the back of her neck were leaving marks. She kicked Piat hard under the table.

Piat turned his head and met her eyes for the first time. "I think you guys should rest up tonight," he said to her. "And stay by the phone. I doubt we can try anything here—anything at all. But we won't know until I see the lay of the land."

Dinner arrived and was eaten quietly.

Piat changed into an antique linen dinner jacket and black wool trousers. He felt like an extra in a Bogart movie, but the clothes, product of the high-end used-clothing shop in London, fit. He watched the man in the mirror—too much shadow on his cheeks, but he couldn't be bothered to shave again. That guy got older every day. But not so bad. The clothes were attractive. In fact, they were too attractive. He was in danger of standing out. And the bow tie looked daft no matter how often he put it on. He pocketed a slim digital camera and forced himself to walk out the door before his stage fright and the wine in his belly led him to do some more drinking.

He walked to the casino feeling as out of place as a boy going to his first high school dance. The presence of other men on the street in the same rig reassured him, but it was the floor of the casino itself that finally relaxed him—it held the biggest crowd he'd seen in Monaco, and he wasn't the only man alone. The male from the French couple in the Metropole's bar cruised by, his eye on a pair of women young enough to be his daughters. His partner was nowhere in sight. Piat wondered if she had moved on or merely developed a headache.

He played roulette, lost, played cards, lost. Gambling in all its forms had always seemed one of the stupidest ways to waste money he'd encountered, but it did facilitate operational activity. It allowed him to move freely through the crowd of people, participating as much as he could tolerate and never sticking out, except that he was conscious of the croupiers and the security men and the undercover dicks and the cameras. Everywhere, the cameras.

At eight thirty-five, Piat got up from the table where he was breaking even at chemin de fer, excused himself to a man who was holding forth on big game hunting, and walked out. He allowed himself a cigar as he walked through light rain to the Metropole. The palm trees had floodlights on them, which symbolized something about how Monaco gilded every possible lily. He stopped and watched one for more than a minute, noting the camera attached to the trunk and the play of the lights on the leaves. Then he went and sat in an outdoor café for ten minutes and drank an espresso while he finished his cigar.

He was watching the promenade in front of the Metropole.

When the six big cars pulled up, he had plenty of time to observe the retinue as it extricated itself from the limousines and began stacking its luggage and bullying the staff. He gave them five minutes, watching every detail of their numbers, movement, and security, until it became plain that the whole party was finally moving inside. He took six photos just the way he had been taught twenty years before, from the camera resting on the table, without ever bringing it up to his eyes. Leaving a euro on his saucer, he got up and ground the butt of his cigar under his heel, swore to run the next day, and walked slowly toward the hotel, cursing the rain. He jogged up the steps to the Metropole's lobby and passed rapidly through the party of Saudis. None of the women were veiled, and their shrieks of appreciation and amusement drowned all other sound. He saw four security professionals, all of whom saw him. He saw the uncle, and the uncle's immediate circle of "friends," and then he finally saw the nephew.

The prince was not a tall man, but he was alder-thin and very plainly dressed, the only man in the entourage who did not have a gold watchband. He wore jeans and a blue rain jacket and he looked, amid the bustle of the arrival of forty people, as if he were alone. He had a bag in his hand, and near him stood another man, an African, with a bird on his wrist that Piat thought was an American red-tailed hawk.

Piat knew that he had missed an opportunity. The reserved man in the Gore-Tex, the attendant with the bird—easy targets for a chance encounter. Hackbutt could have had a minute or more to try and charm the prince—with the bird as the setpiece.

Earlier in the day, Piat had counted the steps from the baroque entrance to the bar. He had timed himself on his movements. He didn't deviate. He didn't stare at the prince or move his head.

Sometimes, Fortuna smiles on a good operator. Ten feet from the Baroque archway of the bar's entrance, Piat spotted the argumentative Frenchwoman from his earlier visit. She might never have moved from her table.

She lifted her eyes, met his, and smiled. She was somewhere in the mystical realm between forty and sixty—attractive, perhaps a little bold. Perhaps a little tired.

He took his chance. He went straight to her table and sat, and thus he vanished off the radar of the security in the lobby.

Luck. Fortuna. Operational daring.

"You look as if you could use some entertainment," Piat said as he sat. "May I buy you a drink?"

She smiled and raised her eyebrows. "Of course," she said.

Piat rose and walked to the bar. From that vantage point he caught the very end of the entourages packing the elevators, a string of Arabic and English invective aimed at the bird, and the prince, waiting with his falcon and his attendant.

He watched the prince's body language, his aside to the attendant with the bird as the elevator doors closed. And he thought, *He despises his uncle and all the rest of them.*

For an entire minute, the prince and his man were alone in the lobby, without security, without friends. While paying for two drinks, Piat fumbled finding his wallet. Using his jacket for cover and working as fast as he could, he managed to shoot four photos. The bar attendant waited impassively.

As he dropped the camera back into his jacket, he found that the prince was looking at him.

Piat smiled, collected his drinks, and returned to the table. His hands were shaking. He sat closer to the woman and with a better view through the arch, just in time to catch the prince's back disappearing into the elevator. For the first time, he believed that the scheme might work.

He set himself to charming his companion.

She declared herself charmed when she went off to bed—alone. "I'm past having affairs," she said, laying her hand on his arm with a smile. "Now I prefer just to enjoy some sleep."

Piat laughed and told her she was a woman after his own heart.

Despite the booze and the nerves, Piat rose with the dawn, put on a disreputable pair of shorts and shoes, and went for a run. He ran up the hills behind the town until he crossed the border into France, and then he ran down the main road along the coast, passing a string of second-rate hotels and restaurants before turning back to the water and running back into Monaco on the beach.

In his room, he downloaded the photos from the camera to his computer. Despite his best efforts, most of them were useless—too dark, too light, too blurry. But he had one photograph of the prince and his attendant standing with the bird.

Their faces wore the same expression—disgust—and all three of them had their eyes fixed on the elevator doors. Piat blew it up, encrypted it, and saved it. He also had a dark but useful photo of the four security men on the curb in front of the Metropole, the first to have got out of the cars. He encrypted that and saved it as well.

At ten, he arranged to pick Irene and Hackbutt up at their hotel in a car. By eleven, they were already high in the alps behind the town, parked at a scenic overlook that faced down a valley toward the sea.

"That's the target," Piat said. His laptop was open on Hackbutt's lap.

"That's the biggest red-tail I've ever seen," Hackbutt answered. "No hood, in a hotel lobby. That's a good bird."

"The guy," Piat insisted. He pointed at the prince.

"Sure," said Hackbutt.

"Can you recognize him?" Piat asked after a while.

"I can," Irene said. She was sitting alone in the back and looking for attention. Or command. Or whatever she craved. "I can pick him out of a crowd of Arabs. Eddie's lucky if he recognizes *me* on the streets of Tobermory."

Hackbutt shrugged. "I'd recognize the bird. That's one hell of a good bird. People get all worked up about peregrines and big hawks and heavy falcons. This guy knows his stuff. Red-tails—easy to train, they like people, they travel well. He's got the best one I've ever seen, and he's got it out in public. Tells me a lot." Hackbutt glanced at Piat. "Wish I'd been there. Lots to talk about."

Piat winced. "I couldn't know," he said. He shrugged. "Water under the dam. Today, we just look for a little luck. Play in the casino. Eat in the Metropole bar. Don't push it and don't act without my say-so. Let me be clear on this, folks—if we don't have a solid opportunity to approach the guy, I *don't* want him to see any of us, and I *don't* want his security to see us. Okay?"

Hackbutt nodded. "So—all three of us? Today? In the casino and the bar?"

Piat nodded. The bird had got Hackbutt interested.

Irene leaned forward from the back seat. "You boys have fun. I'm going for a swim and a massage." She widened her eyes at Piat. "This place is duller than I thought it would be."

Piat and Hackbutt walked and played, ate, talked, and played some more. There were Saudis in the Casino—one woman who had definitely been in the entourage the night before, others who seemed to be her attendants. But not the uncle and not the prince. Piat drank a glass of wine and wished for a surveillance team and the cooperation of the local security service, both far beyond his means. So he was doing what he could.

Despite his efforts, no chance encounter materialized. Whatever the uncle and the nephew were doing in Monte Carlo, they were doing it behind closed doors. The other Saudis circulated, gambled, swam, read books, and walked along the promenade. Piat and Hackbutt saw them all.

At three o'clock, the prince's attendant appeared in the lobby with the bird on his fist. Piat and Hackbutt were in the bar.

"Look at that bird," said Hackbutt, moving to rise.

"Don't move a muscle." The elevator behind the attendant remained frustratingly empty. Taking his time, Piat paid their tab and took Hackbutt out the bar entrance. Twenty meters away, the man with the bird emerged from the main doors. He walked toward the beach with the bird on his fist. He was a curiously medieval figure in a very modern place, and he drew stares.

"He's going to exercise it," Hackbutt said, pointing.

Piat wanted to restrain him, but Hackbutt wasn't the only person on the promenade pointing at the hawk.

"How often does he have to do that?" Piat asked.

Hackbutt looked at him with a raised eyebrow. "Every day, of course. Jack, sometimes I think you don't listen to a word I say. Hawks and falcons need to fly every day to stay in shape. A big bird like that needs a lot of exercise to be in top form. *Oh!*"

The African had walked down the ramp to the beach, apparently uninterested in the attention he was getting. He slowly unwrapped the bird's jesses from his gloved left hand, talking to her as he walked. And then he raised his fist.

Hackbutt was pointing again. The bird was climbing rapidly, free of the wrist. Every eye on the beach watched it climb. Habit made Piat glance around—but the hawk was the only show to watch.

"He's going up—he's waiting on. That's wonderful; I don't think I've ever seen a red-tail waiting on." Hackbutt flicked his eyes off the bird to Piat. "Waiting on—it's like being in ambush. Up high. It requires patience, which most birds don't have much of. Right?"

Piat nodded, his eyes on the hawk.

The big bird was circling over the beach, the curling feathers at its wingtips just moving in response to changes in the wind, the head moving back and forth, the rest of its body still, gliding.

"To fly that bird here—on the beach, with all these noisy people—that's trust. That guy trusts his bird completely." Hackbutt was shaking his head. "Or he's a complete idiot."

"Or he can just get another one," Piat added. He'd known a few Saudis.

Hackbutt shook his head. "No way. Not that size."

The big hawk rose and rose, riding the sea breeze, flying without any apparent effort. He rose high enough that Piat had trouble following the bird's motions. The Pretty People on the beach began to lose interest. A single gull flapped past from the landward side and started to watch the shallow water for its own prey.

"There he goes!" Hackbut shouted.

The hawk plummeted, caught the gull and pulled it from the sky. The gull thrashed once, tried to turn, and died in the air. In five seconds, the gull was on its belly in the sand with the big hawk standing on its neck, head bobbing to seize more meat. The attendant approached and lured the bird off its prey, knelt to feel the bird's crop with a thumb, and began speaking rapidly.

The spectators had shied away.

A small man in dirty white overalls appeared and began to clean up the remnants of the gull. The crowd went back to their conversations and the joys of a cool winter beach. The bird's handler walked back up the ramp to the hotel, talking to the hawk all the way and smoothing her feathers with his right hand.

"I want to *talk to him,*" Hackbutt said.

"Nope. This isn't the time. You'll get your chance."

"I *want to talk to him, Jack.* You got me all the way here, dressed in all this stuff, away from my birds that need me, you show me a performance like that—god damn it, Jack, that was one of the slickest displays of hawking I've ever seen, and bam—the guy just walks away and you aren't going to let me talk to him!"

"That's right," Piat said gently. "He's not the target. He might talk to you all day and never get you closer to the prince. Okay?"

Hackbutt pursed his lips and blew out some air in frustration. "Target-shmarget. I want to talk birds. That guy *knows stuff.*"

Piat nodded. "I'll bet he does. *Later.*" He put a hand on Hackbutt's shoulder. "We're waiting on."

Hackbutt's head snapped around, eyes locked on his, and then he laughed. "I get it," he said.

Irene was waiting in the casino. She looked her part, but her posture and the constant motion of her hands said there was trouble before they were in hailing distance.

"I want to go for a walk," she said. Up close, she looked clean and bright and very much on edge.

Piat shook his head.

"I mean it, Jack. This is important." Her eyes were going back and forth—to the entrance, to the croupiers.

Piat knew that all of them had bad body language just then. Somewhere on the casino security monitors, they were all being marked—three nervous people standing in a group.

"Okay," he said. "Let's walk."

Irene's idea of security was to get outside in the sun and then to scrutinize everything she saw while talking too fast.

"I just saw your prince," she began. "In the lobby. With somebody I know."

Hackbutt was staring down the beach. "You should have seen this guy fly that red-tail, Irene."

Piat didn't stop in his tracks—quite. "Someone you know?"

"George Kwalik. Republican. Ohio. A big shot in certain circles. He was—probably still is—a congressman. Very conservative. Did business with my father." She continued looking around her. Piat could see that she was spooked and wished she could hide it better. Finally she said, "Oil business."

"He was *with* the prince?" Piat asked.

"I'm sure. They were talking. Kwalik was talking. The prince acted as if he was barely listening. He was looking out the windows. I was afraid Kwalik would look at me."

Piat glanced back at the lobby windows. "When was this?"

She looked at him with irritation, her flow broken. "Thirty minutes ago. Kwalik—what's he doing here? I think he saw me, Jack."

"So what?" *So what* wasn't on the list of Agency-approved phrases in dealing with an overwrought agent, but all of Piat's balls were in the air. *While we watched the damned bird, the prince was right there in the lobby, watching through the window. Watching his bird. Or watching us. And talking to some American heavy hitter about something.* Reason said that there was no way the prince could be on to him so quickly. Reason said it, but that didn't calm the bubbles in his belly or the sweat under his arms.

Irene was glaring at him, and he suspected that there was something here he ought to know and didn't—was she on the lam? Had she done something really fucked up before leaving mom and dad?

Christ, the things he didn't know.

He made a snap decision. Actually, he made a whole series of decisions, on the wing, right there on the promenade. "Okay, let's get out of here," he said.

Irene's face relaxed as soon as he said the words. It was Hackbutt's turn, however, to be annoyed. "We just got here. I want to meet this guy!"

Irene was dismissive. "Last night all you wanted to do was get back to your stupid birds."

Stupid birds hung in the air between them like a veil of poison gas.

Piat stepped between them—literally. "Okay, everybody. Keep your voices down. We're all wound up tight and in a minute we're going to start drawing attention. This is *not the time,* Digger. Okay? Everybody saddle up and go. We'll go together—we haven't tried to hide anything, no need to start now. My car. Go to your room, pack, and check out. Don't rush. Don't get panicked. There's nothing at all to be afraid of." Both of them were spooked.

Hackbutt looked past Piat at Irene. "Birds aren't stupid," he said quietly.

Piat tried to dredge up the right way to motivate both of them to fucking *obey*. "Digger—we'll have another chance at our guy. Soon. I promise. You can talk birds with him until the sky falls."

Hackbutt was still staring at Irene as if he'd never seen

her before. "They aren't stupid. And neither am I." He looked up at Piat. "Sometimes you both think I'm stupid." He turned his back and started toward the hotel. "It pisses me off."

Irene stood on the sidewalk, her jaw working and a blood vessel throbbing on her temple.

"I'm sorry!" she shouted. "Fuck, I hate this place!"

Somehow, he got them alive and unbroken to their hotel. He was tempted to stay and watch them pack, but they might make up if he left them, and he needed them to make up.

Christ, he needed a little luck.

He opened the door to his room still wishing for a little luck and found two middle-aged men sitting in his easy chairs. Neither was very tall or formidable, but they were grave, careful men with receding hairlines and guns. The guns were holstered under excellent Italian tailoring, but Piat knew they were there.

"Mister Michalis?" the nearer one asked. He rose to his feet.

Piat knew his cover. He always knew his cover. Jack Michalis was the name on his new passport. He said, "Is there a problem?" as bloodlessly as he could manage.

The graver of the two remained seated. "We are very sorry for interrupting your privacy, Mister Michalis," he said. "Would you please join us?" He indicated the seat vacated by his companion.

Piat didn't want to take it, but they had every advantage—guns, numbers, local knowledge. So he sat. If they were going to arrest him, they wouldn't have troubled to let him sit.

Probably.

"We work for the casino, Mister Michalis."

Piat nodded.

The graver man reached out a hand. "May I see your passport, Mister Michalis?"

Piat handed it over. He'd already passed on the option to

bluster and protest—these struck him as men who were past masters at dealing with bluster. So he limited himself to a single question. "Can you tell me what this is about?"

The graver man flipped the passport open, glanced at the photo and looked at Piat. Then he closed it and handed the passport back.

"We have a great deal of very serious security in the casino," he said carefully. "Also the hotels, yes?"

Piat nodded.

The grave man gave a small, grave smile. "I don't know who you are. I'm quite sure you are *not* Mister Michalis. You understand?"

Piat decided to die trying. "There must be some kind of mistake—"

The man shrugged. "Of course. But no. As I say, I don't know who you really are. But my computer tells me that you are *not* this man, or perhaps there never was this man. You see my trouble? And my own eyes tell me that this passport is real. Terribly real, yes?"

Piat started to rise. Busted in fucking Monaco.

"Please sit down, Mister Michalis. If I may call you that? So my computer and I, we would like you to leave. And please, never come back. Do I make myself understood? Right now, I cannot be bothered to think of anything with which to charge you—perhaps if you came back, or didn't leave, I would change my mind. Yes?"

Piat watched them. The younger one was to his side, not actually behind him. Not as threatening as he could be. The graver one was—grave. But not hostile. Piat reviewed his options, including the option to play the hidden card—the Interpol card Partlow had given him.

But he passed. Despite the liquid in his muscles and the sweat in his armpits, besides the humiliation for any spy at getting caught (never mind about what) by a *casino*—it just didn't matter a damn. They wanted him to leave.

He wanted to leave.

"Fine," he said.

He signaled Partlow from south of Paris. "1."

He caught the noon ferry the next day to Mull.

He called Digger. He checked his pager. And then he slept for sixteen hours.

The alarm crashed on his dresser across the room, and Piat swung an arm at it. Failing to find the snooze button, he woke up enough to get himself out of bed, shut off the alarm, and took stock.

After his usual struggle with the mechanics of the shower, he dressed and walked around the corner to the Island Bakery for coffee. His brain was working. It was working too hard.

In Piat's experience, the case officer's view of an operation went through three phases. In the first phase, the case officer made his plans and met his agents, and everything seemed possible. In the second phase, reality began to affect his plans. Difficulties arose. Personalities clashed and potentials failed to be recognized; outside factors that had been ignored suddenly rose up to get in the way of the operation. The simple cleanliness of the original plan became a dirty muddle of exigency and compromise. In the third and final phase, the case officer either succeeded or failed in his attempt to meld the original plan and the patchwork of reality.

Piat leaned against the steel railing along the edge of Tobermory's main pier and confronted the fact that he was squarely in phase two. For whatever reason, the security of the casinos of Monaco, and by extension, the French security services, had developed an interest in him. His agents were discovering fissures in their relationship. Piat grimaced as he considered that he might, himself, be responsible for the fissures.

On the other side of the balance, the target was not unapproachable. The target really did have a passionate interest in birds. The target had obvious, visible contempt for his uncle and the rest of his uncle's entourage.

Piat spent the whole of his double espresso weighing the balance. Since the value of every item, good or bad, was intangible, he could judge them only from experience. He could, by manipulation and self-control, get Irene and Hackbutt to the next meeting. And perhaps after that, from meeting to meeting, for as long as Partlow required. He couldn't guess what effect French security might have. He didn't think that they had any notion of his actual purpose.

It probably didn't matter.

Unless, of course, it did.

On the other side of the ledger, he had a package of manufactured antiquities in the trunk of his car that could now be "found" at the crannog. The apparently illegal looting of the ancient site would lend them cachet and provenance to certain collectors. And from that, he would make a great deal of money.

On balance, it was worth continuing.

Before he left for the farm, he read a chapter from one of his falconry books on hunting from trees and waiting on.

In Washington, Abe Peretz had invited himself to the Craiks' for dinner. He was a good enough friend to be able to do that. He'd called Rose at her Pentagon office and asked her when she was cooking and could he come, and she'd laughed and told him that she cooked less nowadays, but for him she'd do it any night. He specified Italian; she asked if pasta with broccoli was acceptable; he said that from her, he'd take even broccoli.

"The thing is, it's fast. You throw the broccoli in with the spaghetti while it boils, heat some garlic in oil, and you're done. I don't get home until eight or nine now, Abe."

"I can take you guys to dinner."

"No. No, you're too good a friend, and the kids love you,

and so do we. Come Friday." She didn't say that she worked Saturdays, and Sundays were for lying in bed if neither of them had to work that day, too.

And she promised him a baked apple with boiled cider, which wasn't Italian but was as good as it gets. And so the date was made.

Rose and Abe sat late at the table, well fed and wined. Alan was upstairs, making sure the two older kids were doing homework; the baby was already in bed. They talked about his family, his troubles.

"Abe, if it happened—if you could—would you take Bea back?" Bea was Abe's wife.

"Not for a second." He had been playing with some crumbs and a knife. "It sounds sexist to start with, doesn't it—the idea of a husband 'taking his wife back.'"

"I said it; you didn't."

"I couldn't. The kids, in a heartbeat. But her—" It was as if he couldn't pronounce her name. "It's worse than if it had been some other man. She's a *traitor*, Rose."

"I thought, maybe—" She smiled almost apologetically. "Love conquers all?"

"Well, it doesn't."

When Alan came back, Abe offered to help with the dishes, said he'd become a good dishwasher since his daughters had left. Alan said he threw things into a machine and let it do the work, and he began to demonstrate by carrying dishes away from the table.

"Could Al and I have a little private talk, Rose?"

"God, yes!" She had no jealousy about such stuff—now. She started to carry things to the kitchen, too. "Go, go—!"

Alan actually had something like a study. The house was big, what used to be called a stockbroker Tudor—two captains' salaries. As they were settling in big chairs, Abe said, "Two sexists we—women cook, men talk guy talk?"

"Rose and I split the duty. She shops and does the meals and I do the cleaning-up and the kids. When I can." He grunted. "When she can."

Abe had a long envelope in an inner jacket pocket. Alan wondered if he had carried it that way so he wouldn't be seen arriving with a briefcase or an attaché. But seen by whom?

"I got your list of the people who worked for OIA. I looked around a little," Abe said. "Or I had somebody look around. Big-time law firm, they have some dynamite investigators."

"My God, Abe, billed to who?"

"Billed to me. No, don't tell me a lot of nonsense; I wanted to do it. Anyway, I get a cut rate. And in-house, it's entirely discreet. The woman we use could find Judge Crater if she had to." He looked up at Alan over a pair of half-glasses. "Judge Crater? Have I got so old my references don't mean anything? Before your time. Before *my* time, in fact. A guy who disappeared, okay?" He was taking things out of the envelope and arranging them on the fat, padded arm of his chair. Alan saw a typed page, several pieces torn from newspapers and underlined, a hand-written note. The papers were like a metaphor for a cluttered, disorderly mind. Abe was brilliant, but again he wondered if he was entirely sane anymore. His hands, Craik saw, were trembling. "Okay! What all this impressive paperwork is about is, I know where the folks from the Office of Information Analysis went."

"Abe, I didn't ask you to do this."

"I know you didn't, so you're off the hook." He opened his hands. "You want to know what I've got or don't you?"

"Of course I do!"

"Okay then." Peretz leaned forward. He was pretty much trapped in the deep chair, and whenever he handed anything to Alan, he had to grunt and struggle forward. "It's all written down, but I want the pleasure of telling you about the good ones. So you have to listen to me. Okay—you know what the Office of Information Analysis was, right?—do-it-yourself intel, a bunch of amateurs proud of their virginity. In the beginning, they were in it only to channel raw intel to the White House. Raw intel of an acceptable kind, of course. Then, maybe—this is what you're into, right?— then maybe they got into a more operational kind of intelligence.

"And that's where maybe it gets interesting. I know I said to look for people who moved somewhere after the first term, but there were actually some maybe relevant moves much earlier. Three people, for example, went to your current shop, the Defense Intelligence Agency, in 2002."

"From *OIA*?"

"Am I talking about the Government Printing Office?"

"But my God, Abe—you're saying they had no background in intel, and they came over into Defense Intelligence?"

"I can even name names: Herman Ritter, Alice K. Einhorn, Geoffrey Lee. Ring any bells?"

Craik shook his head. "I'll check the DIA phone directory. It could just be the way people flow through government. Or the administration placing their own people everywhere." He wiped a hand down his face. "But that isn't supposed to happen in intelligence agencies."

"Then there's Ray Spinner."

"Spinner was a munchkin."

Abe held up the hand-written note. "She had to do a little tracking on him. They fired his ass out of OIA right after the clusterfuck in Tel Aviv." He handed the note over. "February, 2002. He didn't go anywhere else in government. Sort of dropped out, in fact."

Alan looked at the scribble. He had known Spinner slightly, years before, hadn't liked him. "Grad school?"

"That's where she found him."

Alan folded the note along its old lines and put it on a desk. "Spinner might know some things. Maybe he's bitter enough that he'd talk to me."

Abe made a disgusted face. He'd go to his grave believing that Spinner had got him shot. He shrugged, as if to rid himself of Spinner, and went back to his notes. "Okay, to the important people who moved after the first term ended. Until 2005, OIA was under a guy named David Sasimo, a deputy assistant secretary. Big-time dome-head, lots of think-tank credentials, wrote Op-Ed pieces, all that crap. Okay, comes the second term, when OIA was eliminated—work is done, mission accomplished, onward and upward—he went to Havers University as president. Five times the pay, double the prestige."

"I never heard of Havers University."

"Neither did I. But he's the third highest-paid university president in California. Okay? Okay.

"Under Sasimo at OIA, and in direct charge of the intel work, was somebody named Frank McKinnon. McKinnon has been in and out of academe, several books, blah-blah-blah. In late 2004, he went from OIA to something called the Petroleum Education Council as 'director of creative projects.' If you can figure out what that means, you get a free box of Crackerjacks.

"Two other people—I'll skip names now because it's late—one man, one woman, went to Hooper and Gretz. You know Hooper and Gretz? What we call a 'K Street firm.' Lobbyists, to the vulgar. Clients include one major automobile manufacturer and two oil companies, plus some defense-contract firms—stars of the military-industrial complex."

Abe held up his hand. "Now the biggie." He grinned. "Three people with OIA connections show up in a security company called Force for Freedom. You like that—'force?'" He rattled one of the newspaper articles. "Two of them *founded* the company in 2001; the other, a guy named Stern, joined the board in 2004. The L.A. *Times* did an investigative piece on civilian contractors in Iraq. Force for Freedom got two no-bid contracts from the provisional authority, both to provide 'military-spec' security for entities inside the Green Zone in Baghdad. They wear camo battledress, reportedly have better body armor than the military, and they pack weapons all the time. They're 'highly respected in the field.'"

"Rent-a Grunt, Inc."

"Pretty good for a company that was formed within a month of Nine-Eleven by two guys with no security experience, wouldn't you say? Two *young* guys with no security experience—one was twenty-four, the other twenty-seven. Nothing in their past suggests they had access to big bucks, either, but they got a PO box and a phone and, so far as my gal can tell, started making big money immediately. They now have an office suite in McLean, Virginia, and a 'training and exercise compound' in the Blue Ridge. No IPO yet, but they're making big money, not just in Iraq." Abe held up another hot-lined newspaper clipping. "An article in the *Post* on private police in New Orleans after Katrina lists them as having upwards of forty people in Plaquemines Parish to guard a refinery." He waved the other clipping again. "Investigative reporter tracked down a former employee, says that a 'typical' Force for Freedom guy is ex-military, either special forces or operational intelligence, at least five years of service, young to young-middle-aged, very focused. Typical pay is seven hundred to a thousand *a day* out of country. And they get *way* out of country: the *Times* says they were able to track one guy in Iraq, Bulgaria, and Thailand." He handed Alan the newspaper clippings, grunting as he struggled with the chair. His hand was still trembling.

Alan had his elbows on his knees, his hands joined in front of him. He was looking at Abe's chest. "So Force for Freedom was set up in—what, October?—2001, before my suspect document was written. OIA is listed as the originating source on the document. Then in the middle of 2002, three OIA people go to DIA, and about then a task number was generated that then got put on the document, 'superseding' a number that's meaningless to the intel community but could have been an in-house number, the house being OIA."

Peretz grunted. "And then they could have put all sorts of black crap into the pipeline under a legitimate task number and outsourced the actual ops to Force for Freedom."

"I don't want to jump to conclusions, Abe."

"These people deal with black ops the way they deal with everything else—bury it under the flag! And reclassify it so nobody else can see it."

Craik shook his head. "Whether they were doing dumb stuff like sending Spinner to Tel Aviv, or whether they were really into black stuff, they'd have to have seen pretty quickly that they were going to have to get their operations into the system, much as they might have hated the system. You can hide crap like that for only a little while before you've got so many accountability problems you're spending more time covering up than you are working. That's why they would have 'superseded' their own numbers with the legit task number. But that they even could do so meant that they already had clout in DIA—they were able to get their shit a DIA code classification." He shook his head. "I don't believe it."

He looked up at Peretz. "The classification code that blocked my access, by the way, is 'Perpetual Justice.' I thought that Perpetual Justice was just somebody's wet dream under one of those goddam names they pick out of computerized lists. A single operation. But it could be that it's more like a program. A way of doing things." He sat back. "Illegal things." Alan was looking at Abe's chest again. "But that raises a question: would they *still* be doing some sort of Perpetual Justice thing, or is that over?"

"Perpetual Justice may just be a way of *thinking*, Al, not a way of doing. If in OIA you thought preemptive war is swell and your enemies have no rights, then yeah, you'd still think it if you went to DIA. Like I said to you before, these people are true believers. They're *committed*. This isn't the nutcase fringe, muttering about black helicopters and close encounters. These are very smart, very, *very* sincere people."

Alan thought about that, then smiled. "I have a hard time believing they're breaking the laws that real intel people have to live by."

"That's why they hate people like us."

Alan looked at the newspaper clippings and the typed page, his frown deepening as he read. "There were also people who went to other parts of DoD?"

"Yeah—DoD, a couple to State, one woman to NSC, some to jobs here and there. Two of them—where is that? It's on the typed stuff—" He tried to read upside down, and Craik spun the page around and Peretz jabbed with a finger and said, "There—Crennan and Kravitz. They went to a congressional staff. Congressman—Kwalik. Ohio." He tapped a newspaper photo. "House Intelligence Committee."

"Just good people moving to other jobs, or true believers spreading the gospel?"

"No way to know." Abe pushed himself out of the chair's embrace. "I've got to go."

They found Rose, and then they stood there talking for a few last minutes, the Craiks sounding apologetic about never being home: Rose saying she had to go to Germany with her admiral for five days, Alan adding that he had a London trip coming up. Rose said she had to work tomorrow. Abe said, "How come you two are such lousy parents and have such great kids? It isn't fair."

They all laughed. It was a good joke, if painful.

14

"He's with Bella," Irene said from the doorway. "Naturally." She was back in work clothes, her hair wet, her cheeks flushed in the cold air.

The dog nuzzled his hand and barked, pushed its head into his thigh and barked again and ran in a circle. Piat wanted to avoid Irene as much as possible. He knelt by the dog and started to give him a good scratch. Piat looked up at Irene and smiled. "I—" he managed before she gave him a thin smile and closed the door.

Piat found Hackbutt half a mile up the ridge that loomed over the cottage by the simple expedient of looking for the bird. He had no trouble guessing what Hackbutt was doing, either. He was trying Bella at "waiting on."

He prepared himself during the climb. While his eyes watched the ground in front of him, seeking the easiest path between the damned tufts of coarse grass, his brain was evaluating what he had seen of Irene (puffy eyes, pot smoke, anger) and guessing at what he would find in Hackbutt, and how he could make them work. Together. Apart. Whatever.

Hackbutt hailed him when he was still more than fifty meters below them. Piat cast well to the south of the pair and then came back to them carefully. He'd learned not to spook a bird or a falconer.

"Did you see her?" Hackbutt said as he came up. "Did you

see her?" Of course, he didn't mean Irene. He meant Bella.

"Sure did, Digger." Piat smiled at him. "Waiting on. I saw her do it for what—five minutes?"

Hackbutt stroked the eagle on his wrist and cooed at her, and then cocked his head at Piat, his face still split by his smile. "I told her! I said you knew birds, that you listened to me. That you'd know just what I was doing. She said you didn't give a shit about birds, and I said you did. And look! You knew what we were doing from the valley!"

"You training with the lure?" Piat asked. He knew that big birds like eagles seldom took to waiting on in captivity when there was so much food available so close by and with less work. Because he'd just read about it.

"You really know your stuff, Jack. You have a glove?"

Piat pulled one from the pocket of his oilskin coat. He flourished it and put it on.

"Take her. This'll be better with the two of us. I wanted to call Annie, but Irene's in such a mood—"

"I noticed." Piat took the weight of the eagle on his wrist. She had her jesses, decorated with the new silver bells, but no hood, and she looked at him, turned her head as if to consider him from another angle, and then started nipping at his glove. Piat took a little tube of chicken from Hackbutt's bag, squeezed it in his gauntlet so that only a fraction was visible, and Bella began tearing at it.

"Don't give her too much—I want her keen. She's smart, Jack—smartest bird I've ever seen. But unless she's hungry, she'll just watch you like you're a show.

"The new command is 'up!'" Hackbutt said. "Give her a try."

Piat rolled his fist to hide the chicken. Bella turned her head and gave him a look—anger, disappointment.

He raised his fist smoothly, not so much throwing her as indicating the way to the sky. He'd never flown Bella before, and for a second he thought she wouldn't rise, but just at the top of his fist's arc she exploded off his wrist.

She was a big, heavy bird and she didn't climb like a hawk. She climbed in circles that grew and grew with every pass. For the first few seconds, she didn't appear to gain any real altitude at all, and then suddenly she was climbing away.

"That was beautiful," Hackbutt said. "I've never watched her—I've always been the one."

Piat realized that he still had his left hand sticking up in the air. He felt foolish, but he understood about falconry. It was in that one, explosive moment, when Bella left his fist and reached into the sky, her wings tearing the air with such strength that every beat fanned a wind through his hair.

She climbed for a long time. "That's excellent—most birds will never go beyond a hundred feet or so. Look at her!" Hackbutt couldn't keep still. "I should have done this months ago."

Piat watched her. "What if she sees real prey?"

"All the better!" Hackbutt exclaimed.

"Digger," Piat began.

"I'm going to leave her for six minutes, and then I'm going to start the lure going."

Piat set his watch alarm. It was like a student exercise at the training school. *You have six minutes to make your pitch.* "Digger," he said again.

Hackbutt flicked his eyes to Piat and then went back to watching Bella. "She's so high, I have to worry that she'll just fly off. I'm not sure we've ever been this far apart before."

Piat had planned a speech. He dumped it. Instead, he said, "Would that be so bad?"

Hackbutt gave Piat his full attention. "What are you saying, Jack?"

"The purpose of raising her is to release her into the wild. Right? And she's almost at her full growth—she's huge. She's fully trained. Right? So what would be so wrong with her flying away? You're going to release her in—what, two weeks?"

Hackbutt nodded slowly, as if a harsh truth had been revealed—perhaps a terminal cancer. And then he raised his eyes to the sky. "Sure, Jack. You're right."

He's going to cry.

"I need Bella, Digger." That statement had been meant to be the cap of an emotional appeal, but to hell with it. "I need her for the operation, Digger. And if you agree, she'll be with us for a lot longer. At least a month. Maybe longer."

Hackbutt's face turned back from the heavens. Tears were running down his cheeks, but his voice was strong. "The wildlife program would freak out, Jack."

What Hackbutt had really said was "I really want to do what you suggest, but—"

"I can fix that." Piat spoke with authority.

Hackbutt's eyes were back on the sky. "She's the best thing I've ever done, Jack. I don't want to lose her. But—but I've only *done* it when I let her go. When she has a mate and a clutch of eggs."

Piat nodded. "I need her, Digger."

High above, Bella turned suddenly but took no other action. She had caught a hint of movement far below. A hare, perhaps, just a little too bold on the hillside.

"She sees something. What do you want her for?"

"As the lure. For the target. To get him to come out of his tree," Piat said. "Only if we have to."

Hackbutt watched Bella. He raised his binoculars, shutting Piat out. "And the wildlife people would agree?"

"Sure," said Piat.

"And when we're done, you'll help me let her go?" Hackbutt asked.

"Sure," Piat lied.

High overhead, Bella saw the hare again. It had tried to become invisible by immobility, but it was young and it moved too soon. This time, its movement was much too bold, and she dropped.

The hare bolted from its cover and ran along the hill, bounding a meter in every stride.

Bella made a minute course correction.

The hare sensed her. He changed his direction, heading uphill at right angles to his original path.

He did it too soon, while she was still well up in her flight envelope with room to maneuver and lots of speed.

Her wings spread like a parachute and her talons reached for the hare while her wings reached for the sky, and in one beat of the terrified heart of the prey she had him in her talons and in the air.

When he got back to his room, Piat left a message for his divers requesting a meeting. Then he spent the evening on the internet, learning about a conservative American congressman named George Kwalik.

Alan Craik had called the Marine analyst, Sergeant Swaricki, and Rhonda Hope Stillman, the Southern earth mother, into his office. He made a point of asking Swaricki to close the door; a flicker of something—panic—passed across Mrs Stillman's face. One reason that she was so good was that she was afraid she'd do something wrong, and now, Craik saw, she thought she was going to be reamed out.

"This is something that I don't want to travel," he said. He hoped to mollify her with that. It didn't. He added, "This isn't personal or about anybody's performance or anything."

She settled her pretty bulk. "Well, that's a *considerable* relief! I thought you were going to scold us!"

"You're the two best people I've got—why would I scold you?" He had the fitness reports approaching final draft. They had both seen theirs, as they had to by law; what had they to fear? Swaricki, nonetheless, was scowling, which Craik put down to Marine culture.

"I've got a task that I'd like done," Craik said. "It's over and above what you're both already doing, which I know is a lot. But this has to be done, and I want it done right." He looked at her, then at him. They were waiting before they'd commit themselves. "This has grown out of a recent tasking we signed off on." He twirled a yellow pencil between his fingers, watching the gold lettering flash past and then wheel up toward him again. His left hand was missing two fingers; once, that damage had made him wince every time he saw it, but now he hardly noticed. He glanced up at Swaricki. "Sergeant, you've already seen a little of it." He leaned back in his desk chair and turned to Mrs Stillman. "There was a reference in a tasking that seemed a little funny. No headers or footers, and the contents were pretty well blocked out. The sergeant thought that one of the lines that was left referred to torture."

He let that settle in. Mrs Stillman was frowning again, now probably over the reference to torture. Everybody was pretty gun-shy about torture by then—Abu Ghraib, White House legal quibbles, the Senate trying to hammer out an anti-torture statute and getting blindsided by a presidential signing letter. He linked his hands behind his head and looked at the ceiling. "I ran the date-time group past one of the DPs downstairs. He came up with a limited-access classification named Perpetual Justice." He looked at them without changing his position. "Ever hear of it?"

They moved their heads from side to side.

"I went to the CIA officer of record on the tasking. I learned two things: the document does refer to torture, and it does have a task number. But the task number looks like it was added to the document after the fact."

Mrs Stillman's breath hissed in. She lived for accuracy, and postdating was not only illegal, it was also *inaccurate*.

Craik pulled himself up and put his elbows on the desk. "Torture isn't our business. I'll say personally I think it's wrong, and I think the sergeant believes the same thing, but this office isn't here to deal with torture. Okay? So it isn't the torture part. It's the task number. 'It's the task number, stupid.' Where did that come from? Anyway, if it's true that somebody's been backdating tasking approvals, then this office has a problem. The whole system has a problem. If a task number was backdated, then the activity was done without approval—it didn't go through the process—and there's been opportunity for breaking laws and opportunity for misusing funds, because, as you both know, when you don't go through the process, there's no oversight. Mrs Stillman?"

She had been fidgeting. Now she said, "Is this one of *our* taskings?"

Alan knew he had to be cautious. He said, "I don't know. The limited-access classification appears to be ours. Other than that, I don't know." He was twirling the pencil again. "Here's what I want." He looked at both of them. "I want the two of you to go through the system looking for the task number that was added to that document, and looking for anything that has 'Perpetual Justice' in it. I want you two to do it because you're the best and because you're discreet, and I want two of you because two heads are better than one. Plus you'll check each other." He looked at Mrs Stillman. "Can you do it?"

"We don't farm it out?"

"No. I want this kept close to the vest. Just the three of us."

Swaricki said, "I don't mean to question you, sir, but, uh—this is a legal order?"

"It is, and I'll give it to you in writing if you want." Swaricki nodded: he wanted it in writing. Another victim of Abu Ghraib—trust.

Mrs Stillman said, "This is on top of everything else we're doing?"

"I see it as part of the Green Book review. So I suggest that Sergeant Swaricki put aside some of his Green Book work while he does this, and, Mrs Stillman, you can hand off the training sessions to somebody for a while. I mean, this isn't going to take all year, is it?"

Mrs Stillman looked at Swaricki and back at Alan and said, "Part-time, maybe a week, I'd think. If it's limited-access classified, we're gonna be closed out of a lot. It's really a computer search."

Alan looked at Swaricki. "Can we say a week?"

Swaricki shrugged. "I don't even see a week. If it's all limited access, we'll be done in an hour."

"Well, try. Okay?" He looked at Mrs Stillman. "Okay?"

"Starting now?"

"You'll both have to carry all your other duties, remember. All but the Green Book work. Just fit this stuff in." He was writing "Perpetual Justice" and the task number he had seen on Partlow's computer on two slips of paper. "Report to me verbally when you've got something, and then I'd like a report in writing when it's over. Sergeant—well, both of you—you'll get a written request for the information from me later today." He handed over the pieces of paper and stood. "Make notes. Keep a paper trail. If this turns into anything, I want it all on the record."

They started out, but he called Mrs Stillman back. When Swaricki paused at the door, Alan nodded, and the sergeant went out and closed the door after him.

"Sit down for a second more, will you?" He took the desk chair again, waited until she sat. "Who's the best Saudi analyst you've got?"

She blushed. "It sounds vain to say it, but me."

"You've got enough on your plate. Who else?"

She named a civilian in the office. He remembered the man's fitness report—all excellent, except for relations with his coworkers—and his own meeting with the guy, which had made Craik dislike him but therefore work hard not to show it. "I want a bio on a Saudi." He had the name from

Partlow's taskings, Muhad al-Hauq, already printed out. "Get everything there is. Open source, classified, Google, whatever. Have him do a Lexis Nexis, the whole nine yards."

"That's easy." She got ready to get up. "That it, captain?"

"Just a sec more." He smiled at her, because he thought that again she'd think she'd done something wrong. "This has to stay just between you and me. Not in writing. If that bothers you, tell me now."

She looked startled. "Is this something different?"

"I think it's connected. But it's, mm, iffy."

"I can't say if it *bothers* me till you ask."

"That's fair. Okay. Three people came to DIA from another government office a couple of years ago. That office is shown on the document I've been talking about as the originating one—that is, before the task number was backdated. I'd like to talk to those three people, but they're not in the DIA phone book. The security officer 'can't comment.' Mrs Stillman, you've been here since before those people came on board."

She blushed and giggled. "*Many* years before."

"I thought you might have an idea of how to locate them."

She sat slightly sideways, resting much of her weight on her right hip. She joined her hands in front of her. She was wearing pink, a good color for her. She said, "We're not supposed to know about the HUMINT people or where they are. Are they HUMINT?"

"I don't know."

"HUMINT are not in the phone book, that's for sure! And I don't think Human Resources would have them, either, or Finance. They pretty much a law unto themselves. Still—" She smiled.

"Yes?"

"People are people. We talk, and we say things we don't think about first. You get to know more than you should if you stay here long enough. You want me to try to find these folks?"

He wrote the three names he had got from Abe Peretz, the people who had moved from the Office of Information Analysis to DIA in 2002—Herman Ritter, Alice K. Einhorn, Geoffrey Lee—on a piece of memo paper and pushed it across the desk. She read it and shook her head. "Never heard of them."

"Could you ask around?"

"Asking's free." She stood up. "I don't want to get anybody into trouble."

"I don't think you will. As you say, asking's free."

She stopped before she got to the door.

"Are these folks *dangerous*?"

He laughed.

Her made-up eyes met his. "Why do we care so much? This is office politics, captain. It doesn't seem your style." Her pronunciation of the word *style* had three short a's and a diphthong.

He nodded. "We signed off on this operation," he said. "This office did. *I did*. Now, I think the whole thing is illegal."

Partlow sent a signal giving Piat a meeting in Paris. Piat declined. The simple codes didn't give him a chance to say why, but Piat had no intention of going to France again any time soon.

In less than an hour, Partlow signaled him again, this time for a meeting in Italy. Piat opened his laptop, did the numbers, and decided it could be done. He packed in two minutes and drove to Glasgow. He was at the airport at four a.m. Friday morning.

All he saw of Milan was the highway ring. He took the A4 east to Vicenza, pushing his Audi rental to one hundred and sixty kilometers an hour because no limit was posted. Having pulled any prospective surveillants into a long tail behind him, he got off at Vicenza.

Vicenza was an industrial town around a medieval core.

Piat wanted to see the medieval part and he had to make sure that no one had picked him up at the airport. Monaco had made him even more cautious than usual. He stopped and had coffee, admired what was left of the town wall, and got on the highway convinced that he was clean. He followed Partlow's directions and drove well out beyond the town's highway ring to a conference center that had Clyde Partlow written all over it—it was new and it gleamed, from the black marble of its two-storey foyer to the black granite of the conference room tables. Where, in due season, he found himself.

"Good to see you again, Jerry," Partlow said. They shook hands. They were the only people in a conference room big enough for a meeting of the Joint Chiefs. There was no bottle of scotch and no sign of happiness from Partlow. "This place is secure. It was built for NATO."

"That's reassuring," Piat said with an artificial smile. He wanted to say that just driving up to such a place was bad security—but what the hell. "Good to see you, too, Clyde."

"You turned down my French venue, Jerry. That puts me on the hot seat—I'm due for a meeting in Paris in twelve hours." Partlow raised an eyebrow. "Do we have a control problem, Jerry?"

Piat shook his head. "It's not like that, Clyde. Wait'll you hear it before you decide I'm a control problem."

Partlow nodded—the renaissance prince withholding judgment. "Please tell me."

Piat flopped back in his chair. It was a nasty chair—hard, angular, shiny. "I said Monaco was a rotten venue. It was, and I got burned by the casinos. I'm not trying to ditch the blame—whatever it was, I probably did it." He shrugged. Partlow watched him, impassive.

And angry.

Piat told the story. The cameras. The problems. And the denouement in his hotel room.

Partlow spread his hands on the table. It was not a gesture that Piat had ever seen him make. "Jesus Christ," he said.

Piat sat still.

Partlow clasped his hands over one knee. "We're dead, then. And I'll have to tell the chief of station in Paris—something."

Piat smiled. "Blame me. I'm a well-known loose cannon." Only after the words left his mouth did he remember that he was no longer that well-known loose cannon. Now he was a man who shouldn't be involved in operations at all.

But Partlow had moved on. "No. No, it's not your fault, Jerry." Partlow was making a real effort not to shout or pound his hand on the table. "I'd never have expected them to be on to you so fast." The content of his statement was "How did you fuck this up?"

Piat hesitated. Partlow was bristling—looking for a fight about the passport and about security. Piat didn't see anything to be gained by giving him one. "I agree. So let's move on. I saw the target, I saw his uncle and the entourage, and I saw the target's bird. We can do it. The falconer can do it. The venue in Mombasa is as good as we'll get. I want to fly down and see it, scout it, and get the right rooms. In Africa, that can be done with straight-up bribes."

Partlow raised an eyebrow. "We have acquired the interest of French intelligence and you want to go on?"

"This is your new world order, right? Screw 'em, Clyde. They probably thought I was there to run a game on the casinos. Right? If they thought I was there to scam a guest, that's okay, too. Right? Otherwise, who gives a fuck? By the time the wheels of the Deuxième Bureau grind, we'll have this guy on the payroll."

Partlow nodded, but his mind and his eyes were elsewhere. "I think perhaps it's time to pull the plug, Jerry." Partlow spread his hands again.

Piat didn't like that physical sign one bit. Partlow only

spread his hands when his resources were depleted. So Piat shrugged. "Sure, Clyde. If you've got cold feet, let's ditch it."

Partlow rubbed his eyes, ran his fingers through his hair. "I just don't think it's going to work, Jerry. And I don't want the scrutiny. Not now."

Piat leaned forward. "Sure, Clyde. Look, you've kept me out of all that—and you've also kept me out of the background data. I don't know what you have on the target—whether it's solid, whether he's tertiary to the terrorist thing or a heavy hitter. But I do know this, Clyde—it can be done."

Partlow sat, elbows on the table, his forehead resting on his left hand. "So you say," he said wearily.

"I have other stuff to talk about. If we're not going forward, it doesn't matter." Piat sat back and watched Partlow, who wasn't meeting his eyes and looked like hell. Partlow looked worse every time he showed up.

"Tell me. I might as well hear it all." Partlow crossed his hands over his knee, but he did it slowly, like an old man with aching joints.

"The woman spotted an American in contact with the target. I didn't want to make anything of it at the time, but it raises some concerns."

Partlow shrugged. "Most Saudis know some Americans."

Piat tossed a computer printout on to the table. "His name is George Kwalik. That's Congressman Kwalik to the likes of us. He's quite prominent on the internet—has his own blog, gets a lot of play."

Partlow leafed through the printout. "I know who he is," he said carefully. His face flushed and his eyes dilated. "Jesus Christ. Jesus—Jerry, he was *in contact* with the target?"

Piat knew he had hit Partlow very hard. He hadn't intended to, and he didn't know what the connection was, but Partlow was reacting as if he had been punched in the gut. "They were seen talking together. Mano-a-mano. Tête-à-tête. Pick your cliché." Piat leaned forward. "Come on,

Clyde. We're not exactly buddies, you and me—but we're *on the same fucking side this time*. Who is this guy, and why's he talking to my target, and why does that make you turn as red as a beet?"

Partlow shook his head. "Jerry—I'd love to. I really would. But some secrets aren't mine to tell." He sat, still turning the pages from Piat's download of data. "Jesus—*what are they doing*?"

"Who, Clyde? What is who doing?" Piat hushed his voice.

Partlow shook his head. "Forget you heard me say that." He sat up, shot his cuffs, rubbed a hand through his hair again. "You think this can be done in Mombasa? Let's try it, then. I'll trust you implicitly. What do you need?"

Piat was a little stunned by the change in Partlow's manner—and attitude. "Just like that, we're back on?"

"Just like that." Partlow opened his briefcase and withdrew a laptop. From around his neck he took a crypto-key. "I have most of the reservation information you requested for Mombasa."

"Whoa, horsey. Thirty seconds ago we were done."

Partlow spread his hands, palm up. "Now we're not."

"Because of George Kwalik?" Piat asked.

"Need to know, Jerry. Need to know. You don't, I do, and that's the equation." Partlow raised an eyebrow. He was trying to convey something.

Piat didn't get it. And his curiosity was fully aroused. He sensed that Partlow was using the operational data on the laptop to lead him away from the subject. But there wasn't much he could do about it. So he read the target's travel information on the computer. Flight reservations, hotel reservations, cars, a truck. "Who rented the truck?" he asked.

Partlow got up and looked over his shoulder. "No idea."

Piat shrugged. "It sticks out. What do they need a truck for? It's not big. I'll check with the rental agency. Can you afford for me to go down in advance?"

Partlow shook his head. "Go a day or two early, Jerry, I'll pay for that. But—I can't afford to have you buy another set of tickets. Do you know how far over budget this thing is already?"

Piat shrugged again. "Operations cost money. Good operations cost lots of money." He glanced up at Partlow. "Do I get a cup of coffee, or are you still so pissed at me we're just going to sit in this basketball court until I'm done reading?"

Partlow raised an eyebrow. "Basketball court?"

Piat waved his arms to draw attention to the size of the room.

Partlow disappeared and came back with a tray of coffee and pastries.

Piat took one, bit into it, and kept reading.

Partlow poured them coffee.

Two sips and two bites later, Piat raised his head. "Clyde, do you like food?"

Partlow was still looking at the Kwalik information. "Of course."

Piat held up his styrofoam cup and waved it. "We're in fucking Italy, Clyde. The home of the finest coffee in the Western world. A place where bakers make pastries that make French pastries look lame. Why the *fuck* are we drinking Maxwell House and eating microwaved American shit?"

Partlow leaned back and drank some coffee. "This is a secure facility."

"Yeah?" Piat asked. "Secure from who?"

When he was done, Partlow gave him an email address for more frequent communications. And he said, "I don't imagine I'll see you again before—before it's done. Before you make contact."

Piat nodded, the taste of bad coffee sour and bitter in his mouth. "I'll want a meeting the second I'm out of Mombasa. One way or the other."

Partlow shut his briefcase with a snap. "Let's do Germany."

Piat thought about it for a moment. "Yeah. That suits—it's on my way. Frankfurt?"

Partlow hesitated. "Stuttgart," he said.

A major American military base. Another "secure facility," no doubt. "Give me the particulars."

Partlow rattled through a meeting spot, a set of recognition signs, a fallback. Solid tradecraft, the stuff that made espionage work. All the stuff that Partlow hadn't wanted to do in Athens. Another red flag. Piat created a mnemonic for the comm plan "Okay. Stuttgart. I'll signal you when I'm out."

Partlow offered his hand. "Good luck, Jerry. I really, really hope you succeed."

Piat took his hand and they shook. "*Hakuna matata, bwana,*" he said. "No problems. What do you want me to do if I run across the congressman?"

Partlow's grip tightened for a moment. "Run like hell," he said.

On the way to the airport, Piat stopped at an "illy" sign and drank two cups of espresso. Because he was in Italy and because he was more than a little scared, he wrote Mike Dukas a postcard. Then he drove back to the airport, dropped his rental car, and flew to Glasgow in time to catch the last ferry to Mull.

15

Saturday morning, Piat woke to his alarm and got himself out the door as quickly as he could. He hadn't run in so long he was feeling like a slug—a slug who lived on airport food and slept in hotels. He ran up the long hill from the Mishnish to the antique pile of the Western Isles Hotel, and then he ran through the less touristy parts of Tobermory at the top, where 1950s housing jostled the older cots and cottages, and then out into the countryside past the Dervaig road. The day was cold, but the sun, where he could find it, was warm, and by the time he'd made his loop and started down the long hill from the traffic circle to the town's waterside main street, he felt better. He sprinted along the front of the eighteenth-century buildings, the shops and pubs and restaurants to his left and the sea to his right, without a thought in his head beyond the euphoria of movement and exercise.

Even the shower was easy.

While the hotel filled his thermos, Piat called the farm and got Irene.

"Why don't I take you guys for dinner tomorrow?" he said.

"Dinner, or some kind of training?" Irene sounded as if her patience was sorely tried.

"Dinner. Just dinner. Italian, over in Salen." Piat tried to convey calm reassurance.

"Eddie says you want him to keep Bella," she said. "Sometimes I wonder if you and I are on the same side."

"This isn't the time to have this conversation, Irene. Yes, we're on the same side."

Piat packed his fishing gear in the boot of his new rental (a spaceship-shaped Renault product too damned wide for the Mull roads) and drove south toward the hills. He parked in the valley and started the climb to the loch, immediately aware of the length of his run and the age of his legs, but pleased nonetheless to make the top, and its view. He stopped, as had become a habit, and drank tea from his thermos. Dykes was standing on the crannog, fishing. McLean was fishing from the bank, well around the loch, more a shadow against the bright surface of the water than the shape of a man.

Piat slugged back the last of his tea and started down the hill. He noted that the path, a barely visible sheep track when he had first come to fish, was now well beaten down. He walked down to the shingle by the crannog and looked for signs of activity. The only thing he could find was the tarp covering the pumps—and he'd helped to place it. There was a small refuse heap—if a pool of mud could merit the name—and a single PVC pipe that ran down through the grass and vanished into the water. Not much to see.

Dykes waved. He flourished a small brown trout. Piat rolled his eyes and began to set up his rod.

McLean hailed him from across the water. "Anything?"

Piat shook his head and shouted back, "Little browns!"

McLean gave him a resigned nod.

At noon, they met behind the crannog for lunch. Dykes had an American gas stove and he used it to cook the little brown trout like anchovies or sardines. Piat wasn't sure the proprietor would approve, but then, he wasn't likely to approve of the dig, either. The fish were delicious.

McLean fetched a heavy plastic bag from under the tarp.

"Not a waste of time at all," he said. In the plastic bag was a Reicher mount with two bone fishhooks, a bead of lapis, a gold disk and a bronze pin.

"There's more," said Dykes. "That's the best shit. We got some arrowheads and some broken stuff."

Piat had to laugh. It was the irony of the thing. He laughed and took another bite of fish. "You guys are the best. No, really. Okay, when I sell this, you guys get a cut. But now that we actually found something, I guess we ought to document it for the buyer—a couple of photos. Can you get a few underwater?"

It was McLean's turn to laugh. "Well, I could," he said. "I have the camera. On the other hand, you could just take a picture of a piece of brown felt. That's what it looks like under there. We're finding stuff by touch and feel. Most of it is old twigs and pebbles. God only knows what we're missing."

"I have one more hole to do," Dykes said. "Then we're just taking your money to fish." He shrugged. "Not that I mind, but I've got bills to pay and shit to do at home."

Piat took out two envelopes and handed one to each. "That ought to cover pay to the end of next week," he said. Both men counted the money right there.

"Thanks," McLean said. He looked out at the crannog. "I could get a couple of shots if they were posed—if we didn't actually have the pump on."

Piat smiled. "The whole thing is posed, Tank. Doesn't matter if the pictures are posed." He laughed again. "Last thing I expected was a genuine artifact. But it'll make the whole thing easier to sell."

Dykes poked him with a hard finger. "Come on. You was hoping."

Piat smiled. "Okay, I was." He looked up at the clouds coming in around the summit of the mountain. "How much longer do you think you guys'll need?"

Dykes and McLean exchanged a glance. They both

shrugged. "A week?" said Dykes. "Two if we string it out."

Piat nodded. "Do you mind stringing it out?" he said. He poured tea from his thermos and handed it around. It started to rain.

McLean shrugged. "It's your money. Sure, I can stay two weeks."

Dykes flourished his envelope. "If I send this here home, I can probably stay another two weeks. What for, though? If you don't mind my asking? 'Cause we're just about done, like I said."

Piat knew that he kept them there for two mutually exclusive reasons—as a trip wire against investigation, and as muscle in an emergency. He wasn't entirely logical about it. He shrugged. "I don't know myself. Insurance. Just in case. Hey, it's my money, right?" He looked back at them. "Any problems? Anybody come by?"

McLean sipped some tea. "His lordship came by. Nice chap—came up on his ATV, watched us fish, came down to the water's edge. He drove right over the pipe—I had to replace her. Either he didn't twig to it or he didn't give a shit. All he wanted to hear about was the fish."

"I sent him home with one of his own sea trout," Dykes said. "Only one I've caught."

McLean cocked an eye at Dykes. "That's because you're a hopeless caster."

"Fuck you," said Dykes, serving up another pan of fish.

Piat stayed most of the afternoon, casting in the cold rain, freezing his hands and arms, his nose and ears almost numb, happy. He didn't keep anything he caught, and he ended his day with a warm bath in his hotel.

When he got into bed, he realized that he hadn't thought about Hackbutt, Irene, or Partlow since the morning.

Mombasa was four days away. He fell asleep thinking about Mombasa, and he dreamed of an empty hotel where someone was hunting him.

The next morning, Piat made reservations for Mombasa by computer. He spent Partlow's money. He read websites on hotels and took the operational plunge of putting his own party at the same hotel as the target. With all the issues Irene and Hackbutt had, with all of Partlow's reservations, with whatever shadow the congressman cast, Piat had to figure he had one shot.

Mombasa.

Late that afternoon, he drove to the farm and collected his agents. Irene looked different—neither the shapeless dress of their first meeting nor the wool skirts of her "rich girl" persona nor the cargo pants and flannel shirts of her "art". Instead, she had fitted jeans and a raw silk shirt with baroque buttons, set off by a necklace of African trade beads. She wore it with a jacket from her operational clothes.

Now, she looked to him like an artist.

Hackbutt had on his oldest sweater with a pair of stained climbing pants and hiking boots. But he didn't look like a refugee or a bum. The change was subtle but evident, not just in his own behavior but also in how the hostess greeted them. Hackbutt, for instance, smiled at her. She smiled back.

Piat wondered if the feeling Hackbutt gave him was anything like the feeling Bella gave Hackbutt.

"We're going to Mombasa," Piat said, when they were seated.

Both of them tried to talk at once.

"I have work to do!" Irene said.

"I'm training Bella!" Hackbutt said.

That got an older and meaner look from Irene. But instead of commenting on Bella, Irene turned to Piat. "You said no spy games." She said it loudly enough for the restaurant's handful of late-season patrons to hear her.

Piat had to restrain himself from turning to look at the patrons' reaction. He leaned back, feigning indifference. "I lied. But that's for later. I just wanted to get it out in the open. You'll leave Thursday." *Oops,* he thought. *Mistake.*

It was Hackbutt who continued to surprise him. He leaned forward, almost a conspirator. "Time for that later," he said. "It's our night off."

Piat made himself relax. "You're absolutely right, Digger. Apologies all around."

The food was excellent, and so, for once, was the company. Irene rattled on about her contacts in France. "They take me seriously," she said, for perhaps the fifth time. She was drunk on it—on being taken seriously.

She was into her fourth glass of wine by the time she began to describe her next installation. "Tools," she said. "I'm going to get a lot of old tools. I mean, a *lot* of old tools. Don't ask me why." She looked around. "Women and tools. Something about women and tools." She sneered. "I *hate* the idea of being 'about' something. It isn't *about* women and tools, it *is* women and tools. Maybe I can get the Bush administration to give me an NEA grant," she said. "What do you think, Jack?"

Piat flicked his eyes around the room. "I think maybe we should call it a night."

Irene laughed again, a rich, horsey laugh, tough and happy and brave and far, far too assertive.

With Hackbutt's aid, he got her into the car. He drove the long way, to give her a chance to sober up a little, and he started telling stories because she was in the mood to laugh, and then Hackbutt told a story from Jakarta that made both of them look like fools, and she laughed all over again. All three of them did. Piat looked at Hackbutt in the electric blue light of the instrument panel and tried to remember if he'd ever heard the man make a story funny before. Hackbutt laughed, not a nasal whine but a head-thrown-back full-throated roar. The car raced along a two-hundred-foot drop to the sea below, the occupants laughing like teenagers hearing their first dirty joke.

Piat and Hackbutt each took an arm and helped her to the door of the farm. Just on the stone sill, she turned and kissed Hackbutt, a passionate kiss.

"I think I'll save the briefing for tomorrow," Piat said.

She took all her own weight on her own feet, stood straighter, chuckled. "I'm not as think as you drunk I am," she said.

Piat caught Hackbutt's eye and flicked a glance at Irene.

"I think you are," he said, and headed for his car. When he looked back, they were kissing again in the doorway, He stamped too hard on the accelerator, so that gravel flew from the wheels despite the weeks of wet weather.

Alan Craik was down in the DIA cafeteria, staring through a tilted sheet of glass at a big metal tray full of something that had to be eggplant. It was Italian day—eggplant, pizza, spaghetti. He had his doubts. The women who cooked and served were all friendly and willing and probably talented, but they weren't Italian.

"How's the eggplant?" he said to a black woman in a white hairnet who was waiting to serve somebody.

"It's good, you like that kinda thing."

He thought of Rose's eggplant with black olives and tomato sauce. It wouldn't be like that. It probably wouldn't be like anything, except maybe boiled greens with hog jowls. He said he'd take some.

He swayed around chairs, heading for a table where a woman he knew was sitting, Nice woman, forties, Air Force. Targeting specialist. He put his tray on the table, established that she wasn't saving the place for somebody, and sat down. At the same time he watched half a dozen people join the cafeteria line, recognized one of them, couldn't place him, and then did and said out loud, "That congressman again."

"What congressman?" He liked her voice—husky, like his wife's.

He bobbed his head toward the line. "That one—the silver-back in the expensive suit."

"Kwalik," she said. "And his entourage."

"Kwalik?"

"Representative Kwalik. Ohio."

"How do you know something like that?"

"He's on the intelligence committee. I got sent up there to brief them because everybody else in my outfit had already gone and they said it was my turn to blow smoke."

"What's he doing here? Hard to believe he comes for the food."

She laughed. "Have you tried the eggplant?" she said. She laughed again. "Don't."

He did anyway. If you didn't think of it as Italian, it wasn't so bad. He listened to her talk about somebody in her department, and he ate and watched the congressman go through the line. Kwalik. He remembered the face from Abe Peretz's briefing. People from OIA had gone to Kwalik's staff after OIA was disbanded.

Which brought him back to his question: *What's he doing here*?

In the morning, Piat went out to the farm, headache and gut ache and all. Irene looked fine—in fact, she was drinking orange juice and was ready for work. Hackbutt looked like hell—but a happy hell.

"Mombasa," Piat began. He told them about Mombasa and its beaches and resorts. He bored them with maps and diagrams. He finished by saying, "The target's uncle and his entourage have booked twenty-six rooms for five days. They have conference rooms, a section of private beach, their own restaurant in the hotel and their own pavilion outside."

Hackbutt was lying on the sofa like an invalid. He nodded with every sentence as if he already knew everything Piat had said, but now he rubbed his chin. "What are they doing there? Mombasa?"

Piat shook his head. "Hard to say. The uncle has some appointments—among other things, his family have paid for a mosque in Kilini, up the coast." Piat decided that a digression on the various types of Islam on the east coast of Africa wasn't suited to the audience. "He's going to shoot some animals in the game park. Illegally, of course. And there's an Islamic film festival in town, and it's possible the uncle is a heavy hitter among the donors."

Hackbutt, however, was not to be led astray by talk of film festivals. "What about the birds?" he asked. "What about the man with the birds?"

Piat clicked to a still picture of the Nyali. "He'll be somewhere in the hotel. I assume he'll have birds with him—if he took them to Monaco, I think he'll take them to Africa. I think he'll fly on the beach. And I think that's where we'll get him."

Hackbutt rubbed his head, which obviously hurt, but when he took his hand away, he had a light in his eyes. "I want to talk to that man about his birds."

Piat nodded.

Irene finished her juice and stood with her hand on her hip. "So we're going to a beach resort in wintertime."

"High summer there."

"And a film festival," she said.

"If you like Islamic film."

"Maybe I will. This sounds a *fuck* of a lot more satisfying than Monaco." She shot Piat a smile—enigmatic.

"Always happy to please," Piat replied while sorting their tickets.

"And I need to be back by Tuesday. I have an installation to complete. And I'll need some of my money, too."

Hackbutt pulled himself up on an elbow. "We both do."

Piat handed them their tickets. "Half up front, half on completion, bonus for success. That was the deal."

Irene scowled. "But I need the money next week."

Hackbutt nodded. "Jack, it's really important to her. And I need some cash too—I have costs. I have to pay the girl who takes care of my birds."

Piat snarled inside at the eternal mercenary nature of agents, but he nodded. "That's an operational expense, Digger—we need Bella fed and flown. In top condition, like you said." He glanced at Irene. "I'll see about some money for you."

Irene looked out the window at the stream which ran past their drive and out to the small loch at the base of the hill. She seemed to be lost in contemplation of the interplay of grays—gray sky, gray water, gray grass. "I need the money soon," she said quietly.

"It's not due until we land our fish," Piat said. It never worked to give an inch on payments.

She raised her eyebrows at him. "Well, then. I guess we'll need to land him in Mombasa."

That night, he drove to Glasgow. At four a.m., he flew to Mombasa via Brussels and Nairobi. He thought that he knew everything that could go wrong.

Ray Spinner was the youngish man who had been in OIA and who Abe Peretz believed was responsible for his having been shot. Alan Craik had known Spinner vaguely a few years before and thought he was too feckless to do much of anything. The skinny on Spinner in the Navy was that if it hadn't been for his father, he'd have been working at Jiffy-Lube. His father was a partner in one of the heavy-hitting Washington law firms, one that always had connections in government, no matter which party was in power, although it was said that they were particularly tight with the current bunch. Ray Spinner should have done well, then, but he hadn't: resignation from the Navy over a screwup that involved his tipping his father off about privileged information; abrupt discharge from the Office of Information Analysis for the data-gathering trip he'd made to Tel Aviv that had ended in the disaster when Peretz had got part of a bullet that had hit somebody else first.

"So I got fired—even though it was my boss's idea. To go to Tel Aviv. And be a spy."

Spinner and Alan Craik were sitting at a table in a Thai restaurant near American University. Craik thought that Spinner had changed for the better—physically thinner, but maybe psychologically so, as well, as if he'd lost pounds of self-confidence and self-love.

Craik said, "Pretty dumb, sending somebody to a foreign country that way."

"Yeah, well—" Spinner gave him an embarrassed smile. "Greta says it was my own fault and I should suck it up. I mean, I didn't say no, she says."

It had already been established at the beginning of lunch that Spinner had married. It was also evident that somebody had taken him in hand, given him a good talking-to, made him understand he'd been a shmuck and had to do better from now on. The hand would be Greta's, Craik guessed, a woman who apparently had Spinner under tight control: he'd mentioned doing the dishes and the vacuuming as "my share of having a home."

"Who was your boss?"

"The great Frank McKinnon."

One of the people Peretz had given him notes on, now doing something "creative" at the Petroleum Education Council. Craik nonetheless pretended ignorance. "Do I know him?"

"*Nobody* knows McKinnon. You just know *about* him."

"Like what?"

"Big-time neocon, academic when it suits him, published *American Millennium*—you read it? Very persuasive. Actually a wonderful book, as Greta says, until you do the math and see what it would cost to keep the US as the world's only superpower forever. McKinnon's a big thinker."

"So he sent you to Tel Aviv as Ray Spinner, Boy Spy, and then fired you because you got caught?"

Spinner flushed. "Well, there was more to it than that. But yeah, he waited a month and then fired me. I didn't take it very well at the time. I thought—I was accustomed to having my dad bail me out." He looked away and then back, directly into Craik's eyes. "Greta says I have to admit my dependence on my dad."

"Like a twelve-step program."

Spinner laughed. "Greta'll love that! Wait till I tell her. Losers Anonymous." He filled his fork with something that had coconut and pork in it and then held the fork in the air halfway to his mouth. "McKinnon firing me was the best thing that ever happened. Reality check."

Alan ate a little of his peanut-sauced chicken and said, "The Office of Information Analysis was a sort of off-the-cuff intel project when you worked there, right?"

Spinner nodded, chewing. "Finding nuggets you guys had 'suppressed.' Don't get mad! 'Suppressed' was their word, not mine. Actually, I bought into it while I was there. It was my job. After I got bounced, I wasn't so crazy about it."

"Just finding nuggets, or did they do operations, as well? Other than yours, I mean." Alan smiled, making it a little joke. Spinner hadn't been in intelligence in the Navy; Craik didn't know how much he understood about the field.

Spinner forked more food into his mouth. He ate, Alan thought, like a hungry graduate student. Spinner said, "Everybody in OIA was really close-mouthed. If they did operations, I didn't hear about it. Everything was top-down, need-to-know, classify it Secret or above if you possibly can."

"Ever hear of something called Perpetual Justice?"

Spinner looked at him in a different way. Maybe it was

the moment when he realized why Alan had asked him to lunch. "Is this official?"

"I'm in the US Navy; the Navy has an interest in something called Perpetual Justice. I'm not on some sort of legal case, if that's what you mean."

Spinner moved his lower jaw way over to one side, his cheek bulging where his tongue was. He looked perplexed. Maybe he was wishing that Greta were there. "I saw a folder on McKinnon's desk once with 'Perpetual Justice' on the cover. I had to read it upside down."

"Read anything in it?"

Spinner shook his head. His bowl was empty, but he made a point of going around the sides with his fork, picking up the last gobs of sauce. Alan changed the subject back to Greta and learned that Greta was a nurse, and Spinner was studying to be a physician's assistant. It was such a revolution in his goals that Alan wondered if he would really stick with it. Then Spinner told him that becoming a physician's assistant was Greta's idea, so Craik thought the chances of his becoming one were pretty good.

"How's your father?"

"We don't communicate much. He doesn't like Greta. The feeling's mutual."

They both had more tea, and Spinner had a brightly colored, gelatinous dessert. Alan allowed a silence to grow, and then he said casually, "So what's OIA up to now?"

"They closed up shop. There was an agenda there about invading Iraq; once that went down, probably the big guys looked for new worlds to conquer. Especially with the aftermath in Iraq going to hell—I can't see McKinnon wanting to be associated with that."

"So where's he now?" Even though he knew the answer.

"Oil industry."

"What's he know about oil?"

"He doesn't have to know anything about it. One, he's tight

with people in the White House; two, he's big on international policy. Looking ahead ten years, fifty years. Big thinker."

"Sending you to Tel Aviv wasn't big thinking."

"It was early days. He was trying stuff on. I was part of his learning curve."

"Little hard on you."

"Yeah, but not on him." Spinner laughed. "When I'd completely fucked up in Israel, I sent him an email and said we'd made a mistake. He wrote me back. 'We don't make mistakes, and when we do, they become triumphs.'" He laughed again and shook his head.

Alan signaled for the check and took out a credit card. As if as an afterthought, he said, "When you were at OIA, ever hear of an outfit called Force for Freedom?"

"Funny you should ask." Spinner had been ready to get up; now he put his forearms on the table. "It's a big security company now—you know that, I guess. In 2001, it didn't exist. Two guys I knew slightly in OIA started it. After I got fired, I went to them and asked for a job. They wouldn't even talk to me." He smiled. "McKinnon."

"What were these two guys at OIA—security people?"

"Nah! They were analysts, like me. Shit, one of them was only two years out of college. But they were incredibly gung ho. They were into what OIA called 'direct action'—preemptive strikes, military solutions to everything. I heard the older guy say in a meeting that the President should declare martial law—this is right after Nine-Eleven—and take over the National Guard from the states. *That* kind of guys." He sniggered. "And had either of them been in the military themselves? Ho-ho-ho."

"Did they talk about intel operations?"

"Never heard them comment on that. We weren't friends or anything. Sorry."

"Any idea where they got the money to set up Force for Freedom?"

Spinner shifted his shoulders, almost a wiggle. "Private money, probably."

"Any chance it was DoD money?"

Spinner seemed uncomfortable with that. "There was a lot of off-the-books money, I guess. Like sending me to Tel Aviv. But about the two guys that set up Force for Freedom, no, that wasn't the scuttlebutt." Clearly, he didn't want to say more. Old loyalty, or caution?

Craik didn't want to let it go. He said, "If it was private money, where did it come from?"

Spinner frowned and fidgeted. Finally, he muttered, "Energy sector. That's all I'll say about that."

They stood and made their way to the door.

Before they went their separate ways, Spinner said, "Did you get what you wanted out of me?"

Alan smiled. "Greta would say you're being paranoid."

They laughed.

16

No operational plan survives first contact with the enemy. Taught by instructors, repeated by superiors, often a joke, sometimes in earnest, and never more true than on a sunny morning amid the palm frond-dappled shadows of Mombasa's Nyali Beach.

Piat lay on a deck chair with coffee and a bottle of ice water at his elbow. He was only one of hundreds of pale slugs trapped beneath the white heat of the sun. The hotel was full to overflowing, and only bribery had secured him the two rooms that his reservations had supposedly insured. And that was the least of his concerns.

A fence had been built from the hotel's "garden lodge" down to the beach. The fence was three meters tall and heavily built, with woven mats stapled over teak. Piat had walked all the way around the enclosure and he knew now what it meant.

It meant that the uncle, the target, and their entire entourage were completely walled off from unbelievers. They were due to arrive at Daniel Arap Moi International airport in six hours and then they would be driven by limousine over the potholed road from the airport to the hotel. They might be visible for a few moments in the lobby during check-in, just as they had been in Monaco. They might then be vulnerable, however briefly, except that Hackbutt and his priceless bird-oriented brain were still in transit and wouldn't arrive for a further five hours.

And then the whole entourage would slip through a heavily guarded door in the north end of the lobby and occupy the garden lodge, as secluded from the other guests as the occupants of a seraglio.

Piat sat in the sun, sipped coffee, and debated various tactics of desperation.

The lead idiot plan was to attempt the contact himself. Six weeks of Hackbutt on falconry had taught him enough to know that it was a sport at least as demanding as fishing, with its own cant and its own techniques, from the knots on a bird's jesses to the way a lure was tied and flung. He knew how men sounded when they attempted to pass as "anglers." He knew how he would sound if he tried to pass as a falconer. And he knew what Partlow would say if Saudi intelligence made him on his first pass.

So he considered trying to buy a hotel staffer. Really buy the guy—ten thousand US, cash and carry. Big money on the beach in Africa. But for what? And at what risk?

Bad idea. Really bad idea. Except that Piat was constitutionally unable to simply surrender to the inevitable and walk away. Rather than abandon the whole thing, he'd take some insane risk.

Which Partlow really ought to have known. Ought to have watched out for. The more Piat thought about it, the more he thought that he was being his own case officer, and that left him with no shoulder to lean on, much less cry on. He allowed himself a lot of traitorous thoughts on the beach at Nyali—for instance, he reminded himself that he'd already made a fuck of a lot of money off Partlow and there was no reason for him to give a shit whether they got the target or not.

Except that he was wired to focus on the needs of his agents and the realization of his operational objectives, and the wiring held. Despite the money and the risks and the fact that nothing about Saudi money or "possible al-Qaeda" terrorists stirred his blood by an iota.

So he sat in the shade of the palms and watched the fence and thought.

One of the few attractive bonuses associated with the hotel for a man in Piat's position was that the café had a plate glass window that looked in on the lobby. It was not an arrangement that Piat could recall encountering in other five-star hotels, but it made his second reconnaissance of the entourage a matter of alertness and discipline rather than the high-risk maneuver he'd had to use in Monaco. He sat at the coffee bar against the window and watched the guests arrive in neat pulses, to the tune of airline arrivals. His own familiarity with the evening's schedule allowed him to note them silently as they arrived—Air Kenya, Lufthansa, British Airways. Different looks, different luggage, different cabin crew.

The entourage arrived on Gulf Air, and their limousines beat the hotel's buses by quite a margin. Two of the security men—by now Piat thought that they were Saudi intelligence officers—came through the door as soon as the limos stopped outside and walked to the desk with a stack of passports. Both of them glanced over the lobby. They weren't thorough, and they weren't interested in the glass window to the café.

Behind them came a solid phalanx of women. They were expensively dressed, and just as in Monaco their laughter could be heard through the window and over the omnipresent air-conditioning. Piat recognized the first woman through the door from Monaco—she had Chanel sunglasses, dark red, perched atop her black hair, and she was over fifty, handsome in a craggy way, and loud. Imperious. It struck Piat that despite the differences in culture and race, Irene might very well become that woman in ten years.

Piat assumed she was the principal wife. The uncle had four of them, all political choices, all brought to him as tribal connections, according to Partlow's reports. Piat knew a lot more about the uncle this time, and he used his new knowledge to try and match names to faces.

Each of the other wives had her own retinue. The four of them did not congregate, didn't laugh together or share conveyance. They had probably come from the airport in separate cars. Piat watched them come in and wondered what reptilian security guru had decided that the uncle could use his wives as bait in the event of an ambush, because the great man himself came in last, flanked by the rest of his security. He came in fast, as if they actually feared a threat in the lobby of the Nyali. By the time he entered, the check-in was complete—the great man himself never stopped moving across the lobby, only pausing at the teak door to the garden lodge to acknowledge the bow of a senior manager, and then he was gone.

Piat's heart beat harder. He forced himself to sit still for five more minutes until the very last attendant had passed from the lobby to the garden lodge, until the red taillights of the five limos had faded into the warm African night. Then he walked out of the café to the lobby terrace and then down the steps and then all the way down the drive to the three-lane-wide main road, where a party of hotel staffers waited in uniformed dignity to be picked up by their buses and whisked away to their huts, far from the eyes of the tourists.

He was thorough, and he looked everywhere. He walked through the unlit darkness of the African night, located the tea shop where the matatu drivers waited for their fares and where he asked who had been at the airport, but he'd known the truth from the moment he had seen the uncle.

His target, his lawful prey, the object of his operation, Prince Bandar Muhad al-Hauq, had not arrived at the hotel.

After an hour in his room consuming alcohol, Piat remembered the truck. The anomalous truck, the one mentioned in Partlow's report that he'd read in Turin so many weeks before that it seemed like another lifetime.

Piat bludgeoned his memory, already a little the worse for wear from booze, until he decided that the truck was supposed to come from Avis.

Once he'd established this fact to his own satisfaction, he stopped drinking.

He hadn't planned to meet Hackbutt and Irene at the airport. He had planned to send Mike, the driver he'd acquired for the week with recommendations from Partlow, to collect them. But now he had reason to be at the airport, and the security concerns that had prevented him from wanting a public meeting with his agents were now running a poor second place to his need to reacquire his target.

By the time Hackbutt and Irene landed in Mombasa late that night, Piat had moved down the beach to the Serena. There was no longer any reason to expose himself, or them, to the Saudis at the Nyali. He arranged for his driver to meet them in arrivals carrying a sign with their names that Piat wrote out himself in heavy magic marker to avoid surprises.

Piat himself went to the Avis counter with a wad of twenty-dollar bills. It was, by a miracle, manned. The occupant was there only to service his reservations coming off the London flight, but he was happy to take some of Piat's money—more than he earned in a week's work—and doubly happy to tell Piat that the truck had been rented to an African with a Sudanese passport and a Saudi driver's license, but the prince had been two steps away, had provided the credit card, had been polite. The Sudanese was the driver of record. When the Avis counter rep had been paid his fifth US twenty-dollar bill, he copied the whole form for Piat on his office copier. The form contained a lot of useless detail—but it gave their destination.

Nguri Lodge, Tsavo East—a game park a couple of hours' drive inland.

"Sorry we're late, Jack," Hackbutt called around his wife. "We sat in Brussels forever." He looked like hell. "One of my birds got sick. Carla—a buzzard. You remember her?"

Piat gave them both a tolerant grin. "I'm just glad you're here. We've had a few changes in plans." He picked up one of Irene's bags. Mike picked up the rest.

Piat waved Mike over. "Can you get us a four-wheel drive, Mike? Since we're here at the airport?"

Mike was a tall, thin man with a deeply serious expression. His English was excellent, as was his Italian and German. Mike was a good driver, and he'd come recommended in a number of ways. He seemed to consider for several seconds. "You want to go on safari, bwana?"

Piat nodded. "I want to go out to Tsavo East tomorrow, Mike."

Mike looked at his watch. He looked at it a lot, as it was clearly one of his prize possessions, a big Seiko chronograph, the gift of a former customer. "Not tonight, bwana. I'll get it in the morning, okay?"

Piat knew that "getting it in the morning" meant that Mike would have to rise before four, to walk to the bus stop from which he could get to the airport—all so they could have a car by eight. And it was nearly midnight now.

Piat gave him a twenty off his roll. "That's okay, Mike. We'll want it early."

At eight in the morning, the three of them left their hotel with boxes of sandwiches and hats, binoculars and bug repellent and shorts and shoes—and all their luggage. Luck and telephone charm had got Piat a reservation at Nguri Lodge. It was a much smaller hotel with only fifty rooms. He was taking a number of chances. First, that his hunch was right and that the prince would go—virtually alone—to Tsavo. To this hotel. Second, that he would still be there. On and on—more risks than he wanted to face, but this was the stage of an operation where everything became one long set of risks—some avoidable, some not.

Hackbutt started the ride in the dumps but he recovered as soon as they had left the litter and pollution of Mombasa behind them and turned north into the countryside. Hackbutt kept referring to the road as a "country road," when in fact the two-lane tarmacked strip was the main highway from Mombasa to Nairobi. There weren't any support services on the highway except tea shops and petrol stops with ill-spelled signs and single windows for service. Towns were infrequent and looked like boom towns in America's old west—a single street of shops painted in garish colors with tall false fronts. Blink and you missed it—that was Mariakani.

They stopped for a late breakfast at a truck stop. Piat wolfed down two heavy cakes laden with sugar and drank a cup of excellent coffee. Kenya didn't have bad coffee anywhere. Irene watched him eat the cakes with something like horror, and Hackbutt raised his hands as if in surrender and ate from his hotel lunch.

It was noon by the time they reached the gates of the park. A line of matatus and four-wheel-drive vehicles was queued up fifty vehicles long. Mike sighed.

"Jesus," Piat said. He had been impatient since he had got in the car, various nightmare scenarios playing out in his head: the prince was at Tsavo for one night—was already back—would pass them on the road.

Mike shrugged. "You want me to get us in the gate, Bwana?"

"Sure."

"Cost you fifty dollars." Mike shrugged, as if the venality of his countrymen was a source of perpetual astonishment.

Piat counted out the money.

Mike drove past the waiting vehicles, pulled up into an apparently closed bay, and honked his horn.

The man from the first bay completed his altercation with a matatu driver and then crossed over. Other drivers in the line honked, then shouted. Matatu drivers tended to be free spirits, or even rebels—and they didn't like to wait. The gate guard shouted a phrase that was so heavily accented that Piat couldn't even recognize the language. Mike grunted and replied calmly in his own clearly accented Swahili. Piat's Swahili ran to about fifty words, and he understood nothing of Mike's rapid flow.

Then Mike handed over the fifty dollars.

The guard brightened up, took the money, and raised the barrier. "*Habari*!" he shouted at the occupants of the car. Irene waved. Piat called "*Habari ya leo*!" and they were through the gate. Mike gave Piat a big smile.

Piat clapped him on the shoulder. "Nicely done."

Mike nodded. "I told them you were all citizens, yes? And you say—*Habari ya leo*! Just like Ki-setla. Now the guard, he thinks maybe you are citizens."

Piat nodded. "Except that we bribed him."

Mike shook his head vehemently. "No bribe, bwana Jack. We paid for tickets. Perhaps we overpay or perhaps it slips his mind to give us change. Perhaps he doesn't *have* change. Perhaps he doesn't know the exchange rate for US dollars. But there was no bribe." He gave Piat a look that he knew well from the corridors of the Agency, a look that meant *Please cooperate with me in this little deception*.

Piat said, "My brochure says everyone has to show a passport to enter the park and put their name down on some sort of register."

Mike drove for a few minutes, avoiding the mammoth potholes that nearly filled the road and pointing out the first watering holes to the north of the track. His eyes were flicking between the horizon and the surface of the road. Finally he cracked a smile. "I think maybe you'd rather not show passport," he said.

Piat could see why Mike came with such recommendations.

Before they had driven for forty minutes they had seen two prides of lions and enough zebra to satisfy every tourist in Africa.

"I didn't know they were all so fat!" Irene shouted over the noise of the car. "I thought they were just fat in zoos!"

Piat turned around. "Zebras are the method nature uses to store protein for predators," he shouted.

Hackbutt thought it was funny, and Irene did not.

For an hour the terrain had grown more broken, the flat, dry savannah giving way to the first hills of the plateau. A small river crossed their track. The ford was flooded and deeply cut by heavy tires and tracks. Mike drove well north of the ford to spare his undercarriage. In the process they found a herd of more than a hundred elephants, and they stayed with the animals for another hour. Irene was delighted, alternatively speechless and then babbling with something like ecstasy—so many, all together, the old bulls and the young bulls and the matriarch and her daughters, eating and playing and walking.

Hackbutt was less interested in the elephants than in the birdlife. He kept up a running commentary on a migrant falcon he saw in a tree and couldn't identify, and he kept interrupting Mike's dissertation to Irene on elephant habits with questions about nesting birds.

"That looks like a grouse," he shouted.

Mike stopped the car.

"What do you call it? It looks like our grouse at home."

Mike glanced at the bird and said patiently, "We call it a sand grouse, bwana."

"But it's *different,*" Hackbutt said with a hint of his old whine. "It has a black face. Look at it, Jack. That's a big bird."

Piat, despite his impatience, hadn't torn his eyes off the elephants. He followed Hackbutt's eyes and saw nothing. Mike, old in the ways of tourists, pointed accurately at the bird in the dust. "Sure looks like a grouse," he said, since Hackbutt seemed to expect a reply.

"That's a good prey bird," Hackbutt said, as if satisfied that Africa had something to offer.

Mike got the vehicle across the river on a gravel shingle. His crossing didn't wet the hubcaps. "This car—not really tough enough for safari. No clearance. I have to drive carefully, okay?"

"Sure, Mike," said Piat. "How far to the lodge?"

"Not far, now."

They drove for another hour over hard-packed gravel and dusty rock with mesas rising in the distance, cone-shaped hills rising from the flat plain. Piat didn't know whether Mike was lost or taking great care with his driving because of the car, a small Suzuki, and while he was considering the possibility of asking outright, Mike's shoulders relaxed and they bounced down a steep incline and arrived on a road.

"Not far now," Mike said again.

Ten minutes later, they rounded the spur of a low mesa to see a much greater mound rising from an alien landscape studded with bigger cone-shaped hills, as if the anthills of the open plain had grown to fill the horizon. The man-made shapes of the lodge hotel and the white walls of its compound contrasted with the smooth organic shapes of the biggest mesa and the table-flat plain at its base. Two small lakes filled the near end of the plain, surrounded by lush green grass—and herds of zebra and antelope.

High above, two vultures circled, but even they were not as high as the top of the mesa that held the lodge. And above them, turning circles, there waited another predator.

"He's here!" Hackbutt shouted. He had his head out the window.

Piat glanced back at Hackbutt and then out his passenger window and up into the sky. "Who's here, Digger?"

"The prince!" Hackbutt shouted. "Can't you see his bird?"

Irene pulled him back into the car. The shoulder of the great mesa now cut off the view. The car was toiling up the switchbacks to the lodge. "You can't tell that's his bird, silly man."

Hackbutt shook his head. "I can."

Piat asked, "How?"

Hackbutt shrugged. "Like you can tell someone you know way off on the hillside. Hard to say. Big bird, not a vulture, keeping station over the mountain? That's his bird. Okay? Want to make a bet? That's the big red-tail he had in Monaco."

Piat wanted to ruffle his hair. "No bet, Digger. I hope you're right."

"I am," Hackbutt said.

He was.

Irene decided to have a bath. Their rooms were festooned with signs recommending caution in water use, and Irene allowed as she would accept a quick shower.

Piat and Hackbutt hurried to the bar.

From the bar, they could see the prince and his tall black falconer standing alone at the edge of the escarpment. A few tourists on the bar's deck were already watching them. Hackbutt and Piat bought drinks and joined them.

Hackbutt turned to a small man who was watching the falconers through a pair of low-light binoculars—very expensive optics indeed. Hackbutt waited until the man took the glasses from his eyes.

"What prey is he finding?" Hackbutt asked.

The man looked at Hackbutt as if he had spoken a foreign language. "Huh?" he said.

"Has the bird killed?" Hackbutt asked.

Piat felt as if he were watching a sitcom. He was glad—very glad—that Hackbutt was bold enough to approach a stranger and ask a question, but he could see that Hackbutt, the same old Hackbutt, seemed to think that every onlooker would share his knowledge and passion for falconry. Why not?

"I should hope not," said the man with the expensive optics. "This is a game park. It's not here to allow the slaughter of wild things."

That's what you think, bud, Piat thought. The report had said that the uncle would be hunting here. Hunting what—elephants, perhaps? It had certainly happened before. But even Piat, who was against such shenanigans, couldn't see that a single red tailed hawk, regardless of size, could do a lot of damage to a park the size of Wales.

Hackbutt chuckled. "I can see you aren't a falconer," he said. "He's got the bird off the fist—that means she's free to hunt. What she makes of all this—the height, the wind, the strange animals—I don't know. But when she's hungry enough, she'll kill, even if it's only a mouse."

"Shouldn't be allowed," grumbled the man, whom Piat now had pegged as a birder.

In fact, Piat was surprised to see the bird hunting so publicly. On the other hand, that's just what the prince's falconer had done in Monaco. Piat wondered if this was a character thing—if the prince liked to make these kills in public. A demonstration? A gesture of contempt? Or perhaps he was so much a prince that it never occurred to him to do otherwise?

The rich are not like you and me. That wasn't Shakespeare, but somebody had written it, and it stuck in his head all evening as they watched the bird hover and land on her master's fist, go aloft and land again, all without a kill.

"She doesn't really know where she is," Hackbutt murmured. "She doesn't like it here. The falconer—the black guy—he gets it. He's trying to gentle her. And I think he wants to feed her. The prince isn't having it."

Piat sipped his scotch. "What would you do?"

Hackbutt shrugged. "I'd give her a feed and let her settle for a day. She's going to spook at this rate. The falconer knows it, too."

Eventually the falconer said something. He must have been speaking strongly, because for the first time in an hour the prince looked at him while he spoke. Then the prince nodded, turned on his heel, and walked back up the brick walk to the bar.

Piat's heart began to beat faster. He touched Hackbutt's elbow.

The prince entered the bar and glanced at the group of people watching his bird, his face expressionless.

Piat willed Hackbutt to move. The prince—*the target*—was ten feet away, and his eyes flicked over Piat. Piat stood immobile, like a hare on a hillside, hoping that the predator would not notice him.

Hackbutt's attention was still on the bird. Piat had time to think, *He's going to blow it,* and then the prince walked through the bar and into the lodge.

Neither Piat nor Hackbutt saw him again that night.

"Digger—why the hell didn't you say something?" Piat paused in his pacing.

Hackbutt was peering through the drapes of Piat's room at the watering holes, now deep in shadow.

"Say what?" Hackbutt muttered. "There are a lot more birds here than I first thought. Look at those vultures! They're huge!"

"Digger," Piat said softly. He couldn't let himself be angry. "Digger, why are we here?"

Hackbutt rubbed his jaw with his right hand. He avoided Piat's eye like a kid caught out by a teacher. "Uhh—to contact the Arab guy. Right?"

Piat nodded and sat heavily on the bed. "You watched him for an hour. You had all kinds of comments to make about his falconry and his bird. How hard would it have been to approach him? Say something like—hey, your bird's nervous, isn't she? Something like that. Right?"

Hackbutt leaned against the window, the red light spilling across his face and making him look very young. "I'd hate it if somebody said something like that to me," he said. "I mean—I'd be criticizing him. He probably knows the bird is nervous. Why tell him that? He's got his own ways. I can see that."

Piat was tired, and the air-conditioning was giving him a chill, and he'd already had too much to drink and maybe too much of Hackbutt. He wanted to put his head in his hands. "Digger—we're here to contact the guy. You've got to find a way to pull the trigger."

Hackbutt nodded. "Not a criticism, though. It's got to come naturally."

Piat shook his head. "It's never natural. It isn't natural to approach a stranger when you do it from the most innocent of motives. There won't *be* a natural moment. This is a powerful man who we'll hardly ever get to see, much less talk to. We'll be lucky if we get another shot at him at all. He was *alone* in the bar. No security, no falconer, just him, standing ten feet away!"

"Why didn't *you* do it?" Hackbutt said. It was real curiosity, not the Hackbutt nerd whine. "You're so much better than me. I used to watch you in Jakarta—girls, guys—they *want* to talk to you. Even Irene—" Hackbutt trailed off.

Piat got a jolt from his adrenal gland at Irene's name, but he stuck to his subject. "Digger—listen, man. Listen up, as they say on sports teams. *You* have to do this one. Just you. I shouldn't even be standing near you. I look like what I am—a spy. I know a little about falcons and a lot about people and I'm smooth. Smooth will not cut it with this guy. You aren't smooth—but man, you love your birds. So does he. That can't be faked, Digger. It's got to be real."

Hackbutt nodded. "I guess I could go to his room and ask to help with his bird," he said.

Piat shook his head. "Too abrupt. It's a subtle thing—as natural as you can make it."

Hackbutt looked distraught. "I blew it. I could have just asked if she was off her feed. Just like that." Hackbutt sagged. "I didn't even think about it. I was worried about the bird. If they keep flying her, she's going to bolt. And because we're so high, she'll be able to go a long way."

"What do you mean, bolt?"

"You know what it's like to lose a bird. She flies too far from you, and then she can't see you, and bang—she's gone. Some guys use radio collars."

"I suspect the prince is too traditional for radio collars." Piat rubbed his forehead. "Okay, tomorrow is another day and all that. I'm wasted."

"I need to call Annie. I have to know that Carla is better." Hackbutt was back to looking out the window.

"Digger." Piat caught himself on the edge of doing something stupid, like yelling. "Digger, we're operational." Even as he said it, he thought—fuck it, Digger's not in any cover here. Why can't he call home? "Okay," he said. "Call Annie. Do it soon. Then get some rest."

Hackbutt said, "Thanks." He grinned. "Not sure why I need your permission—but there we go." He let the drape slide shut. "I wonder where they'll go tomorrow?" he asked. "They're just too high up here. They need to get down on the plain."

"Probably too dangerous. The park might not let that happen."

Hackbutt raised an eyebrow, no longer the guilty schoolboy, now the submarine captain. "You say these guys can bribe the park to let them hunt elephants, but they can't get permission to do a little falconry down on the plain?"

Piat nodded slowly. "Touché, Digger. That's good thinking."

Hackbutt went to the door. "I'm going to go find Irene." He paused. "Do you want to eat with us?"

Piat shook his head. "Better if we don't spend too much time together in public. Besides, I'm going to go find Mike."

Hackbutt reached out and touched Piat's arm. "Sorry, Jack. I know this means a lot to you."

When he was gone, Piat spent a moment considering that last sentence. *He's doing this for me.* Despite the money and Irene's installation and another month with Bella, Hackbutt was doing the whole thing for him. Piat didn't do guilt most of the time, but just then, with the red sun light bleeding all over his room and too much scotch in his system, Piat glanced in the mirror and didn't like what he saw.

It's a nasty business, boys. Some pompous snot had said that at his graduation from the Ranch.

Piat went out to find Mike.

The three shacks had lights on and the front door open. *Of course,* Piat thought, *the drivers don't get air-conditioning.* Piat walked over to the middle hut.

"Mike?" he called out.

Mike appeared behind the door. "Bwana?" He looked past Piat. "Is there a problem?"

Piat shook his head. "*Hakuna matata,* buddy. No problems. I need a favor."

Mike made no move to let him in. "Sure," he said. His tone was flat. *I'm off hours and this better be good.*

A female voice called something from the kerosene-lit darkness behind Mike. And a laugh.

Piat felt like a fool. "Sorry, bud. I'll come back later." He took a step away from the door.

Mike shook his head. "No—sure, I can help you. You shouldn't be here. If you need me, you can just call the desk, right?"

Down on the plain, a hyena howled. The woman's voice laughed again.

"This is a special thing." Piat hoped that sounded right, that Mike got the nature of the call.

"Sure," Mike said. "Sure. Give me ten minutes, okay, boss? I'll meet you at the car."

Piat passed the ten minutes reviewing all the bad operational decisions he'd made, first on the one op, then over the course of his career. Mike was a driver—a paid hireling, even if he did come recommended by Partlow. Piat was about to use him operationally, a big no-no. Like kissing one of your agents, or two-timing another agent—hell, it was a pretty long list, and involving Mike didn't seem the worst of it.

"Sorry, boss." Mike materialized by the driver door. His shirt was ironed and it glowed in the late evening light.

"No, I'm sorry, Mike. I didn't mean to haul you out of your rack time (and your bedmate). And I don't like to be called bwana, or boss. Just Jack."

Mike stood a good four inches taller than Piat. He smiled, a flash of white teeth. "Sure, bwana," he said.

Piat had heard special forces guys in Afghanistan use ranks as an insult (Right away, *Captain*.) Mike was giving him the gears.

Whatever. "Mike, I need to know where the prince is going to hunt tomorrow. Can you find that out?"

Mike glanced at his watch. "Sure, Jack."

Piat peered through the sudden darkness at him, looking for hidden meaning. "Sure, as in, *sure*? Or sure as in, I want to get back to bed?"

Mike laughed. "*Hakuna matata*, Jack. Everybody back here knows what everybody does." He laughed.

Piat had expected that was the case. And he knew what that implied for his own operational security.

But what the hell. "I need to—stay close—not too close. Tomorrow."

Mike slapped the car for emphasis. "Sure. Sure. No problem. I come to your room—maybe an hour? I'll know then. Okay?"

"Sure," said Piat.

Mike was as good as his word. "I know where they'll go. It's close—maybe ten miles. One of the rangers—KWS guys, right?—says they go to hunt with the bird, yes? Where the people in the lodge can't watch. They're taking food, flasks of coffee—big day. Out all day. Easy to find. Maybe with some money, easier to find."

Piat waved Mike into a chair, poured him a scotch. Mike made a curiously British gesture—on taking the glass, he raised it in the air as if toasting his host.

"How much money?" Piat had a fair amount, but he'd never tried to bribe a Kenya Wildlife Service ranger before.

"Fifty dollars," Mike said.

Piat paid him fifty and another fifty. "That's for you and the girl you left behind."

Mike slammed back the rest of his scotch. "Sure," he said.

"There is one problem. Okay? We're supposed to stay on the roads. Everybody is. We lose our park license if we go off the roads. Okay? And—bwana—Jack—it is sometimes no picnic, yes? Off the roads?"

Piat took a drink. He wished that Mike were an expert falconer—he was clearly a man who thought things through. "So what do we do?"

"Rent one of the lodge trucks, so we can drive where we want. That Suzuki we have from Mombasa is useless out here. Okay? And let me get a ranger to say we can drive around. Cost more money—but they hate the Arab guy. You know?"

"I don't know." Piat leaned forward. "Tell me."

"All the rangers—all used to be poachers, right? And when KWS gets them, they train them to protect the animals. Right? Sure. And when rich Arabs come to kill the animals, rangers get to be the guides. Right? Sure." Mike sounded increasingly vehement. It was obviously a subject about which he felt strongly.

Piat counted two hundred dollars from his dwindling supply of US twenties. "That enough?"

Mike made the money vanish. "More than enough," he said, and downed his second drink. "You don't want this Arab guy to know we're out there, right—Jack?"

"Right."

Mike nodded, straightened his neat white safari shirt in the mirror and smiled at his own reflection. "We should leave late. Okay? Ten o'clock. Maybe you want to talk-talk this Arab guy?"

Piat tossed his operational security over the cliff. "Yeah, maybe. If it happens that way."

"Sure," said Mike. He smiled.

"You're in charge," said Piat. He had just felt the first cool breeze of a wind change. Luck. Operational daring.

"Sure."

* * *

Al Craik had got the report he had asked for from Mrs Stillman and Sergeant Swaricki. The report on Perpetual Justice task numbers was short: they had found eleven listings under the suspect number, all buttoned up tight with the Perpetual Justice code classification. The system wouldn't kick out data the other way, however: going in with "Perpetual Justice" produced no hits, so if there were more operations under it—and he was sure there were—they were, in Abe's words, buried under the flag.

Mrs Stillman's report on Muhad al-Hauq, the target of Partlow's operation, was fuller. It told him a lot he didn't find useful (al-Hauq had three wives and seven children; he swam in a saltwater pool every morning; he wrote poetry) but several things he did: Muhad al-Hauq was the nephew of the governor of Saudi Arabia's Eastern Province. His uncle was said to be both lazy and ignorant, and the nephew was effectively the region's governor. The Eastern Province was the poorest in Saudi Arabia; its people were mostly Shiites (which might explain why they were kept in poverty); but it was the location of most of Saudi Arabia's oil. It bordered the Persian Gulf, a bit of the Emirates, Kuwait, and Iraq.

Muhad al-Hauq was a devout Sunni but not necessarily (the sources weren't sure) a dedicated Wahhabist. He was believed to support financially jihadists going into Iraq, but the little that was known of him suggested that he wanted to get an invader out of an Arab state, not that he was either in favor of restoring Saddam or (virtually the opposite case, so weak was the intelligence on him) of helping al-Qaeda. His alleged support for al-Qaeda was based on a CIA list put together in 1997; an intelligence summary of pre-Nine-Eleven 2001 that, if read carefully, used the word "assumed," meaning that the evidence wasn't there; and the contact report that had started Alan down this trail.

The information made him wonder why Clyde Partlow

thought that al-Hauq was a good target—and for what. The use of falconry as a contact suggested recruitment. Would a devout Sunni who funded Iraqi jihadists be a likely recruit, a likely agent? Or was Partlow cynically using the name and the alleged al-Qaeda link as a way of floating an operation, fulfilling a task, justifying an appropriation?

Or did Partlow have something else in mind?

That question raised the further question of what you might have in mind for the effective governor of the Eastern Province. What might you do in a region that had most of Saudi Arabia's oil, and on the other side of whose border stood thousands of American troops?

Or, perhaps, what might you do there without him?

Irene made no protest at staying behind at the game lodge. One part of Africa was as irritating to her as another: where she wanted to be was in her studio.

At ten a.m., Hackbutt and Piat were in a white Land Rover Defender, a vehicle so old the Toyota Land Cruisers parked on either side dwarfed it. It had the green shield of the lodge on its doors and a heavy luggage rack on the roof. Piat, dressed in khaki shorts and a khaki shirt, felt as if he were playing a part in a movie. Like Monaco.

Hackbutt had acquired a pair of pants whose legs zipped off—shorts, trousers, and shorts again by turns as the weather changed. He loved them and couldn't stop talking about them.

Mike felt much the same way about the Land Rover. "This is a car to drive in Africa," he said. He enumerated its features, most of which amounted to a lack of gadgets and robust engineering.

They drove down the mesa from the lodge, took the main road north, and drove ten miles before Mike turned off the road across the plain.

"I thought we were only going a few miles," Piat said.

Mike flashed him a smile. 'I promised the ranger that we wouldn't be seen from the lodge. And you don't want the Arab guy to see you, right?"

Piat thought, not for the first or last time, that Mike knew a good deal more than he ought. "No, Mike, I don't."

"So we go around," Mike said, one hand on the wheel and the other tracing a wide arc on the map in his lap.

"Do you have a compass?" Piat asked.

Mike shook his head. Piat produced one out of his bag, but Mike shrugged it off.

Away from the water holes, the plain was a desert. There wasn't an animal to be seen, and the sun seemed to come through the car's white roof to grill them inside. Below his shorts, Piat's knees stuck to the seat every time he tried to change position. He was sweating sitting still.

"There's another grouse!" called Hackbutt. "That's what he ought to be hunting."

"Probably is," Piat said.

Mike had slowed while he looked at the map and then swiveled his head around, comparing it with the big mesas in the middle distance. He didn't seem to like to stop the car. Then he drove on a distance, past a dry water hole and a deep wadi, and then he slowed to a crawl again and checked his map.

"Okay, Jack," Mike said. "See this ridge? See the anthills there—see them? Just past that. They'll be there."

There was a ridge that rose eighty meters tall, rich dark red soil and sand and rock. A climber's paradise. Piat said "Over the ridge?"

Mike nodded. "There's a mound—not so tall. This wadi has water in it. So there will be animals. That's where he will have lunch and fly his bird. And Jack—the talk at the lodge is that tomorrow the other Arab comes."

"Shit," said Piat, who knew that the uncle's arrival meant

more security and less opportunity. He looked up the ridge. "We'll be pretty naked out there."

"Sure, Jack."

Hackbutt was restless. "What are we doing?"

Piat looked up the ridge, popped his door, and pulled out his binoculars. "We're going to climb that ridge."

Hackbutt pursed his lips and nodded. "Okay! Then what?"

Piat looked at Hackbutt. "We wait until we get lucky." *Or we try something desperate.*

Despite its forbidding appearance, the ridge was an easy climb. It was so easy that Piat narrowly avoided crossing the central contour line into full view of the party at the wadi on the far side. He and Hackbutt found a pair of rocks that looked like rubble from a glacier (unlikely at the top of a mesa in Africa) and hunkered down with their binoculars.

The prince, his falconer, and two men with rifles were on a twenty-meter-tall mound in the valley below, the men with rifles squatting in the shade of rocks. The prince and the falconer stood under the full weight of the sun. The bird had the only shade on the mound, a parasol set up just for him. Beyond, in the shade of the big trees on the wadi, were three vehicles: a gleaming white Toyota Land Cruiser, a dingy green Land Rover with KWS markings, and a small rental truck. *There's the truck,* Piat thought.

"They still haven't fed him," Hackbutt said. "He must intend to try him on something really big. A vulture? No, that's silly. Maybe a mammal? I've heard Arabs fly falcons at ground game."

"Like antelope?" Piat could see a handful of wary animals moving through the thorn trees to the covered water of the wadi at the base of an enormous, castle-shaped baobab tree.

Hackbutt took the binoculars from his eyes with weary patience. "Give me a break, Jack; you know better than that. That's a big red-tail, but he can't take an antelope. He wouldn't know what the hell to do with it." Hackbutt put the binoculars back up to his eyes. "Bella wouldn't know what to do with an antelope."

Piat went back to staring through his own binoculars. "They have some small antelope here. Dik-diks."

After fifteen minutes of watching the prince eat his lunch, Hackbutt sat back. "So—now what?"

Piat continued to watch. "We wait."

"What are we waiting for?"

Piat said, "Something. I don't know what. We're as close as I dare get. If we don't get lucky, we'll just drive up and 'encounter' them. Hey—Digger—don't wave your binocs around. Somebody might see the dazzle off the lens."

"Pretty boring, if you ask me. He's not even flying his bird."

"What does that tell you?" Piat asked.

"He's waiting for something. He's probably waiting for a particular prey. Maybe even your miniature antelope."

Piat raised his glasses and peered off into the middle distance. "I don't know anything about big-game hunting in Africa," he said. "Fuck, I wish I knew something about all this. What's he waiting for?" Piat changed position, restless, angry at his own shortcomings. "Digger, what's he doing?"

"Eating lunch. Not a bad idea, if you ask me." Hackbutt started to use his binoculars to watch birds in the valley behind them. "I really like these," Hackbutt said. "Better than my glasses at home. Can I keep them when we're done?"

Piat peeked at the party below them. Despite the cover of the rocks and anthills, he felt exposed, and had a presentiment of doom. His whole idea was based on Hackbutt's prediction that the prince would lose his bird. In the hot light of day, it was revealed as a stupid idea.

Piat changed position four times in an hour. The prince and the falconer continued to eat. Then they drank tea from a thermos. They stroked the bird and watched the plain at their feet and were in turn watched.

Piat fidgeted and tried not to infect Hackbutt with his anxiety. He felt less and less confident in his luck.

"How about some lunch?" Hackbutt whispered.

Piat sent Hackbutt down to the car and he returned with their lunches. They retreated partway down the ridge and ate them. Piat drank off two bottles of water in a few seconds, and climbed across the scree to find a place to take a piss. His watch said that it was a quarter to three in the afternoon. It was a magnificent day with high, clear skies. He was starting to think about high-risk approaches to the prince. He had to set a time—five o'clock sounded about right. If they hadn't got lucky by five—or maybe they should just drive home and lurk in the bar. Maybe the prince would fly the bird at the hotel at dusk.

So many intangibles. So many opportunities to make the wrong guess.

Sound carried thinly from the valley on the other side of the ridge. Clear as a bell on Sunday morning came the cry of a hawk, and voices—shouting. Piat froze in mid-thought and placed his hand on Hackbutt's shoulder.

More shouting. Another hawk cry.

Piat climbed back to his rocks and lay full length on the sandy scree. As soon as he put the binoculars to his eyes, he saw that everything had changed while they ate.

The prince was still on the mound, his gestures dramatic. He was shouting orders. The black falconer was down in the wadi.

The bird was not under the parasol.

The two game rangers were also down in the wadi. One

of them was sitting on a branch of the baobab tree. The other was climbing the far bank.

Hackbutt slid up to his elbow and pulled out his own binoculars.

"I knew it!" he said with the satisfaction of seeing someone else fail—not an attractive trait, but one Piat could forgive. "They lost her. They got her too hungry and they flew her from that mound and she's treed."

Piat started sweeping the tree line with his glasses. "If we can find her before they do—"

Hackbutt was looking up. "They think she's in the trees by the wadi." After a minute he said, "They're probably right. She's not up high and she's not going to go out on the plain. See the falconer? He's making noise—trying to flush her out of the trees. I guess he's trying to get the guides to help."

The prince was standing alone on the mound, arms crossed. The falconer stopped shouting and waving his arms and came up the mound, climbing quickly. He asked a question, pointing to the trees. The prince hit him across the face, a single blow, and after a second elapsed, the sound carried to them like the breaking of a twig.

The falconer continued asking, apparently indifferent to the blow.

"I don't think I like that guy," Hackbutt said. Hackbutt's views of the world were often reduced to the simplicity of adolescent black and white. His moral disapproval was reduced to dislike.

Piat had learned to appreciate Hackbutt's apparent simplicity.

"I don't like him much either," Piat said. "If we went down there, could we help him recover the bird?"

Hackbutt nodded. "Sure. Those two goons are useless. A couple of falconers to help him and we can lure the bird down in no time." Hackbutt was assured. His body inclined to the situation below like a pointer's at a pheasant.

Piat nodded. "Okay. Let's go." *Win or lose, this is the throw,* he thought.

As they climbed down, Hackbutt asked, "What do we tell them about why we're here?"

Piat had thought about that all morning. "Nothing," he said. "They won't ask, at least now. Later, we make it sound like chance. Listen—" as they climbed into their truck, "just let Mike handle the first contact. He'll talk to their driver—right? Until then, we act like we don't know what's wrong."

Hackbutt looked at him wryly. "I think that's pretty obvious, Jack. We certainly don't want them to know we were watching them."

Piat sighed inwardly. Then he crossed another line of the hundreds he had crossed in making this operation. "Mike?"

Mike smiled in the rearview mirror. "Ya, Jack?"

"Play it cool with the drivers, Mike. Okay? Ask if something's wrong. Get *them* to tell *you.*"

Mike's answering nod and smile were eloquent of just how much Mike understood of what was going on. The book said that unless Mike was a recruited agent, Piat couldn't use him like this, giving specific direction on operational issues. Piat just chucked the book out the window.

Piat picked up a book on the birdlife of Tsavo and pretended to read. In fact, he could barely breathe.

Three minutes later, Mike pulled the Land Rover up next to a gleaming Toyota Land Cruiser and called out to the driver in Swahili.

The driver laughed and gesticulated at the patch of trees by the water. Mike handed him a cigarette—an American Marlboro—and the driver called to the truck. The driver from the truck came trotting up to Mike's window but stopped when a shout came from the trees. He shouted back—Piat caught the verb "take"—*nataka* something something. Mike lit a cigarette and tossed it to the newcomer, who caught it and put it in his mouth. He pointed down the wadi and laughed and talked, and Mike laughed with him.

Piat leaned forward. "What's happening, Mike?"

Mike turned around. "Bwana, the drivers work for a man who has a special license to hunt. He's hunting with a bird. The bird has become lost."

Piat thought that Mike was being a little too thorough, like all newcomers to deception. Nonetheless, he was effective. "Tell them one of your passengers is a falconer—a hunter with birds. Ask them if they need help." Piat knew that the drivers wouldn't take it on their own authority to agree or disagree. In fact, he was counting on it.

Too much time was passing. This had to be *just right.*

Both men listened to Mike and both started talking. To Piat, they seemed to talk for a long time. Then the second man, the truck driver, pinched out his cigarette and tucked it behind his ear and ran off toward the wadi. A dusty African with a rifle emerged immediately and held his hand up, palm outward—stop.

This is not the way this is supposed to go.

"What's he saying?" Piat asked.

Mike ignored him. He shouted to the man with the rifle, who cupped his ear to listen. That was the action that gave him away—it was an elaborate pantomime. Piat saw through it in a second and hoped that the prince was not so perceptive. Mike and the truck driver had arranged it.

For fifty dollars.

Mike smiled at him. "He says a bird has been lost—a valuable bird. He asks us to help." His face said, *Isn't this what you wanted?*

Piat wanted to hug him. Instead, he slapped Hackbutt on the thigh. "Hey, let's go help find this bird."

Hackbutt was out of the car as fast as Piat. Piat's knees were weak and his heart was pounding.

They jogged to the edge of the wadi. Piat looked for the bird, but Hackbutt located the slim shape of the prince's falconer and called out.

"Hallo there!" Hackbutt called. "Your driver says you've lost a bird!"

It was remarkable. Digger had just spoken *exactly* the right line.

The slim black man in the wadi glanced over his shoulder—toward the prince still standing on the mound, invisible to Piat. And of course Piat wasn't supposed to know he was there.

Then the black falconer made up his mind—a balance of things that would anger his master, Piat suspected. His English, when he called, was heavily accented but fluent. "Please move quietly!" he called. He sounded more Indian than African.

Hackbutt slid down the slope of the wadi and moved carefully to the falconer's side. Piat took his time. It was now all down to Hackbutt, and Piat wanted Hackbutt to know it.

Hackbutt joined the other falconer, and Piat could see them both pointing up into the branches of the baobab tree. The prince's falconer was speaking quickly, and Hackbutt was nodding.

Piat watched the tree.

The prince's falconer went up the wadi at a trot, headed toward the mound, leaving Hackbutt standing at the base of the tree, watching it. He backed away slowly, still looking up, almost tripping over a rock and never taking his eyes off the tree.

Piat, his attention divided three ways—Hackbutt, the African falconer, the tree—yet caught a flicker of pale movement in the tree, close to the inverted cone of the trunk. And another. He even recognized the motion, nearly identical to Bella's shows of anger and bafflement.

In a low voice, he called, "Digger?" No response. He didn't want to take his eyes off the bird. "Digger?"

"I hear you, Jack." Hackbutt was at his elbow, his binoculars on the tree. "Good eyes, Jack."

"She's mad."

"He, I think. Yes. Mad as hell. Going to be quite a piece of work to get him down." Hackbutt sounded pleased with himself and the challenge. Piat was reminded of Hackbutt on the birds in Scotland. And Mike, talking to the other drivers.

"What do you want me to do?" Piat asked.

Hackbutt kept his binoculars on the bird. "Clear the wadi, Jack. Get the drivers and the rangers back by the vehicles."

"Where's the prince's man?"

"He went for his bag. Fancy coming down here without it. I think he's scared, Jack."

Piat nodded, which, of course, Hackbutt couldn't see. "Okay, Digger," he said, almost whispering. "Clear the wadi. Anything else?"

Hackbutt smiled beneath the binoculars. "No. I'll take it from here." That, too, was like Hackbutt with his birds, a sudden, surprising authority.

Piat cleared the wadi with the help of Mike's voice and Mike's language. Then he confined his activities to handing out cigarettes and watching Hackbutt and the prince's falconer work. They laid out a long lure and cast it, the falconer whirling it over his head like a sling and then letting it travel until the chunk of meat at the end hit the dust of the wadi floor. The first three casts, the bird shifted his weight and opened his wings, clearly interested, but anger and bewilderment overcame hunger and training, and he stayed in his tree.

Piat tried to get a glimpse of the man on the mound. He couldn't see him, no matter how he shifted his position.

When Piat returned his attention to the wadi, Hackbutt had the lure. He spun it through the air differently, slowly, the meat at the end making a low whirring noise as it passed through the long circle above his head. Twice, Hackbutt managed to entangle it in thorn trees. The third try, Hackbutt whirled it with the meat almost on the ground.

The bird shifted his weight, then shifted again, leaned out and gave a low cry of frustration.

Hackbutt kept whirling the lure. He didn't let it touch the ground. He didn't speed or slow his motion. After a minute, Piat wondered how long he could keep it up.

After five minutes, he wondered how strong Hackbutt was. The bird in the tree was in constant motion now, walking back and forth on his branch, spreading his wings and then furling them, over and over.

Then Piat saw the prince. He came slowly into the wadi, picking his way down the opposite slope, using cover to hide him from the bird. He moved like an athlete.

Hackbutt let a little more cord out on the lure and spun it even more slowly, changing his slow circle to an oval so that the chunk of meat on the end almost stopped for a heartbeat at the apex of the oval. And then, as the prince emerged from behind his cover, Hackbutt reversed his lure, a move like a fly-cast with a heavy rod, so that the lure turned over in the air and reversed direction—

The bird leaped into the air and rolled under a branch, feet already extended for the strike—

Hackbutt pulled the lure like a fisherman retrieving a cast, so that the lure changed direction again and fell to the ground almost at his feet—

The bird lunged, turned on a wingtip and struck the lure, two feet from Hackbutt's leg—

The prince's falconer knelt fluidly, passed his hand under the bird's feet and seized her jesses and the lure in one motion and rose with the bird captive on his fist and yet feeding on the meat. The bird glared around, once, and then put his head down and started to eat.

The prince, now standing behind his falconer, gave him a powerful slap on the back. He was smiling. He said something with authority in Arabic. Piat's Arabic had never been that good, but the tone was one of gentle malice. Like *You've ruined my day's hunting. But at least you got the bird back.* Something like that.

Before Piat had climbed down the wadi to congratulate them, the prince had asked Hackbutt to dinner.

"You sure know some swell places," Craik said. The coffee house was in Adams Morgan, trendy but grungy, hints of iconic hippiedom in the waitress's unbound breasts and flowered, floor-length skirt. Next door was a defunct African restaurant, its exterior now decorated with panhandlers.

"Old guys get around." Peretz had been there ahead of him, was looking down into a cup with a lot of froth. "I think my coffee has hydrophobia."

Alan let himself into a chair and said, "We used to come up here for Ethiopian food."

"A lot of Ethiopians went home when their war ended. That's what it means to be the world's superpower—other people get killed and we get ethnic restaurants. I think we have a lot of Iraqi food in our future."

Craik got himself a double espresso and a muffin that was big enough to feed a family of four. It was mid-morning; he'd missed breakfast, what the hell. Back at the table, he said, "I hope there's a reason why we're meeting here."

"You don't like my favorite coffee shop? Shame on you." Abe tried a little of the froth on a spoon, made a face. "You look bad. What's up?"

Craik shrugged. "Little business meeting with my boss this afternoon." He shook his head. "I need his okay on this stuff I talked to you about. Putting my nose in." He shrugged again. "Fuck him."

Peretz started to say something and then seemed to decide it was better to change the subject. "I was right about Leah."

Alan looked his question.

Peretz sniffed his fingers. "I have new neighbors."

"That's nice."

"They are, in fact. Really nice. A couple, my age. Funny coincidence, they're liberal, reformed Jews. What a nice fit."

"You don't think it's a coincidence."

"They want to go to Israel. They've never been to Israel, they say. Wouldn't I like to go with them? Safety in numbers. We can be liberal and reformed together." He pushed the coffee aside and took a small piece of Alan's muffin. "I sent a reply to Leah's email. I put it off and put it off. I was scared, scared of what I'd find. It took me three weeks to get up my courage. Then I had to be half sloshed. I just said I was glad I'd heard from her and I loved her."

"And?"

Peretz's voice got angry. "Comes back an answer. 'plzplz cum 2 c me luv luv.' Broke my heart." He looked away, blinked, sniffed his fingers. "Then my new neighbors showed up." He tightened his mouth and looked off through the shop's window at the grubby street. "We eat dinner together sometimes."

"You think they're a plant?"

"Do cows give milk?"

"Abe, you don't *know* that."

Peretz snorted. "I told one of my buds from the Bureau; he checked them out. In fact, they've been to Israel nine times. They're nice people, but they're lying to me." He shifted gears. "Enough about me. Let's talk about what I'm doing for you." He opened the small paper napkin that had come with his coffee. "I've been looking into the OIA–Force for Freedom–K Street circle jerk. It's practically neoclassical, it's so symmetrical." With a felt-tipped pen, he drew a circle. "You want to hear this?"

"All ears."

Peretz made a mark on the circle. "Hooper and Gretz. Lobbying firm. Two OIA people signed on with them. One of their clients is—" he made another mark—"the Petroleum Education Council. OIA's McKinnon went there as a biggie, you remember." He blacked in an arrowhead pointing at Hooper and Gretz, then drew another arrowhead pointing the other way. "Part of lobbying these days is buying Congress members with what are wink-wink, nudge-nudge called political contributions." He made another mark on the circle. "Congressman Kwalik, Ohio. Got sixty thou from the Petroleum Education Council. Two OIA people went to him as staffers, you'll recall."

"I've seen Kwalik at DIA. He's on the House intelligence committee, so maybe it's legit."

"Probably checking to see that everybody has enough rubber bands. Our elected representatives never sleep." He made another mark on the circle. "Force for Freedom is also a Hooper and Gretz client." He drew more arrowheads. He drew another arrowhead pointing at Kwalik. "Force for Freedom gave Kwalik eighty thousand of its hard-earned dollars over the last two years." Peretz looked at his diagram, improved a couple of arrowheads, put in dollar signs in several places. "A cynic would say it works this way: lobbyists work on congressmen to get what their clients want, and the clients kick in the bucks to the congressmen to make sure it happens. The congressmen use their oversight to forward the client's agenda.

The agencies that actually get the job of forwarding the agenda farm out some of the work to private companies that then—surprise!—employ the lobbyists and give more money to the congressmen. And the money goes round and round."

"I don't believe it's about money."

"I don't either. It's about political theory and ideology and conviction, but it's sweeter if everybody makes money in the process." He tapped the paper. "Not to brag, but when they got the White House and the House and the Senate, I said this would be the most corrupt administration since U. S. Grant. Was I wrong?"

"What's your idea of the agenda?"

"Power. US power. More, more, more. And oil, without which a military force can't operate. F-18s don't fly on solar."

"American power isn't necessarily a bad thing, Abe."

"No nation's power is a bad thing until they get too much of it. Lord What's-his-name was right: absolute power corrupts absolutely. And always in the name of the most admirable goals. Democracy! Homeland security! Justice!" Peretz sniffed his fingers, smiled. "We're a flawed species, Al. We have intellect but we don't have the wisdom. We always blister our fingers because we build our fires too hot, ever since we discovered that fire makes meat taste better." He sighed. "Even us. Even the good guys. Even the *best* of the good guys."

Craik sat slumped in his chair. He picked up muffin crumbs with a wet finger and ate them. "I always feel so cheered up after I've been with you."

All the way back to the lodge, Hackbutt refought the luring of the red-tail in extraordinary detail. Piat had expected Hackbutt to be excited, but this level of postmortem combined the operational details and his passion for falconry into a monologue that was still droning on when Mike stopped the car in the lodge's drive.

Piat couldn't give enough, nor could Hackbutt get enough. When Hackbutt slid off the seat to find Irene, Piat turned to Mike. "Brilliant, man."

"Sure," Mike said.

"You're doing a great job, Craik."

"Thank you, sir."

"Don't mess it up."

"Sir?"

"Let me give you some advice. There are, what?—eight captains in naval intel? One of them, maybe two, will get promoted. The rest will get honorable retirements. You're on the track to be the one. When you get to this level, you're good or you wouldn't be here. From here on, it's political. Take it from me." He smiled. "Don't waste time on stuff out at the periphery."

He was an Air Force two-star general with movie-star looks and a good smile. He looked a lot younger than he was, and even then, he was young for his rank. He hadn't got to be the commanding officer of the Defense Intelligence Agency by bothering with things on the periphery. "You understand what I'm saying?"

"Are you telling me to back off, sir?"

"I'm telling you to focus on your job, which you've been doing really, really well. A hundred and ten percent. 'Top officer of a thousand' kind of fitness report."

Craik had made an appointment with General Raddick and had laid out what he had found about Perpetual Justice. The general's answer seemed to be that it was out there on the periphery, and he should look straight ahead.

"I believe that everything involving task numbers falls under my responsibility, sir."

"What you're doing with the Green Book is great. Great!

Concentrate on that." General Raddick shifted a brass elephant two inches to his left on his desk. "I'm not going to ask you how you know what you know, because it's on *my* periphery. But Perpetual Justice is highly classified, something unauthorized people shouldn't even know exists. You're a dedicated officer; you stumbled on this; you've brought it to my attention. Good." The general had pale blue eyes that added to his handsomeness but didn't do anything to suggest warmth. "Now you want to go back to your own home ballpark."

"Are you telling me to drop the matter, sir? Even if I suspect that my office signed on for an illegal operation?"

"I'm giving you some career advice. Focus on getting two stars and taking my job." The smile flashed. "Okay?" Raddick stood. "I'm glad we had this talk. In this job, I don't see enough of the officers who really run things. Come to me any time."

A few seconds later, Craik was out in the corridor.

Piat had gathered Irene and Hackbutt in his room before they went to have dinner with the prince. He found that he was nervous, tried to keep his tension out of his voice. "We need another meeting with him—somewhere else, and at least a week from now. We've talked about this, Digger. This is the operational plan. We've made the contact. Now we need to build a relationship."

Hackbutt nodded. "Okay." He was still high on the success of the day; he looked wonderful in the used dinner jacket that Piat had bought for him in London. Admiring himself in the mirror, he said, "I'm ready."

Piat walked them down the corridor and then across the lodge's atrium toward the restaurant. Hackbutt paused in front of another mirror and tweaked his black bow tie. "What do I talk about?" he whispered.

"Birds," Piat said with a little too much force.

Irene hissed.

The restaurant had vanilla walls and heavy teak tables the color of cinnamon, scraps of African tribal décor and white linen, and an unparalleled view of the valley and the parkland beyond. A red sunset tinted the room a rich salmon.

The prince was waiting at a corner table. A young Saudi man in a business suit stood at the corner of the broad windows, watching the patio outside, while another stood at the bar without a drink in front of him. His falconer stood behind the prince's chair.

The prince rose to his feet

One shot, Piat thought, again. *It's this or it's over.* He said, "Show time," and they walked in.

17

Piat walked into the bar of Stuttgart's Le Meridien exactly on time, at least according to the signal he had sent. The walls were painted a deep red brown, like bloodstains, and all the furniture was black. It was a disconcerting room.

And Clyde Partlow wasn't in it. Piat wandered through the empty bar, presided over by a stunning blond, and ordered a beer. Still no Partlow. Piat finished his beer and ordered a second one. The window to meet Partlow closed on his third gulp, and he began to consider the fallback meeting a day later in a different location. He didn't think he had a day to waste. In fact, despite the quality of the bar and the woman behind it, Piat couldn't help running through all the things that might happen with Hackbutt—or Irene—while he cooled his heels in Germany.

Partlow came in midway through the third beer. He was twenty minutes late—millennia in espionage terms, an unsafe margin. Piat himself should have been long gone, except that he didn't have anywhere to go.

Partlow sat at the other end of the bar, ordered a beer, asked the bartender in accurate German if he could smoke. She shook her head. He drank his beer while reading a paper and walked out, leaving his black pack of Canadian cigarettes on the bar.

Piat ordered chips, and while the bartender was distracted,

lifted the cigarettes. Fifteen minutes later, he followed the directions on the inside flap of the packet to Partlow's room. The level of tradecraft worried him—Partlow was seldom so careful about such stuff, and the extra effort suggested that something was very wrong indeed, especially in Germany.

The door was open with the bar lock folded against the jam. Piat pushed in silently. Partlow was sitting facing the door, looking as well groomed and well-to-do as ever. He rose when he saw Piat and extended a hand. "I gather congratulations are in order?" he said as soon as Piat had the door shut.

"Eight out of ten. What's with all the spy shit?"

"Additional precautions may be called for." Partlow sat, waved Piat into a facing chair at a table piled high with food.

Piat poured coffee from a flask and took a fat-laden croissant sandwich from the pile. "Better than the food at that place in Italy."

"My choice of venue in Italy was a mistake. The food was the least of it."

Piat, his mouth full, shrugged and chewed.

Partlow sat back. When Piat took another bite, Partlow started to drum his fingers on the table.

"You in a hurry?" Piat asked.

"I'm more than a little eager to hear what 'eight out of ten' means," Partlow replied.

Piat nodded and took another bite, savoring the reaction he was going to get, setting up his arguments in his head. He popped a mineral water with his thumb, drank half, and used a napkin on some crumbs. The he smiled.

"I was hungry. Okay, here it is. The target is not recruitable. We contacted him, he bit, we got a second meeting on the spot, made social contact, all that jazz. He didn't like us, didn't like what we had to say or how we said it. Despite that, using the bird I told you about, we arranged a follow-on. He's offered the falconer a million dollars, cash and carry, for the bird."

Partlow, whose face had slumped at the first news, brightened. "That's great, Jerry. Well done."

"The falconer was incredible, if I do say so myself. I'd like to take all the credit, but a lot of the stuff he did himself. It's in my contact report."

Partlow stiffened. "Your what?"

Piat tossed a cheap 56K memory stick on the table. "Contact report. You know, the kind of thing case officers file. I know—I'm just an agent. But you needed more than just a debrief. I wrote the report. It runs forty pages and it'll give you a blow by blow of the meetings."

Partlow picked up the memory stick. "Bad security."

Piat shrugged. "You're welcome. I just saved you five hours of work. Seriously, Clyde, this is complicated shit, and I wanted it in writing."

Partlow nodded. "Try not to do it again. What if you'd been picked up in German customs?"

"Well, first they'd have had to find it, and then they'd have had to open it without my crypto-key, and then they'd have had to gather what it all means. Give me a break, Clyde, it's done." Piat picked up a second sandwich, this one with a lot of Brie. "Do you want to hear this, or not?"

Partlow sighed. "Go on. Why is he not recruitable?"

"He doesn't like the West, Clyde. I could tell you all kinds of pop-psych crap, but let's just take that as read, okay? He shows all the signs of a serious convert. I kept expecting him to tell me that America was the far enemy, or something. He's a gunner, and he's into some heavy Islamic stuff, and that's that."

"Fundamentalist? Wahhabi?"

"I can't put a tag on it, and the leopard doesn't change his spots overnight—he went hunting on Friday, ate dinner with us, showed no signs of fasting I could see. But he's in it—in the political shit. I'd swear to it."

Partlow shook his head. "That's why we want him, Jerry. Don't be simple."

"I'm not simple. I just know what can and cannot be done. This guy cannot be done. He didn't like Hackbutt, he didn't like the girl, he doesn't drink, he hated going to school in the US, and he doesn't have any easy vices or handles."

"Gay?"

"What's gay? What's gay in Saudi?"

"Point taken."

"The biggest problem with our approach is that our fundamental information was flawed. He's into birds—but they're not his life. In fact, our falconer didn't think much of him."

"Oh, Jesus. How bad was that?"

"Not bad at all. I'm telling you, the falconer was great. He went out with the prince the morning after we had dinner—a really bad evening—and they flew birds together, and he was great. No, I'm saying a different thing. I don't have any evidence for this, but if I had to guess, I'd say the target was seriously into falconry until his conversion opened a wider world for predatory power. He's not a nice guy."

"Terrorists so seldom are." Partlow offered a thin smile.

"Hmm. Terrorist? Whatever. He's a tough target, and I don't think he's worth an approach—which, if I read you and this op right, means no go. Because if he listens politely and burns us to the king, careers end. Right?"

Partlow turned his head away, avoiding eye contact. "Something like that. Jerry, I'm sure you're bang on the money, but I fail to see how this adds up to eight out of ten. I confess that you've done your part—admirably—but it appears to me—"

"Not there yet, Clyde. Stick around for the good part. He has a servant—more like a slave. His personal gofer. Also his falconer. Sudanese. If I had to guess, I'd say a southerner, either a convert to Islam or a forced convert."

Now Partlow leaned forward.

"I thought that would interest you. The sale of the bird—if it goes through, if you care—gives us opportunity to contact the servant. The falconer—that's our guy—made excellent personal contact with this guy. It was really our guy and this guy who flew the birds; the prince just stands around and watches with a sneer on his face. In my report, I call the Sudanese 'Bob.' Bob's young, he doesn't seem to love his master, and his master doesn't seem to see any of the resentment. 'Bob' went to Monaco and to Mombasa—I think he travels everywhere with the target. And, Clyde—I think he'd take the hook as soon as it was offered. Money and a US passport for some stated time in place and a retrieval."

Partlow nodded. "Will he have access, though?"

Piat crossed his arms. "I don't know. He stands behind his master's chair at meetings. What do you think?"

Partlow smiled. "I think you may have just pulled a pearl out of a cesspool."

"Me, too. I look forward to the bonus. Listen, Clyde. This isn't in my report. It's just between us."

Partlow crossed his legs. "Go ahead."

"The prince was never recruitable, Clyde. No way. In fact, without luck and more luck and some brilliant improvisation by me and my hand-built African network, we'd never even have got a shot at this guy. He's big league, he doesn't like Westerners or the West, he has his own contacts—he's beyond hard, Clyde. He's fucking impossible." He held Partlow's eyes. "Who told you this could be done?"

Partlow's look was bland and unreadable. "Need to know, Jerry."

"Sure—whatever. Keep it to yourself. But I only see two possible scenarios, Clyde. Let me lay them out for you. One—you're so fucking desperate to get a counterterrorism op that you sent me, because I'm totally expendable, to contact an impossible target in the vague hope that somehow I'd make it fly. That'd be annoying and flattering at the same time, but it's bullshit, because you couldn't take the blowback if I fucked it away, and because you were going to have Dave run it—and Dave would've died the real death just now in Mombasa. Right?"

Partlow's face was as readable as a gravestone.

"Two—somebody else turned you on to this op and you really had no clue what you were up against. In which case, something stinks, 'cause I think we—or is it you—were set up to fail."

Partlow poured himself a plastic cup full of mineral water. "Both fascinating scenarios. Why didn't we ever send you to the Ranch as an instructor?"

Piat rolled his eyes. "Because I'd have been drunk and disorderly every night in the bar, and I'd have tried to make all the chicks. Oh, wait—that's what all the other instructors do, too."

Partlow glanced at his watch. "I assume you have a plan to carry on?"

Piat waved at the memory stick. "In my report. We shift focus to 'Bob.' We sell the target the bird. We use the negotiations and the sale to make contacts with 'Bob.' We pull the trigger and see what we get. Our falconer can probably work up an extended relationship with 'Bob,' if only by email—and we use that for comms if we land him. Worst case, 'Bob' burns us to his master—and he's a no-status, third-country national, and nobody gives a rat's ass. The ambassador in Saudi mumbles an apology while he's handing over parts for their F-15s."

"You realize that now I have to go back and sell a new target and a new budget." Partlow rubbed his chin. "But I like it. It can be done."

Piat had done it. Partlow was going to buy the

operation—now Piat's operation. He said, "I need to arrange to move the bird—that's all very, very illegal and you can fix it with a phone call."

Partlow looked pained. "More than one phone call."

"Sure, whatever. Make a dozen. I need the bird moved to Bahrain. You know what that means—I need legal-looking paper to show to Hackbutt, and we'll need it to move the bird—there's got to be some sort of export license, a waiver of shit like the CITES treaty, permission of the Royal Ornithological Society—Christ knows what all. You're going to take care of all that, right, Clyde?"

Partlow nodded.

"Okay, I need to set up another meeting with the prince. For the sale. Once it goes down, we tell 'Bob' to call if he needs help—if the bird gets sick, for instance."

"And we just wait?"

"If I do it right, he'll call. He wants us—he just doesn't know we exist yet. I mean it, Clyde. Some guys are born to be agents. 'Bob' is one." He paused, not wanting to oversell, but needing to make sure that Partlow understood. "I think he hates the prince, Clyde. I think he'd love to see him take a fall."

And Partlow grinned.

Half a bottle of scotch later, Partlow asked, "How much difficulty will the Brits make about the bird?"

"Lots." Piat shrugged again. "Hey, I can't sugar-coat it. The bird is protected, there's about four hundred breeding pairs out there, and she's a magnificent specimen. So give the Brits a share of the take. What the hell, they must be in on it, anyway, if it's all terrorism stuff." He grinned. "You didn't run an operation on British soil without asking their permission, did you?"

Partlow said, "I think you are in danger of telling me how to do my job."

Piat thought of all the usual jibes. *Somebody has to do it* came to mind. But he passed. Again. Instead he said, "I want to do the recruitment on Bob. Myself."

Partlow raised his eyebrows. "How much will that cost me?"

Piat grinned. "Lots. But nothing compared to somebody else fucking it away."

Partlow almost grinned back. "I'll take it under advisement. It may be time to take you off this, Jerry. I'm not made of money." Partlow straightened his tie. "I'm of a mind to let you do the recruitment, nonetheless," he said. "But I make no promises. As I said, it may be time to retire you."

"Hey, I just got you a fucking miracle."

"Eight out of ten, Jerry."

Jerry threw his head back like a disgusted teenager. "When will I find out if I can do the recruitment?"

Partlow scribbled a number. "Call. It'll take a while."

"It can't take very long. We've got to move the sale of the bird along or he'll lose interest. I'm going to set up that meeting for the soonest date I can get. If you dick around, it'll be too late and you'll lose 'Bob.' And me."

"We certainly wouldn't want that to happen, Jerry."

"Oh, yeah."

Craik's time with his family was too short, he knew—he should be spending hours with them, not minutes—but he squeezed in what he could. Coming home at nine, he saw each of his children, then clumped downstairs to eat something and was met by Rose at the bottom of the steps.

"I was just going to call you." She kissed him. "There's store-bought meat loaf and frozen green beans. Without a microwave, we'd starve."

"I was going to get a sandwich."

"God doesn't want you to eat a sandwich." She put an arm around his neck. "You look so tired."

"God knows why; all I do is sit on my ass all day." He debated telling her about the meeting with General Raddick and decided it was the wrong time. They put their arms around each other's waist, steering themselves into the kitchen. It was a big room, tiled halfway up with white ceramic in the twenties, the suggestion that it might be an operating room mitigated by antique copper pans and baskets hanging from the ceiling. They had meant the kitchen to be the center of their family, and they had succeeded: the room was warm and profoundly, usually untidily, informal.

"This is the best house we've ever lived in," he said. He sank down on a stool by the island, where she had set two places, two glasses of dark wine. "You haven't eaten yet?"

"Sure, but I thought I'd be friendly. I'll suck on a piece of bread or something." She put a heaped plate in front of him. "I've got a confession to make." She was standing close to him, wearing blue jeans and a putty-colored sweatshirt with the sleeves pushed up. She was forty-two, and he thought she was gorgeous.

"How'd you like to have sex with a sailor?" he said.

"I'm shocked, shocked at the very idea! And both of us captains." She leaned on him. "Eat first, and no nuzzling until I confess." She removed the hands that had slipped under the sweatshirt.

"Okay, confess."

"Eat."

"Confess."

"I forgot to tell you that you had a phone call."

"Oh, Christ, not the unit!"

"Some woman. She wouldn't say who she was. Somebody you got on the side?"

"Southern accent?" He was thinking of Mrs Stillman.

"God, no, more like Syracuse." Rose was from Utica, New York; Syracuse was to her the poor relation. She made her voice lugubriously heavy. "'Sorta like dey talk in de old prison flicks.'"

"That's Chicago."

"No, she had the Upstate nose. Very nasal. Anyway, she's going to call back. I apologize. I should have told you when you came in."

"I'm glad you didn't—one less thing to think about." He was shoveling in the food. It was pretty much like what he got at the DIA cafeteria. "If it's important, she'll call back. Otherwise, what the hell."

"She sounded nervous."

"I have that effect on women. They go all weak."

She was sitting opposite him now. She crossed her eyes and tipped her head. She said, "I'm going to drink this wine and then I'm going to be squiffed and I'm going to bed. Not alone."

She had ice cream and frozen strawberries for dessert, and she was just putting them together when the telephone rang and they both shouted, "I'll get it!" and Alan got to it first. It was a wall telephone right in the kitchen, left there by some earlier owner from the days when telephones came with the house. Its location allowed them to communicate—looks, grimaces, hands—while he talked.

"Alan Craik."

"*Captain* Craik?" Rose had been bang on. The voice was both nasal and heavy, not at all Chicago but quite possibly Syracuse.

"Speaking."

Pause. Then, "You don't know me." Pause. "I called earlier."

"I'm sorry; I was working."

"This isn't—I'm not a telephone salesperson or anything."

Pause. Alan yawned. He made a face at Rose, who was eating his ice cream and strawberries.

"I need to talk to somebody."

He didn't know what to make of that. Some wacko? Why him? "I guess you need to tell me who you are and what this is about."

"No, no, I can't do that. Not over the phone. That's why I called you at home. I figured—" She didn't say what she figured. Rose had certainly been right about the nervousness, too—her words came in bursts, jagged, her voice sinking sometimes almost to inaudibility. "This is very sensitive."

"Well, mmm, unless I know something about you—"

"I'm an Air Force officer, okay? This is straight, Captain, nothing funny about it. This is serious. Would you meet me someplace so we can talk?"

Rose was halfway through his ice cream. He was thinking of their being in bed. It had better be soon, he was thinking; he was really tired. "You'll have to tell me what you want to talk about."

Pause. Then: "Perpetual Justice."

His fatigue was pushed back by a jolt of adrenaline. He frowned. "What do you know about that?"

"A lot. But we have to be careful. Please. All I want to do is talk. I've got to talk to somebody!"

She wanted him to meet her right then, but he said he couldn't, and he said it in a tone that made it clear he wouldn't. She wanted to meet him in a parking garage at White Flint Mall, an idea that told him that she'd seen too many spy movies but wasn't in operational intel herself. He suggested lunch the next day at a fast-food joint near Bolling, but she said that was too far for her, and she named one in Bethesda. He named a Chinese restaurant in a ratty shopping center farther around the Beltway toward his office, guessing that she was in the Maryland part of the DC sprawl and the Chinese place would be halfway between them. She said reluctantly that she'd meet him there tomorrow at noon and hung up.

When he had settled the phone into its cradle, he shook his head at Rose. "I've made a lunch date with a strange woman." He went over and put his arms around her. "I'm nuts."

"I ate your ice cream."

"Fuck the ice cream."

"That would be so messy. And cold."

"You're warmer."

"And not messy. Come on."

18

Alan got to the Chinese restaurant where he was supposed to meet the woman almost fifteen minutes late. He was thinking that she should be grateful he had got there at all; at the same time, he knew that if she was really an Air Force officer, she was busy, too, and she might have given up and left. Sheer nervousness might have made her do that anyway.

He looked around. The place was only a quarter full—a bad sign at the busiest time of the day. It wasn't much: tatty paper lanterns and the little paper parasols that went into drinks that came in things like coconut shells, Formica tables, tubular-steel chairs from the sixties. Still, the place had been there for years; he'd had it filed away as a good spot for a semi-clandestine meeting. He thought of Abe Peretz.

A broad-faced Oriental woman was smiling and half-bowing at him and saying something that suggested that she wouldn't bother to learn English, no matter how long she stayed in the restaurant trade. He had already spotted a woman sitting alone, and, when the woman ducked her head away as their eyes threatened to meet, decided she was the one. Craik grinned at the Chinese restaurateur and headed for the lone woman's table.

She was in civilian clothes, an unremarkable dark dress

that was a nod toward dressing for success but didn't put much faith in the idea. She had swagged a blue and beige scarf around her neck and one shoulder; she had brown hair, shiny, probably washed that morning; small, neat hands with chewed nails and only clear polish; an expression of fear when she looked up at him.

Alan sat down. He had his Navy ID card ready in a pocket, and he put it down on the table as if he were trumping her hand. "Alan Craik," he said.

She licked her lips. She had food in front of her but hadn't touched it. She put her head out a little so she could look at the card. "Thank you."

"Now I'd like you to return the favor."

"Oh, no—" Her hair swung back and forth as she shook her head.

"I need to know who you are. You know how it goes—my security officer gets to know who I talk to. Sorry."

"I'm not going to report this to *my* security officer." The voice was definitely nasal, the t's and d's hard and punchy.

"Bad move."

"I don't want people to *know*."

"Ma'am, the security officer is the best friend you've got if you're doing something on the sly. At least if you report it, you've got it on the record if it goes bad later." The idea of something's going bad shook her; her eyes went to her shoulder bag, which was standing on the table next to her. She was ready to bolt. "We've both come all this way," he said. He made his voice sound pleading. "Please. I have to know who you are."

She chewed on her lower lip, ruining what was left of the pale lipstick there, and then she went into the shoulder bag and burrowed until she came out with a wallet, from which she extracted an ID card. Craik retrieved his own ID and looked at hers. Sarah Berghausen, captain, US Air Force. The photo matched.

He gave it back. "That wasn't so bad, was it?"

She snatched the ID and forced it back into the wallet. The Chinese woman came up then—she had been lurking back by the kitchen door, perhaps thinking she was watching a marital spat—and put down a menu and a pot of tea, and he glanced at the menu so fast that he was able to say "Number sixteen" before she had moved away again. When she was gone, he said, "Okay, what can I do for you?"

Sarah Berghausen cleared her throat and said, almost whispering, "I heard you went to General Raddick about Perpetual Justice."

It stunned him. He and Raddick had had a private meeting only yesterday. "How did you hear that?"

She fidgeted. She shrugged. She whispered, "I overheard something."

"Somebody else saying I'd talked with General Raddick?"

She nodded. He tried to hold her eyes, but she didn't want to look at him. "That meeting was private and the subject was classified." She nodded again. He sat back and folded his arms. "Who'd you overhear?"

She shook her head. He lunged forward and said, "Look, Captain, you wanted to talk to me! So talk!"

She licked her lips again. She looked at her hands while microwaved chicken with cashews and three spices was put down in front of him, then a bowl of rice. The Chinese woman poured him another cup of tea. She looked as if she wanted to stay and offer marital counseling, but he thanked her and she backed off.

Sarah Berghausen said, "I'm a financial officer in a classified branch of DIA."

"Perpetual Justice?"

She picked up her fork and probed the food in front of her, now cold and glistening with a milky sheen. "Not its official name."

"Okay."

"The reason I called you—" She tried the food, or at least the sauce. "I can't do my job. They're doing stuff without sending it through me. I can't keep track of the money! If GAO ever came down on us, all hell would break loose and I'd be the first one they'd go after!" GAO was the General Accountability Office, financial watchdog of the government. Classification and priority meant nothing to them. GAO had a reputation for humorlessness and dedication, and "forgive" was not in their vocabulary.

"Why would GAO come down on you?"

"They just do!" She waved her fork, then put it down. "I can't eat. I can't sleep anymore. I'm a bean counter, right? Well, the shits I work for don't let me see the beans."

"So you came to me because you heard I'd talked to General Raddick. But you must have overheard *what* I talked about with General Raddick, otherwise how would you know I was the one to come to? And, because I know what I talked to Raddick about, I'm putting two and two together and guessing that you think there's funny stuff going on with Perpetual Justice. Am I right?"

"I don't know that it's funny stuff. It's just that they don't go by the book. I'm in the dark. I was ordered to this unit six months ago because I was due for this kind of rotation. I didn't know anybody when I got there; I didn't know what to expect. The guy I replaced had everything in a mess. I wouldn't sign off on some of it. I still haven't signed off on some of it. I complain to the officer-in-charge, he goes, 'Don't sweat the details.'" Her face was like an angry child's. "My job is the details!"

Alan ate some of the chicken-in-library-paste and forked a lot of rice into the rest and said, "I'm going to run some names past you. Wave when you recognize one." He mixed the rice into the library paste. "Herman Ritter."

She jerked. It was a comical reaction, except Alan didn't

dare laugh. She looked like a bad actor playing astonishment. "How do you know that?"

"Alice K. Einhorn."

She moaned. She gulped cold tea.

"Geoffrey Lee."

She chewed on her lower lip. Now, she couldn't seem to unlock her eyes from his. After several seconds, she muttered, "That's fantastic."

"Tell me about Herman Ritter."

"I, uhm, shouldn't—"

"Yeah, you should. If GAO comes down on you, you're going to look awfully good for talking to me. But you have to *talk.*"

"Ritter's the officer-in-charge of the unit. He's a civilian, but there's a light colonel under him."

"Not unusual. Tell me about Ritter."

"Well, he's— He's pretty snotty, you know the type? He likes to bully people. He blows up, screams at people, gets right in your face. But he's got a good reputation on the outside, as I understand it—he writes books—"

"What does the unit do?"

"I can't tell you that."

"Are they cooking the books or are they just sloppy?"

"I don't think they're—" She frowned. "It isn't cooking the books, exactly. It's like Ritter can't be bothered with stuff like that. It's—for all his reputation, the truth is that from where I sit, he's incompetent. He can't do things *right.*"

That sounded to Craik like the people who had sent Ray Spinner to Tel Aviv. He said, "Alice Einhorn?"

"On her door, it says 'Policy and Tasking,' but I think she's into everything. Some of the older guys, the military guys who have been there a while, they complain that they can't tell what the lines of command are. The truth is, it looks like Ritter and Einhorn run everything from the top down, and the organization chart doesn't mean squat."

"What about Lee?"

"He's a lawyer, I guess. At least he's listed as 'Legal Affairs.' I went to him once to ask about some money that was being authorized—I mean, I thought, Well, if he's the legal guy, he can tell me if it's legal. He bullshitted me, and the next day Ritter called me in and screamed at me that I was questioning his judgment. I was asking about things that weren't my business. I tried to tell him the finances were my business, and I thought he was going to hit me. He's a big guy, and he loves to intimidate. I got nowhere."

"Did you take it up with the lieutenant-colonel?"

"Fat chance. He's tight with Ritter. Worried about his own career." She had pushed her plate far away and now leaned forward with her elbows on the table. "Why did you go to General Raddick?"

"You know what a task number is?"

"Of course! Is there a question about a tasking? That's just what I've been talking about! Oh, God. When they've spent money, the paperwork is like they sprinkled amounts on the task numbers with a salt shaker. The numbers *can't* correspond with what actually goes on. I mean, they charge stuff to taskings that were completed a year ago. *Two* years ago."

"Ever seen expenditures for a company called Force for Freedom?"

She gave him the bad-actor astonishment again. "How do you *know* all this?"

"How much money?"

She shook her head. "You wouldn't believe me. A lot. I mean, a *lot*. And it's no-bid. I see the contracts. The amounts are big, but I think they're slippery—Force for Freedom is billing stuff against one contract when I'm sure as can be that it's part of another. It's just a can of worms."

"Does their money come through a DIA pipe?"

"Well, some of it does. That's what I'm supposed to be

there to monitor. But they spend more than that. There's money coming from another source. I can't tell you."

"DoD?"

She looked irritated.

"Secretary's office? One of the undersecretaries?"

"It's got a number and a name but I don't know what it is, okay? But it's a lot, so it isn't somebody's office coffee money." As if the talking had made her feel better, she pulled her bowl of cold rice toward her and began to dig into it with her fork. After a mouthful, she grabbed the salt shaker.

Craik asked her if she knew what sort of operations the unit was into, but she said she didn't. Everything was coded. She knew nothing about the operations themselves except what would be implied by the task number, and they were so general that they didn't help any more than to tell her that the unit spent a lot of money on antiterrorism and "control and exploitation of enemy combatants."

"And it's all called Perpetual Justice?"

"Ritter and his cronies call the unit Perpetual Justice. See, below Einhorn's level, the unit's split into two camps, sort of pro- and anti-Ritter. If you're for Ritter, you call it 'PJ;' if you think he's a shmuck, you use the official name. Which I'm not allowed to tell you."

He tried to get her to tell him anyway, and he tried to get her to tell him where the unit did its work, but she'd made up her mind by then that she'd said enough. She was clearly feeling better, but as they paid for their dismal lunches and headed out, her nervousness came back and she seemed to sag. She wouldn't give him a telephone number.

"I really wanted to ask you—what—what you think I should do." Even now that she had talked, her question was still hesitant.

"You ought to think about going to GAO," he said. "You'll

be better off to be the whistle-blower than the financial officer who let things get worse."

"It'd be my career," she murmured.

"Quit. You have a detailer? You know him?" Craik tried to hold her eye.

She shrugged. "Her. Sure, I know my detailer."

"Call her today and tell her you want a new job immediately—anywhere. You won't have to say why. Listen, Captain. I may not be Air Force but I know the system. If you tell her you'll go anywhere, she'll know that something is really, really wrong—and she'll move you."

She turned away, fiddled with her purse, and then got up. "I'm afraid to leave. Afraid that I can't pass my accounts."

Craik stood up with her. "I know it is easy to say, but stop being afraid. Don't do wrong just because you are afraid of the consequences of doing right." Even as Craik said the words, he realized that they were for him. And that his career, his hunt for flag rank, was over. Maybe to himself, and maybe to her, he said, "All the people at Abu Ghraib—who were afraid to speak up—they'll go to jail, too. And have to live with what they were part of."

She shook her head without any other last word and headed for a silver Hyundai in the middle of the mall's scruffy parking lot. Craik headed for his own car but kept an eye on her. He saw her repairing her lipstick with the help of her rearview mirror, and by the time he was behind the wheel of his own Toyota she had her backup lights on. He waited until she was ready to exit to the highway and then pulled slowly out of his parking spot.

He let her get well ahead of him. He risked being wrong about where she was going and took the ramp to the Beltway heading west. Within a mile, he saw the silver Hyundai ahead, and he pulled in several cars behind her and waited for her to take an exit ramp. She got off at Silver Spring, and he followed her down to Georgia Avenue, then toward

Bethesda. When she turned into a parking garage, he cut into a side street, couldn't find a place to park, went on around the block, and came out in time to see her go into an office building that might have been put up in the seventies by somebody short on money.

He went into the same parking garage and stowed the car, then walked to her building. The street side stood on massive pillars with aluminum facings, ugly as could be. Craik went in through the glass doors and found a one-storey lobby with two elevators. No security desk. A building directory that took up part of one wall told him that the Office of Geophysical Excellence occupied one of the building's seven storeys. A couple of dozen other enterprises were scattered through the upper three floors. He guessed that a lot of the building's space had no tenants—just the kind of place the government looked for. He studied the names, rejecting any that were clearly things like law firms or one-man shows. That still left more than a dozen, most with made-up names like Gotrex and ExcelHunt, or old-fashioned, iron-assed names like Spalding Machine Imports and Fawcett Human Services Management. He leaned toward the made-up names but thought that a classified DIA operation might disguise itself as something like a human services firm, although it would be embarrassing if somebody came in looking for career counseling. In the end, he scribbled the room numbers and the names of all fourteen in his notebook and headed for the elevators.

The corridors had the look of all unclassy buildings—floors with too much polish slopped on the baseboards; flotsam lines of dirt that had hardened into the old wax; lettering styles that had missed the last twenty years. Still, he was able to reject most of the offices on his list—some had unlocked doors; some were obviously too small; some were too well maintained. In the end, he settled on three—

Gotrex, on five; Franzen Acoustics, also on five; and something called Elastomer Engineering Limited, on six.

Back in his own office at Bolling, he looked the three firms up in the civilian telephone directory. Gotrex and Franzen were there. Elastomer Engineering wasn't.

Score one for low-tech investigation.

Craik stayed late to write a one-page report on the meeting with Sarah Berghausen for his security officer. He was specific and factual. He included what she'd said about Ritter and the others from OIA, and what she'd said about financing. He mentioned his following her and the building's address. He said that she'd "heard" about his own meeting with Raddick and suggested that there had been a violation of security, because he and Raddick had discussed classified matters. He didn't say that only Raddick could have committed the security violation.

He printed out two hard copies of the report. One went into a file called Perpetual Justice. The other went into inter-office mail for the security officer, but it wouldn't reach her until at least noon tomorrow, and by then it wouldn't matter if she went to somebody with it and the shit hit the fan.

The after-effects of the Mombasa trip were to stay with them, although Piat didn't see that it would be that way. When they got together for the first time after they returned, he thought that there was new tension. It might be Irene's guilt about having drunk too much during dinner with the prince; some of it might be Hackbutt's irritation with her because of the drinking. But under it all was something new: the prince's offer to buy Hackbutt's sea eagle. The offer—actually a demand—had come during that dinner. The prince had made it quite clear that it was the only reason that any relationship between him and Hackbutt could continue. He had as much as said that he didn't like Americans and he didn't like Western men whose wives got drunk and pushy. It was going to be Bella or nothing. Sell the bird or abort.

And then there was Irene's "art." She had been back at work before Piat got to the farm. Hearing the sound of a power tool from the studio, he looked at Hackbutt, got raised eyebrows and a pursed mouth. These were signals; they suggested to him that Hackbutt and Irene had been fighting. It might be about the drinking; it might be about her show; but it was probably, he thought, about the sea eagle. Which side was Irene coming down on, he wondered—sell, or abort? And he was a little amused that Hackbutt had used those signals with him, signals of intimacy and a kind of established code, suggesting that the two men had the sort of intimacy that Piat envied in Hackbutt and Irene. Things had got *very* complicated.

But they said nothing about the bird that day. Piat knew he had to get the commitment, but he'd have to go at it delicately. And he didn't want Irene around when he did. He wanted her neutral, at the worst, preferably pro-selling, but he wanted Hackbutt to himself. He spent that day reviewing what had happened at Mombasa, stroking Hackbutt and asking his advice for the next step. Both of them avoided mentioning the bird. They sketched the possibilities for another meeting with the prince. Piat didn't say that he was sure that the prince was a lost cause and the only point in going on was to get next to Mohamed, his falconer.

When he came back next morning, the sun was shining—a rarity—and the house was bright. To his surprise, the studio door was open. He heard Hackbutt's voice; he could tell from the tone that he was trying to please Irene.

"Come on in, I won't bite you." She was standing by the far wall with Hackbutt. She had on her working clothes but she wasn't working. The two of them had been looking at a colored drawing that was pinned to the wall. The floor had been cleared, even swept, and what Piat took to be the "installation" was laid out on it.

"It's finished," he said.

"That it is."

"Come look at this, Jack. It's incredible."

Her finished drawing of the piece was done with the skill and precision of an architect's rendering. It showed the installation as it would be, the perspective perhaps a little exaggerated: the floor with the large, mounded piece somewhere near the center, the other things in an undulating line leading to and away from it; three big rectangles overhead, their planes slightly angled to the floor; ranks of uprights on each side with small rectangles set into them.

Piat looked at the big central mound, which he knew now was really humanoid and incorporated some of the sheep skeleton that Hackbutt had boiled down for her. "Where are the photos?"

"In the standing mounts." She tapped the uprights along the sides.

"I thought they were going to be attached to the center thing."

"Oh, that was a lousy idea. I gave that up."

He turned to look at the real thing. The bloated-looking mound that he had once taken for a mass of jelly was now a glistening pinky-white that looked both lustrous and horrible, like something almost phosphorescent with decay. Seen up close, it showed swirls and cloudy loops almost like writing. Seen from the same vantage point as her drawing, it was a woman's bloated belly, the spiral core of a seashell set into the navel, the vagina shading into deeper pink and blue, then purple, the labia like fronds, like sea anemones. Two thighs, equally monstrous, quickly shrank before getting to where the knees should have been; one disappeared altogether, as if into the floor; the other shriveled down like dried skin and became a sheep's thigh bone which, in its turn, seemed to plunge out of sight. At the shape's other end, BX cable curled to become a kind of spinal cord ringed with the sheep's vertebrae, leading to the sheep's skull, the nose pointed skyward, the back flowing into a big piece of driftwood that spread like hair. Beyond the figure were, at intervals, the condoms, a block of diseased-looking styrofoam, other detritus—but all now crafted from fiberglass. Seeming to have emerged from the vagina and leading down the room were a plastic baby doll, the pearls and diamonds she had said her father had given her, a board with rusty nails, shells. Most of the objects, like the legs, seemed to be half buried in the floor. As if in sand.

The female figure had no arms. Springing almost from each side of the BX cable was a yellow rubber glove of the kind women used in washing up. He touched one and found it wasn't rubber but fiberglass. Even he could see that the work was meticulously done.

"*The Body Electric,*" he said.

"What? Oh, God, I gave that title up ages ago."

"What does it mean?" He was pointing at the rendering.

"I'm not a conceptual artist, Jack."

"What's it called, then?"

She looked at the central figure. "Fucked if I know. The gallery wants a title, though. I'll have to think of something." She made a gesture toward the door. "Okay, you've seen it, now I have to go to work. You guys, too, I'd think."

Hackbutt walked to the door and stood there. He looked back at her, then at Piat, jiggling something in his pocket. Piat said, "I thought it was finished."

"It has to get from here to France by Saturday. That means I have to pack up every bit of it, including the rough drawings and the rendering. If you think I'd trust the packing to somebody else, you're out of your mind."

A bell went off when she said "Saturday." He murmured, his tone as light as he could manage, "We've got to set up another meeting with the prince by then."

"Go ahead. I'll be in France."

So he knew what she and Hackbutt had been squabbling about. He was angry but hid the anger. "Irene, if you'd told me—"

"I've told you for the last two weeks that the gallery had moved the date up to the twentieth! But you don't listen!"

"Yeah, but—"

"But nothing. I have to be there! I've got three flat-screen TVs that have to be ceiling-mounted. Do you think I trust anybody else to do that right? I haven't even bought the materials for the standards to hold the photos yet—for Christ's sake, I'm going to have to make them on-site! I've got a month of work to do in one week after I get there, and I don't give a fuck about another meeting with your fucking prince!" Hackbutt was looking miserable. Piat was standing his ground. She moved a step toward him, dropped her voice. "I hated that sonofabitch. And he hated me! So I drank too much wine—big deal! What was I supposed to do, put on a burka and ask him to stone me to death? Fuck him. And fuck you and your operation!"

"Well, Irene—we had a contract—"

"Sue me."

Hackbutt looked as if he was going to cry. Piat realized that he was making a probably bad decision because he didn't want to lose her. He said, "I'll work it out." He managed a smile.

Outdoors in the sunlit cold with Hackbutt, he said, "What're the flat-screen TVs for?"

"Oh, they go overhead. To show the video of the dead sheep being boiled down. It plays on a loop the whole time the show is open."

* * *

He went back to the farm when he hoped Hackbutt would be busy with the birds. He touched the dog's nose, then crossed to the porch. Distantly, Irene's "music" seemed to be playing—or was it the wind in the trees along the stream? He turned his head, saw the trees were indeed blowing, and behind him the door opened.

Irene had a kerchief on her head; a rivulet of sweat ran down along her nose, another down her throat into the unbuttoned V of her shirt, hugely provocative but not intentionally so, he knew: she had been packing the installation. She would be off soon.

She looked at him, glanced over at the dog still lying in the grass, back at Piat. "Eddie isn't here." She apologized to him for the day before, but she didn't say she was going to take part in the third meeting. She simply said that she was sorry she'd got angry but her mind was made up.

He followed the established line. "I'll miss your help with Edgar."

She smiled. It wasn't phoney. The smile said, *We could still be on*. She said, "You're still getting my help with Eddie. I told him he should sell Bella to the prince. We had kind of a fight about it, in fact." She grinned. "I'm glad the prince didn't want *me*. I think Eddie'd let *me* go before he'd give up that bird." She held his eyes. "Let's hope so, anyway."

"Where is he?"

"He's on the hillside with Bella," Irene said. "Saying goodbye. Be gentle, Jack. I hate the fucking bird and I *still* feel for him."

Piat nodded, but he stood in front of the door with his hands in his pockets. For the first time in a month, he wanted to smoke. Instead, he stepped into the half-open door and kissed her.

"I'd like a way to meet when this is over," he said.

"Do you mean my life with Edgar, or your spy game?" She slipped out of his arms.

"Both," Piat said

She looked at the dog. She looked at Piat. More sweat trickled down along her nose, and she wiped it away with a knuckle, the gesture like brushing away a tear. Behind her, the sound of her "music," now clearly not the wind, groaned, menacing and orgasmic. "You better go." Her voice trembled.

"Irene."

"*Don't.*" She looked furious, but what she said was, "Not now." He wondered if she meant "Not in Eddie's house" or "Not until my installation is complete." He wondered if she knew herself.

"Irene!" He hadn't meant to speak again, but there it was.

"Not now!" She swallowed hard. "Eddie'd know, and I won't do that to him!" She shook her head, as if denying the validity of what she'd just said, her grip tightening on the edge of the door. "You think he's stupid; you think he doesn't get things. You're wrong! You think you know all this crap they taught you about body language and dilated eyes and *shit*, but you don't know anything about people!" Her voice dropped. "Eddie's intuitive. He isn't manipulative, like you; he doesn't look people over for signs and symptoms and run them through a computer. *But he knows things*! He doesn't always know them until all of a sudden they jump out of him, but he knows! His feelings are very deep—not like you, you don't have feelings; maybe I don't either—and it takes him a while to sort them out, but he gets them and he gets them right. Do you know he worries about your drinking? Do you know he thinks you've got something else going on on the island? That's how he thinks! So don't kid yourself he wouldn't know if you and I crawled into bed while he isn't here."

"I wasn't suggesting it." His voice was hard. She had frightened him with what she'd said about Hackbutt's thinking he had something else going on; he didn't want her to see it. And something between them—had it ever been more than flirtation?—had just died.

She withdrew deeper into the protection of the door. "Yes, you were." She said it as if she were pronouncing sentence. "But not here. Not now. When this is over. When your operation is over."

The door closed. Piat took a step backward off the stone porch. Distantly, her music moaned. He turned to the dog, snapped his fingers, and it bounded to him. "Never give your heart to a woman," Piat said.

Then he went up the hill.

Lying in bed, Alan Craik wanted sleep but couldn't reach it. He was turning over the meeting with Sarah Berghausen, his following of her. He had told Rose about it while they ate. Now, lying beside him, she was quiet, and he listened for her breathing and, not hearing it, said softly, "You awake?"

"Uh-huh."

"Thinking?"

"About you."

They turned toward each other; he put a hand on her bare shoulder. "What about me?"

"What a good guy you are. And what a foolish one."

"Ouch."

"Charging at windmills." She moved closer. "But don't try to change. It's who you are."

He said, "I'm thinking about the stuff Abe Peretz got for me. It's great if it's solid, but—Abe's seeing far-right conspiracies everywhere. He's a good friend, but he's just got crazy on the subject."

"Abe isn't crazy. He's hurting. What are you doing about his problem? About Leah?"

"What can I do about Leah?" Craik had his hands on the muscles in her neck.

"Call your buddy in Tel Aviv." Craik had met the current head of Mossad during a diplomatic incident. They had had some things in common. Craik had all but forgotten. He said, "Okay. I didn't think about it."

"Too busy tilting at windmills."

He massaged her shoulder and neck, an unconscious action. "I'm trying to figure out what to do next." He could feel her breath on his nose and mouth; it was warm, sweet with toothpaste. He told her about the meeting with Raddick. "General Raddick warned me. He meant that if I make a stink, there'll be no promotion."

"That bother you?"

"It ought to bother you. If I get dropped to the bottom of the list, so will you. You know how it goes."

Rose had always been ambitious. Her goal for years had been to be an astronaut; when that had collapsed, she had tried to throw herself into staff and command work. Some of her fire may have cooled, however. Once, after dropping out of the NASA program, she had said, "You learn a lot from failure," and when he had said she hadn't failed, she'd only shaken her head. Now he said, "What do you think I should do?"

She sighed and stretched and moved over to make contact with him down the length of their bodies. "Two retired captains. We could raise our kids like normal people. Live in the same house for the rest of our lives. Have a dog. Three dogs."

Rose had said she'd never have another dog after a black Lab named Bloofer had died. But time and what she called failure might have changed her mind. "Write our memoirs," he said.

"Start a business."

"Not security."

"A country store. Or a gas station. In the middle of some desert, where nobody ever came."

"Tough on income."

"Nah. We could retire to Utica tomorrow and be the richest couple on any street in the city. And low on taxes."

He felt her breathing smooth out. The small, warm breeze was on his throat. He thought she was asleep, and then she murmured. "I can live with it." She settled her head on his shoulder and fell asleep.

19

It took three sets of phone calls to and from Saudi Arabia to complete arrangements for the transfer of the bird and the payment of the money. Hackbutt handled the calls well enough—he was distant and touchy on the first one, but the prince delegated the rest of the matter to his falconer, and Hackbutt and the African talked longer than circumstances required both times—until, in fact, Piat all but punched his fist in the air. Mohamed was like a ripe fruit ready to be picked.

He got on to Partlow to do the paperwork and the moving of the big eagle from Mull to Bahrain, the only location the prince would consider.

Craik was back in the parking garage opposite Sarah Berghausen's building at seven-thirty the next morning. He had a cup of convenience-store coffee in the cup holder and a bagel he'd taken from his own freezer. Home had been the usual morning frenzy. It was supposed to be his day to take Annie to day care, but he'd traded with Rose for the week after he got back from London. She had been too busy to argue.

He watched other cars come in for a while, noting the physical types of the people and the old stickers on the rear windshields. He was looking for ex-military. For a while, there were none, and then a man in his forties showed up in a Taurus with a Cherry Point logo on the rear window. Then several women drove in, none military that he could identify, and then three guys in an Explorer with a Bush–Cheney bumper sticker. They had sidewall haircuts and discreet middle-aged spreads, and Craik got out of his car and headed for the exit behind them.

He was wearing a blue blazer and chinos and a blue button-down with a mostly gray tie. He carried his Navy attaché case, which had no markings but would be as recognizable as a tattoo to other military. This time, he didn't linger in the lobby but followed the three right into a fast-filling elevator and up to the sixth floor. Other people got off at lower floors. Some people knew each other, the usual workday chatter. The three got off with him on six.

He followed them at a little distance straight to Elastomer Engineering, saw them go in. He'd noted the door's coded lock yesterday; now, he wanted somebody careless enough to open it for him. And he knew somebody would. There was a war on terrorism and blah, blah, blah, but many people were generous or craven or both, and if you smiled at them and looked white and middle-class, they'd let you in and never think about it. They'd let in Osama bin Laden if he'd shave his beard and join a car pool.

She was about thirty and flirtatious. There he was, a pretty good-looking guy, government attaché case, good shoes. She gave him a questioning look that meant, "Coming in?" and he grabbed the edge of the door and held it for her, and they went in together.

"Thanks."

"You new?"

"I'm meeting Ritter."

"Oh, wow. Well—see you around—"

The offices were mostly empty; it was early. There was no receptionist and no security guard. Where a corridor branched from the entrance vestibule, an unattended desk stood. It would be the night duty officer's, he thought; nearby would be an office with a cot. Mostly, security began and ended with the coded lock and the phoney corporate name on the door.

He walked the quiet hallways. The long corridor from the vestibule ended in a T, the two shorter arms running from the back to the front of the building. They were functional, drab; no attempt had been made to carry out the fiction that elastomers or engineering were of any interest here. Craik walked the long hall, then the short ones, poking his head into open doors and smiling when he found somebody looking at him. By the time he headed back he could smell coffee, and more people were filtering in. He hung his DIA badge on his breast pocket but didn't put much faith in it—some of the people coming in had badges, and they didn't look much like his own.

"I'm looking for Herman Ritter."

He'd picked out another over-pretty woman. A little too made up, a little too dressed, like one of the women from *Friends*.

"Oh, hi!" Smile. Toss of the head. "The *big* office down the hall, hang a right, third door on the left." She opened and narrowed her eyes like a flashing light. "Corner office!"

He said that was great and tried to imply that she'd lighted up his day. As he was walking away, she called, "He's already in there! He comes in at six!"

I'll just bet he does. He walked the corridor, turned right, counted doors. Bingo. The door was unlocked. Inside was a small space with a desk that probably belonged to an assistant; this bunch clearly didn't go for receptionists. The room had no windows. In the back wall was another door—Ritter's office, he thought. Probably L-shaped, with a private bathroom jutting in this direction and denying the little outer office a window.

He opened the inner door.

A big, rather strikingly good-looking man in his late forties was sitting at a large desk with his crossed legs up. He had a telephone at his ear. He looked up at Alan and frowned and then ordered him out with a gesture—the sort of gesture that comes from never having people disobey. Here was a man who had been imposing his will on the rest of the world since infancy.

Alan went in and closed the door behind him and sat down.

It was, indeed, a corner office, and there was, indeed, a door back there that would put the bathroom about where he'd thought. Ritter hadn't hired a decorator to do the place, so it didn't look as if it belonged in *Architectural Digest*; on the other hand, it looked a lot classier than a government-issue DIA office. The wall behind the desk was hung with trophies—Ritter with the vice-president, Ritter with the new secretary of state, four diplomas, five plaques displaying awards for illegible accomplishments, a Yale pennant that you were probably supposed to know was from some period well before Ritter's youth, and various framed things that couldn't be puzzled out at a glance.

"Get the hell out of my office." Ritter had covered the telephone to say that.

"I'm Captain Craik, DIA Collections."

"Get-out-of-my-office!"

"We need to talk. When you're off the phone."

Ritter thrust his lower jaw forward. Craik suspected that Ritter liked confrontation, wasn't really upset yet. Perhaps was even looking forward to a good shouting session to get the day going. He growled into the phone, "Get back to you," and reached way over to put it down where it belonged, not taking his eyes from Alan. "Harry!" he called. "Goddamit, Harry!" He had a good, loud voice. But Harry, who was probably the assistant, wasn't there yet. "I'm going to throw your ass out of here," he said to Alan.

"Perpetual Justice." He gave Ritter a full second to react, but the man didn't. Ritter seemed utterly confident but bad-tempered. Alan went on: "Eleven task numbers backdated to cover operations that in fact weren't DIA's."

"Who the hell *are* you?"

"Oh, you know who I am, Ritter. Come on! Backdating task numbers is strictly illegal and can be—"

"Get a life! What the fuck are you talking about?" The words brought his feet off the desk and his torso upright, head forward. He really was a good-looking man—dark hair with some gray; tall, lean body; a good tan; clothes several notches above whatever GS rating his job had. "Just get the fuck out, will you?"

"Backdating task numbers is illegal and can be prosecuted. It's a security violation. However, it tends to include money crimes, as well, because task numbers drive both appropriations and expenditures. Want to tell me about it?"

Ritter stood. Framed by his trophy wall, his old Yale pennant above his head like the banner in a Renaissance engraving, he looked great. Alan thought of his own meager office and his chinos and wished he could look half as good. A quarter as good. Ritter said, almost chattily, "I don't have time to waste on trivia. We do important work here. Go do whatever it is you do. I don't want to have to have you thrown out."

"Why not?"

"Look—" Ritter pointed a finger. "You're going to be in trouble. *Career* trouble. As far as you're concerned, this office doesn't exist, and if you want to talk about security violations, you're committing one by even being here!" He didn't ask how Craik had found the place or how he knew what Perpetual Justice was. He was too good and too confident for that. He couldn't be bothered with such questions (although he might later direct somebody else to pursue them).

"The door was open. You people have lousy security. And a lousy legend. If you were at all careful, you'd at least have your cover company in the phone book." Craik smiled. "And I'm bulletproof, so save your threats."

Ritter came around the desk and leaned back against it, arms folded. He seemed almost interested. He said, "Do you know who I *am*?"

"Absolutely."

"Do you know how important what I do is?"

"I know that, however important you think it is, you don't know how to do it right." Craik smiled again. He wasn't aware of it, but he was grinning. Confrontation had that effect on him. "And despite your assurance, you don't do a very good job."

Ritter seemed almost amused. He leaned forward, still clasping himself in his arms. "Do you know whom I was just on the phone with?"

"The guys at Force for Freedom?"

For the first time, Ritter seemed threatened. He snapped erect. "Get the fuck out of here."

"You'll do better to talk to me now than later. When the GAO goons show up."

"I said get the fuck out of here!" The voice was rising now. The time for fun, the voice said, was over; the tantrum was on its way. Craik could see the Ritter whom Sarah Berghausen feared.

"No-o-o-o," Craik answered. He drawled the no. He realized at a remove that he was antagonizing the man, because he'd found his enemy. "Not yet. You haven't heard what I want."

"I don't give a fuck what you want!" Ritter was pumping himself up to full blast. Viewed objectively, it was a significant performance, practiced and yet fresh, deliberate and yet, to many people, frightening. Although controlled, it looked as if he was out of control. The tantrum must have started in infancy when the burgeoning will was frustrated, had evolved into a weapon, perhaps the major one, in the will's arsenal. Ritter was leaning forward now, then moving two steps closer, now looming over the seated Craik but not touching him, like an attack dog being held on a leash. "You're a nothing! You're a fucking nobody! You're not getting anything here and I don't give a shit what you want! You're done, finished; you're toast! Get out! Get the fuck out!" Screaming now at what was probably the top of his voice—or had he saved a little?

Alan didn't move. He wasn't physically intimidated, figuring that Ritter almost certainly didn't touch people when he was in this state or he'd have a slew of lawsuits and he wouldn't be in this job. And if Ritter really did get physical, Alan figured he could take care of himself, although that was never certain. Ritter seemed very fit, although fitness and street-fighting weren't necessarily connected, and street-fighting was what Alan would go to directly if a hand was put on him. "I'd like to see your documentation of the eleven backdated operations, to start with," he said. "Or shall I just get the GAO?"

Ritter's face was red. A vein thickened in his temples. He was looming closer, all mouth up close. Shouting, "What did I say? What the fuck did I say? Are you too stupid, you jerk, you nothing, you goddam third-rate military hack? There's a million of you, captains, Jesus Christ, captains come out my ass when I shit! Are you too stupid to understand what I say? You're a disgrace; you're a military moron; you're—" Spittle flecked Alan's blazer in little white spots. He didn't move.

"Get *ou-u-u-t*!" Ritter did have more voice, now pouring out in an almost operatic scream. Then he lunged back at the desk and hammered the telephone and screamed into it, "Get somebody to my office, now! Now!" He turned to face Alan, his face bloated with his now genuine rage.

"And I'd like to go over with you and your Mister Lee the legal basis for the activities in the tasks that had superseded numbers," Craik continued. Sometimes, bureaucracy was the weapon.

It seemed to wound Ritter and he started to holler again, now almost an animal scream of deep pain, as if he felt Alan's words physically, rage now joined by righteous outrage.

Alan's voice rose to counter it as he went on. "If those activities were illegal in 2001 and were backdated under a different task number, then there are further violations—"

Three men burst into the office. They weren't going to be amused and they weren't going to be impressed by anything Alan said or did. One of them—the least threatening—was from building security; the other two were either serving or former military. Alan held up the DIA badge that had been hanging from his pocket. "Craik, Captain, US Navy." He had to say it three times. It did keep them from jumping on him, but it didn't keep him from getting hustled out. Ritter followed them, still screaming. Nobody came out of the offices to see what it was about. Maybe they were used to it. Three women in the corridor shrank back against the walls.

Outside the code-locked door, Ritter now inside and seeming to wind down, they checked his ID. They weren't sympathetic—he'd been in their space without authorization—but they had to admit he was a Navy captain.

"So you were here without authorization, *sir*, and Mister Ritter says you were abusive, *sir*, and a report will have to be made, *sir*. So get out of here and don't come back, you follow me? *Sir*?"

He laughed. "I'll be back," he said.

It was barely nine when he got to his office. The work was piled up; people wanted to see him; the phone was ringing. He didn't take off for lunch but used the time to write a report of his encounter with Ritter, then filed one copy and sent another off to the security officer. Late in the day he looked up the number of the Director of Naval Intelligence and dialed it on his telephone. He had worked for the Director when he was younger, and he could call him by his first name. Then he called Mike Dukas on a STU.

The breakfast table in Dervaig was covered in artifacts. There were as many of them as there were pancakes. Piat ate and fondled, ate and read from a book, ate and tried to talk. He was tired, running on nerves, and pretty much unable to form a coherent thought.

"Wow," he said for the third time.

Dykes turned a chair backwards, put his own tower of pancakes down on the table, and started to eat.

McLean didn't light his pipe, but he fondled it. "What do you suggest we do, Jack?"

Piat stared at a lapis pendant and a perfectly preserved wooden plate. They were the best items. The plate had a clean break across the surface, but the heavy oak was otherwise untouched by a few millennia of immersion.

"Wow," he said for the fourth time. He drank some coffee and rubbed at his chin, where two scars reminded him of his accelerated awakening process, prompted by the alert on his pager and the seven codes contained on it. He couldn't remember shaving—just bandaging the result.

"I think it's all Bronze Age." Piat fingered his chin again. He picked up the lapis pendant. "You think there's *more*?"

Dykes stopped chewing for a minute. "I'm not an archaeologist. Fuck, man, I'm not even a grave robber. But I read books, and McLean knows a thing or two. We think it's a trove-like, somebody dumped the family treasures off the patio 'cause the barbarians were at the gates."

Piat rubbed his eyes. "Okay. So there's more."

"What do you suggest we do?" McLean leaned forward.

Piat shrugged. "It's going to get pretty complicated if we

come up with more stuff. I've got a guy selling the other stuff. The stuff I bought to sell off this dig. You with me?"

Both of the divers nodded.

"I never expected there to be actual artifacts. Or rather, I hoped there might be some, but I was prepared for the other eventuality." He rubbed the lapis pendant again. It was good enough for the Louvre.

"Obviously," Dykes said.

"I'm worried that too much stuff will make the dig look fake. Trust me—irony and all, if we dump all this into the pot with the other items you found and the stuff I bought to sell, the whole thing will look like a put-up job."

"Which it was," Dykes said with a slow smile.

"But now it isn't," McLean said. He took a match out of his pocket but just stopped himself from lighting the pipe.

He really wants to smoke. "Go ahead and smoke," Piat said.

McLean jerked his chin at Dykes. Dykes shook his head. "No way. I mean, no way. I put up with twenty-four years o' that shit in the Nav. Smoke when I'm done eating."

McLean looked at Piat and shrugged.

Piat filled the ensuing silence by eating more pancakes. The he scraped his plate and sucked the golden syrup off his fork. "Okay. Fuck it. I'll get my guy to sell this stuff, too. It's funny in a way—the stuff you guys found is better than the stuff I seeded. This pendant—it's a home run."

McLean set his pipe down. "I want somebody real to be notified. Back door. So the site gets salvaged." He looked at Dykes.

"He's been saying that for three days. I say we hold it for a year and then sell it off," said Dykes. "But I admit, I been paid, and you never said shares. I only say that you never said shares 'cause there wasn't anything to share. Or so you said."

Both men were watching him carefully. It was a dangerous

kind of watching—the kind of intensity that meant that the wrong answer would have serious repercussions. Piat's problem was that he didn't know what the right answer was. Thinking was like walking in a dark fog.

"How long to clean up and get out?" Piat asked.

"A week. Maybe more, because I have to go down south for two days and Dykes can't do it on his own. And we can't work in the daylight." McLean had his pipe in hand again.

"And it is *fucking* cold," Dykes put in. "We got to clean up around the stack—the crannog. And that water is cold." McLean shoveled his last forkful into his mouth and chewed.

Piat rubbed his eyes again. "Okay. I need sleep. Sure, I can find a way to tell somebody in the halls of academe. When the coast is clear. And I'll give you both shares in the pendant—you found it. And what the fuck, gentlemen—there's really going to be plenty of money to go around." Piat looked at the assortment of artifacts—the pendant was much more like a work of art, and he thought briefly of Irene—and thought *I probably won't ever have to work again.* The pendant might earn seven figures. Other items, already sold—the two gold beads, a polished stone axe head, and the fakes—had already filled his Greek bank account. He shook his head, unable to get his mind around so much success. He looked up at them. "My own free pass to move this stuff could expire any time now. Yeah. Pull the plug."

Apparently, it was a good answer. Both men nodded. Dykes swallowed his last bite and nodded. McLean scraped his match on the scarred wooden tabletop and waited while the sulphur burned away before lighting his pipe.

"Of course, you're going to help carry it all down," McLean said.

Piat rolled his eyes. "*After* I make a little trip that's coming up." He wanted to keep them there until he was done with Hackbutt and the prince. Talismans? Good luck tokens? Muscle, at any rate. "Hang around for a week or so, okay?"

"It's your penny."

The next morning, Hackbutt announced that the weather was perfect to check his eggs.

Piat looked blank, and Hackbutt gave him a big grin. "I'm part of the sea eagle project, Jack. Remember? I have a nest that I watch up on Glen More. It's a hell of a climb—takes me half the day. Annie's coming over to feed the birds."

Piat still had to struggle with all of the differences between the new Digger and the man he had known in Southeast Asia. He glanced at Irene. "Go ahead. I can have a day without spy shit in the studio. Praise the Lord."

The dog was less forgiving. He wanted to go where Piat went now. Twice, Piat had taken him in the car and then up the long haul to the loch. Ralph had thought it was heaven.

So Piat found himself driving to the great glen of Mull without the dog and with Hackbutt babbling happily about the sea eagle reclamation project. "I've had two birds."

Piat was negotiating a lay-by. He wanted to make a point about how useful such enforced stops could be for locating surveillance, but he didn't like to interrupt Hackbutt, especially the new Hackbutt.

Piat was enjoying the road—it was early, and he had the glen road all to himself. He was going too fast, and he knew it. Hackbutt was boring him, but listening to Hackbutt was part of the game. Listening, being interested, being involved. "I remember the program, Digger. So what're we doing today? Looking for another chick?"

Hackbutt shook his head. "No—nothing like that. This time of year, I just keep an eye on the nest. I try and check every month. I feel like I know them."

"Are these birds Bella's parents?" Piat asked, glancing by habit down at the river below. Water was high. Good fishing.

Hackbutt grunted assent, eyes on the mountaintops.

As soon as Piat had the parking brake on, Hackbutt was

out of the car, a pair of binoculars up to his eyes. Piat took out his heavy walking boots and put them on.

The day was bright and clear, with some high clouds moving fast from the east. The mountains rose into the clear air, the sun sparkling off the water on their rocky slopes. The great glen seemed as vast as the steppes of Russia. From where Piat sat tying his laces, he could see nine miles to the most distant mountain slope.

"I can see them!" said Hackbutt. "They're on the nest! Jack, I'm going to be able to show you something extraordinary. You'll be amazed. Come!"

Piat was pushing spare socks into his pack. "Lunch? Water? You have all that?"

Hackbutt plucked his pack out of the trunk. "Of course. Water, thermos of tea. Irene made us a crock of guacamole. Jack, I never knew you to be so slow. Come on."

The Hackbutt he had known in Asia would never have remembered to pack a lunch, much less to pack for someone else. Piat rolled up a rain jacket, checked that he had a compass and map (old habits die hard) and pulled a sweater on.

"Where are we going?" he asked.

Hackbutt thrust an arm into the sky. "Look for a tree—the only tree on the hill. Just below the last big rock outcrop. See it?"

Piat looked and looked. He raised his own binoculars, found the peak, and then located a single tree growing precariously from the crotch of a washed-out chimney just a few hundred meters below the peak. "Jesus, Digger. We're going all the way up there?"

Hackbutt raised an eyebrow—a gesture Piat had never seen him use before. Just for a second, Hackbutt, in his tweed trousers and vest, looked a little like Clyde Partlow. "I told you it would take us half the day. Are you ready? Can we get started?"

And they were off.

It was hard walking. The solid gravel-based path gave out in fifty meters and was replaced by sheep trails of the kind that Piat had experienced getting to the crannog. The grass was the same coarse stuff he'd seen elsewhere. Generations of sheep had cut the turf down to bedrock in places, so that a misstep could plunge a hiker knee-deep in mire.

There was no one path, and sometimes the two men diverged, choosing different lines to get up the slope. After the first mile, Piat called a halt to pull off his sweater and swallow tea from his thermos. Hackbutt stood by like a pointer waiting for the first bird. The paths continued up and up, steeper and steeper as they climbed, until around mid-morning they encountered the first sheer rock face. Hackbutt skirted the boulder field and stayed with the sheep, moving quickly and confidently from hummock to hummock until he found a better line up the slope. Piat took a different route born of years spent rock climbing—he went straight up a fissure, skinning his knee but gaining ten meters on Hackbutt as he shinnied over the top of the outcrop.

It was a race. Piat hadn't realized it until that moment, but Hackbutt was off again up the slope, sparing Piat just one glance. He hadn't imagined Hackbutt would attempt to compete with him—Hackbutt had always been such a nerd that he didn't do macho at all.

Until today.

Piat had done some rock climbing—enough that he could take a straighter line to the tree, but every face he negotiated squandered energy, and Hackbutt didn't seem to slow or tire. Somewhere on the top third of the mountain, Piat had to concede that Hackbutt was in better physical shape than he. Piat's arms were burning; his upper thighs felt as if they were made of lead; and he had to take a Hackbutt route around a rock face because he didn't think his body could take another rock climb without a rest.

"Jack!" Hackbutt was suddenly above him. "Bear left, Jack! We don't want to scare them. Follow me!" And he was off again.

Piat hauled himself to his feet, defeat conceded. Hackbutt was still bounding with energy. Piat was at the point of glancing too often at the tree to see if it was any closer. His breath was coming in gasps.

"You're not tired? Jack? Are you all right?" Hackbutt was close above him now, and whispering.

Piat took two deep breaths. "I'm fine," he said.

"We have to be quiet from here, Jack. Take it easy—and don't climb the rocks. They know we're here—but we don't want to upset them. I have a hide up here, just on that stream—follow the line—other way. See? I'm going to cast farther left to keep the hide between us and the birds. Follow me. Okay, Jack?"

"Okay," Piat said.

The hide consisted of a dark green PVC tarp covered in dry bracken with a thick layer of cut grass on the floor for comfort. It sat on a miniature bluff over a deep cut in the rock where one of the mountain's hundred burns rushed under their feet.

"The sound of the water covers me. I can move around, change position, take pictures—the birds won't care. Like I said—they know we're here, but we're not in their faces."

Piat was full length on the bracken, a cup of tea in a trembling hand. He waited for Hackbutt to go on but the other man was suddenly silent. As if aware that the silence was wrong, Hackbutt snatched up the binoculars and began to search the rocks and the sky. Piat, exhausted, was happy to let him do it; it was just Hackbutt being Hackbutt.

But it wasn't. After the silence had extended and extended and then snapped and been replaced by Piat's own thoughts, a desire to sleep, Hackbutt put the binoculars on the ground and said, without turning around, "Irene and I had a fight last night. She slept in her studio."

Piat heard a warning in the voice. *About me*?

"I wanted to make love, as a way of—" He waved a hand. He still wasn't looking at Piat; his eyes were on the nest. He laughed. "There's an old joke about two newlyweds. They put a jar at the head of the bed, and every time they make love for the first year, they put a penny in it. Then, for the rest of their lives, every time they make love, they take a penny out. And they never empty the jar." He shook his head and pulled at a piece of bracken. "I've always thought that's the saddest joke I ever heard." Now he turned to look at Piat. "We've been together five years." He went back to plucking at the bracken.

"Is she still mad?"

"She was never mad. She's thinking of leaving me." He smiled back at Piat, his head tilted so that the smile looked furtive. "I don't think she knows it herself, but it's what she was fighting about."

"You can't know that, Digger! She loves you!"

Hackbutt didn't seem to hear. He looked out over the vast expanse below them, all the way down the mountain, over the thread of road, the flattened, green land, to the sea and the islands far off in the haze. "It's like I'm seeing Irene through a zoom lens, getting smaller and smaller, going away— I thought it was about you, but I decided that it wasn't."

"Me!" He tried to cover, talking fast. "Irene and I got over disliking each other, Dig; she's not upset about me being there all the time anymore."

"I thought it was you." He turned and looked at Piat. "But you wouldn't do that, would you, Jack." It wasn't a question, but a statement. Perhaps, just perhaps, a warning.

Piat thought about equivocations. He probably thought too long. He shrugged. "No," he said after too long a delay.

"It would sink the operation. And that's what you care about." He picked up the binoculars, but he didn't put them to his eyes. "And—I don't think you'd do that to me."

He looked back and their eyes met. Piat said, "This is why you got me up here."

"Yeah, I guess so." Hackbutt frowned at his thought. "I can say what I mean up here."

Then he began to watch the eagles, and after a few minutes he began to talk about them and then to point out the islands and tell Piat which was which. Piat, still weak from the climb, let himself be silenced by the display of authority he'd seen. But Hackbutt wouldn't stop, and Piat pulled himself together because that was what Hackbutt expected.

I like him, Piat thought. It was a revelation. But he couldn't say so. He didn't even know how. Instead, he said, "Holy mother of God, Digger, is that Ireland?"

"No, Jack. That's Ulva. There's Iona—see? I forget the others—the big islands. Ulva has another nesting pair. Iona has some unique terns." Hackbutt passed his glasses over the infinite spaces behind them and then lay down and pointed his binoculars up the mountain at the nest.

"Both of them. Oh, Jack!" he whispered. "Look!"

Piat looked. The birds were big, well developed. Their nest was a pile of offal and bird shit at the top of the cleft, supported by two big rocks. There were bones and bloody bits scattered over the top of the nest and coating the rocks all the way to the base.

"Old nest?" Piat asked.

"I think so. I think they've been here for*ever*. The old Ordnance Survey calls that feature Creag na h-Iolaire—that's the eagle's crag, in Gaelic. Gaelic! How long have they been here, Jack? Two thousand years? Five thousand years?"

"Fantastic," Piat said. In fact, it was better than fantastic. The two birds—Bella's parents—were huge through his binoculars. They were quite clearly repairing the nest.

Hackbutt was beaming at him. "I'm so happy you came," he said. "I've tried to get Irene to come—but it's not her—"

"Cup of tea?" Piat murmured, the binocs still perched on his nose. "It's a tough climb, Digger. I'm wasted. You're not even breathing hard."

Hackbutt laughed. "You're so good at everything, Jack. You're so surprised to lose at anything. You remember that night in Jakarta—in the bar? You sang 'Roland the Headless Thompson Gunner.' You turned off the karaoke machine. You remember?"

Piat nodded. He remembered that there had been such an evening. He must have been pretty drunk.

"And I thought—God, he can even sing."

"You're embarrassing me." Piat shook his head.

"No, Jack—you started it. You made me see that I needed to do something—something worth doing. Here I am."

Piat found himself looking at a man who could climb a mountain and handle a wild eagle. He thought of the same man's crying on the gravel drive. Without thinking it through, he said, "Digger—why can't you always be like this?"

Hackbutt had started to root in his pack, and now he stopped, and a slow smile spread over his face.

"Like what?" he asked. But the smile suggested that he already knew.

It was dark by the time they made it down the mountain. Piat was obscurely pleased that Hackbutt had forgotten to bring a torch—he might have thought that every trace of the nerd had been washed away down the mountain. They didn't talk much, climbing down or in the car. But when Piat pulled up at the farm, he gave Hackbutt's shoulder a squeeze.

"That was a great day," he said.

"Yup," Hackbutt replied. "You said it, Jack."

"Take the weekend off, Digger. I'll see you Monday." Piat had other plans in motion and some other work to do, and he already dreaded what his leg muscles would do in the morning.

"Don't you want to come in and see Irene?" Hackbutt asked. Piat wondered what, exactly, Hackbutt was asking.

"No," Piat said. And then, realizing that he'd made a gaffe—"Just send her my regards, Digger. I'm beat."

Hackbutt leaned back into the car with a wide smile. "You need to get more exercise, Jack."

Piat laughed as he drove away, because it was the phrase with which he'd ended almost every meeting with Digger in the old days.

The next day, Piat awoke with aching joints and the thin memory of a dream. As he washed his face, flashes of the dream came up at him, as if from the water in the sink. Something about Irene and Partlow—Hackbutt had been in it too.

He drove to the farm, equally afraid that he would see her and that he wouldn't. He wasn't sure he had anything to say to her. He still wanted to say something.

But she wasn't there. She was moving the first load of boxes to the ferry, and Piat found Hackbutt on the hillside. Hackbutt was standing in a circle of beaten grass with Bella on his arm. He smiled at Piat when he came up, but otherwise the big bird had his complete attention. He was talking to her quietly, and she had her head turned a little away, as if she only had one good ear and were listening carefully.

Piat moved until he was at Hackbutt's elbow.

"You want to hold her, Jack?" Hackbutt asked.

Piat reached out and took her. She hesitated only a moment before stepping from Hackbutt's arm to his.

"I'm saying goodbye, Jack," Hackbutt said. He had the tracks of tears on his face, but his voice was strong and soft. Controlled. "I thought about what you said. About everything you said. I guess I'm willing to give up Bella—to save people. That's what it is, isn't it? Because that guy—the prince—he's a bad man. I can tell."

Everyone's the hero in his own movie, Digger. Piat almost said it, because it was the truth, and terms like good and bad had no meaning to Piat. Except that, while causes didn't move him, people did, and right now, with the big eagle on his fist under the slate-gray sky, Piat didn't feel like lying to Hackbutt at all.

So he stood with the man and the bird and the sky, and together they said goodbye by saying nothing at all. And then they walked back down the hill.

The next day, the cartons that had filled the house's corridor were gone, and so was Irene. She hadn't told him when she was going. It was better that way, he thought: with Hackbutt standing by, they could hardly have talked about where they would meet when he was back from Bahrain. If they were going to meet at all. Piat already had the uneasy feeling that the prospect of wealth would change him. And that the Piat who owned his own future might not have much to offer Irene. Or was it the other way around?

Then there were two days of marking time, when he took long walks with the dog and walked for the twentieth time through Tobermory's shops and sat in the Mishnish bar and nursed some single malt he hadn't tried before. Without Irene, Edgar was both edgy and elated: he missed her, but no relationship is perfect, and without admitting it he liked the freedom of being alone. He asked Piat to make macaroni and cheese for supper, a dish he liked but Irene wouldn't make ("Redneck food, Eddie"). Yet the imminence of parting with Bella had him staring out of windows at the rain and moving through his own house like a restless ghost.

The next day, a man appeared in an aging green van to get Bella. Piat had helped Hackbutt find the perfect travel cage for her: they had sat together going through the back pages of his falconry magazines, looking for advertisements. When they found one Hackbutt thought he might approve, Piat would make a note and later look it up on the web. Hackbutt had had almost impossible requirements, but Piat had told him that he had to choose because they were in now and they had to go through with it. In the end, he had ordered a huge, dome-topped cage of ABS plastic with screened windows and cast-in food and water dishes that could be filled from the outside.

The pickup man was sandy-haired, middle-aged, cheerful. Piat thought he had a look of the long-time sergeant, probably one now double-dipping for MI6. It made sense that Partlow had informed the Brits, particularly to get the paperwork on the strictly illegal shipping of an endangered bird to a foreign country.

"Sign, if you please," the man said. "Six places—there's a little red arrow stuck to each one. Hard to miss." He looked around, stretched. "Beautiful day." They were outside; it was sunny with a few big clouds like puffs of cigar smoke. The dog was running among the three of them.

"*Thank* you," he said. He produced another sheaf of papers. "Your copies of the shipping packet—customs forms, letter from the ministry, letter from Foreign Affairs—" Piat glanced at it and read "... for transfer of a rare avian female to another government for breeding purposes—" Well, close enough.

The man was going on. "—letter from the Royal Ornithological Society—waiver of CITES treaty requirements—" Piat handed each one to Hackbutt. He didn't want to hear about breaking laws or violating a trust after the bird was gone.

Partlow had done his part well. Barring a personal note from the prime minister, a nation could hardly have put more clearly on paper its willingness that its laws and international treaties be violated.

"Well, then." The man checked over the signed documents and removed the little red stickers, which he rolled between his fingers and thrust into a pocket. "Let's have this bird then, shall we?"

Hackbutt turned away. Piat went with the man, who dragged a red dolly behind him, to the bird pens, where Bella was already in the new, commodious cage. Hackbutt had been trying to accustom her to it. The man looked at it, looked at Bella without getting too close, whistled in appreciation. "Do you a right wound with that beak, wouldn't she!"

He began to work the dolly under the cage.

"You're driving her to Glasgow?"

"Holy Loch." He gave Piat a look that meant he'd say no more about that, but if Piat had any sense he'd see that Bella was going to be flown out by military air.

Better and better. Holy Loch to Bahrain, one way, no customs.

When they were back in the front yard, Hackbutt had his own bundle of paper to hand over. He'd written out in painstaking block printing instructions on feeding, watering, petting, flying Bella. He'd in fact written a monograph on the care of traveling eagles.

The man took it all. "Right. Going to ask you about this sort of thing." He'd already found the cast-in pocket on the side of the cage for documents. He put the feeding and watering instructions in it and taped them down with a roll of black tape from a pocket. "Don't you worry, sir," he said. He seemed to have grasped at once who the real owner of the bird was and how he felt. "She'll be cared for like she's a baby." He put the rest of Hackbutt's writings with the legal papers. He brandished the packet. "This'll ride with her every step of the way." He winked at Piat. "Wouldn't want to get in trouble with the powers that be, would I?"

He and Piat lifted the cage into the van; the doors closed, and Hackbutt winced. The dog, sitting nearby, cocked his head.

"I'm to be contacted when she arrives," Piat said.

"Not my area of responsibility, sir, but I'm sure that if that's the arrangement, then that's the way it will happen." Then he waved at them and got into his vehicle and drove away.

They looked after the van long after it had climbed the hill and disappeared. Piat put an arm around Hackbutt's shoulders. Tears were running down Hackbutt's nose.

20

The London Conference came around every year, and if you were one of the ones who went you pissed and moaned but in fact you knew that you were one of a very select group in the intelligence community. It was what one old hand had called a "love feast with the cousins," but there was a lot of acrimony these days, too. Nobody on either side had come off well after Iraq; blame was inevitable.

For Alan Craik, it was a first time, and he was therefore a little apart from the old Anglo-American irritations. Nonetheless, nervous that he do it right, he had scheduled himself to go over early, learn the ground, taking with him a lieutenant-commander and Sergeant Swaricki as backup. He landed at Heathrow on the Friday morning, less jet-lagged than most because he was an old hand at sleeping on aircraft, went right to the obligatory four-star hotel and was checked in by eight-thirty. Uncle could pay for the extra half-day. Uncle was getting his money's worth.

Leaving Swaricki to catch up on his sleep, he went to the American embassy to touch base and introduce the lieutenant-commander around, then MI5's glass castle on the Thames to do the same, then out to an obscure suburban business park where they went over the meeting rooms, got briefed on security, found the johns and made sure there would be coffee. Swaricki met them there and Craik left him and the lieutenant-commander to establish a beachhead. By lunchtime, he was ready to meet his British opposite numbers—four of them—and the US deputy naval attaché at somebody's club. He was back in his hotel by four.

He sat on his bed and let himself be tempted by the idea of a nap. Another idea was more tempting, however: the island of Mull, where Dukas said Partlow's perhaps kinky operation was supposed to be preparing, only a few hundred miles away: *Mull, Piat, Falconer*. He admitted to himself that that proximity was the real reason he'd come to London on Friday and sailed through his London responsibilities, the idea of a visit always at the back of his mind. He could still be in London in plenty of time for Sunday's pre-conference brief—plenty of time, for that matter, to see Partlow if he had to. Partlow was a fixture at the London Conference.

He pushed a pillow aside as if it represented the idea of a nap and picked up the telephone. He could fly to Glasgow, but not to the island, and a sleeper train left London at ten-thirty and would put him in Glasgow sixish; he winced at the price but made the reservation—no having to hustle to and from airports, no super-early wake-up. Another call got him a rental car, and a few minutes on his laptop brought him a ferry schedule to Mull and a reservation on the early ferry. Piece of cake.

Then he called his wife and explained how easy the expense was on a captain's salary.

He rolled the little car up the welted steel of the ramp and off the ferry, and he was on Mull. The island had risen around them as the ship had got close to it; then, coming to it with his back to the sea, it looked like its own small mainland, solid and self-sufficient. There were a shop and a tourist center and a gas station and a pub, a big parking lot and a lot of people waiting to walk on board—weekend shoppers headed to the mainland, perhaps. He thought he knew on sight that they weren't an American crowd, something about posture and maybe clothes, although any notion that the British were any longer bound by jacket-and-tie dress codes was nonsense. The faces looked pink—sea mist and cold air—hospitable, very alive. The women in the information center were absurdly helpful and—the only word for it—*nice*.

Craik drove north toward Tobermory, the only town of any size (all of a thousand people?), wondering where Piat was right then. To find out, he'd have to start where he and Piat had last left off—fishing. Piat had seemed pretty dedicated to the sport; if he was living on the island now, Craik thought, he had to be doing some fishing. Unless he was that good—so adept at cover that he could completely shed the old skin of himself, including even his hobbies.

Tobermory's Tackle and Books was the place for fishing, according to all the tourist brochures. It was at the far end of the town's main street, thus not easy for the novice to find by sight. Nevertheless, a few minutes' walking found it. He took it in at a glance, made sure Piat himself wasn't in there, entered; a tall man looked up from a counter and grinned and went back to explaining something about a USB stick to a frowning, middle-aged woman. Alan waited, hung about, looked at a book or two, came back when no customers were at the counter.

"Fishing?"

"Oh, yes, lots of fishing. Sea or freshwater? Awfully good sea fishing now, couple of big skate the last few days."

"Fresh. A friend recommended it."

"Oh, I'm glad to hear that!" The man went down a list of waters, pros and cons, then got a flat book like a ledger from under the counter and went over a couple of pages, a long finger tracking down a set of columns. He seemed to have great enthusiasm for his work. And for the fishing, a lot of which he seemed to know firsthand.

"Salmon?" Alan said. He thought that Piat had been salmon-fishing in Iceland.

The man made a quick clown grimace. "Not much right now, I'm afraid. The Aros, maybe—" He sounded doubtful. "Lots of excellent trout, though! The Mishnish Lochs—"

Somebody else was asking a question; the man excused himself and moved down the counter to the other customer. Alan without hurry spun the book around and glanced down the open pages. Days of the week across the top, fishing down the left side. Here and there, names penciled in—not many people fished, he thought—with now and then the number of fish caught. One set of entries jumped off the page—a single venue where somebody had fished again and again. He turned back a page and saw the same pattern; back another, and back to the week when he had called Dukas because Partlow had wanted Piat back. That's where the entries started; the week before, there were none.

"Find anything?" the man behind the counter said. "Sorry about that—somebody's computer problem—where were we?"

"This loch—you say loch?—where this, I suppose it's a man, Mister Michaels been fishing every other day."

"Oh, yes, yes, Jack Michaels! Yes! He *loves* it up there! Hard spot to reach, half an hour's walk in and it's mostly uphill, but he *loves* it. Getting quite nice trout, too, he says." He gave Alan his big grin and looked apologetic. "But if you're just here for a day or two, there's lots of easier places to get to. If it's a matter of time, I mean."

Alan asked where the loch was; a map was produced, the loch identified. He could see from the contours how rugged the walk in would be. If "Michaels" was in fact Piat, he was in good shape. The loch wasn't big but would be magnificently isolated, certainly a virtue for somebody like Piat. At one end, there was a small extension of the lake, almost a second, smaller lake, and a penciled circle.

"What's that?"

"Oh, that's the crannog. Michaels was interested in it, too. They are rather neat, actually—man-made island. Bronze Age. Bit special." The grin came again. "Long walk to see it, though. There's a more accessible one in Loch Squabain."

Alan said he'd think about the fishing, and he veered off to the flat boxes of flies that sat on the counter, bought a mixed dozen, bought an Ordnance Survey map, and said he'd be back after he'd talked to his wife. This seemed to please the man behind the counter as much as if he'd taken all the fishings for a month and he liked nothing better than spending his time explaining things to strangers.

The path to the loch would have been almost invisible except for recent use. Craik supposed it was all Piat's comings and goings. He'd seen at the bottom of the hill where Piat parked his car—flattened strips in the coarse grass—and had left his own nearby. He was chancing Piat's seeing it, but the book in the tackle shop had told him that Piat never came here on a weekend. And if he saw the rental car, he mightn't get too wrung out over it. The island was full of rental cars.

His respect for Piat's fitness grew as he climbed. The path was steep and rough, in places no more than broken, pale grass growing in uneven tussocks. Sheep used it, too; in muddy spots, there were deeply stamped hoof marks, and, in one high above the gorge of a small burn, clear human footprints. Piat's, he was sure, but somebody else's, too—there were two tread patterns. He was careful not to add his own to them. He found himself walking too fast, pushing himself, feeling the exhilaration of a completely free day and a completely new place. He was smiling.

He came in at the head of the loch, which lay in a bowl with at first shallow sides, then rapidly steeper ones as the mountains loomed above it. A stream ran out on his left, doubtless the burn he had seen below. Ahead at the far end of the loch was the little extension and its supposedly man-made island. He headed for them.

He knew that Piat sometimes dealt in antiquities. He knew that Piat was a crook. Those things might add up to interest in a Bronze Age island in the back of nowhere. Something other than trout must be bringing Piat way up here, he thought, and there were no houses to hold attractive women.

He used some harsh navy language as he came around the loch: there was no track, foul footing. The wind blew in his face, rippling the water so it looked dark and hostile. A light rain was falling. At the top of the mountain on the other side, water began to run down slender rock faces like silver threads.

Everything was rock, so there were no footprints near the water. The little loch was shallow, however, and sheltered from the wind; he could see rocks under the water that looked like stepping stones heading out to the crannog, which looked to him quite natural, eternal, wild, except that it was perfectly round. And had those stepping stones leading to it.

He walked along the bank, studying the crannog through binoculars. Something yellow showed between the clumps of grass. Bright yellow, the yellow of slickers and plastic technical gear. Not natural or wild or eternal. Near it was a cone of what appeared to be mud. Like the crannog itself, it was round, but unlike it looked man-made—too perfect, too bare of grass.

He looked at the stepping stones and guessed that the water was too deep to jump from one to another. And too deep to wade. He looked up into the drizzle of rain. Cloud was blowing up the valley and swallowing the mountains.

Craik sighed. Then he laughed. He was going to do a silly thing for the sheer exuberance of the day.

He stripped down to underwear and T-shirt and waded in.

The water was even colder than he had expected. The bottom was ooze with rock under it, gooey and insecure. He waded deeper, feeling goose flesh rise on his chest and arms. The water reached his groin. He groaned, leaned forward, and pushed himself into a glide, the cold like a harsh embrace; then three hard strokes and he was pulling himself up the crannog's side. Close to, its rock structure showed—an island piled up stone by stone three thousand years ago.

The mud cone that he had seen was some kind of tailing made up entirely of tiny particles. Rubbed in the fingers, it felt like wet dough. *Sifted,* he thought. Nearby, as if tossed aside, was a wooden frame with a wire-mesh screening. *Not very high tech.* Still, it would work—one or two men shoveling mud into it, then shaking it, wetting it.

The bright yellow he'd seen was the tube of a snorkel. *Careless.* That didn't sound like Piat. The other footprint in the path meant that he had at least one helper—a somewhat careless helper. Or, more likely, more than one, to work while Piat did whatever he was doing with the falconer.

Under a camouflage tarp was a machine with a plastic hose and a funnel-like end. The big, bulging part was an air compressor, he was sure (a metal plate on the side said "Hibernia Compression Limited"). A paste-on label told him the name of the rental company that had supplied it. He didn't need to be an underwater specialist to see that the thing was a kind of vacuum cleaner—the mud went in the wide end of the funnel and got spat out—perhaps into the sifter—at the other. *At least two men.* Under the tarp with the contraption was a metal detector, two sets of black swim fins, air tanks. He wondered if they used the compressor to refill the tanks, too—it was a long haul up here with more of them. It must have been a long haul getting the stuff here in the first place.

He was shivering almost violently by then. His exhilaration persisted—near-naked under a threatening sky, wind blowing, rain; it was *great*!—but his body was objecting.

He swam back, rubbed himself as hard as he could with

his sweater, put his digital camera and a pencil and a scrap of paper from a brochure into the plastic sack he'd carried lunch in, and went back into the water. When the water hit his chest, he knew he should have done it all in one trip.

One of the brochures he'd picked up at the tourist center was for a place called Wings Over Mull, which raised and showed falcons. It wasn't all that far from Piat's fishing loch, in fact. He didn't think that it would be where he'd find Piat's falconer—he didn't *want* it to be where he'd find Piat's falconer—because it looked too public and too smooth. His hair was still wet from the loch when he pulled into their parking area; although he'd got over shivering on the walk out, his skin still felt damp and clammy to him under his clothes.

He walked around a couple of buildings, looking for life. The wind was raw now, the drizzle turned to real rain. He started to shiver again. At last, life found him.

"Help you?" a girl said from the corner of a building. She might have been fifteen, might have been twenty-two, pink-cheeked, small-chinned, smiling. "You're a bit wet."

"Been swimming."

She laughed. "Feels like it, doesn't it." Her voice went up and down like the island roads. You could *really* learn to like living here, he thought.

"Mister Michaels said this was the best place on the island to see the birds."

"I don't know a Mister Michaels. Is he a falconer?"

"Friend of mine. American."

She shook her head. "No, sorry. But we've lots of birds! We're closed just now, but we're doing an exhibition at four o'clock; you can come back and see them flighted."

"Well—" He was trying to play the confused tourist, but he was shivering so hard he was having a hard time concentrating. "I'm sure my friend said there was this falconer on

Mull he knew. That was the idea—a personal friend. Let me get close to the birds."

"Oh, we couldn't do that."

"Um." He tightened his back to stop the shivering. "Is anybody else on the island into birds?"

"Well, there's the sea eagle project at Craignure. And there's bird-watchers galore." She giggled suddenly. "Well, there's old Mister Hackbutt up at Killbriddy. But he's—" She stopped as if it would be impolite to say what old Hackbutt was.

"Yeah, Jack said he was a little—" Alan put a shaking hand out, rocked it back and forth.

She giggled again. "I've never seen him m'self, but I've heard he can be a little dee-ficult. He's American."

"We're a difficult lot."

She laughed, not a giggle but an older, womanly sound. She looked at him and blushed, as if she might be saying, *You're far too old for me, but still—* He got out his map and she showed him where Killbriddy was. He saw the double lines of the "highway"—a single-lane road—then the thread of what might be a sheep track leading to old Hackbutt's farm. The rental-car company wouldn't be pleased with what he was about to do, he thought.

"You really helped."

"Come back at four."

"I'd like to." He really meant it but knew he wouldn't. But he left smiling, thinking how much he really would like to come back.

The road to Hackbutt's was not as bad as he'd feared, paved after a fashion, helped by the lack of other cars. He drove past the house that corresponded to Hackbutt's location on the map and went over a hill, up and up, not passing another house, at last finding a place to turn around where a pasture gate made a little lay-by. He headed back past the place and pulled in over the brow of the next hill and walked back off the road, his pant legs wet from the knees down from the grass.

He found himself a kind of snuggery in a rock outcrop and sat down. His waxed-cotton coat gave him a dry seat, but when he tried to stretch his legs out, the backs of his thighs were immediately soaked. He put his binoculars to his eyes and tried to look like a man watching birds.

After an hour, a girl he thought to be in her teens came down the road on a bicycle from the other direction. She turned into Hackbutt's and propped the bike against the house, prompting great enthusiasm in a black-and-white dog who had been lying near a fence. She didn't go in but patted the dog and went around the back, then reappeared heading for some sort of shed, from which she emerged after fifteen minutes with a bucket whose weight pulled her far down to that side. He thought she was probably like the young girls you see around stables, who wouldn't run a vacuum cleaner at home but were delighted to muck out horseshit for free. He watched the girl go to a series of pens, some invisible behind trees or other buildings, the bucket getting lighter as she worked. It took her forty-five minutes. He saw only two birds; the rest, he guessed, were inside the ramshackle coops that dotted the terrain behind the house. Then she took the dog for a quick walk beyond the fence and got back on her bike, rubbing her hands on her wet blue jeans—blood, he guessed, from raw meat for the birds—and pedaled up the long hill and out of sight.

The falconer and Piat weren't there, then. And they were away for at least the day and maybe more, or they wouldn't have needed the girl.

Craik walked down to the farm and looked in the house windows. A few items from Bali or someplace similar, souvenirs—Hackbutt had lived in Southeast Asia, perhaps. Another window showed him a not particularly clean kitchen, another a bedroom. The bedroom told him that a woman lived there, too.

He caught the last ferry of the day and was on the late plane out of Glasgow for London. No sleeper trains on Saturdays. He was thinking about what he would tell Rose when he called home. He would say, *I've found us a place to retire to.*

21

To begin with, Piat's flight was two hours late getting to Bahrain.

Bahrain was, as usual, full of surveillance—it just wasn't directed at him. He passed through several bubbles and noted their activity—local police, local military, American. All busy watching somebody else.

He went to his hotel, a faceless modern high-rise, and right to his room to shower and try to wash off some of the jet lag. He put a cell phone where he could reach it from the shower—one call and the cell phone would be finished, but the call was an important one. It was the comm link with whoever had brought Bella into Bahrain.

He had finished the shower and had dressed again and was lying on the bed thinking about how he would recruit Mohamed when the ditzy little jingling went off.

"Yes?"

"Uh—I'm calling about a bird."

That's what the man was supposed to say, silly as it sounded. Piat said that birds could be found at the Manama zoo, which also sounded equally silly but was supposed to satisfy the guy at the other end.

"Uh, yeah—well—"

"Where and when?"

"Uh, sir, well— Uh, there's a small problem."

Small problem never meant small. Piat cursed silently and felt his blood pressure go up. What he was supposed to do next was walk the route he'd want Hackbutt to take next morning. "What kind of problem?"

"Uh, sir, the bird is, uh, sick."

"Sick! Sick how?"

"He *looks* sick. He isn't eating. He's, uh, kind of shaggy—"

"It's a she, not a he. Where have you got her? Is she in the animal quarters?" Bella was supposed to be in the special animal transfer facility at Manama International, or at least that was where Piat had expected her to be. They had a vet there, and they should know how to care for even an eagle that was off its feed.

"No, sir. She didn't come in to Manama. We have her at another location."

Unless she'd come over the causeway by truck or in some cockamamie boat by sea, that meant she had been landed at the Navy airfield. Piat could feel his blood pressure rising still farther. *We spies avoid military installations like the plague. One or two visits to a military base, and you're made.* Then he realized that Partlow had probably saved money, and maybe time and trouble, by consigning Bella to the military.

"I want to see her."

"Yes, sir, that's why I'm calling."

"At once."

"Yes, sir."

It was poor procedure. They were supposed to deliver the bird to him, and he was supposed to hand it over to Hackbutt. Piat had left a few hours for contingencies, although nothing like this; Hackbutt would fly in four hours from now. By then, Bella was supposed to be at Hackbutt's hotel, which had been alerted that he would have a falconing bird in his room. Arabs understood things like that.

Now this. So, the first phase of the op plan went out the window, and Piat heaved himself off the bed and went downstairs to wait for a man named Carl. When he appeared, Carl looked like somebody who might have come to fix the air-conditioner: he had thinning brown hair, a stoop, granny glasses, and a gray golf jacket that looked as if it ought to have his name over the pocket.

"I'm Carl." He pushed his glasses up his nose. Piat was to see a lot of that gesture in the next couple of hours. Carl offered ID, which was useless to Piat; it said his name was Carl Trost and his face looked much like that of the man in the glasses and the jacket. So what?

"Let's go."

"I got my car."

Piat didn't want to get into Carl's car—bad security, bad tradecraft, and danger. Getting into a car with a stranger was as stupid in an agent as it was in a teenage hitchhiker.

Piat did it anyway. He did register the fact that Carl's car was a rental. Significant? Did he care?

Once they were in the car and rolling, Carl started to say again how sorry they were. Whoever "they" were. The transfer company, Piat thought. He was trying not to show signs of impatience or nervousness, but in fact he was in a rage because he wanted to focus on Mohamed. This part of the operation was supposed to run on automatic.

Carl navigated a roundabout and passed Bahrain's largest mosque. Piat was pretty sure they were headed for the military base. "Where are we going?"

"Navy base. You know it?"

Yes, he knew it, but he didn't say so. It had been a while, because it was one of many places in Bahrain where he shouldn't be seen. Piat changed the subject to Bella's condition, which lasted for only a few seconds; then there was silence until the car rolled to a stop at the gate of the base. Carl showed a plastic ID. Piat concentrated on it—it wasn't a military ID, and it had a red edge and a photo. Other than that, he didn't recognize the type. Not State Department, not diplomatic security, not military. Absolutely not Agency. But as American as apple pie. Carl was passed through with a wave. Nobody had even requested Piat to show ID.

Okay, so Carl had easy access to the base but didn't live in Bahrain, if he could judge from the rental car.

Carl drove too fast along the base's crowded streets, past Fifth Fleet headquarters and the NCIS office, to where the pavement gave way to a dirt track lined with warehouses, then trailers. He stopped next to a trailer. "Not very upscale," Carl said with an apologetic bob and a push at his glasses.

They had to cross a plank over a foundation to get to the front step of the trailer, which was a only piece of plywood nailed across two supports. The interior was warm and smelled of bird shit. Bella was sitting on a Navy-issue desk with newspaper, perhaps originally spread under her, scratched and pulled into loose wads around her.

The cage in which she had left Mull was on the floor. It had a crack running from the top of the door all the way across to the back, with a hole the size of a grapefruit punched in the top.

"Sick, bullshit!" he shouted. "What the hell happened?"

"Uh, well, as I understand it, the guy with the forklift—uh, Arab guy—there was some kind of uh accident when they unloaded—"

Piat went straight to Bella. She was underweight—he could see her weight loss from the doorway. And she was dirty. But she was not, so far as he could see, injured.

"Get me some water," Piat snapped.

Carl snatched a gallon plastic jug and walked down the trailer. "I don't know a thing about taking care of birds. *Is* he sick?"

Piat took the whole weight of her on his arm—his ungloved arm and wrist. Bella was quiet. He stroked her head. "Turn up the goddam air-conditioning! And get me some raw chicken. And a heavy glove. Any goddam glove."

"Yes, sir." Carl was back with the water—and another man.

A very different type—older, a bit of a gut, muscle. Dark-skinned, "African American," but maybe Latino, as well. "Raw chicken," Carl said. He looked at the other man, who looked back and shook his head. He didn't do raw chicken, he meant.

Carl was out the door. Carl was good at obeying.

Piat poured water into the cap of the jug and held it while Bella poked the water with her beak. He repeated the process again and again. Bella developed some energy as she drank, and her wings stirred, and her talons began to lacerate Piat's wrist.

Piat had heard the car start outside and heard Carl drive away. He walked up and down the trailer, ignoring the lances of pain from his wrist, crooning to Bella, stroking her feathers. He found a heavy web belt in a kitchen and shifted Bella while he wrapped the belt around his left arm and wrist and then put her on it. He gave her more water. He sang "Roland the Headless Thompson Gunner" for her.

The whole time, the dark-skinned guy watched him. When Piat walked Bella out of the office and down the trailer, he followed. Then he followed them back. Piat said, "You got a name?"

"Yeah."

Piat decided not to make anything of it. He had problems enough.

Piat wanted to build her a real perch. He started rifling the trailer, moving carefully with the bird on his arm from countertop to desktop. The nameless man followed him. Piat removed a curtainless rod from a window, and jammed it into a corner, supporting one end on a window ledge and the other on a hole he seemed to have punched in the wall-board. He found an aluminum foil tray from somebody's takeaway lunch under the packaging and warranties for a couple of international pagers in the wastebasket, washed it out in the kitchen sink and wired it next to the perch with wire he found on spools from another desk. He filled the aluminum tray with water.

Bella watched him work with her head on one side, then hopped up on the rod and began to drink again. Piat salvaged the newspapers from the desk and laid them on the floor under her. Under the newspaper he found the extensive packaging for the two international pagers. He made a food tray from one of the heavy plastic bubbles. He put all the rest of the packaging into the wastebasket on the crap from the pagers. The other man watched him all the time and, when he was finished with the wastebasket, put his foot on top of the contents and pushed them way down. Human trash compacter.

Piat heard the car outside and went back to Bella.

Carl held out a bag as soon as he was through the door. "Don't know about the gloves. Chicken's fresh." He saw Bella and pushed his glasses up. "She going to be okay?"

"I'm not a vet. She could *die* for all I know. And then you guys are responsible. Understand?" Piat pulled a pair of gardening gloves out of the bag. Better than nothing.

The other guy grinned, and Carl shot him a look and he went blank, so maybe there was some question about who was in charge here. Carl, at any rate, was the one who made the apologies and said it wasn't their doing, and they were sorry, and he thought the bird looked better already. And so on.

Piat fed her some chicken, concealing most of the chicken breast in the glove as he had seen Hackbutt do. "I can't feed her too much. It'll hurt more than it helps. She'll need to be fed again tonight." Piat was trying not to think of anything but Bella. He needed to get over this hurdle; then he'd worry about the rest, Mohamed most of all.

He fed her some more and then put her on the perch. Carl took the rest of the chicken off to the kitchen. When he came back, the dark-skinned man went off to the back of the trailer. He had said one word—yeah.

"I can't use this cage for her," Piat said. He had been looking at it. Bad enough that it looked like hell—the prince would be put off—but a lot worse that she could catch her neck in the crack if she tried to put her head out the hole. He didn't want a strangled bird. That would end the operation before they ever got to Mohamed. He looked at his watch, making sure he had time to get to the airport to meet Hackbutt. "You guys owe me a cage."

"And we're on it. I've got my girl right on it. She's found one that we think will be okay, but she's still calling around because we, uh, because we know this is on our nickel and we're obligated. Really. We'll deliver her to you in a brand-new cage. I swear it."

"The bird was to have been delivered to me two hours ago. You bring her to me and I find her underweight and scared and with no water! You know what this bird is worth?"

"Uh, yes, sir, no—I can hazard a guess but I don't know. She's a valuable bird. We're on it—really. We'll deliver her in a new cage by five local. Honest." He looked hard at Piat. "Are you born again?"

"Oh, come on—"

"I am. We don't say 'Honest to God,' but when we say something we know we stand in Jesus' sight. I mean this, sir. Five o'clock."

Piat was looking down at the desk at an untidy litter of correspondence. He could see three dates from several months before. All three had a letterhead for Force Air. Glancing at it, he had thought it said Forced Air, and he thought how funny it would be if Carl really was an air-conditioning man. But it said Force Air. He said, "You with Force Air, Carl?"

"Yes, sir."

That made some sense. Maybe one of the Agency's in-house airlines. That would be Partlow's style, he thought.

"Well, I know who to blame, then. Five o'clock. You better

be there with the bird and new cage, or you're up shit creek. Can you get her into the new cage?"

"Uh—well, if I have to—" Carl was looking at the glove, which Piat had tossed on the desk.

"Don't try to handle her. Don't try to feed her until then. Then, put a little of the chicken in the new cage. Let her see it and smell it before you put it in." He was thinking of Hackbutt in Kenya, luring the red-tailed hawk out of the tree. "Maybe she'll walk right in. If she doesn't, you call me, same number you did before." So the one-call phone would become a two-call phone. Bad procedure, bad security. It was a clusterfuck. "Okay?"

Carl pushed his glasses up his nose and said "sir" several times and "yes" several times, and, staying away from Bella, he circled around to Piat and asked if he wanted to stay in the trailer with the bird or did he want to go into Manama?

He checked his watch again. No point in letting Carl know anything about what he was doing. "Take me back to my hotel." He'd get a cab there to the airport.

Yessir, yessir.

Piat walked into the airport and went straight to a washroom, where he sat on the can and thought about the potential for disaster that faced him. He'd wanted these hours to think about recruiting Mohamed, and instead he had an operation that could fall to pieces because of a bird. On top of that, he'd compromised his own security by going to a military base and was going to do it again by letting Carl call him a second time, and then he'd have to get Bella—if she was alive and well—and transfer her to Hackbutt without letting Carl see Hackbutt or even know about him. What he needed, he thought, was a backup team; in fact, he had needed one to check Carl out before he had even let the little man pick him up.

Too late, too late.

He had about fifteen minutes before Hackbutt was due to

land. He drank some water form the tap, splashed some on his forehead and washed the chicken off his hands. He felt used up, and his brain wouldn't work. He had the terrible feeling that he was too old for what he was doing.

He thought *This is the last time I do this.*

Hackbutt was one of the last people off his flight, appearing just as Piat had begun to think that he might have missed his plane. He looked more dignified than the other passengers, older, better dressed. And not much like Edgar Hackbutt.

"Digger," Piat said, taking his hand.

"Jack. Nice of you to meet me." Hackbutt was wearing a tropical suit and had a leather case over his shoulder. He looked like an ad for senior adventure travel.

"Something's gone haywire, Digger." Piat spoke low, steered Hackbutt away from the rush to the exit and into a coffee shop. "Something's come up."

Hackbutt went right to his main concern. "Is it Bella? Is she okay?"

"How long can Bella go without food?"

Hackbutt started and got red. "What are you saying? Where is she? What's the matter?"

Piat put a hand on Hackbutt's. "She's fine. I just saw her. She didn't like the shipping process, that's all, and she's pissed. I sang to her and gave her half a chicken. Was that too much?"

"Too much to fly, but fine after a long time without feeding. What d'you mean, she didn't like the shipping?"

Piat cut him off. "Can she make it until tomorrow on that feed?"

Hackbutt nodded. "A week, if she had to. Jack, what's *happened*?"

Piat rubbed his chin. "There was some screwup with the cage. It's okay, it's okay! I checked her over; she's not even bruised—she didn't react when I touched her, nothing like that. But they cracked the cage."

"Cracked it! You couldn't crack it with a sledgehammer!"

"Apparently they used a forklift. Anyway, she's okay, but we're getting a new cage."

Hackbutt didn't like that at all. "She was just getting used to the one we had." His face was puckered up like an angry baby's.

"You can't give the prince a goddam million-dollar bird in a cage that looks like a cracked egg, Digger! Jesus! We're getting a new cage. Suck it up."

"I'm just thinking of Bella, Jack."

"Well, start thinking about Mohamed. *Focus*, Digger!" *Christ, it's getting to me*! He changed his tone. "I'm sorry, Dig. I got a lot on my mind."

"It's my last night with her, Jack."

"Yeah. Right. I understand. Of course, you're absolutely right. So, here's the deal: I'll get her and the new cage at five o'clock; I'll bring her—"

"You haven't *got* her?"

"Jesus, Christ—! Dig, the transport guys have to buy a new cage. Bella's in an air-conditioned space; I saw to it that she had water and a perch and she's *okay*. Give it a rest, will you?"

Hackbutt pouted. "You seem awfully jumpy, Jack."

"Yeah, pre-menstrual tension. It's Mohamed, Dig. That's where I've got to focus." He met Hackbutt's eyes. "You, too. Okay?"

Hackbutt looked away. He was hurt. He slumped. "She's my *favorite*."

"And you'll see her in about an hour." He tapped on the Formica tabletop. "I get the bird and the new cage and I bring her to your hotel. Now listen up, Dig—unless you hear otherwise from me, I want you at the loading dock of the hotel from five-thirty in the morning on. Got me? With a handcart or something to move the cage with. And maybe somebody to help. Yeah, get a porter with a handcart or a dolly; it doesn't look good for you to be moving a big object. You're rich; you pay other people to move your stuff. The hotel's expecting a bird, okay? They won't be expecting a fucking eagle. Try to go up in a freight elevator—get a porter who understands you, okay?" Piat was sweating. He thought he was making it up as he went along, although he'd always intended to do it this way, had in fact briefed Hackbutt on it before they'd left. But it was different now because of the cage and the bird's condition. And because he was spooked.

"I'll meet you at the loading dock. Then she's yours for the night. Okay? Just focus on how great she'll feel when she sees you. She'll know. It'll be great for both of you."

But Hackbutt wasn't cheered. "The last night."

Oh, Christ, don't have second thoughts! Piat touched Hackbutt's hand. "Five-thirty? Loading dock, porter, hand truck. Act like a king, Digger. Act like you expect people to do things your way, and they will." He lowered his head so he could look into Hackbutt's eyes. "Are we together on this?"

Hackbutt stared at him, then broke out of his mood and straightened. "Sure, Jack. It'll all be fine!"

"Good." Jesus Christ, they'd switched roles—now it was Hackbutt supporting *him*. He took out a piece of paper with the number of a cell phone he'd bought in the souk. Another one-time—or two-time or three-time if he couldn't pull his socks up. "You can reach me any time at this number. Once I've turned Bella over to you. Okay? If there's anything, *anything*, you call me. Okay? I don't want any surprises in the morning, Dig. Okay?" Hackbutt was nodding. They had been over and over this stage. Did he get it? "In the morning. We meet at six outside the front door of your hotel. Okay? It's like a drive-by, only I'll be on foot. You come out, you see me, you walk to your left—your left, okay?—and I'll check your back trail. Go four blocks and stop and wait for me. If I don't show right away, call me on the number I gave you. Okay?"

"This is so you can brief me."
"Right."
"Just like we planned."
"You got it."
"Where's Bella all this time?"
"In your room."
"What if somebody says I can't keep her in the hotel?"
Piat suppressed a sigh. "Be a king, Dig. Tell them it was all arranged and don't take no for an answer."
"But what if they won't?"
"Then call me."
He went over it again. And then again. And then he said they'd see each other at the loading dock between five-thirty and six, and he hoped that he was telling the truth.

In the event, it went like a well-tuned car. Carl called him just before five and was at the meeting place Piat had picked out a few minutes early—Piat knew because he was earlier still. He parked where he could watch Carl's approach and check around them for a bubble. All this, when there was no reason why there should be a bubble or why he should feel the unease that seemed to have gripped him.
He waited another five minutes and then pulled his rented van behind Carl's car. The transfer took two minutes, the slowest part getting the cage out. Carl was driving a Land Cruiser this time; the rear seats had been taken out, but still getting the cage out was like pulling a worm out of a hole.
"Big cage," Piat said.
"The best."
Also a heavy cage. Through wire mesh that would have resisted bolt-cutters, Piat saw Bella's angry eye. She looked okay.
Getting her into the van was easier, but the two men were winded when they were done.
"We're really, really sorry," Carl said.

"The new cage looks okay."

"We try to do the right thing. It's how we do business."

Carl seemed eager to please. Piat wanted to pat him on the head and tell him he was a good dog, but instead he held his hand out for a pen and began signing his cover name to manifests and insurance forms. He looked up from one and said, "If she isn't one hundred percent, your company's ass is grass."

Yessir, yessir.

He drove a careful countersurveillance route back to Hackbutt's hotel. He couldn't leave the car to make real stops, and it limited his observations. Bella kept him pinned to the car.

The countersurveillance route didn't make him feel better. He wasn't sure he was clean, nor had he seen anything to prove that he was dirty. The ambiguity of the situation wasn't the result of nerves. Piat was a careful spy, to whom trade-craft and precaution were a lifestyle. He felt that he was under surveillance, and the feeling was on the edge between intuition and observation.

If Carl had brought somebody to the exchange, then they'd have been all ready to follow him. Ideal surveillance conditions. Piat sat in the parking garage of his hotel, rubbing his face.

So he drove a second route to Hackbutt. It made him late. That was too bad. He still didn't see anybody and he couldn't shake the notion that he was being watched, or that the watchers had picked him up when he took the bird.

On his second pass, he tucked into the mean street that led to the loading dock and saw Hackbutt, in tropical suit and safari hat, standing there with one hand in his jacket pocket and the other on a big dolly whose other end was being tended by an Arab in what appeared to be a French Zouave uniform. The two of them went together pretty well—an image of imperialism past and present.

Piat felt better.

The transfer was peaches and cream. Hackbutt stood by, hand in pocket, looking like a monarch trying to decide which of them deserved the Order of the Garter and which a lashing. Piat and the porter handled the big cage with a certain amount of grunting. Hackbutt resisted rushing to Bella. Nobody came screaming out of the hotel to say that they didn't take sea eagles.

For any onlookers, Piat gave Hackbutt some papers to sign.

"The van will be here tomorrow at seven, sir," he said.

Hackbutt nodded almost absently, as if to say, "Of course the van will be here at seven."

Piat was impressed, as much with the success of his teaching as with Hackbutt. It had worked. It was all going to work. Why, then, did he feel so worried?

Piat slept deeply, woke to stagger to the bathroom, realizing that he was exhausted. By the last few days in Mull, by Irene, by tension. And by sleep that, while deep, was horrible—dream-ridden, hag-ridden. He felt as if he were getting sick. A terrible gloom hung over him, certainly the result of the dreams, none of which he could remember. Trying to recall why they were so unsettling, he fell asleep again and into their toils.

He struggled up toward his wake-up call at five-fifteen, the last dream like some gluey fluid in which he was drowning. Irene had been in the dream, something erotic but bad that he recoiled from. But there had been a lot more—a memory of looking for a place, a room, a place where things would be all right, then experiencing its constant withdrawal as the city or town around him changed its shape and he could never find his way back. And then a beach. Horrible things. Stuff on the wet sand—yellowing foam, ugly seaweed with stems like tubing. Something dead—a child? A dog?

Bella.

He was up by then, trying to shave without looking at himself. He looked dreadful—old, baggy, burned out. He tried the shower.

Bella. Bella was on the beach. Dead. That had been it. The sea eagle half-awash in the tide. Tangled in wire the way seagulls got tangled in monofilament. Her feathers were wet and bedraggled; one eye was gone, pecked out or rotted out. Wire wrapped around her.

He tried a cold shower to bring him out of it. The after-effect of the dream was smothering him. Pushing him down. Dragging at him.

At twenty before six, he was sitting in a taxi in a line of three up the street from Hackbutt's hotel. He studied the street, windows, cars. He tried to ignore his depression. It was terrible.

Hackbutt came out at six. He looked spry, almost dapper, his long hair a nice touch of eccentricity. Without looking around for Piat, he turned right and walked away.

Piat looked for somebody to follow him, looked again at the street, windows, cars. Nothing. Of course there was nothing. Who would care? Unless the prince wanted to run an advance surveillance on them, who gave a damn what they did on the streets of Manama at six on a Sunday morning?

Except that Piat's effort to detect any surveillance was both passive and simple. He'd catch an amateur. He suddenly wished he'd laid on a mile of intense shopping and switch-backs. He wanted to be reassured.

Piat paid the taxi driver and followed Hackbutt. He found him where he was supposed to be and led him into another hotel and another coffee shop. One that, he had already determined, opened at six.

"You don't look good, Jack."

"How's Bella?"

"I think okay. She settled right down with me. You hung over, Jack?" He grinned. "You should get more exercise."

Piat rubbed his eyes. "I'm okay." He began the final briefing. Nothing was put on paper. He went through it all three times, even though they'd been through it in Mull: the meeting would be at the Tree of Life, a landmark baobab out in the desert where people sometimes went to fly falcons. The choice had been the prince's, approved by Piat. Hackbutt had to find his way there in the van with Bella; Piat went over the route, but he had made Hackbutt memorize it in Mull, and this was simply reinforcement.

"How do I behave toward the prince?"

"Respectful but dignified; I let him set the pace."

"Good. What's your real target?"

"Mohamed."

"What do you want from him?"

"A meeting if possible, a phone number if not. Phone number regardless, I mean. But meeting first."

"Try to find out if the prince is going to stay in Bahrain. Find out if he has a house here, or maybe he's using a house of his uncle's. I don't see the prince rising early and sprinting across the causeway to make an eight a.m. meeting. I think he's already here. So try to find out where."

"From Mohamed."

"Right." They went through it again, poked at it, looked at possibilities. Hackbutt asked if he should offer money and Piat said no, that was later. "But try to find out his real name. See if you can get a rise out of him by asking about family. If you get any response, even an expression, maybe he looks at the prince and shuts up—say something about maybe you could carry a message for him. You get it? We want to plant the seed that we're his connection to the world outside Saudi Arabia. Okay? Nothing heavy-handed, Digger. Light. Nuanced. If you get anything adverse, back away. Okay?"

Piat couldn't eat. He couldn't even drink coffee; the first mouthful was like acid.

"Okay, what's the gimmick—the connection?" Hackbutt, on the other hand, was putting it down pretty well.

"Bella."

"Damn right. Is she eating okay? Does he understand how finicky she is? How varied her diet is? How—"

"I got it, Jack. She's my bird."

"I just want you to bore in on the idea that you're Mohamed's expert when it comes to Bella, and he's to telephone you a lot."

"Jack, you're like a water drop on a hot pan. I've never seen you like this? Opening-night jitters?" Hackbutt gulped coffee. "It'll be all right. I'll be fine. The hard part for me is saying goodbye to Bella, and I did that overnight." He patted his mouth with a napkin. "You're making me nervous, Jack."

Still, he went over it once more. The mood dumped on him by the dreams and the surveillance remained, a curtain through which he tried to be the seasoned professional doing his job. He was just alert enough to keep from spooking his agent, turning his own black mood into a virus that would infect Hackbutt. In the end, it was Hackbutt who looked at his watch and suggested they move on, and Piat gave up and walked out with him.

Piat had left the van in his hotel's garage. Now, he drove it through the waking streets, looking for surveillance, finding none. He backed it to the loading dock. Hackbutt and the same porter were already there, nodding as if in approval of his driving. Piat handed over the keys, helped load the bird into the van, and walked away.

There was always this moment when you walked away and left the agent to do it or not do it. He, a man who had never had a child, thought it must be like leaving your child for her first day at school.

He was back in his room just after seven.

Something was wrong.

Alone, he knew that something was wrong. It wasn't Hackbutt and it wasn't the meeting and it wasn't his mood. It was—

He didn't know what it was. He had got out his running clothes, meaning to try to run the dreams out of his head, out of his body. He was sitting on the bed, a T-shirt in his hands. There had been no hitches after the business about the cage; there had been no surveillance, no problem with the agent. He was a basket case, but the briefing had gone okay. What, then?

Something, something that bothered him. He went over the briefing, then tracked the cat back through yesterday. Carl, the bird, the trailer, the cage—

The cage.

The damage to the cage. She hadn't been hurt but the cage had been ruined. Yet they had called him, fixed it with a new cage; she had been okay, if rattled. Was it the cage?

His mind called up a kind of memory photograph: correspondence lying on the desk in the trailer.

Force Air.

He put down the T-shirt and picked up the telephone.

A woman answered. Her voice was thick with sleep. It was only five in Naples.

"Can I speak to Mike?"

"No, I'm sorry." He could picture her, sitting up, running her hand through her hair, waking. Pretty woman. "He's not available right now. Can I take a message?"

Piat contemplated hanging up. She was an NCIS officer, Dukas had said. Let's see. "Leslie? I doubt you remember me. We met on Lesvos."

Silence. "Oh," she said. Then, "How have you been?" Without saying a name.

Even through his panic, Piat thought, *That's one quick girl you've got there, Mike.* "I need to talk to Mike. Could you tell him that? Something's a little—off—and I'm trying to reach him?"

Pause. She was chewing on something—a pencil? And writing, he thought. "Is there somewhere that he can call you?" she asked.

Piat wasn't that desperate. "No. But listen—it's just something, a name, maybe he'll recognize. Tell him 'Force Air.' Okay? Not Forced—Force, no D." She was waiting for more. He hadn't intended to give more, but he said, "Tell him I'm in a place that has one of your offices and a lot of sand."

"Oh, sure."

After he'd hung up, he thought he'd done a stupid thing. He should have called the emergency number that Partlow had given him, but he had dismissed that idea without even thinking it through. This wasn't an emergency. This was a *feeling*.

He ran. He headed out the way Hackbutt must already have headed, not meaning to go anywhere near the meeting, only being drawn that way by it. He ran hard; he wanted the mindlessness that comes with exertion. He wanted his brain to let go, the mood to let go; he wanted relief. Instead, the dreams seemed to come with greater clarity, and he found himself running in the early heat, sweat pouring down him, and seeing the Bella of the dream, dead on a beach and wrapped in wire.

They'd called him because she was sick. Except that, aside from losing a little weight, she wasn't sick. The cage was ruined—the fork from a forklift had gone right through it.

Bullshit. He'd helped Hackbutt select the damn thing. To get a forklift to spear it, it would have had to be welded to the floor. Otherwise, it would just move. Not to mention how unlikely it was that an Arab would hurt a falcon.

He was well out of the nice parts of Manama, running through a district that mixed low-income Shia and warehouses. He turned, following old pavement marks for a hash run, a local expat running sport. He automatically took the opportunity of the left turn to check his back trail.

He was under surveillance. The knowledge went through his brain like a lance of ice. The red Toyota crawling along the side street had been around his hotel earlier. Same driver.

Simultaneous with that realization came another.

Bella.

Wire. There had been wire in the trailer. He had used it to make her something. It had been thin, braided of many strands. He could see it wrapped around the dead bird in the dream. Communications wire.

Bella is wired.

It came to him in that form—the dream as pun. And he saw it all. Including the reason an American in a Toyota was watching him.

Bella, wire, the wrapping for two new pagers in the waste-basket, the new cage.

The new cage was a bomb.

22

"Craik." It was the middle of the night to him; he had been deeply asleep in his London hotel room.

"Al, Mike Dukas."

He started to say, *What the hell time is it and what are you doing to me?* but he knew that Dukas was calling because he thought something was important—Dukas would have called Rose, who would have given him the number. He looked at the bedside clock. It was not quite three-thirty in the morning. "Shoot."

"Get on a STU and call me back. My office."

"Sunday? At this hour?"

"We never close."

Cursing, he plugged in the STU he'd brought with him and thought would be useless, got the tinny buzz of encryption.

"That was quick," Dukas said.

"I didn't want to ruin my entire night. What's up?"

"Piat called me. Something's going on."

Craik groaned aloud. "What happened?"

"Leslie talked to him."

"He say anything specific?"

"He asked what I know about Force Air. I didn't but I checked—it's the air wing of a security company called Force for Freedom. That ring a bell with you?"

"I'm afraid it does."

"Looks like he was in Bahrain when he called. That significant?"

Craik thought about how much to tell. "Bahrain could be a meeting site."

"Al, I don't want to find I've got one foot in the shit just because I helped Partlow with Piat. If Partlow's running something that's got Piat worried, I need to know."

"That makes two of us. I'll get back to you."

The Tree of Life was Bahrain's most uninspiring landmark. Except that it was far from anything else in the desert, and people went there to fly falcons. And it was overlooked by cliffs more than a mile away. Cliffs where a man with a cell phone could sit and remotely detonate a birdcage.

Piat knew where to find the Tree of Life.

And Piat knew what to do with his surveillance, too. *Walk.* Or in this case, run.

It was a long run. It wasn't the longest run of his life, but it seemed that way, and he hadn't run in the desert enough to recognize the difference between good footing and bad, or the difference between short distances and long. He ran easily on hard-packed gravel, and then he was twisting his ankles in shifting sand.

Of course, the well-groomed man in the red Toyota and his partner in the little Mercedes couldn't, or wouldn't, come across the sand. Piat was careful to run toward the sea until he crossed a small ridge and disappeared from their sight. Then he turned east.

He peeled his jacket over his head and tied it around his waist. And ran on.

After three miles, he was winded, his ankles hurt, and he didn't have much hope of arriving on time. His watch told him that he had eighteen minutes until the meeting.

Somewhere within a couple of miles, Edgar Hackbutt would

be wondering where his good friend Jack was when it mattered.

Piat put his head down and ran faster. He was covered in sweat—lathered in it. He was thirsty and hungry and the curry he'd eaten didn't agree with the running.

He pounded on, stretched his stride, cursed the sand and his lack of recent exercise and all the thousands of mistakes he had made in this operation, in this year, in his whole life that had led him to this moment.

Then he saw the tree.

Partlow was staying at the same London hotel and was even less happy than Craik to get his telephone call. At the same time, Craik thought that Partlow sounded awake and alert and as if he was expecting a call from somebody else. He was, however, irritated to find that this one was Craik. Craik cut him off and said, "I need to talk to you. Right now."

Partlow was wearing pajamas, a velour robe, and slippers that cost more than most shoes. He didn't look like a man who had been sleeping; in fact, he looked like a man who needed sleep. And he was annoyed. He swelled up and vocalized. But he was worried, too.

Craik said, "Tell me what you know about what Jerry Piat's doing right now."

Partlow dropped that quick half-beat that meant he'd been surprised. "I can't possibly—"

"Piat thought enough of Dukas—not you—to call him from Bahrain. Something's going on. Tell me about it, Clyde." He waited. Partlow looked at his watch and gave a little jerk. "He mentioned Force Air, which is the in-house airline of Force for Freedom. I'm mentioning Perpetual Justice. What the hell is going on, Clyde?"

Partlow's face started to contract; then, through some exercise of will, it smoothed again, but he looked at his wristwatch, and Craik would have sworn he was feeling something like panic. They were still standing, as if Partlow was going to give him ninety seconds and go back to bed.

"Clyde, if you've involved Dukas and me in an illegal op, you're dead meat. If Dukas doesn't see to it, I will. And don't tell me I haven't got the clout!"

"Nothing I do is illegal." But he sounded unsure—as if he were listening to some other conversation that was more important and what he said to Craik was on autopilot.

"Something smells. Smells enough that you let me see some information about it so maybe you could share the blame with me if it went bad. Perpetual Justice, Clyde—tell me about it!"

Partlow pulled himself a little together. "I've no idea why Piat would be so irresponsible as to call Dukas about anything, but it's nothing to do with me."

Craik changed his tone. "Clyde—I did you a favor. I brought Dukas in; together, we got Piat for you—twice. 'Give a little to get a little.' As a favor to me, then. Please. Clyde, I'm asking you as nicely as I can—what is Piat is doing?"

"I'm awfully afraid I don't know what you're talking about."

Craik pulled up two chairs. He sat. After several seconds, Partlow sat, but he looked at his watch again. Craik said, "Perpetual Justice is a DIA setup, Clyde. They do a lot of business with Force for Freedom. What is Piat into in Bahrain?"

"Even if I knew, I couldn't tell you, of course."

"Perpetual Justice gave you a backdated contact report on an interrogation that probably involved torture. So far as I can find, that report is the original source of interest in Muhad al-Hauq. Isn't it? Did Perpetual Justice set you up in this operation? Are you just the front guy for a DIA clandestine op that smells enough that the point man has to call on an outsider?"

Partlow murmured, "So far as I know, DIA doesn't do clandestine operations."

"Have they known the details of your operation all along? About me, Dukas—Piat?"

Partlow laughed. He had found his groove—comradely condescension. "You ask the most remarkable questions!"

"Contact reports? So they knew exactly what was going on day by day?"

Partlow looked pained. "I've no idea who 'they' are."

"I thought you said DIA," Craik said patiently. "I know every approved tasking that DIA touches. This is something else. And you know it. This is the bunch over on Mulholland Avenue."

Partlow looked at him. He hadn't been able to keep his eyes from reacting. But he was able to laugh again, not very convincingly. "You have a frame of reference I just don't understand, Craik."

"They've screwed up, Clyde. They've screwed up their paperwork and they've screwed up their finances, and maybe now they've screwed up your operation. Maybe they've screwed you, too. But they're not going to screw me and they're not going to screw Mike Dukas!"

Partlow waved his hands. He might have been trying to quiet an unruly crowd. "You don't have— I really can't—" He dropped his arms. He looked hard at Craik, a kind of test run of one Partlow style, found it wasn't going to work. "I have no comment to make."

Craik studied him, gave up. Partlow might have known more, might tell it another day, but probably wouldn't now.

Craik stood, thinking about flying time from Bahrain to Glasgow, then the trip to Mull. Would Piat come back to Mull with his falconer? And there was a woman—was she with them? He said, "I'm going to have to miss some of tomorrow's meeting. You're going to cover for me." He smiled. "As a quid pro quo."

"I'm sorry, my friend, but—"

"I have a good officer to stand in for me; I'll clear it with DNI. He won't like it, but I'll persuade him. This officer can handle most of the stuff, but if it gets sticky, you're going to make it happen that everybody waits until I get there. Okay, Clyde? To keep me from being unhappy?"

Partlow smoothed his robe over his thighs. He stood. "I suppose so." He checked his watch.

Craik headed back to his room and the STU. Maybe Dukas could track Piat and the others out of Bahrain. Or maybe they were still there.

Or maybe Piat's call had been ado about nothing—but Craik didn't believe that. If Piat had called Dukas, he thought something was going on.

He knew the tree was huge, alone on the floor of a desert valley dominated by low, rocky ridges. He knew, too, that it was home to a swarm of flies and not much else. He'd been there before.

But now he could see it.

Twelve minutes. Two miles at his best running pace. How big did a big tree look at two miles?

At the eight-minute mark he picked up a gravel road and stayed on it. He was taking long strides, was running as well as he had ever run over such a distance. He was aware, like a man gambling his last chip, that at the end of this run, whenever he stopped, he'd have nothing left—that the running was all that was holding him up, even now, and when he stopped it would be to fall.

Tough shit. *Suck it up, princess.*

Four minutes to eight. Might get a minute or two if he was lucky or some part of the op—the other op, the enemy op—was slow. His thinking was completely clear, his head was clear. He saw the whole thing. Somebody—it didn't matter who—had played Partlow from the start, because the op, the contact op, was never a recruitment. It was an assassination. Except that Partlow—and Piat, of course—had done such a good job that instead of walking away, they'd found a way to make it work, and so here he was.

Partlow was in it, but knew nothing of the bomb. Otherwise, he wouldn't have been so pleased by "Bob." Partlow had a good poker face, but he couldn't hide pleasure.

Piat wished he knew who it was who wanted the prince dead.

Now he could see two clusters of tiny people near the tree. A white SUV. A van like a toy car.

Don't jump the gun. Don't just hand over the bird, Digger, or you're dead. Stand there. Don't let the prince near the cage—that's when they'll trigger it—

Five hundred meters. More than a quarter of a mile. The human body looks like a speck at that distance. A good high school athlete can run it in just a little over a minute.

Four hundred meters. Where was the man with the pager? Was Carl with him? Carl of the eyeglasses and the yessirs and the shit-eating manner? Carl, who'd blindsided him? Led surveillance right to him?

They could be anywhere on the north–south ridges. Anywhere within sightline. They'd have wonderful optics and the pager and nothing else to give them away.

Three hundred meters. Carl must see him—except that he was on foot, running—not what Carl would expect. Except that their surveillance should have alerted them that he had run off.

If Carl cared about him at all. Almost close enough to shout now.

Two hundred and fifty meters, and the human body is as tall as the distance between the quick and the tip of a thumb held at arm's length.

Two hundred and twenty meters, and two of the minuscule figures were bending to take something big from the van. Wired Bella.

Piat threw himself forward into the stumbling remnant of the sprint he didn't have left in him, but he covered ground until he could recognize Hackbutt's face and Hackbutt's straight back as he and Mohamed carried the heavy cage in both arms toward the white SUV. The prince, recognizable by the men clustering around him, was standing to receive them.

Fifty meters. Five seconds for a world-class sprinter. More for a tired spy of fifty. The standing figures were as tall now as the whole nail of a thumb held at arm's length.

Piat knew that the man on the ridge would need several seconds to dial the number that would detonate the bomb. *Seconds.*

He stopped running. He was gasping. He wanted to put his hands on his knees, rest. He tried to get enough breath to shout. "Digger! The cage is a bomb!" His voice seemed to stay in his throat. He fought for air. "Digger! *Bomb! Get out!*"

Mohamed did hear him—younger ears. Hackbutt didn't. Mohamed turned his head, looked at Piat, and dropped his end of the crate. And ran.

The prince heard him as well. He focused on Piat, and then he was running for the white SUV, and his security men were trying to get between him and Hackbutt.

Hackbutt had held on to his end of the cage and had even tried to catch Mohamed's end before it hit the ground. The thing was too heavy. He staggered and lost his hold, and the cage hit the sand and tipped back, and Hackbutt kept it from tipping over with an effort that almost pulled him down.

Piat wanted to run to him, but he was done. Panting, he managed to shout, "Digger! The cage is a *bomb*!"

Hackbutt heard him this time. He looked once at Piat, and then he reached and wrestled with the latch of the cage's door. Piat was screaming but didn't hear himself. He was trying to shout *Run, run!* but he wasn't making the words.

Hackbutt pulled Bella out of the cage by the jesses, and

then, a huge effort made possible only by adrenaline and passion, he swung the big bird up, up, running two steps forward, and threw his arms at the sky, and she clawed for the air, at first feebly and then more strongly, seeming to sink and then to rise, up, up, sweeping up into the first circle that would carry her far above them all, and Piat saw Hackbutt simply stand there to watch her, his arms still raised as if he were accepting some tribute, his long hair blowing, until he was wrapped in the flame of the explosion.

23

Piat had got out of Bahrain hugger-mugger, not sure who might be after him or even if anybody cared. His clothes were thrown into his bag; his sweaty running clothes were still on him under a five-dollar Ahmadinejad jacket and blue jeans. He took the first flight he could get a ticket for and flew to Karachi, from there started backtracking. He tried to call Irene twice from Karachi, again from Prague. He practiced old routines of evasion.

He called again from Frankfurt. This time, she was in her hotel room in Arras.

"Oh, my God!" she said. "At last!" Before he could say what he had to say, she was rushing on. "It's fantastic, the show's fantastic! It hasn't even opened yet and a Paris gallery wants it; it's going to be even better, they're promising me much better lighting—the lighting here sucks; but anyway it's fantastic! The local rag, which isn't really bad, the art critic has a reputation, she came yesterday even though I wasn't ready, she called it 'a profound meditation on death and womanhood!' How's that for meaning!" Excited, happy, she stopped. He said her name, but she interrupted, her voice now almost harsh. "Where the hell is Eddie? He was supposed to call me. He was supposed to call hours and hours ago. Where's Eddie?"

Piat cleared his throat. Even so, his voice was hoarse. "Edgar's dead, Irene."

She didn't say anything for what seemed like minutes, could have been only seconds. Then: "How can that be?"

"I can't tell you anything over the phone. I'll tell you when I see you."

She said nothing. He didn't hear breathing or sobbing—nothing. He said again, "I'll tell you when I see you. All about it." He waited. "Irene?" He waited again. "Irene—I'm going to see you. Right?"

She was silent for so long he thought they had been cut off, and then he heard her mutter, "Jesus Christ," and she hung up.

Later, sitting numbed in the airport lounge, he knew that she had meant that they were never going to get together. She had meant what he had known from the moment the bomb had gone off but hadn't been able to admit to himself: she could fuck him if Hackbutt was alive, but she couldn't go near him if Hackbutt was dead, because that would be fucking on his grave and being glad he'd died.

He had hoped he'd be changing his flight to Paris, a train to Arras. Now, he went on to London, then Glasgow. He picked up his rental car there and caught the last ferry to the island. He didn't go to the farm or the Mishnish but made a phone call and then went to the cottage in Dervaig and sacked out on the divers' floor.

He didn't know who might care about what had happened or what they might do. "Carl" wouldn't be happy about his screwing up the bombing. The prince might not be happy, either, although if he had any sense he was thinking that Hackbutt was a hero, and so was the man in the running shorts who'd done the shouting. But one or the other might be vindictive, and Piat didn't want to be surprised by somebody's lust for revenge.

In the morning, he told the two divers that he wanted them to cover his back for a day or two.

"Wot? We're supposed to be humping that gear down from the crannog."

"Give me a day or two. I want to see who shows up."

He still had a hope—or a fear—that it would be Irene—that she would come back to the farm for things she valued, for the money she was owed. He didn't want her to arrive and find a couple of "Carl's" tough guys or a couple of Saudi specialists.

He drove out to the farm with the divers tailing him, pulled off where he had waited the first time he'd ever come there, and watched the house. He was pretty sure that nobody had got there before him, or the dog and the birds would be showing signs. Nothing happened for several hours; then, Annie came down the hill on her bike, stayed for an hour, walked the dog, and pedaled her way back up the hill.

"Come on."

"Now what?"

"We're going down to that farm. Park the van around back where it can't be seen from the road." He drove down. The dog was ecstatic. He let himself in and went straight to Hackbutt's bedroom and the closet where he knew Hackbutt had kept a shotgun. He found it leaning in the corner behind clothes that smelled of dead chickens and bird lime. Two boxes of shells sat on the floor beside it.

"One of you take the shotgun. The other go up on the hill where we stopped and keep an eye out." He handed over his own cell phone. "You see anything headed this way from either direction, you call. I don't want to be surprised."

McLean looked like a man who was ready to bail out. "How serious is this, chum?"

"You've been getting your money for doing nothing the last week."

"Yeah, but there's jobs and jobs. I've done a tour with the hard ones. That was enough."

"Then take off. Leave me the gun."

But they didn't go. Instead, both of them went up to watch and Piat was left with the shotgun. Not the kind of backup he'd hoped for.

In the middle of the afternoon, he let the dog in. It was suspicious of the house. It went from room to room, sniffing, backing away from things, suddenly trotting, then standing still. In the end, it threw itself down at his feet, ears alert. When he touched it, it winced.

"Hey, it's me."

One car passed in the whole day. It was Annie's dad, heading out and then returning two hours later. The divers took turns coming down to eat. They foraged in the kitchen cupboards, found cans and frozen things—Irene food. They were apologetic, but they weren't going to change their minds about getting killed for him. At nine, with darkness falling, he told them to go home. He'd call them if he wanted them next day.

"Sorry to draw the line, chum."

"It doesn't matter."

Dykes lingered in the door. "How bad is it?" he asked. He had I'm sorry written all over him.

Piat shrugged. "Like McLean didn't say, it's not your problem. Not your op. Something else went very, very wrong. Go home, Dawg. Get out of here."

Dykes hesitated. They went back together, and he was thinking about that.

Suddenly Piat realized he didn't want Dykes and his wife and college-bound daughter on his conscience. "Seriously, Dawg. As soon as the lapis sells, I send you a cut. Get gone."

He ate standing in the kitchen; a canned potpie of some indeterminate meat that said it was beef. He washed it down with beer, then took out a bottle of single malt that he had brought when the dietary rules had started to crumble. It seemed a long time ago—the two of them just starting to eat meat, nibbling at it; then Irene drinking more, smoking. Coffee. A long time ago. Teaching Hackbutt stuff that didn't matter a damn now.

Role model.

For a dead man.

He went into the sitting room with the dog and the bottle and the shotgun. The dog, he thought, would hear anybody who came close now; he'd certainly see any car lights himself.

He sat in an armchair in the dark. He drank the salty, seaweedy scotch. After a while, he slipped down next to the dog, sat with his back against the chair.

"He was a good guy, Ralph," he said aloud. His voice was rough with whisky and emotion. The dog lifted its ears; he could feel the movement under his hand. "He was a better man than I am, Gunga Din."

He was drinking the scotch from the bottle now; his glass was up above somewhere. "You think you're pretty good, and you think you do something just right, and then—" He swallowed hard. His eyes felt hot. "I was behind it the whole time. He did all that shit, put up with all my shit, so that he could—so he could stand there and let his fucking bird go. And I didn't protect him." He put his face down into the dog's long, silky hairs. The dog was warm and responsive; his breathing rose and fell, and, answering Piat's contact, he rolled back, exposing his side and part of his belly.

"Oh, Christ, doggie, doggie—!" Tears ran into the dog's fur, and Piat sobbed. Only for seconds, but he hadn't cried in a long time and he was surprised. He said, "Shit." He sat up, exhaled, wiped his eyes on his sleeves. "My God." He still had a ball in his throat, his nose now stuffy. "Oh, God, doggie!"

That was his mourning for Edgar Hackbutt. And for himself, because, as Hopkins more or less made clear, it is always ourselves we weep for.

* * *

He woke at six on the floor. The bottle was mostly empty. The dog lay against him, snoring lightly. Piat was cold, but the dog was warm where they touched. He remembered the tears, added them to the list of things he wouldn't tell other people. Now, he knew, came the hardening of the heart: first, an instant of surrender to feeling, then the hardening. You hardened your heart against women you were going to leave, against death, against the claims of other people's lives. It takes practice.

He went to the kitchen and put on coffee, then went to the bathroom and tried to vomit but couldn't; he took four aspirins from the medicine cabinet, showered, rubbed himself hard with the towel, felt like hell.

"How about a walk, Ralph?"

The dog jumped up. He quivered, wagged, raised his head and made barking motions but no sound. He backed toward the door and sneezed. It was raining out, but he didn't care.

"I think the answer's yes."

They went up the hill as far as the place where Edgar had flighted his birds. Up here, he had told Edgar about wanting Bella for the operation. Now Edgar was dead, and Bella was soaring over the desert or the Arabian Gulf, or she was sick and hungry and hiding somewhere. Mohamed, he thought, would try to coax her down the way Hackbutt had coaxed the red hawk in Kenya. It had all gone to shit—the prince, Mohamed—and it was his operation and it was his fault, and he was back to thoughts he was trying not to think.

He came back down the hill, head pounding, nauseated. He clipped the dog to his chain again and went inside. He put the shotgun across the arms of a chair and sat in another one with the rest of the coffee. He didn't believe anymore that anybody was coming. He'd panicked because of the shock of his failure.

And she wasn't coming back, either. Maybe she'd come back eventually, two or three months or a year from now, but not now. Not for so long as she thought there was a chance that he might be there.

He was sitting there, the cup empty, when the dog started barking. Piat stayed low, looked out the window, saw a car he didn't know. He went out the back door and hung at the corner of the house until he saw who was in it.

He waited until the men were out of the car and dealing with the dog's enthusiasm before he set the gun against the house and stepped into view. One man—the Navy captain, Craik—was wearing the same thing he had been the last time Piat had seen him: yellow slicker, bucket hat, old corduroys. Craik looked up from the dog and saw him, smiled. Dukas, lingering behind, stared around him. Then he started toward Piat.

Dukas came close enough to speak, then came a step closer and said, "What happened?"

"You're late," Piat said. "Too late."

"You know what I mean, Jerry. With your agent and the Saudi. Hackbutt. What happened?" Craik, still kneeling by the dog, was listening.

"Is it on the news yet?"

"Al-Jazeera says there was an attack on a Saudi official in Bahrain and an unidentified man was killed. We think the Bahrain government and the Saudis are sitting on it." Dukas hunched his shoulders and pushed his fists deeper into his pockets. The rain was like cold spray. "You were in Bahrain. What happened?"

"I got blindsided."

"Muhad al-Hauq. What happened?"

Piat looked up at the gray sky. "Ask Partlow."

Craik came over, shook his head the way a dog does, fast, as if he were trying to shake the water off his hat. "I don't think it's Partlow. The people who did it have been in it since the beginning. They've been waiting. You got them to al-Hauq. What did they do?"

It wasn't that he saw any professional reason not to tell them. It was that the moment was so wrong—he wanted time to be alone, time to get over Hackbutt. Time to get over Irene. He didn't want the little obscenity of talking about it. "I'll put it in my final report. When Partlow pays me."

Both men looked at him. Craik shook his head again and then took the hat off and shook it with his hand. Piat guessed that water had been dripping down his neck. Craik put the hat on a little off-line. He said. "I know about your archaeological dig up at the loch. I've already been by there today. Didn't see your car so figured we'd find you here." He squinted into the rain, as if somebody else might turn up to make trouble, and he said, "I was up at your crannog on Saturday, too. I got enough from what I found up there so I guess I can pull in the people who're working for you. They'll rat you out to save themselves. Tell me what happened."

Piat let the possibilities speed through his mind—tell Craik to fuck off and risk the cops; run for it; or tell Craik what he wanted to know, the unseemliness of it, but on the other hand the symmetry of it, because Craik was the first one he'd seen when all this had started in Iceland.

"That's rich," he said. "You got me into this. Now, you'll burn me to the cops to make me talk about it." His bitterness filled his voice, so that he sounded like a stranger even to himself. "Why'd you come looking for me here?"

Dukas grunted. "Because you aren't in Greece and you aren't in Bahrain and the cousins say you were on your way here as of last night."

He remembered the probable MI6 man who'd picked up Bella. Of course. "You know who lives here?"

"The falconer."

"Yeah." He decided then to stop being a horse's ass and tell them. What the hell. "Well, he's dead."

"In Bahrain?"

"Yeah." Piat lifted one side of his mouth in a mock-smile.

"He died for love." He scratched the dog's ears and told them the story of the bird.

When he was done, Dukas was incredulous. "They killed an American citizen as part of an operation?"

"First-class clusterfuck." Piat shrugged, watching the hillside. "From what little I saw of them, they were idiots. Except that they fooled Partlow, but maybe he wanted to be deceived."

"What the hell were they thinking of? No, belay that, they weren't thinking. Jesus! Who were they?"

"The ones I saw were all Americans. Force Air." Piat shook his head. "It probably looked neat on paper—kill al-Hauq, hustle me and Hackbutt out of country, fade away. They didn't even get the first part right—what they got was kill Hackbutt, miss al-Hauq, scare the shit out of me, and leave evidence all over the place."

"Why the hell did you come back here, then?"

Piat could have said several things, but he didn't see any point in dragging all that into it. "The crannog," he said. He patted the dog.

Craik took a small tape recorder from his pocket. "Let's go inside. We want you to go through it in detail, and then I want it in writing, longhand, signed, and we'll witness it." He glanced at Dukas. "Both of us want it."

Piat held the door to make it perfectly clear he could keep them out if he wanted to. He suspected that Craik didn't care what he wanted. Dukas looked solemn and perhaps pitying.

They sat in the kitchen, the dog under the table among their legs, his tail slapping the floor. Piat turned the heaters up, which were in the energy-saving phase and would respond only slowly. He made more coffee. Craik fussed with paper and a pen and the tape recorder, and then Piat gave each of them coffee and got ready to rat out his own operation.

"Expecting company?" Dukas said.

Piat realized he had been looking out the windows a lot. He thought he'd been discreet. "That's my business."

"Anybody from Bahrain likely to come after you?"

"Why?" Piat glanced out the window at the end of the kitchen. "I didn't kill anybody, they did."

"Witness?"

"There were lots of witnesses."

"The Saudis?"

"The Saudis probably want to give Edgar and everybody who was connected with him a medal. He saved their guy's life."

"What about the wife?"

"She's in France. She's an artist."

Craik turned on the tape recorder and said who he was and where they were and who Piat was, only he called him by his cover name, Michaels, surprising Piat. Dukas, watching him with the pitying look, turned the tape recorder off. "You're going to sign the paper as yourself. That's for Craik's personal safe, photocopy for mine. The tape's for DNI." Dukas kept a hand on the tape-recorder switch. "Jerry, we're sorry. About your guy. I know what it's like when you lose an agent." The pitying look got more so.

Piat shrugged. Harden your heart. But then he thought that he'd never have a better chance to say the words, so he said them. "He was my friend."

And Dukas nodded. He said, "Like that, uh?"

Piat nodded back, and said, "Just like that."

Craik had never run an agent. So he just sat quietly for a minute.

Dukas turned the tape recorder on again and they went through the whole tale, or as much of it as Piat wanted to tell. He gave everything about Edgar's death, maybe was even a little maudlin, he thought, leaning hard on the nobility of saving the bird. "He was heroic."

"Did he know he was going to die?"

"I suppose he did. Or he thought saving the bird was what mattered and he didn't care."

Then he answered Craik's questions about the attackers.

"Were they pros?"

"At the bomb part, yes. Blindsiding me, not so good—if I hadn't had my head someplace else, I'd have put it together. I should have put it together. They weren't all that good."

They talked some more and Craik said, "That's it," and snapped the tape recorder off. He nodded at the paper and pen. Piat had gone on looking out the window, checking. Maybe for Irene, maybe for somebody else, because no matter what he'd told himself about the attackers, one of them might have a bean up his nose and decide that taking revenge on whoever was in or near Hackbutt's farm would ease the pain of failure. He started writing but kept checking the window. He was still a little worried, was the truth.

Edgar's shotgun was still outside.

"I gotta piss."

Piat walked to the bathroom, the dog at his knee—he wasn't going to let Piat get away from him again—flushed the toilet, stepped out of the back door, and got the shotgun. He left the gun open and put it on the kitchen table. "Think I was going to shoot you?" he said.

"No."

He went back to writing, finished, read it over, signed his cover name and threw the pen down. Craik read it over, got to the signature, shook his head. "Real name."

"Suppose I tell you to fuck yourself." Piat realized he wanted an opportunity for anger—maybe violence.

"Your crannog is still there, with all the evidence your guys left. I took photos."

Dukas said, "Look, Jerry, Partlow's got to be pissing his pants because he's afraid he'll be tagged with your guy's death. The tape pretty much exonerates him of the worst of it, although he'll get hit for being suckered out of his own operation. Your real signature on the paper nails it down. I'll go before Congress and swear, I'll go to court and swear, that the tape is genuine and I have it in writing, but I won't give it up. If you'll feel better, I'll let Craik bury it somewhere in ONI."

"And someday somebody will put your back to the wall and say we want the signed statement or you're doing ten years in Leavenworth."

Dukas shrugged.

Piat thought it over. "What the fuck." He signed his real name.

Craik folded the paper and put it in an inner pocket and climbed into his yellow slicker. "How long you going to stay here?" he said.

"I want to square things away. There's a kid comes in to feed the birds, I need to pay her. There's the dog." The dog, now under the table again, thumped his tail on the floor.

"What about the wife?"

Piat shrugged.

"There's stuff at the crannog."

"Mind your own business."

Craik and Dukas went down the corridor and opened the front door. The rain had turned to a finer drizzle. They stood in the little porch, looking out at the vast, wet landscape. Craik said, "Believe it or not, I think I'd like to live here."

"That's the first likable thing I've heard you say." Piat almost smiled. He found Craik easy to dislike.

Craik lifted the corners of his mouth. "The beginning of a beautiful friendship."

Dukas gripped Piat's shoulder. "Jerry, I know it's tough. It'll get better, okay? Stay in touch."

They got in the car and drove away.

Piat spent the rest of the day cleaning his own things out of the house and trying to conquer his hangover. He slept that night in a bed, the dog stretched out at his feet. In the morning, he went to the loch with the dog in the car. It was a cold, windy day; the rain was gone but heavy cloud lingered. When he parked, he couldn't see the tops of the hills.

He and the dog made the climb. His legs still hurt from the run in Bahrain.

From the top, Mull spread away to the north. He could see the mountain where Bella's parents lived, and he could see the opening of the Great Glen, and everywhere, the sea.

With the dog, he walked down to the crannog. He walked around the beach. The cleanup was good, and by now, Dykes and McLean were gone.

Piat drove back to the farm and made a last check around. When he came out, Annie was just wheeling her bike in. She was startled but looked severe.

"I didn't expect you, Mister Michaels."

"I was just getting a few things, Annie."

"Where's the Hackbutts, then?"

He had the story prepared, went through it smoothly: Hackbutt had been in an accident and was now in a hospital in France. Irene was with him.

"Oh, that's terrible. How bad is he?"

"I think he'll be back in a week or two. She wasn't hurt."

"Oh, the poor man." Then she asked what had become of Bella, and he told a prepared tale about the ornithological society and a breeding program in another country. Even if she believed him, she didn't like the story much.

"Irene wanted me to ask you if you can go on caring for the birds for a couple of weeks." She looked annoyed—there were only four birds now, but she had a long ride each way, and taking care of them was a lot. It had been Hackbutt's full-time job, after all. He said, "She knows you deserve more, so she asked me to give you this." He held out a hundred pounds.

"Yes, well." She took it and looked at the money and then

shoved it into her wind-cheater. "Well, goodbye, then, Mister Michaels." Her severity was for him—the severity of the superior morality you get to practice at sixteen. Piat thought of the moralist he had been at that age, the idealist—the war-lover too young to go to Vietnam and for whom, when he was old enough to go, there wasn't any more war. He had settled for spying, which had suited his adult morality better, as it turned out.

He went back inside and waited until she was gone. He put the shotgun and the shells down, then stood in the doorway of Irene's studio and looked around at it. Inhaled it. Some of her beach combings were thrown into a pile against a wall: he saw the arm of a doll, a bottle, a battered log. He'd never understood what it was she did or how she decided what to put in and what to leave out. He never would.

After Annie had left, he took the dog outside. He walked it to its improvised kennel, stopped over for the chain, and clipped it to the collar.

"Time to go, Ralph." He caressed the silky ears. "You're a good, good dog. Somebody'll take you, for sure. A dog like you, you can't miss." He stood up. There was no point in trying to find something final to say to a dog. "So long." He turned away and walked to the car.

The dog lay with his head on his extended paws for a long time. The Man had gone away before and had come back, so now he was gone away and he would come back. Before The Man there had been somebody else, somebody he no longer remembered but would know if he saw or smelled him, but now there was The Man and that was enough. He would lie here and wait and The Man would come back.

He slept. He smelled a fox going by far up on the hill and he woke. Sat up. Sniffed. He filled his mouth with the scent, but it was weak and it came and went with the wind. He smelled the birds in their hovels, smoke from a house a mile away, something dead down the burn. He smelled the remnants of the man and woman who had been here and who hadn't liked him. He smelled the girl and the tires of her bicycle, even though she had ridden away.

He lay down. Dusk began to fall. He put his head on his paws and slept.

He woke to the sound of the car. It was almost dark now, and he saw the lights as they turned into the farm and came toward him. The car stopped. The door slammed.

The Man stood over him. "Well, come on, then," he said. He unsnapped the chain from his collar, and the dog raced for the car.

Epilogue

Craik led Abe Peretz across Mulholland Avenue and through the entrance of the building where Perpetual Justice had its offices. Peretz had trouble keeping up because of his left leg, and Craik turned and waited for him inside the door. He led the way to the building directory and pointed out Elastomer Engineering.

"Their front company. They're sloppy about it. Somebody even held the door for me to go in."

"They going to hold the door for you today?"

"Probably not. Unless it's on the way out."

They went up in an elevator and got out at the sixth floor and walked along the corridor. It was the middle of the day, but nobody seemed to be about. Nothing looked any different until they got to Elastomer Engineering's door, and then Craik saw that the electronic keyboard was gone.

"Shit."

He pulled on the door's handle. The door swung open. Inside, the floors were uncarpeted. The night duty officer's desk was gone. The place was empty. Stripped.

"My guess is it wasn't like this the last time you were here," Peretz said.

Craik strode down the long corridor to the T and turned to the door that had led to Ritter's office. It stood open. The room beyond was bare—no carpet, no desk, no nothing. The inner door was open, too. Inside Ritter's office, a man in a white cap and paint-spotted coveralls was leaning over a bucket.

"Hi," Craik said.

"Hi, there. You not the new tenant, I hope. It ain't ready, if you are."

"No, no—in fact, I'm looking for the old tenant."

"They're gone."

"Since when?"

"I been here since yesterday. Nobody here then. I paint the walls; I don't ask questions."

"Fast work."

"They come and they go." He thrust the end of a wooden pole into a roller and began to roll paint across the ceiling.

Craik backed into the lee of the doorway and said to Peretz, "The guy died in Bahrain only four days ago. Jesus."

"Fast work, as the man said." Peretz shifted his weight to look around Craik at the painter. "This kind of shop, the shit hits the fan, they're very fast." He grinned. "'They fold up their tent like the Arab, and as silently steal away.' Except that they weren't Arabs, were they."

Craik walked back through the offices, looking in every door, staring out of windows and studying up close the nail holes where somebody's photos or diplomas or posters had hung. "Right to the floors."

"Lot of shredding, I imagine." Peretz looked pained. "My bladder needs a john. How much nothing do you want to go on looking at?"

Craik directed him to a men's room he'd looked into. "Or, there's a ladies' room the other way."

"I'll stick with convention." He limped off. When he came out, Craik was standing by the front door. They went down in silence, crossed to the parking garage, and climbed to Craik's car. Peretz said, "Is Dukas going to investigate?"

"DNI has everything. He's going to pass it off to Dukas if

Dukas wants it. The connection with NCIS is thin—it looks as if the bomb was made on the Bahrain navy base—but it's enough."

"FBI?"

Craik looked down the long, gritty gloom of the garage. "I think there's a feeling of 'Who can be trusted?'"

"You going to push it with DIA?"

Craik smiled. "I've been relieved of my duties at DIA." He leaned back on the vehicle and folded his arms. "I'm going to DNI for my final tour. Two years and retirement."

"Al, I'm so sorry."

"Me, too. But you pays your money and you takes your choice. I made my choice. And I still have some friends." He put his hand on the door handle. "Where can I drop you?"

"Oh, my office," Peretz said.

They got in and Peretz, once settled, said, nodding in the direction of the building where Perpetual Justice had had its offices, "You going to follow these guys?"

"Well, as the painter said, 'They come and they go.'" He eased the car backward, then drove down the ramp and to the exit. He stopped with the car's nose almost in the street. "They come and they go." He looked left and right, turned his head back to the right toward central Washington and its highways and byways of power. "The question is," he said, "where do they go?" He turned left.

Force Protection

Gordon Kent

While his carrier USS Thomas Jefferson patrols the Indian Ocean, intelligence officer Alan Craik flies to Mombasa to assess security. But no sooner has he arrived in the Kenyan port than a US Navy support vessel is blown up at dockside.

In the ensuing mayhem, violence erupts in the ancient streets, rapidly spiralling out of control – until Craik steps in, risking his life to prevent further chaos. When the dust has settled, he receives orders to investigate the apparently motiveless attack, and is assigned a special team from the Jefferson, with full aerial back-up.

Rumours suggest the involvement of Muslim terrorists. Alan has his own ideas, but when a car bomb explodes outside a US agency in Cairo, it becomes clear that someone objects to the US presence in the area.

Nobody knows where or when the next attack will come. And with a new battle group heading to the Suez Canal and a massive storm brewing in the Indian Ocean, Alan Craik must act fast.

ISBN 13: 978-0-00-713172-3
ISBN 10: 0-00-713172-0